DELIVER
HER

DELIVER HER

PATRICIA PERRY DONOVAN

LAKE UNION
PUBLISHING

Published by Lake Union Publishing, Seattle
www.apub.com

Amazon, the Amazon logo, and Lake Union Publishing are trademarks of Amazon.com, Inc., or its affiliates.

ISBN-13: 9781503934511
ISBN-10: 1503934519

Cover design by Shasti O'Leary-Soudant

Printed in the United States of America

To my own precious cargo:
Maurice, Molly and Nora

Let the powers that be warm the path you will tread;

No journey's harder than the one in your head.

Amphibian, "Cloud Path," *Rainmaker*

PROLOGUE

The music. I can't hear the music.

"This isn't a good idea. It's not what we planned."

"Relax. I've got this."

"But her mother . . . she'll worry. We'll be so late."

"We'll be fine. I'm the driver, remember?"

Half-dozing in the backseat, Alex craved sleep, and yet the girlish whine beside her persisted like a mosquito's drone. She longed to swat it away, but her hand wouldn't cooperate.

A lurch of the car triggered fresh anguish.

"What was that? Be careful."

"I told you. I'm not used to this car."

Shut up. She dug deep for those words, and a caution echoed in Alex's head, a memory: *Don't express your emotions so freely.* Alex's hand pressed open like a book, a woman's roughened finger tracing faint markings from pinky to pointer, her kohled eyes beseeching.

Maybe now was one of those times, Alex thought, when she should just *be.* Summoning every ounce of energy, she shifted toward the window, shoulder belt slicing across her chest, silky softness cushioning her cheek. Another shimmy of the car triggered more high-pitched dismay from her seatmate.

"I said, 'I don't *want* to.'"

"It's too late. We're almost there."

"We can still turn around. Please stop. For *her* sake."

Who was *her*? Was *she* her? Muddled, Alex floated back down to where it was soothing and lovely and quiet, a sanctuary shimmering with love and tranquillity, radiating energy so potent it could carry her across the cosmic divide. She was ready to surrender, to unburden herself, to be transported—when the car's jerk lashed her head against the window.

Beside her, the girlish pleadings gave way to a mournful scream, severed by the deadly scrape of metal on metal.

Protests choking her throat, Alex clung to the seat belt, powerless to stop their descent, a plunge more menacing than the Dragon Coaster's familiar dive that terminated with the winged demon swallowing its prey. In those terrifying seconds before this leaden, unknown beast exacted its revenge, Alex opened her eyes, meeting the reptile's garnet gaze: seeing all, judging none.

SATURDAY

MEG

"Right, Meliss. Like Mom would ever have fallen for . . ."

Meg Carmody's voice trailed off at the sight of her house, her smile fading as they pulled into her driveway, the sheen of the day's happiness already evaporating.

Not again.

Every light blazed. Beneath her forearm, the car door throbbed with the bass track reverberating from the modest colonial. As she stepped out of her sister's car, Meg neatly crushed the stem of a wineglass under her heel; one of her favorites, she noticed as she walked around to the driver's side.

"Can you believe this?" Meg asked. She gestured to the van angled tipsily beside them, windows wide open. "Somebody even drove my car."

"You're being paranoid," Melissa soothed. "It was probably Jacob."

"Jacob never takes the van. Says he's not a 'soccer dad.' Which leaves Alex."

"She doesn't drive."

Meg pursed her lips. "No, but plenty of her friends do."

"Be serious. Would they really steal your car?"

A year ago, Meg wouldn't have thought it possible. But a year ago, they were living different lives.

"Didn't you say she was babysitting?"

"That's what she told us." Meg rubbed her neck. "Anyway, thanks for today. I really needed it." The matinee in the city, a frothy remake of a seventies Broadway show with a pair of TV stars as leads, followed by cheap Chinese at a place off Canal, had refreshed her. Escaping Manhattan before the evening performances let out, they had sailed over the Robert F. Kennedy Bridge and up 95 to Riverport in under an hour.

To come home to this: another reminder of her sixteen-year-old daughter's pain and Meg's own failure to soothe it.

Melissa tilted her head toward the house. "Want me to go in with you?"

Hands shoved in her coat pockets against the April night's chill, Meg shook her head. "I'll deal with it." Jacob had been in charge of the kids tonight. So far, their separation had been civil—as civil as things could be when they were forced to share the same house. His car wasn't in the driveway.

Meg scanned the street. The only vehicles were her neighbors'; either the revelers were on foot, or whatever had gone down at their house had moved to a new venue.

Melissa gripped Meg's arm through her window. "You've got to do something."

"I know." Meg ached for her daughter, who had lost her best friend, Cass, the previous year. Cass's death had been excruciating for all of them, but there were limits. She glanced back at the house and sighed. "I can't expose Jack to this anymore." He was only seven, but he had eyes. And ears.

Melissa threw the car in reverse. "Jack is fine. For now. And remember, whatever you need, I'm here. Love you."

Meg walked up the driveway, kicking cigarette butts into the mulch. At the front door, she squared her shoulders and turned the knob— unlocked, of course. Inside, the stereo boomed from every corner of the house at a volume Meg didn't know existed, the heavy metal track vibrating in her chest. She turned the sound off on the wall control, clinging to it a moment as she surveyed the kitchen.

She had to hand it to Alex: the path of destruction was pretty uniform. On the granite counter, snacks of every kind pulled from the pantry, sampled and abandoned. Droppings crunched under her feet. Their dog, Angel, would never leave these forbidden treats; she was probably cowering under Alex's bed upstairs. On the stove, thick white fat pooled around a burner; a greasy skillet held charred remains of burgers.

She continued the tour. In the dining room, her beloved mahogany table had been kitted out for beer pong, its top stamped with telltale rings, the floor beneath sticky with spilled beer. Besides this chaos, the room's landscape seemed off somehow; Meg couldn't put her finger on the difference. In the living room beyond, the coffee table served as a makeshift bar, holding mostly empty bottles, cheap brands of vodka, gin, tequila. These kids drank dangerously—fast and hard. She'd heard the ER nurses talk. They practically set their watches by the concert schedule at the Eagles' Nest, anticipating some underage patients before the warm-up act even finished.

On the end tables, more glasses from the china cabinet: fine-stemmed goblets, wide-mouthed pilsners, champagne flutes—the latter a gift from Jacob's mother. Miriam would be happy to see them put to use, Meg thought wryly.

"Alex?" Meg called out while heading upstairs to check, even though she knew she wouldn't find her. All three bedrooms were empty, as was the hall bath.

Downstairs again, she brushed off a couch cushion and sat down to contact Alex. Not even bothering with voice mail, she texted her daughter.

```
Please call me immediately.
```

Given the circumstances, she didn't expect a rapid response. Next, Jacob. He needed to know about this.

"Meg?" Wherever he was, it was noisy.

"Where are you? And where's Jack?"

"He's right here," he shouted. "We're bowling. It's disco night. Jack's loving it."

"It's almost nine o'clock."

"Loosen up. It's Saturday night. And you're having fun, right, Jack?"

Her son's voice poured into the phone. "Mom, you should come. This is soooo cool."

"Hi, honey."

"So, Mom. There's this band playing right on top of the alley, so when you throw the ball it goes right underneath them. And they make you wear these clown shoes before they let you bowl. And Dad got me a chili dog and cheese fries and a giant soda and—"

Meg couldn't help but smile at her seven-year-old's account. "Glad you're having fun, bud."

"See. I told you. He's fine," Jacob said when he came back on.

"I know. He sounds happy. Listen, wasn't Alex babysitting tonight?" Meg asked.

"Yeah. I watched her walk down there." Alex had a standing Saturday night gig with the Millers, a neighborhood family.

"Well, she must have walked back, because she threw a hell of a party here. The house is a wreck. What time did you leave?"

"Right after Alex."

She glanced around the living room. "The carnage looks about right for a few hours of day drinking."

"Sorry you had to come home to that. Where is she now?"

Meg didn't have a clue; Alex hadn't yet responded.

"Huh. She's probably with Shana. I'll try her, too. Wait. Did anybody touch my instruments? Shit. I knew I should have locked them up."

"I don't know. I haven't been down there."

"They better not have. Alex knows damn well what the rules are."

"Maybe, but she ignored quite a few of them tonight. Somebody even drove my car."

He guffawed. "Seriously, Meg. Did you dust it for fingerprints?"

"Funny." She kneaded her forehead, loath to suffer his humor tonight. Lately, his teasing bordered on spite. She missed the Jacob who always had done the honorable thing, starting with making room for her, then Alex and eventually Jack in his carefree life. "We can't keep making excuses for her."

"She's a kid."

Jack whined in the background.

"Still, it isn't healthy for her to act out like this. Even Melissa thinks so."

"You know I love your sister, but this is *our* family."

The family he wanted to break up?

Meg sighed. "I don't want Jack to see this. Take him to your mom's when you're done, please."

"She'll want to know why."

"Yes, and I'm sure she'll hold it against me. But it's the best place for Jack tonight. I'll wait up for Alex."

"Don't you have work tomorrow?"

He was right. She'd promised to cover a shift for someone. "I don't care. Alex and I need to get some things straight tonight." She was up and pacing now.

"You guys will both be exhausted tonight. You know you'll say stuff you'll regret. Let's just deal with it tomorrow."

She might have considered his suggestion, except that more often than not these days, Jacob made an art out of *not* dealing with things.

Like drumming up new business, leading his construction company to go belly-up soon after his father died last year and forcing Meg to suffer the indignity of sharing the same house with him, even though he'd asked for the separation months ago. He couldn't even dump her properly, she thought. Though he'd grandly allowed her the master bedroom while he decamped to the basement couch, he decreed to the entire family that the lower level was now strictly off-limits to all. *Man cave, schman cave*, she'd thought at the time. He was welcome to it.

"I don't know if I can wait until tomorrow, Jacob." As she said this, Meg opened the powder room door and gagged at a puddle of vomit. She dealt with sickness all day at the infusion center, patients retching from chemo, but this was different. She leaned against the door.

"I'll be home then," he said. "We'll talk to her together. Ground her."

"Perfect."

"It's not like you've come up with a better solution. Listen, it's Jack's turn. Gotta run."

Hanging up, Meg rubbed her cheek, wishing Jacob would give her credit for all the ways she'd tried to help their daughter. After the accident, she'd put her own mourning on hold to help Alex cope with hers, offering every support she could think of, from therapy to music camp, only to run into a solid emotional wall. As her daughter's actions and school attendance became more erratic, Meg alternately entreated, cajoled, wheedled and very nearly bribed her to change her behavior, without success.

The day the police officer had showed up to report Alex's shoplifting incident, Meg finally decided to consider other options and began researching her alternatives on the sly. Meanwhile, Jacob had still insisted all their daughter needed was time.

Meg headed downstairs to check on his curated collection of guitars, amps and bulky cables—relics from his Objects in Mirror days. Recently he'd dropped a few hints about getting the band back together. All seemed in place; each instrument upright in its stand, amps at attention below. The only sign the festivities had migrated down here were a handful of LPs out of their sleeves on the ancient wooden crate that served as their coffee table. Meg paused to reunite the albums with their protective covers. Jacob was anal about his records.

About to head upstairs, Meg bent to retrieve a fallen barstool cushion, which rattled like a beanbag when she replaced it. Curious, she unzipped the cover. Nestled against its stuffing was a small plastic bag packed with candy-colored pills. There were pinks, whites, baby blues, circles, capsules, little dots like the saccharine pills her grandmother used to carry in her handbag. A mini-pharmacy.

A flyer from the pediatrician's office about kids ransacking parents' medicine cabinets flashed through her brain. Those pain pills from her dentist for an abscess a few months back: What did they look like? Panicked, she ran upstairs to check her bathroom. The prescription bottle was still there; she thought it felt lighter, but couldn't be sure. A stop in the kitchen: Alex's own antidepressants still on lockdown in Meg's purse.

She ran back down to the basement and tore apart every pillow and couch cushion, coming up empty. She shook the album covers she'd just straightened, then moved to the wall of storage bins, pawing through ancient school projects and baby clothes like a ravenous bear at a Dumpster. When those searches turned up nothing, she flopped onto the floor, massaging the insistent pinch in her neck that flared up when she was stressed. Lately it seemed to be there all the time.

Things were worse with her daughter than she had imagined. What if Jack had gotten his hands on the pills? Or Angel? Clearly, the time had come for Meg to put her plan into action.

She had researched dozens of residential programs over the past few months, convinced the only viable option was to separate Alex from Riverport and its painful memories. After hours of furtive calls, she had settled on The Birches in Silver Mountain, New Hampshire, hoping its mix of therapeutic treatment and academics in a postcard New England setting would bring her daughter back to her.

Melissa was her partner in crime, covering for Meg when she'd driven three hundred miles in the depths of winter to visit the school. Meg had watched students snowshoe to classes conducted in the string of converted cabins bordering a frozen lake.

"Think *The Shining* meets summer camp," she joked to her sister. In all seriousness, however, the camaraderie of the small student body and the staff's tough-love affection were palpable. A few brave students who had traveled paths much rougher than Alex's shared their stories, bringing Meg to tears and convincing her of The Birches' healing power.

And while it would crush Meg's soul to do so, if sending Alex to the snowy, pine-rimmed campus could make her daughter realize there *was* life after loss and inspire her to pick up the pieces, then Meg would carry out her plan.

So Alex could begin again.

Meg might have forgiven the house party, but the discovery of the pills had clinched it. The Birches it was. The question was no longer *when*, but *how*. Jacob might prove problematic; he was dismissive of his daughter's behavior and more concerned with recapturing his own youth.

And then there was Alex. Meg already had a pretty good idea how her daughter would react to the idea. She winced, recalling the recent wintry day when she had somehow convinced Alex to stop for coffee following a dentist appointment. Instead of going for the seven-dollar latte Alex expected, Meg had driven out to the Playland promenade on Long Island Sound, where a handful of vendors stayed open year-round. Shivering, the pair sipped their drinks on a promenade bench for a few minutes in silence, until Meg turned to her sullen daughter.

"I'm sorry things have been so hard for you, honey."

"It's OK. I'm good." Alex had stared straight ahead at the Sound, where a yellowish foam had formed at the water's edge, great clumps of it breaking off and scuttling across the beach like wayward trash. She blew on her coffee. "I'm freezing, Mom. Can we go?"

"In a sec. Al, what would you think about going away from here?" Meg asked.

"You mean, like, a vacation?"

"Not exactly. I was thinking about a new school. It worries me that you're struggling. Maybe a change would be good."

"I'm not going to St. Martin's. Not with those geeky uniforms."

Did that mean Alex *might* consider a change? "I wasn't talking about a school around here. I was thinking more . . . New England."

Alex looked at her mother for the first time since they sat down. "You mean, go *away* to school?"

"A lot of kids do it."

"Live there? Are you kidding?"

"I know it would be an adjustment at first, but—"

"An *adjustment*? You think it would just be an *adjustment* for me to leave?" Setting her coffee on the bench between them, Alex stood and leaned over the promenade rail.

Meg joined her, putting an arm around her daughter. "Listen. What would be the harm in looking? You and I could take a ride, make an overnight of it—"

Wriggling away, Alex turned and glared at Meg. "You really have no frigging idea how hard it would be for me to leave, do you, Mom?" The cold had stamped her cheeks an angry red and drained her taut lips of color. "You must be clueless if you think I could ever, ever leave . . ."

In the next second, Alex bolted, racing toward the parking lot.

"Alex. Wait!" Meg ran after her and found her crying by the car. Despite repeated urgings, she refused to get in the van, standing outside with her arms wrapped around herself and shivering, pulling her phone out occasionally to text. Meg watched her and waited, alternately rolling down the window to plead with her and texting Jacob to contact his daughter, hoping she'd respond to his reason. She had half a tank of gas; she would sit with the car running for a couple of hours if need be, she decided.

It started to flurry; soft white flakes dropped onto the warm windshield and melted away like tears. Meg tried one more time. "Honey, please. You'll freeze out there." Alex continued to ignore her. Minutes later, a young man pulled up in an SUV, and Alex climbed into his car without a backward glance.

Meg considered following them, but worried that it might cause the young man to drive recklessly. They didn't need another tragedy. She sat in the empty parking lot a little longer, berating herself for believing that by cornering Alex in this deserted public place, she might sell her on the benefits of a fresh start.

She drove home alone that night, fearful and discouraged. Alex eventually *had* come home—late, but safe.

Please let that happen again tonight, Meg thought, back upstairs in the living room, sprawled on the couch to wait for her. From this vantage point, she spotted something underneath the love seat opposite—*probably a beer bottle,* she thought, as she got off the couch to investigate. Kneeling, she found the sugar bowl from her silver tea set. *That's* what had been off when she first came in; the little handed-down collection usually sat on the dining room table. She felt around for the creamer, then the teapot, its scrolled front freshly dented, insides rank with whiskey. She arranged the three pieces on the coffee table and knelt in front of them—relics from her childhood, entrusted to Meg and her sister after their mother moved to assisted living.

"What am I going to do, Mom?" she murmured. Her reflection in her mother's teapot was watery, like an old photo. Meg was surprised to see she was crying.

ALEX

The cemetery was pitch-black, but Alex knew her way along the graveled path. "Three more rows," she hissed to Shana, who followed with a beach towel from her car.

"Why are you whispering?" asked Shana.

"I don't know. We just should."

At the appointed headstone, Shana spread the towel on the damp ground, flopped on it, and lit a cigarette. "I can't believe how fast your house cleared out. Never knew you could run that fast, Al."

"I know, right? My heart is still pounding." Alex unscrewed a bottle and held it out.

Shana eyed the offering. "Maybe a sip. I gotta drive." She took a swig. "Still, the party rocked while it lasted, right?"

"Right." Alex licked her lips over the way the night had unrolled. One minute, Mrs. Miller was telling Alex the kids were sick and she wasn't needed; the next, Shana was group texting the world. Things had gotten out of control quickly—like everything else in her life right now. She couldn't summon the energy to shut it down, fake smiling at all the strangers streaming into her parents' house. Thank God, that stupid sophomore had yelled "Po-pos!" The bogus cop sighting had cleared out the house in minutes. "Who was that girl, anyway?"

"Larke, I think. Evan brought her."

"Figures." The tall, skinny senior with the piercing blue gaze and hipstery scruff of chin hair had a history of going for the young ones. Fresh meat, Alex and Shana liked to say. Whenever Evan came by Alex's house, he set off her mother's warning bells.

"What are you doing with that guy?" Meg would ask.

Alex never had an answer, other than that Evan was just there. Although she'd never give her the satisfaction of knowing, her mother was right: Alex didn't know what she was doing anymore. Sometimes it was exhausting just to be herself, or the self everybody thought she was.

She sighed and took another sip as she and Shana gossiped about the night's hookups—none of which had involved them, thankfully. "That short guy with the glasses was kind of hot in a nerdy way," Shana said. "Cass would have made a move on him."

"If Cass had been around, she would've dragged us to some geeky coffeehouse comedy night or something."

"True." Sitting cross-legged in front of the stone, Shana reached out and traced the words etched into its polished surface: Dance Like No One Is Watching. "Do you think she is, Al?"

"Do I think she's what?" Alex was still adjusting to Shana's habit of bursting out with random questions. It got on Alex's nerves sometimes; she wasn't a mind reader.

"You know . . . watching. From, like, up there." Shana pointed toward the sky.

Alex gulped the night air. "I don't know. I guess." Of course Cass was watching—her BFF literally lived in Alex's dreams. But she wasn't about to share that with Shana. They weren't that tight; they were friends, kind of by default. Ever since the accident, Shana had been stuck to her like glue. It got awkward sometimes.

The two sat in silence for a while, passing the bottle back and forth. "I wish I'd been there." Shana's head dropped.

This time, Alex knew what she meant. They'd talked about it so much already: Shana had been injured so badly, she couldn't go to Cass's funeral, even though she had begged to. Afterward, Alex visited her at CareMore, the rehab facility, and described the daisies they had tossed onto Cass's casket and the graveside guitar player strumming "When You Dance," Cass's favorite song.

"She would have loved that," Shana had sniffed. It was true. Cass took pride in being the anti-cool. No Facebook for her ("Farcebook," she called it) and no smartphone—just a crappy flip phone her mother made her carry. It was all Alex and Shana could do to get her to text.

Cass had been the self-appointed expert on all things mystical—her birthright, she claimed. She told them jillions of times how her Greek-mythology-obsessed mother had named her Cassandra for the Trojan princess given the gift of prophecy by Apollo. When Cassandra spurned Apollo's advances, the god had cursed her so no one would ever believe her prophecies.

This did not stop their Cass from making grand predictions herself. It had been her idea to have the palm reader at Alex's Sweet Sixteen— only to freak out about it that night. The woman was giving off toxic energy, Cass had said. Not for the first time, Alex wondered now if things might have been different if they hadn't stopped at the palm reader's station.

Shana stood and popped a mint into her mouth. "Let's go, girl."

Alex took another long sip. "Hang on. I'm not done."

"Al, if I don't get the car home by eleven, I can't use it for school. Which means I can't give you a ride. *Comprendez?*"

School. A commitment Alex made on a day-by-day basis. It just took so much to walk through those doors every morning. She recrossed her legs. "I think I'll hang a while."

"You crazy? You can't stay here by yourself." Shana glanced around anxiously. "What if there's, like, pervs or something?"

"The pervs could get both of us while we're sitting here. Don't worry. I'll just call Evan in a bit."

"Evan, huh? Are you guys, like—?"

"OMG. No. He's just a friend."

"Riiiight." Shana shone a pocket flashlight in Alex's face.

"I mean it," Alex laughed, shading her eyes. "Why didn't you use that thing before?"

"Forgot I had it. Ciao bella." The bright light bounced as Shana walked away, then blinded Alex again when she spun back around. "You're coming tomorrow night, right?"

"Yes. I told you."

"Cool. I promised you would." Shana walked away in the charcoal night, leaving Alex alone with Cass. She leaned her cheek against the granite headstone. The idea of staying there by herself did creep her out a little, but she wasn't about to admit that to Shana. Anything was preferable to going home to the deep freeze, to the freaking war zone her parents had created with their bizarre setup: half the house her mom's territory, the other half her dad's, Jack zinging from one parent to the other like a pinball in a vintage arcade game.

The only place in the house where Alex didn't feel like an intruder, where she felt safe and protected, was her own bedroom.

Outside of that, she'd rather come here. She owed that to her friend. And even though the cemetery visits made Alex gut-wrenchingly sad, Cass's presence was comforting, too. Her friend's spirit was so potent, Alex swore its energy swirled around her as she sat there, bubbling up like a spring. Like a promise.

Alex knew it was selfish. She had no right to come here, to draw even one second of peace from this place. To take anything more from Cass than she already had.

She came anyway. She could only hope Cass was OK with it.

She dug into her bag for a stick of Rainbow Bubble, rolled it into her mouth and snuggled closer to the tombstone. Now she just had to figure out tonight, find a way to stay out until both her parents were asleep. She'd be tired in the morning, but what was the purpose of school, anyway? Wasn't like she needed to get stellar grades or anything. Her father had made that point very clear the night of her Sweet Sixteen.

Great time to be a hard-ass, Dad.

MEG

An angry squeal of tires followed by Angel's barking jarred Meg awake around one thirty. She met Alex at the door, her cheeks tight from her tears.

"Where have you been?" Meg demanded.

"Nowhere." Alex's heavily rimmed green eyes seemed glassy, her breath sticky sweet. Alcohol or Rainbow Bubble? Meg wasn't sure.

"Do you mind telling me what happened here tonight?"

"Just some friends. No big deal." Alex pushed by her, heading for the kitchen. Following, Meg noticed the daisy tucked into Alex's ash-blond braid, tinged pink like the ends of her hair. An unfamiliar black romper hugged her daughter's athletic figure, toned from years of soccer. Meg's throat caught at the sight of the violet satin scarf cinching her daughter's waist. Alex was never without the memento, winding it around her head, roping it to a purse, draping her throat. Shaking off the stab of grief, Meg made herself focus on the matter at hand.

"No big deal? Honey, do you know what happens if someone gets hurt here when we're not home? We could lose everything. There'd be no house, no college . . ."

"I don't care about college. Anyway, we weren't doing anything."

"Right. Just trashing our home and helping yourself to our things." She thought of the pills in her pocket. "And God knows what else." Meg blocked Alex's path to the refrigerator. "Who was here tonight? Shana, I'll bet." The two were thick as thieves lately. It tore at Meg to see them together without Cass. Still, it didn't give them the right to do this.

Alex licked her lips. "Nobody."

"Nobody? Should I start calling parents, then?"

"Mom, no!"

"Fine. I'll just wait for the pictures."

Alex blinked a few times. "So you're stalking me online now?"

"Forget it, Alex. Go to bed."

"Stop yelling at me. Why are you so mad?"

"Because this is our house, that's why. And because you're my daughter, and I'm worried about you. I don't even know what you're doing anymore."

Meg produced the baggie of pills and laid it on the counter.

"Wow, Mom. You going all *Nurse Jackie* now?" Alex cracked a wobbly grin.

"I'm serious. Whose are these?"

"I don't know. They're not mine. I swear."

"Tell me the truth, Al."

"OMG. You're a nurse. You'd totally know if I was taking something."

Meg pocketed the pills. "This isn't over, Al. We'll talk about the consequences tomorrow." She turned to head to bed.

"Consequences," Alex mimicked, opening cabinets and extracting a bowl and a box of cereal.

Take Jacob's advice: discuss it tomorrow, a little voice told her. But Alex's dismissal infuriated her. Before she could stop herself, Meg found herself yelling again. It was like an out-of-body experience. "Put those things back *now*. Do you know what time it is? You need some sleep if you're going to study for midterms tomorrow."

"You're not my guidance counselor."

"It's your junior year. The most important one for college." There couldn't be a more inappropriate time to debate Alex's academic future. But having planted the flag, Meg soldiered on.

"Really? I'm pretty sure if you can write your name, you get into county college." Foregoing the bowl, Alex stuffed a handful of cereal from the box into her mouth.

"You're smarter than county, Alex."

"Right. Ask Dad about that." Alex started toward the stairs with the cereal.

"Where are you going with that? You think this is a hotel?" She grabbed the box.

"I'm allowed to eat." Alex pulled back. The sheer ridiculousness of the scene registered in Meg's mind: *Why doesn't that crazy woman just go to bed?* Already anticipating the regret she'd feel in a few hours, Meg yanked once more, sending the box flying, carpeting the kitchen floor with cereal. With a yelp, Angel swooped in for the kill.

"Happy, Mom?" Alex smirked before leaving the kitchen.

How can I be happy when you're self-destructing right in front of me? Hot tears formed again as Meg grabbed a dustpan to sweep up the mess, ashamed of her adolescent behavior.

Upstairs, the clock glowed its fluorescent admonition: 2:00 a.m. In four hours, she'd have to get up for work, while Alex got to sleep in. Meg tossed and turned at the unfairness of it for a good half hour. She considered going downstairs to apologize. Maybe if they both cooled off enough to talk, and Alex promised to study during the day, they could get their nails done after work tomorrow. Like before.

But just as Meg's feet hit the floor, the aroma of burnt popcorn from downstairs enraged her anew. Giving up on sleep, she slid her laptop from under the bed, typing again the keywords so familiar they auto-populated her search window: *teen, grief, alcohol, drugs, parenting.*

She had her plan, but maybe tonight Google could offer up some advice to help her through tomorrow.

The first page yielded the usual resources, their violet links a reminder of the vast virtual terrain she'd already explored. Who knew there were so many wilderness camps? ("Brat camps," according to parenting blogs.) Meg knew it would take more than cold showers, trust falls and solitary hikes to get through to Alex.

Frustrated, she was about to give up her search for the night when an ad at the top of the page caught her eye:

"Alternatives for Parents of Troubled Teens: Begin Again Transport gives you peace of mind as we transport your child to their residential program."

CARL

The bride sang first. Tonight's was a reedy blonde laughing and stumbling through the lyrics unrolling on the screen. Carl was happy to wait. That's how it went with the hen parties that swooped in to Trinity to toast the bride-to-be. They were one-shots, easy to spot. She wore the tiara, the rest of them pink sashes like beauty contestants. Their table-tops were crowded with pricy pastel drinks.

Carl called her song, too: "It's Raining Men," by the Weather Girls. With these groups, he could virtually guarantee he'd hear that song and one other—"I Will Survive," the Gloria Gaynor anthem, always sung by a wronged bridesmaid spitting on the mike.

He loved karaoke for its routine and ritual: line up, pick a song, wait your turn to sing your heart out. Traveling for work, he sought out karaoke clubs like other road warriors hunted for hotels with in-room Wi-Fi or 24-hour gyms.

There was a decent crowd tonight. Ever since a city guide had anointed Trinity a top New York karaoke spot, it attracted tourists in droves.

Carl bided his time, swirling the stirrer in his ginger ale. He liked to wait until people had a few drinks in them; it made them all the more appreciative. When his turn came, he tucked in his shirt out of habit before climbing the single step to the stage. Once DJ Ken introduced him, he took the microphone and cleared his throat.

"Evening, everyone. I'm going to do a little Amphibian ditty. A favorite of mine from the seventies."

"Phibs! Whoop-*whoop*!" someone yelled.

"Shut up and sing," called another.

Ignoring the catcalls, Carl gave the DJ his cue. The music started; someone recognized the signature opening notes and hollered the title. "Rose Vol-cayyyy-no."

Carl loved it when there were Phibs fans in the house. They exuded their own unique energy. Nodding, Carl began to sing:

> *People warned me to stay away but her power drew me close.*
> *Deep as a river that scorched like fire, that woman's name was*
> *Rose.*

Carl moved easily around the stage, tapping his foot. It took less than a minute for his sure baritone to register with the crowd, for the front tables to shush talkers behind them and start clapping. He didn't need the words on the screen:

> *Though her force could burn and her words could sear, it was*
> *useless to resist.*
> *I learned this truth from her scalding lips the moment that*
> *we kissed.*

He loved all of it, the adrenaline rush, the release, the adoration. By the time he reached the chorus, the whole of Trinity was with him:

*I never knew what would set her off; I was helpless in that
heat.*
*Though she leveled me with a single glance, Rose made my
world complete.*
Rose . . . my Rose Volcano.

By the end, the entire bar was on its feet, stamping and singing
along until the final drawn-out "vol-cayyy-no." The bride and two
friends twirled on a table.

"'Lifeboat'! 'Cloud Path'!" Customers pressed for more Phibs nug-
gets. Illuminated phones in the air begged for an encore.

"Thank you, everyone." Carl wiped his forehead with a crisp
white handkerchief and stepped off the stage, applause ringing in
his ears.

One and done, that was his motto. Back at the bar, Martin set
him up with another ginger ale, then returned to dissecting bar fruit
in front of Carl with military precision, tart citrus spraying from neat
slices of lemons, limes and oranges. "Like I've said before, I've always
pegged you as more Neil Diamond than Ace Ackerman." He aimed
his paring knife at Carl. "I think it's that uniform look you've got
going on."

Carl glanced down at his khaki work pants, pressed navy sport
shirt and work boots—a far cry from the trademark tie-dye of
Amphibian's lead singer—and supposed Martin was right. He didn't
bother much about clothes. He often had to take off on very short
notice; limiting himself to a few staples made packing easier. In spite
of the differences in their wardrobes, however, Ace Ackerman et al
had taught Carl to appreciate a number of things in life, principally
music.

Around 1:00 a.m., shortly after the bride staggered out, Carl
drained his glass and dropped a couple of singles on the bar. Outside
Trinity, Pearl Street was filled with people who had a lot of night left

in them. As usual, he walked. He spent so much time on the road that when he did get back to the city, he left his car in the garage as much as possible. He passed an all-night bodega, its outside stands stuffed with daffodils and hyacinths, and then an after-hours club, its queue of young well-dressed customers snaking around the block.

Twenty, twenty-five years ago, he'd have jumped right in there with them. Today, Trinity was more his speed. He'd found the place by accident after he'd rented his apartment, stopping in to eat one night. Back then, there wasn't much around in the way of entertainment, just a couple of workingmen's bars.

Four years later, 9/11 happened. Carl thought about moving. For a while, New York seemed frozen in mourning, shunned by tourists. Then the city got its groove back, bullied by the mayor's relentless enthusiasm.

Today, Carl could barely get a newspaper without circumventing a stroller or two; his lower Manhattan neighborhood had become so gentrified. Workers hung around instead of jumping on the first train home; residents of ubiquitous converted lofts and crystal towers spilled out of their boxy homes like ants most nights. College students were everywhere, and arrogant.

It was as though secret crews worked through the night on the city's transformation. Often, when he returned from a trip, the local landscape had shifted again—a new coffee place where a bookstore had been, another doggie day care. It was like solving that puzzle in the back of the children's magazine, trying to figure out what was different.

With all the upscale changes, he was just grateful to hang on to one of the few remaining rent-controlled apartments. His buddy Jimbo had turned him on to the building when they'd gotten out of the service. Carl's Pearl Street one-bedroom suited his spartan lifestyle—ideal for someone living alone.

Half a block from home, he ordered a gyro from a street vendor, the 24/7 availability of food a perk of gentrification. Waiting, he reminded himself to drop off the Suburban at Randall's tomorrow for service. Randall was the last of a dying breed, a mechanic who would open his garage on Sunday for a loyal customer. Carl was overdue for a new car, but like everyone else coming off the years-long recession, he was gun-shy, eking out a few more miles from his current vehicle until business picked up again.

His end of the street was quiet. In the vestibule of his apartment, his BlackBerry vibrated, an unfamiliar New York number lighting up the screen.

"Begin Again Transport. Carl Alden speaking. How can I help you?"

SUNDAY

MEG

The testimonials from Begin Again parents had been like a drug. Meg scrolled and scrolled, addicted.

> *Thank you for the very professional service Begin Again provided for us in getting our son Eric to Resolutions Center. You turned what could have been a very emotional and angry confrontation into a very smooth transition.*

> *—Alicia D., Nashville, TN*

> *Your assistance with my daughter Marisol has helped to give us our lives back. I would recommend your transportation services to any parents who feel they have nowhere else to turn.*

> *—Elsa C., Destin, FL*

Nowhere to turn. *That's us,* Meg thought.

She read Begin Again's checklist for parents:

- *Has your teen found new friends and left the old ones behind?*
- *Do you suspect your child is using drugs or alcohol?*
- *Has your teen adopted an "I don't care" attitude?*

Check, check, check.
The last item:

- *Do you feel you are losing your teen?*

A little bit, every day. Swallowing the lump in her throat, Meg watched Begin Again's video of a simulated transport: A mother leads two agents into a teenager's room. They talk with the girl briefly, then lead her outside to a car, the mother watching from a window. Clearly, the mother and child were actors. But the agents seemed real, the whole process humane, possible.

The cheesy two-minute movie gave Meg hope. Too revved up to sleep, she slipped out of bed and shut herself in her closet to dial the 800 number. Despite the ungodly hour, Carl Alden was gracious and professional as Meg tearfully related Alex's story and her own plan to rescue her. It was fate that Begin Again contracted with The Birches for transportation services; Meg had never even thought to ask the school. Alden knew the facility well and spoke highly of it.

They talked for nearly an hour, Meg holding her breath at the sound of Alex finally coming upstairs, though it would have been unusual for her daughter to stop by her room.

Until that moment, all that separated Alex from The Birches in Silver Mountain was a phone call from Meg and a way to get her daughter there. But in Carl Alden and Begin Again, Meg found the missing piece of the puzzle: a transporter. Alden offered references and directed her to complete Begin Again's online Transport Request Form.

All of that had been last night. Today, Meg had printed the form clandestinely at work and had it with her now. She'd come out to the promenade, a detour after work, so she could read the form and think about what she would write. She gazed out at Long Island Sound from a bench and contemplated the ruffle of clouds stitched to the horizon like lace. A few people took advantage of the bonus hour of daylight: a bundled figure chasing a dog at the water's edge, a fisherman sitting low in a beach chair, his twin lines anchored in the sand.

Meg chose a different bench every time she went to the water. She was a few yards away from where she and Alex had fought over the boarding school idea; today's bench was "Your Wish Fulfilled." For five hundred dollars, the town soldered a personalized plaque to a bench. Dedications were strung along the walkway like love letters, bouquets lashed to the benches on birthdays and anniversaries, wreaths and even some battery-powered fairy lights attached at the holidays.

Meg wanted her own bench one day. She'd thought about surprising Jacob with one for their twentieth anniversary. They'd certainly logged enough stroller miles with both kids. After Jack's colicky infancy, they'd jokingly crafted their inscription: "Silence Is Golden."

Obviously, that bench wouldn't happen now, Meg thought, lighting a cigarette filched from Alex. The dog on the beach now obediently fetched the driftwood its owner hurled into the water, dropping it back at its master's feet. Digging in her pocket, she pulled out Begin Again's form and unfolded it. The first part was simple enough: name, address, contact information. Next, the legal mumbo jumbo. *I have full legal custody and rights to place this minor in the services of Begin Again Transport.* She squirmed before checking the box. *Describe any unique custody arrangements.* Meg could state with a clear conscience there were none. If anything were to change, it would be after the divorce. She dragged deeply, rolling the word "divorce" around in her mind. Why was Jacob so willing to take the easy way out?

Next, Alex's physical characteristics. *Height*: five foot five, Meg having lost the height advantage. *Eye color*: green, since hazel wasn't an option. *Date of birth*: September 9, 1995. Seventeen this fall. *Identifying physical characteristics*: lip ring, sanctioned by a well-intentioned Jacob after the accident; no tattoos Meg was aware of.

On to *Transportee history*. "Extremely helpful in assembling the right transport team," Alden had said when he walked her through the form last night. She pondered its questions now: *Is your child a flight risk? If so, please explain.*

The child in the video had gone docilely. Meg had asked Carl what would happen if Alex tried to flee. For kids deemed a flight risk, Carl brought an ex-military or police officer, but from what Meg had shared so far, he told her, that didn't seem necessary. In Alex's case, a female guide would sit in the backseat with her at all times. He trained his staff to de-escalate volatile situations with something called Positive Control Systems. Meg had made a mental note to look that up.

Has your teen exhibited violence and/or aggressive behavior? Alex periodically flew off the handle, but had never gotten physical.

It was obvious Alden painstakingly matched the transport team to the child's physical and emotional state—*like a bizarre dating service*, Meg thought, pocketing the form. Alden had calmly assured her during their phone call that he used no physical force to move the child from bedroom to vehicle, the most vulnerable time of the transport. His secret? With the parents out of the picture, he said, emotions were less likely to flare.

"When the child meets us, they'll weigh their options: run, play possum, fight or cooperate." His team could read body language and act accordingly.

A light wrist hold was sufficient to manage most kids, he had assured her, and the auto's basic child locks contained all but the most hyperactive teens.

If things escalated, there were restraints, but their use was extremely rare—with one in ten boys, maybe one in twenty girls, he estimated.

"Ultimately, your child will realize her best option is to cooperate with us."

Meg had found it difficult to swallow, suddenly. "I can't believe I have to resort to this." Carl was sympathetic as she explained how she had tried to talk to Alex about The Birches. "I know she won't go with me willingly," she said. "But this . . ."

There was a lot of judgment about using a transporter, Carl acknowledged. "I talk to families like yours every day. The best thing *would* be to take your child yourself. But if it puts either your child or your family at risk, is it worth it?"

It wasn't. Carl had made the trip to The Birches several times. Begin Again's time from Alex's bedroom to program would be five to six hours, he estimated. Working together, the school and Begin Again could operate on very short notice, should Meg decide to schedule the transport. He had urged her to think seriously about it.

It was all Meg *had* thought about for the last twelve hours. Alden struck her as attentive, even calling her at work earlier that day to see if he could assist her further.

Meg stubbed out the cigarette and stuck the papers back in her pocket, sure of what she would write.

Arriving home, Meg had all intentions of putting everything on the table. Jacob raised a hand to her from the den. "We left some pizza for you."

She had half hoped Jacob would cook tonight. She loved coming home on Sundays after he and the kids commandeered the kitchen and spent the afternoon cooking. It was worth the mess that remained to see Alex and Jack beaming over their efforts. He hadn't done that in a long time.

Alex was out tonight, Jacob said—something about a study group. Meg could only imagine what they might be studying. Once Jack was in bed, she confronted Jacob in the den, standing between him and the television. He fixed her with a heavy-lidded stare.

"I'm very worried about Alex," she began. "She's really floundering."

"I talked to her about the party, Meg. She promised it won't happen again."

"I know a way to make sure it doesn't." Meg perched on the ottoman. "I found this place in New Hampshire that would be amazing for her."

"New Hampshire? You want to send her away because of a trashed house?"

"Of course not. This isn't sending her away; it's sending her *to* a place where she'll thrive." Meg launched into The Birches' philosophy, its success rate with kids like Alex, its family-focused approach.

"You mean, we'd sit around and share our feelings with strangers? We don't need that touchy-feely stuff." He leaned around her to see the television. The salt-and-pepper waves grazing the neck of his T-shirt were out of character; he usually took such care with his appearance.

Cursing herself for having led with that, Meg changed gears, pitching the school's self-sustaining farm that taught the students responsibility, accountability. She didn't mention she'd seen it in action—droopy-jeaned boys yawning while they milked cows at dawn. "You know Alex is crazy for animals. Remember Clara?"

Clara was the matriarch cow at London's, their local farm stand. They stopped there often when Alex was small, holding her over the fence to stroke Clara's snout.

Jacob smiled. "How about that card she made for Clara's birthday?" The yellowed drawing was still taped to the farm's register. "There are animals here, Meg. We'll get her more hours at the animal shelter."

"She hasn't volunteered there in months."

Jacob shifted on the couch. "How much does a place like The Birches cost, anyway? We've got college to think about."

"If we don't do something soon, she might not make it to college."

"Don't be so dramatic. How are we going to afford some ritzy New Hampshire boarding school?"

Now Jacob chose to be fiscally responsible? He might have begun a few months ago by persuading his mother to scale back the Sweet Sixteen gala she had insisted on throwing for Alex. Their daughter would have survived. If they had to accept Miriam's largesse at all, her funds could have been used to offset their mounting bills instead.

But Jacob had balked. His mother just lost her husband, he argued; they should let her throw a party for her oldest granddaughter. Her mother-in-law had attached one odd stipulation: that her role in Alex's celebration remain a secret, Miriam's way of massaging her son's ego, Meg surmised.

"The Birches is considered therapeutic," Meg continued. "It's in our insurance network. We're covered as long as Alex meets their criteria. They think she will."

"*Do* they? So you've already talked to them." He aimed the remote over her head. They sat in stony silence while a *60 Minutes* reporter grilled an oily haired man about a phony drug cure he'd been peddling to desperate cancer patients.

At a commercial, Jacob muted the sound. "Suppose for one second I go along with this. Do you think Alex will magically agree to go this time?" He stretched his legs alongside her on the ottoman. "She wouldn't even talk to the school counselor. Or Dr. Fallon."

Dr. Fallon had been Alex's therapist for a brief period. Alex had allowed Meg to sit in on the first session, probably because Alex already had decided not to cooperate. When Alex did volunteer something, no matter how trivial, Dr. Fallon would ask, "And how does that make you feel?"

Meg didn't blame her daughter for shutting down, refusing to see the doctor. She went back to the drawing board, setting up appointments with two more therapists, both younger and more relatable, she thought after speaking with them on the phone.

Alex ditched the first appointment and showed up stoned for the second.

Jacob's resistance to The Birches didn't surprise Meg. After the thunderbolt of the separation, she'd suggested marital counseling, which he rejected as "too Oprah." Meg suspected he feared being forced outside his comfort zone. When life got messy, he usually retreated to the basement, to his beloved bass. Consequently, there was a lot Jacob missed, even when it was right in front of him—like his own daughter, curled up on her bed for hours.

"Of course Alex won't agree to go," Meg said. "That's why I thought we should . . ."

He waved his hand. "Forget it. I've been on board with everything so far, but not this. It's too drastic."

"But Jacob . . ."

"She'll grow out of it. We all did. Didn't you do anything crazy when you were her age?"

"Not as crazy as this." Meg dangled the baggie of pills in front of him, the bottom cloudy with fine powder from its travels.

Jacob sat up. "Where did you find those?"

"In the basement. After the house party." She described the exact location.

"Maybe she's holding them for somebody." He fingered each pill as though one might convey some crucial information.

"Come on. Even Alex didn't try that excuse on me."

"I'm just trying to give her the benefit of the doubt." He tilted his head. "What exactly did she say?"

"That she'd never seen them before. That she doesn't use pills." She shook the bag. "There's some lethal stuff here: Xanax, Ambien . . . Oxy, maybe. If she's mixing them with her prescription . . ." Alex had agreed to a mild dose of antianxiety medication after the accident, which Meg closely monitored.

"There were probably a lot of kids here that night. They could be anyone's. I believe her, Meg."

Meg crossed her arms. "Well, I don't."

Jacob stood. "Alex doesn't need a boarding school. She just needs us."

"She's had 'us' for sixteen years." *Us.* A concept Jacob appeared bent on redefining.

Meg leaned toward him. "I'm afraid, Jacob. The partying, self-medicating. On top of the shoplifting, the skipping school. What if she . . ." Meg couldn't verbalize her worst fears.

"She won't. You're overreacting. As usual." He stretched. "I'm gonna catch the rest of the game in the basement. Any objections?"

How much time have you got? There was no point in bringing up the transport idea now; he was already shut down.

"No. Go." The slam of the basement door underscored her frustration. In their early days, she would have followed him downstairs, determined to distract him from his nightly practice, convincing him to set down his guitar long enough for their own personal intermission, Meg languishing on the couch afterward while he polished the band's latest number, the strains soothing the infant in her belly.

She would have followed him in the later years, too, with the freshly bathed Alex and Jack in tow, the kids lugging toy instruments downstairs to join Jacob in lusty, if slightly off-key, jam sessions before bed.

Those days are history, she thought, crumpling the pizza box into the trash. She was about to make Jack's lunch for the next day when the basement door swung open again.

"I was thinking," Jacob said. "Those pills. We shouldn't leave them around. Jack and all. I'll dump them."

"No worries." Meg patted her pocket. "The hospital has a disposal site. I'll drop them tomorrow."

He yawned. "OK. Sounds like a plan."

Only step one, she thought, pulling a clean knife from the dishwasher.

"Hey, Meg."

She turned. Except for a slight swell at the waist, Jacob's body hadn't lost its youthful tautness. In spite of everything, the anguish of Jacob's rejection, she missed him desperately, they way she missed her daughter, their family, the way life used to be.

"Forgot to tell you. I'm heading up to Vermont on Tuesday for a few days with Ben."

"Really?" Meg smeared super-crunchy peanut butter on the cheap white bread Jack liked.

Ben Johnson was a friend of Jacob's from high school who ran a local tree service. Business had boomed since the previous fall, when Hurricane Irene ripped a swath of devastation through New England, downing thousands of trees, washing away homes and roads. Ben had more or less established a satellite location near Burlington and frequently offered Jacob work. The money was welcome, but it meant Jacob was away a lot.

He'd be home Saturday, Sunday at the latest, he said now. "Can you cover things here?"

Meg pressed Jack's sandwich closed. Yes, she could certainly cover things. Four days without Jacob. Ben had no idea of the gift he'd just given her.

THURSDAY

ALEX

How badly do you want it?

"So you see, in an acute triangle, the angles share a side and a vertex but have no interior points in common."

Vertex, vortex. Alex didn't see. She sighed, sliding the textbook across her geometry teacher's desk in the deserted classroom. "There's no way I'll catch up."

"Of course you will. The midterm isn't for two weeks."

"But I've missed so much." Skipping school was almost a daily habit now. She always showed up in the morning, heading resolutely down the main hall toward her locker, but would then duck out a side door and through the teachers' lot, lured by an irresistible force. She'd snuck back in the same way this afternoon, hitching a ride from the cemetery so she'd get back to school after dismissal but before her geometry teacher left.

"I'm not saying it won't be hard," Mrs. Ward said. "But if you come to class . . ."—the teacher aimed her protractor at Alex—"and by that, I mean come and *stay* and do more practice exercises, you'll have a pretty good shot."

Extra help was available every day after school, she said. "But you've got to put in the time." Her teacher held out the textbook. "The question is, how badly do you want it?"

So badly she could taste it. Mrs. Ward's question stuck with her while she walked, like a cartoon balloon over her head. It had taken everything for Alex to approach the teacher after school, but it had been a breeze compared to facing Sunday night's study session at Perk Up. Every nerdy eye in the discussion group for *The Giver* had locked on Alex as she entered the coffee shop. She'd considered bolting, until a dark-haired girl waved madly at an empty chair beside her, leaving Alex no choice but to join the circle.

"Glad you came, Al," the girl whispered.

OMG. It was Shana, unrecognizable under her newly ombréd mane.

"So? What do you think?" Shana had turned her head this way and that.

Shocked, Alex leaned back for a better look. The full-on black was severe compared to Shana's natural red-blond. It was edgy. Thinking that she would have to get used to it, Alex nodded and smiled, then turned to the discussion. Following along was kind of a joke because she hadn't even cracked open the book. *Yet.* From what she could gather, the premise sounded good: a place where there was no war or fear or pain. No choices. *Sign me up,* Alex thought, frantically jotting down essay-friendly sound bites. The group was divided over whether the main characters truly discover a real village in Elsewhere or only imagine it as they fight to survive in a frozen tundra. Alex sided with the realists.

Her attendance Sunday night—she hesitated to call it participation—left just two other subjects where she'd fallen dangerously behind. It was scary how fast a few missed classes and procrastinated projects added up to academic probation.

You can do this, she told herself at her locker. She took the long way out of school, avoiding the auditorium and its stage, hoping to blend in with the after-school jocks. She'd make up the classes one at a time, even if it meant summer school. Get back on track for senior year. Maybe when her parents recognized the effort she was making, it might make up a little for the trashed house. She felt horrible about her mother's tea set; she knew its story and tradition. If only it had been Aunt Melissa's turn to keep it, those stupid jocks wouldn't have landed on it when they were wrestling in the living room.

She didn't know a way to fix that, but if she did really, *really* well in school, maybe she and her dad could talk again about her college possibilities—this time without fighting. Trying to catch up was hard enough; the thought of having that stressful conversation with him again made her feel as if she would puke.

When Alex arrived at the town library, she glanced over her shoulder to make sure no one saw her going in. She hadn't even told Shana she was coming.

Inside, she gazed toward the children's wing with longing. She and Cass had spent tons of hours in its reading corner, even after officially graduating to the young adult room, flopping onto beanbag chairs to reread old favorites: *Miss Nelson Is Missing,* The Lupine Lady of *Miss Rumphius, Pippi in the South Seas. Happy Corner,* Alex thought ruefully, stopping at the adult room desk to reserve a copy of *The Giver* before ducking into a study carrel, determined to attack a few more geometry problems on her own.

Feeling confident, she flipped open her practice workbook, skipping ahead to the advanced section and reading the first problem: *In the figure below, ABC and DEF are triangles. AC = AB, AB // DF, BC // ED, AC // EF and ∠ CAB = 70°. Find ∠ x, ∠ y and ∠ z.*

The figure was a triangle within a triangle labeled with letters and degrees that looked for all the world like a baseball diamond. Alex had no clue where to begin. "No worries," she whispered, fortifying herself with a fresh slice of Rainbow Bubble and heading back to the front of the workbook.

Avoiding the longer word problems for now, she attacked a true-or-false section, evaluating a list of statements:

A parallelogram is never a square.

A square is always a rectangle.

A rhombus always has four equal sides.

Always and never. Mrs. Ward and other teachers always warned the students about these words on tests. They were usually red flags, Alex remembered; things were rarely that black and white. Which meant that the three statements in front of her must be false, Alex decided, about to write *F* beside each when she wavered. What if they were trick statements? Sweat beads popped out on her upper lip, and every detail she had ever learned about squares, rectangles and rhombuses flew out of her head.

Easy, girl. Don't freak out. She got up for a drink of water from the fountain, splashing some on her hot cheeks before returning to her carrel. She smoothed the workbook page and went back to the beginning word problems and read the first one. Its nautical premise might as well have been in Greek:

A naval distress flag is in the shape of a triangle. Its three sides measure 5 feet, 9 feet and 9 feet. Classify the triangle by its sides.

Whaaat? She read it again, then a third time. *Don't be a dumb ass. This is a basic problem.* She had already learned what *classify* meant, only at this moment, she had no clue about its definition. She went back over the problems Mrs. Ward had reviewed with her; none seemed to apply in this case. She was stuck. This entire afternoon had been a waste.

Furious, Alex threw down her pencil, watching it bounce out of the cubicle and onto the floor, where she left it. If she couldn't solve one little geometry problem on her own, how would she cope with tons more work from her other classes? There was no point.

She could send up a million distress flags of her own, and she would still sink.

Loading up her backpack, Alex left the library and walked the rest of the way home, ignoring Shana's texts, kicking random pebbles in her path. Her whole life sucked. She would never be able to turn things around; it had been a waste to even try.

No matter how badly she wanted it.

CARL

Carl Alden sold serenity. Meg Carmody cried a little when she handed him his check.

"I'm sorry," she said, pulling a tissue from her scrubs. "Everything's happening so fast."

Crisis mode was the nature of Begin Again's business. The two had connected barely a week ago. Now, Carl sat opposite his new client in her modest living room, the transport scheduled for the next morning.

"This is an emotional time, Mrs. Carmody. It's understandable." He clipped the check to his file, along with the signed waivers and Alex's school photo. He stole a look at his watch; if he could wrap this up quickly, he might still make it to the bank.

"Please. Call me Meg." Her eyes darted to the living room window.

"Meg, then. My job is to make this as easy for you as possible."

Carl had expected someone taller than this five-foot-four woman, a brunette instead of a bottle blonde. It was a game he played, crafting a mental image from the initial phone contact. He was right maybe half the time. Cancer nurse, she told him. Her voice had a tired, raspy quality. Then again, they all sounded defeated and shell-shocked when they called, often in the middle of the night as she had.

"Will Mr. Carmody be joining us?" Carl asked.

"Unfortunately, no. Jacob is away on business," Meg said, chewing her lip.

Carl shifted on the couch. The absent father concerned him. Legally, he needed only one parental signature on the release. But things went best when both parents were on the same page. Especially if things became too emotional.

Regardless, delaying this transport wasn't an option. Business had been light of late, parents hanging in longer than usual with their kids' dramas. His fees weren't the issue; most could scrape together the few thousand Carl charged. It was the rehab stays: they cost a bundle. The new health-care law was supposed to fix all that, but it was going to take a few years for all the political dust to settle.

This family obviously had the means to cover the daughter's treatment, or he wouldn't be sitting here. The female guide he'd engaged was already on her way.

Begin Again couldn't afford to let this one go.

"All right, then," Carl said. "As long as you are a legal guardian." Behind his client, a family portrait over the fireplace included a towheaded girl of about eight who leaned on the father's shoulder. *A daddy's girl.*

Meg followed his gaze. "That's Alex on the right. That was taken on Rye Beach."

"I'm staying out that way tonight," he said. "Along with Officer Murphy. She's very qualified—former police officer, has assisted on dozens of transports." He softened his voice. "She's a mom, too."

"I'm glad." Still teary, she wiped her nose. "Whatever will make this more comfortable for Alex. She's been through a lot." Her eyes darted to the front window again.

Carl cleared his throat. His client needed to have it together for tomorrow morning. He asked to see the most direct way to the daughter's room. She led him up the stairs into a small bedroom on the right. The space was typical of many he'd entered in the early hours over the past few years, down to the band posters on the wall. One in particular next to Alex's bed caught his attention: Amphibian's distinctive logo commemorating the jam band's watershed moment a quarter century ago. He aimed his pen at the poster.

"Phibs fan, your daughter?"

"Yes. A bit obsessed, I'd say. Her dad's a musician. She inherited that gene from him."

"Not the worst trait in the world." Funny that the girl was drawn to this band in particular. The Phibs crowd was an older demographic, more her parents' generation. Something to do with the resurgence of the whole hippie scene, he guessed. Tie-dye was mainstream.

Carl tapped his pen on his clipboard. "Mrs. Carmody, this is where it's all going to happen tomorrow." Her role in the pickup was brief but critical, he stressed. "Once we're in the house, you'll lead us into this bedroom. Alex has to see that you're in charge. That this is coming from you."

Meg sniffed. "I'm sure she'll figure that out pretty quickly."

"Right off the bat, tell her you love her and that you've asked us to help you." A hug was very important, he stressed—as critical as Meg's prompt departure.

"What if something goes wrong? If Alex needs me?"

"Trust me. Things go best when you leave right away. You can talk to her later in the day, when she's arrived at The Birches. Between now and tomorrow morning, act normal. You don't want to arouse any suspicion." He instructed her to pack a small bag with essentials for Alex's first few days. They would pick it up from her porch tomorrow morning.

"This is all really . . . clandestine," she said, leaning against Alex's closet. "I'll be so relieved when it's over."

He made notes to share with Murphy later and then returned to the hall to identify any unsecured areas. The mother tailed him nervously, apologizing for the state of the house as he peered into bedrooms and closets. Everything seemed straightforward.

Back downstairs, he picked up his backpack. His client's hands were fists in her scrub pockets.

"That's it, then?" She seemed like she might cry again. Clients were always jittery during this phase.

"The next twenty-four hours will be tough, but try to stay calm." At the front door, he gestured to the rental parked a discreet distance from the house. He would have preferred his own, but his mechanic was fixing the essentials—enough to keep the car on the road a few more months. Carl planned to pad the next few transports a bit to cover the expense. He felt justified; he hadn't raised his prices in years. "Assuming she's home by five a.m., we'll execute tomorrow, as we discussed," he said.

"Execute. Sounds like a firing line." Her pressed lips were white.

"Sorry. Jargon comes with the territory." He smiled to reassure her. "Everything will be fine. I've staked my reputation on Begin Again, on providing a hundred-percent-success rate." Carl reminded his client to text him when Alex arrived home. "Get some sleep. Things will happen quickly tomorrow morning."

He ticked off the three check-in calls she would receive: once the transport was under way, during the lunch stop and upon successful delivery to The Birches—about this time tomorrow, he noted, checking his watch.

A final wrap-up call from his hotel tomorrow night would be the last time they'd speak.

"If I make it that long," she said.

There was one more thing: the letter that Begin Again suggested parents write to their child, delivered during the transport when the child would be receptive to it. (Translation: when the teen settled down enough to read the letter without ripping it to shreds.)

Meg's hand fluttered to her throat. "I'm still working on that. I'll have it tomorrow."

Carl hated to leave things until the last minute, but, like the father's absence, this was out of his control. Anyway, the letter was for Alex, not him.

Walking back to the rental, Carl felt his client's eyes on him. He didn't envy her, having to playact through the evening. He hoped, for all their sakes, the girl got home in time to green-light the transport. There was an awful lot riding on one sixteen-year-old's whims.

At the end of the Carmodys' street, he stopped to let a young girl cross. She was bent under the weight of her backpack. In the split second Carl glimpsed her face, he could have sworn it was Alex. And that she was crying.

Back at the hotel, Carl followed up with another transport shaping up for Sunday. A tight turnaround after the Carmody delivery, but doable. He had no choice.

That family's call started out like most others he'd received in his eighteen years of business—something like, "We've tried everything. We don't know what to do anymore."

Clients were initially skeptical that Carl could succeed where they had failed, that a child who rejected all parental authority would respond rationally and cooperate with the transporter. The parents didn't get that Carl lacked their emotional connection, that crazy genetic bond that triggers adolescent defiance and also tricks parents into believing that no matter how much has gone down, no matter how many empties, pipes or pills they discover and destroy, no matter how many heartfelt apologies they hear, that somehow this time *really* would be the last.

He knew this because he'd been one of those kids, subjecting his parents to years of hell, bouncing from vo-tech to reform school (they didn't sugarcoat it in those days) for being a wiseass. He worked odd construction jobs. On rainy days, the work crews sat around, drinking, smoking the occasional joint.

It rained a lot. Somebody hatched the bright idea of hitting a convenience store. Like a moron, Carl agreed to drive the getaway car. Thought he'd be the hero. Except, when the store owner hit the alarm, they all ran, leaving him to take the rap.

Lucky for him, he was under eighteen. After juvie, his record was expunged. But by then he had acquired a taste for the hard stuff, his friend Jack D, a habit rendering him unemployable. His sainted parents finally tossed him out when he was twenty-four. Eventually, when he ran out of couches to surf, he got sober.

Sobriety led him to enlist in the armed forces, ultimately landing him with a military police company out of Fort Benning; its exploits fueled his adrenaline habit. During the intense final days of Operation Just Cause in Panama, Carl's company defended the canal and democracy and fought to end drug trafficking—post-discharge duties as a stateside police officer paled against those heady adventures.

But Carl grew restless and bored, and his ghosts resurfaced. Fired from the force, he messed around for a while before deciding to hit the AA rooms again, and hard.

It took time to do it right. But once he had his blue chip marking six months of sobriety, he took everything he'd absorbed from the military and police duties and poured it into this business, his heart and soul. Begin Again Transport stepped in when families reached their limit—when that one thing put them over the edge: a missing check, the totaled car. When they wearied of sleeping with wallets and purses, keys slung around their necks like wardens.

The realization, finally, that life had become completely and utterly unmanageable led them to Begin Again. A drill sergeant of Carl's had once told him something—barked it at him, actually: *What's the definition of insanity? Doing the same thing over and over, expecting a different result.*

These parents had their own breed of insanity: believing they had even one iota of control over their teenagers' behavior. As soon as they surrendered this fantasy, they found their way to Carl.

He was the answer to their prayers.

MEG

Meg was toweling Jack's hair dry after his bath when Jacob called from the road to say good-night. She made her son answer, afraid she'd slip, that he'd hear something in her voice. After, she nibbled a nail while Jack chose a bedtime story.

"Slow down, Mom." Now that Jack was learning to read, she couldn't fool him as easily. *I'll make it up to you tomorrow, bud.* Finished, she tucked the sheets mummy-like around him the way he liked, then switched off his baseball lamp.

"But I'm not tired." Jack pulled his arms out from beneath the blankets.

"You will be, as soon as you shut those eyes."

"Ms. Traynor said we have to get eight hours of sleep every night." Jack's teacher dispensed a great deal of advice, some of which Meg felt overstepped her bounds.

"Ms. Traynor is very smart. Now, lights out."

"Where's Alex?"

"Out. Now stop stalling and get to sleep."

The sweet sound of Jack singing a lullaby she usually sang to him herself filtered through his closed door, igniting a flicker of guilt. *One more day, Jack.* Once Alex was away, she could devote more time to her son.

Downstairs, she ignored unopened mail and unfolded laundry and collected the things she planned to pack in Alex's bag. All week she'd pulled things piecemeal from her daughter's floor, throwing them in with her own laundry, hoping Alex wouldn't notice. She'd found herself buying the teen new underwear and socks, her usual pre-vacation ritual. "I must be in denial," she'd told Melissa when they met at the diner the night before Jacob left for Vermont.

Her sister was on board with sending Alex to The Birches, mostly. The one point they didn't agree on—and it was major—was telling Jacob.

"You can't keep this from him. He's her father," Melissa had said as she blew on her clam chowder to cool it. "You always do this, Meg. Remember when you sold all the baby furniture on Craigslist without telling him?"

"Jack was five. We knew we weren't having any more kids."

"Still, you made things pretty official. Jacob was really upset."

"That was totally different. It was about *stuff.* And I told you, I tried to talk to him about the transport Sunday night. He blew me off—even after I showed him the pills. Like they meant nothing."

"Listen, I know how much he's hurt you, but—"

"You think I'm doing this to get back at him?" Meg cried. "I would never use my daughter that way."

"I know that. But what about *later?*" Melissa let her spoon fall into her soup. "Jacob could use this in the divorce."

Out loud, the word had stung. Meg still hadn't told many people.

"*He's* the one abandoning us. He'll probably be happier with Alex off somewhere in New Hampshire. One less kid to cramp his 'single' style."

"You know he's devoted to them. Tell him, Meg. Before he leaves for Vermont."

"I can't." How could she convince her sister this wasn't revenge? Meg swallowed. "He'll thank me. I know he will."

"That might be a stretch. And there's still Jack. He could try to take him from you. Use the 'unfit mother' thing."

"If an unfit mother does every imaginable thing to save her child, then I'm guilty." Meg dropped her burger, no longer hungry. "Whose side are you on, anyway?"

"Yours, of course," Melissa had said softly. Picking up a small stainless pitcher of hot water, she poured it over her tea bag.

It reminded Meg of her mother's dented teapot and the set she hoped to hand down to Alex one day, as her mother had passed it on to her. She stared up at the diner ceiling, where tiny lights glittered in the stucco like constellations. "Don't you think if I had any other option for getting Alex there, I would use it? You *know* what happened when I tried to talk to her about it. When *you* tried."

"I know," Melissa sighed. Following the boardwalk debacle, Alex had curtly dismissed the idea of a road trip, as proposed by her godmother. It was an opportunity she would have embraced a year ago. "You think I don't know how you two work?" Alex had snarled.

"I'll deal with the fallout from Jacob later," Meg said. "I'm just so terrified something will happen to her if I don't do something *now*."

Her sister reached across the table to clasp Meg's hands. "It *won't*. And now that I've said my piece . . ." Melissa slid a folded check across the table. "Put this toward the transport."

Meg slid it back. "I can't take your money. I moved some stuff around . . ."

"Please. Let me do this for my goddaughter."

Reluctantly, Meg pocketed the check. "OK, but I'm paying you back. With interest."

They had hugged good-bye in the diner parking lot, after Melissa agreed to come early the morning of the pickup to be with Jack.

Going back upstairs with the things to pack in Alex's bag, Meg realized gratefully that her son's singing had finally ceased. She grabbed Alex's duffel and carefully arranged the items inside, pausing every now and then to peer out the bedroom window, hoping to see her daughter returning home. There'd been a tense moment that afternoon, when Alex breezed in moments after Carl left. Meg had feared the plan was blown. But Alex seemed preoccupied, refusing dinner and pouring cereal instead. Later, Meg could tell by the way Alex bounded down the stairs she was headed out.

"No homework?" Meg had called.

The door had slammed without an answer. Meg hadn't fought her. *Let her have one last hurrah,* she thought now, zipping Alex's duffel shut and hiding it in the garage under some old shower curtains. She found herself thinking about Officer Murphy, the mother coming into her house tomorrow to take her child. Would she judge Meg for this? The mommy court could be brutal; Meg certainly had issued her fair share of judgments.

Walk a mile in my shoes, Officer Murphy.

CARL

Meetings were like karaoke: some nights you played to a bigger crowd than others.

Tonight, the two wings of Riverport's one-story Presbyterian Church beckoned to Carl like open arms. Downstairs, in a dusty classroom festooned with felt Bible banners, the group was small. Step meetings didn't draw a big crowd. He preferred them, mulling over what each step taught him about his own addiction and recovery.

Tonight's was Step Eight: amends. Amends were hard—brutal reparations of relationships shattered by poor choices. For Carl, these included his parents, an aunt whose pearls he pawned, a cousin whose graduation party was the launchpad for his first acid trip. Some forgave easily, some not at all.

Like Diana, after that night at Grayson Lake. The two had been separated when the Kentucky crowd swallowed him; he came to in the litter-strewn parking lot the next morning to find her kneeling over him, crying in relief, only to rage at the discovery that he had lost the van keys and all their money.

He lost her, too, that night—Diana, who set the bar for every woman afterward. So far, none had measured up. It took a special kind of partner to sustain things long-distance, to play second fiddle to his life's work.

Carl had grown to believe things were better this way, his work a protective shell. He loved women, but nothing could compromise his ability to respond to Begin Again's next call. He lived alone and had liked it that way—until recently. Maybe it was all the strollers in his neighborhood or the brides in the bar, but he'd begun to crave companionship. It felt like something, someone, was missing.

He had heard that Diana married a hometown guy, had a couple of kids, ran a graphic design firm. He kept track.

In making amends, Carl wrote a lot of letters. Diana's came back unopened.

Begin Again Transport was one big amends to everyone he'd harmed. Especially Diana. Carl stood, the metal folding chair scraping the church floor:

"My name is Carl, and I'm an alcoholic."

The meeting ended with the usual recitation. Beyond straightening the chairs, he never hung around after. Outside, he read an apologetic text from Murphy. Her daughter's soccer game had gone into overtime. She was here now. Should they meet by the Sound?

He saw her on Playland's promenade, a slight figure waving, standing between two turquoise towers. To his right, mechanics clung to the ribs of the Dragon Coaster, tuning up the old-fashioned roller coaster before the pier reopened for the season. The fierce jaws of the red-eyed reptile gaped open, ready to consume its passengers at the ride's end.

Carl caught up with Murphy at the fountains in front of the Ice Casino. The rink was closing up for the night, exiting hockey players hobbling under the weight of equipment bags, sticks over their shoulders like shepherds' crooks.

Murphy leaned against the railing. "So, chief, we all set?"

"Still waiting for the word from the mom that the kid got home tonight. Otherwise, we're good."

Carl led Murphy to the Tiki Bar at the end of the pier. The place had some years on it. They took a table inside, watching the wind off the Sound ruffle plastic palms on the outdoor patio. A shivering waitress in shorts stumbled over reciting the Tiki specials. She seemed disappointed in their simple orders of sandwiches and sodas.

While they waited for food, Carl sketched the layout of the Carmody house on a napkin. Murphy had read Alex's entire file and bought the snacks and drinks Meg specified. There wasn't much more to cover.

Over Carl's head, Murphy glanced up at the activity in the bar and laughed. "Ah, I get it," she smiled. "Sandwich *and* a song."

He turned and shrugged. "You know me well enough by now."

The machine was set up onstage, a few names already in the queue. Carl got up to add his to the list. A few songs in, when they had nearly finished their meals, the overzealous emcee called his name, teasing out the song's opening chords. Murphy dropped her napkin into her lap with a flourish. "You're on, Carl. I just wish your clients could see you now."

"Might be bad for business," he laughed. On his way to the makeshift stage, he passed a waiter, who offered a fist. "'Oceanus.' The B side. Cool, dude." Carl obliged the employee, then grabbed the microphone to serenade a crowd in which the Tiki Bar staff outnumbered patrons:

> *Oh mighty river from which all tears flow; this libation of*
> *supplant prayer.*
> *Show us your pearls, buried treasures, your secrets; reveal what*
> *truths linger there.*

ALEX

"Come on, Al. You owe me."

Evan was beyond desperate on the chaise longue next to Alex, pleading. They were hanging in his grandparents' garage for the last time before the pair returned from Florida. Snowbirds returning to the nest, he had texted earlier. Tonight's crew included the spray-tanned Larke—the same Larke who had torpedoed Alex's house party.

Evan *had* come through Saturday night, picking her up at the cemetery around midnight—creeped out that she'd stayed there alone, like Shana had been. Alex hadn't bothered explaining to him that once she'd grown accustomed to the dark and the silence, it felt kind of peaceful—the kind of quirky, out-of-your-comfort-zone thing she and Cass would have done together. With Cass, she somehow ended up doing things she never would have imagined. Cass had a way of making everything irresistible.

Like marine-science camp the summer before eighth grade. Standing next to Cass on the promenade reading the sign-up sheet, Alex had wrinkled her nose at the suggestion. "Yuck. Too much work. Can't we just hang on the beach?"

"It'll be cool. Look. It says real marine biologists teach it."

"So what." Alex eyed Cass over her sunglasses.

"Last year's teacher was really hot. My cousin told me."

"OK, but don't you realize we'll probably be the only eighth graders?"

"Yes. Which means *we* get to drive the boat the last day of class."

"What boat?"

"The one they borrow from the college. It has a glass bottom, so we can see all the cool stuff in the water." Cass dug in her bag for a pen. "Do what you want, Alex Carmody, but I'm signing up."

And so, as usual where Cass was concerned, Alex caved. Also as usual, she was glad she had. The soft summer mornings flew as the girls worked ankle-deep at the shoreline, drawing water samples and matching real plants and animal life to images on the gigantic chart leaning against the lifeguard's chair—like assembling a huge puzzle. Who knew this exotic ecosystem even existed? Alex became obsessed with the study of tides, the seining, the sieves—she couldn't get enough of those mesh-bottomed pans, the marine biologist's best friend, her sifting through all the junk to get to nature's heart.

Alex loved all of it, especially their exhilarating final day. Having each helmed the promised speedboat as it skimmed over the Sound, they sat and dangled their legs above the six-paneled clear bottom show-casing the aquatic universe below. After, eating ice cream on the prom-enade, Alex crammed the tip of the cone into her mouth. "By the way, I decided. I'm going to be a marine biologist," she announced.

Cass slapped Alex's thigh. "Go for it, girl."

"What about you?"

"That, my friend, is up to the stars. Maybe I should ask Zoltar," she joked, jerking her thumb behind her. Even though parts of *Big* were filmed on this very promenade, the locals knew that the arcade fortune-teller was a figment of Hollywood's imagination, that a rusty soda machine that randomly ate their dollars stood in Zoltar's place.

Even without Zoltar, Cass would figure it out. They had all the time in the world, Alex had thought, back on that carefree summer afternoon.

Evan was shaking her. "How much time do you need to decide, anyway? I'm gonna be in deep shit."

"Give me a minute," she said, flashing a smile. If she couldn't get through Geometry 101, how would she possibly conquer marine biology? It was useless. Maybe she should just make a career out of helping Evan. It was supposed to have been one and done, her helping him. She'd barely slept the first time she hid his stuff at her house, terrified somebody would find it, even though she was positive her hiding place was foolproof. She told herself she wasn't dealing, that she was just helping a friend—and helping herself in the process. But all along, there'd been that prickle up the back of her neck signaling her that the whole gig was just *wrong*.

And now, just because of a stupid baggie of pills, her mother had decided Alex was some kind of drug addict or pill pusher. Didn't she know Alex at all?

"I'll make it worth your while, Al." Evan waved a wad of bills at her. Alex was torn. She had a serious cash-flow problem: The Millers were increasingly unreliable, and on top of that, she'd lost her job at the surf shop—for calling out once too often or just not showing up. She couldn't remember. She hadn't dared tell her mother; she'd have made her put in a bunch of employment applications around town so she would stay busy, *occupied*. Like having something to do, somewhere to go, made everything all right.

And here was Evan, making her an offer like some kind of human ATM.

"My father's sweeping my room like a *Law and Order* detective," he said. "If he finds anything else, he's gonna throw my ass out." His face was inches from hers; she could see herself in the brown pools of his eyes. "Please hold them for me a little longer?" He kissed her lightly, barely more than a peck. "Last time. I promise."

Alex pulled away, her pulse pounding in her ears, knocked off balance by the senior's attention, hesitating only a second before answering him. Evan sprung off the couch and joined the group huddled around the outdoor fire pit. Larke tossed her annoyingly perfect blond hair and gazed up at Evan adoringly. *Ugh.* He ate it up, throwing his arm around her. A bong began to make the rounds.

Alex rubbed her lips. Her brain knew Evan's kiss was his way of persuading her, but still, she'd felt *something.* How could he go straight from kissing her to flirting with Larke? Boys were so confusing.

Twirling her braid, Alex decided she was more than OK with this snowbirds thing being over. She hadn't even thought about going out tonight until Evan texted her; she'd been planning to dive back into *The Giver.* Shana had stayed home to study, a decision that freaked everybody out, including Shana, judging from her text.

```
I know, right? Aliens have taken over my
body.
```

Shana texted that she was turning off her phone to concentrate. *As if.* Alex didn't get it. They both survived the same horrific night. How could Shana just pick up her life and go on, bouncing back like a Slinky while Alex crashed and burned?

The truth was, Alex was bored hanging out here without Shana. And tired. Though she'd die before admitting it to her mother, she'd rather have stayed in tonight, curled up on her bed with Angel. She'd only gone out to escape her parents' perpetual cold war. Although, come to think of it, she hadn't seen her father in a few days. Back when he and her grandfather worked construction together, he was home every night for dinner. Now, with his tree gig, she never knew when he would reappear.

Bitch Larke's shrill fake laugh rang out over the chatter. Completely over this scene, Alex dug in her bag for her phone. It wasn't *that* late—barely midnight. Maybe her mother could come get her, no questions asked. Then Alex might actually think about dragging herself to school the next day, connecting with Mrs. Ward again.

She pulled up her latest stream of texts with Mommy Dearest (her mother had not found that funny *at all*, but it was better than Crazy Bitch or Psycho Mom, nicknames friends attached to their moms' contacts) and sent off a new message:

Hey can u pick me up?

She pictured her mom sitting on the couch or her bed, her phone beside her; how happy she would be to read this message, to bring Alex home safe and sound. Her mother would drive up all bright and cheery and would pepper Alex with annoying questions on the ride home. Alex wouldn't be surprised if her mother knew Evan's grandparents and remembered they went to Florida for the winter. She would definitely grill Alex about *that*.

Her mom must have been sitting on top of the phone, because her reply came about three-and-a-half seconds later:

Sure. Where are u?

All she had to do was give her mother the address, Alex thought, and she'd be on her way home. *Easy-peasy.*

A burst of laughter floated from across the room. Evan and Larke looked even cozier, if that were possible. If Alex left now, any chance she had with him would go up in smoke—the smoke from the bong making its way around the fire pit. Larke was *not* going to rule.

On her screen, blinking dots meant her mother had more to say.

Alex? Where are you? Tell me address
plze.

Sorry, Mom. I'm nowhere.

Tossing the phone back into her bag, she counted down the seconds until her mother resorted to an actual call. *Brrrrrrrrrrrrrr*—right on cue. She felt a twinge of guilt as the barrage of repeated calls vibrated through her bag's embroidered fabric.

Alex walked across the room and stepped into the circle, between Evan and Larke.

There really was no rush to leave now. No rush at all.

MEG

It was after midnight when Meg crawled into bed to compose her letter to Alex, nauseous with anxiety over whether she would come home tonight. If this transport came off at all, it would be a miracle. She checked her phone again: radio silence.

Pen poised over the blank sheet, Meg wondered if Alex would even read a letter given to her under these circumstances. She never acknowledged anything Meg wrote her—not a word about the notes she had been slipping into her lunch for years. But if a letter were part of the transport plan, she would write one.

Closing her eyes, Meg reviewed the roller-coaster ride of the past nine months following the accident—the partying, the slipping grades, Alex's growing detachment. Like Jacob, she had at first attributed Alex's behavior to the grief process, a natural reaction to the tragic loss of her best friend. Meg could only imagine the depths of her daughter's sorrow. Having watched the girls grow up together like sisters, Meg herself had to avoid Cass's street for months after, knowing she would break down into tears.

Even now, the memory of Cass's funeral caused Meg physical pain. Outside Kennington Funeral Home, the line of teenagers waiting to pay their respects had stretched beyond the parking lot. The girls tugged at borrowed dark skirts and jackets, sniffling and holding each other in their fresh grief, bearing flowers and stuffed animals. Standing beside Meg, Alex was silent and hollow eyed.

The boys, so awkward at that age, years too young to know how to comfort anyone, punched each other instead as they inched closer to the entrance. Meg recognized many of them from Alex's Sweet Sixteen. Inside, parents hung back, overcome by the specter of sorrow. Kennington extended the evening viewing hours to accommodate the throngs of mourners.

A screen at the entrance flashed pictures from Cass's young life: newborn in a crisp white christening dress, a cheerleader holding pompoms aloft. Meg winced at the images capturing the girls' friendship: soccer games, cast photos, the pair crouched at the harbor's edge the summer Alex fell in love with the water. Meg hadn't heard much about her dream of becoming a marine biologist lately.

The montage spun images from Alex's party: Cass, Alex and Shana, arms around one another in their party finery. It was the last time the three were together, just hours before they got in a car driven by Logan, Shana's brother. Cass had absolutely begged Meg to let Alex go on that after-party Slurpee run in Logan's car, instead of their going straight home from the party. It would only take half an hour, Cass had said. *So much loss over frozen soda.*

After the accident, blood tests showed Shana and Alex had been drinking. Cass and Logan had not. The police blamed the accident on distracted driving. Cass's distraught parents hadn't pursued any legal action.

For Meg, there remained many unanswered questions. Why had it been so critical for the three girls to get in Logan's car that night? Why hadn't the beautiful party they had thrown for Alex (or that her dear mother-in-law Miriam had thrown, to be precise)—an event more elaborate than Meg's own wedding—been enough for the sixteen-year-old? Why hadn't the always-responsible Cass worn a seat belt?

The day after, the school assembled a team of grief counselors, making them available all weekend. Alex refused to go. Days later, she spurned her parents' overtures at the cemetery, standing alone as her friend was lowered into the ground under a mountain of daisies. Sorrow had sliced through Meg at the sight of Alex's heaving shoulders, the tears soaking the angry stitches on her daughter's cheek. Meg leaned on Jacob, imagining Alex now walking out of school alone instead of with an arm intertwined with Cass's, realizing she would never again hear Cass's giggles erupting from their kitchen or her van's backseat.

If these losses seared Meg with sadness, what misery must Alex have been enduring?

Meg and Jacob had made many allowances for Alex, providing her ample time and space to grieve for her friend. Bottling her own sadness, Meg pumped coworkers for therapist recommendations for her daughter. That exercise failed miserably, as had every effort since to get Alex to open up. Nearly nine months had passed, and every time Meg broached the subject, Alex's response was the same: "I don't want to talk about it."

Now the time *had* come to talk about it and all that had happened after. The Birches was Meg's last hope for her daughter, whatever the cost. She chewed the pen.

Dear Alex . . .

FRIDAY

CARL

Around 3:00 a.m., Carl's BlackBerry skittered across the hotel night table with the mother's text:

    Alex is home.

All systems go. *The girl would be good and groggy when they woke her,* he thought, tapping a reply to the mother and to Murphy, reminding Meg again about the letter.

He rose easily at five to shower and shave, leaning over the sink to trim the white *O* around his mouth. At 5:30 a.m., Carl and Murphy walked out of the lobby, leaving behind guests in drab business casual circling the breakfast buffet.

Ten minutes later, Carl and Murphy idled half a block from the Carmodys' red house. He made out the girl's duffel on the porch, a good sign. A blue minivan warmed up in the driveway, its exhaust blasting the crust of frost below. On the lawn, daffodils pushed through stubborn snow patches.

To the east, the Atlantic sky hinted at sunrise, salmon rays slicing steel clouds. Carl rolled down the window, inhaling the damp, cool air.

A good day for travel.

"Is that the mother?" Murphy pointed to the house, where the front door had opened. Carl nodded as a coatless Meg Carmody bent to slip an envelope into the duffel, then went back inside, reappearing a few seconds later, pushing a sleepy boy in pajamas toward the van. The dog circled nervously, nearly tripping the mother as she stuffed them both into the car. She clasped an adult hand extending through a back window, then returned to the porch, rubbing her arms against the predawn chill.

Carl tested the rental's child locks one more time, the final item on his predeparture checklist. They clicked into position faultlessly; everything functioned as it should. Adrenaline rippled beneath Carl's skin, the familiar rush triggered by the start of a new transport. He signaled to Murphy to get out of the car.

"Showtime."

In silence, Carl and his partner walked toward the waiting mother.

ALEX

Sometimes the dream was different. Sometimes Cass answered when Alex called, when her own stretcher rolled up alongside hers. Silly Cass, lifting the sheet from her face and sitting up, all smiles, Alex's candelabra earrings gleaming in her ears, so perfect with the dress, reflecting light from every facet. Cass's violet wrap draped over one shoulder like a beauty contestant's sash.

"Gotcha," she would say, like some gruesome Halloween prank. "They checked me out. Said I'm good to go." She would hop off her stretcher and walk alongside Alex's, dangling strappy heels in one hand, clasping Alex's hand with the other. "Happy birthday," she'd whisper. She'd tuck herself inside the ambulance beside Alex's mom, and at the hospital, without a trace of squeamishness, would watch the surgeon stitch Alex's cheek with swift, clean strokes, the dark filament taut in his assured hands, the stainless-steel surgical scissors glittering under the work light.

In this version, her parents brought them both home to Alex's, so furious over the deceit, but so relieved they were safe. Alex would dream that she woke up the next morning and lay in bed patting her bandaged cheek and looking over at her sleeping friend. When Cass finally opened her eyes, she'd fall all over Alex with apologies, pinky-swearing, like a ten-year-old, never to do something so stupid again. Cass would turn serious, sitting up tall and looking Alex straight in the eye: "It's OK. I forgive you."

Awakening from that version, Alex would feel almost human again, daring to think normal thoughts from her previous life: What's going on today? What should I wear? *On a good day, she might even get one foot on the floor before the darkness swallowed her again, reality setting in like a soaking rain:* I'm sorry. I'm sorry. I'm sorry.

Sometimes the dream was different. This wasn't one of those times.

Three sharp raps on her bedroom door: her mother's lovely wake-up call. *As if.*

"Go away. I said I'm not going."

Alex's words tasted like last night. She burrowed deeper into her bed, temples throbbing, regret coursing through her like a jolt of Perk Up's double espresso.

Here it was, like clockwork: the daily standoff. How many times did she have to tell her mom there was nothing for her at that school—that there wasn't one square inch of the place that didn't remind her? She had tried again yesterday, and all it did was drive home how lost she was. And yet her own mother expected her to suck it up and go.

A wedge of hall light sliced across her bed.

"I said, don't come in." It wasn't her mother's fault she felt like crap. If she'd allowed her mother to pick her up last night, she could have shared some of her horrible day. Not a deep heart-to-heart. But maybe a moment on the couch, bonding over Conan's stupid DVR'd jokes. A place to start.

But she hadn't let her. And now her mother approached in those clunky, horrible plastic shoes everyone wore, their stupid charms jangling. *They must give the patients a headache.* She peeled back a corner of the blanket. Alex heard her distinct inhale—the sniff test, her mother's favorite morning ritual. Alex held her breath for as long as she could, until the thud of more footsteps, heavier than her mother's and heading toward her bed, made her exhale.

This was a new approach. Was her dad now in on the negotiation? Alex jerked the covers back over her face. *Why couldn't everyone leave her alone?*

"Alex. Wake up. I need to tell you something."

Even through the covers, the full-on blast of overhead light seared Alex's lids. "Mom, please," she moaned. "Go *awaaay.*"

"I want you to meet someone."

Was she kidding? Who had company at this hour? "Not interested, Mother."

"Alex, Daddy and I love you. We just can't live like this anymore. We want to get you the help you need."

Whaaaat??? Her mother's voice sounded fake, rehearsed—like she was speaking lines in a terrible play.

"This is Mr. Alden and Officer Murphy," she continued. "We've asked them for help. They're going to get you safely to a school in New Hampshire. I love you, honey."

Through the blanket, her mother dropped a kiss in the vicinity of Alex's head.

"Mom, wait. What?" By the time Alex raised herself on her elbows, the plastic squeaks had faded and her bedroom door clicked shut. This was a joke. Alex crawled to the edge of her bed and peered out. Below was a pair of unfamiliar brown work boots—so close she could smell the shoe polish. Above the boots, crisply pressed khakis. She rolled over, shading her eyes against the harsh light, and a man extended a black-leathered arm toward her. A perfect *O* of white hair circled his mouth; in his aviator sunglasses, she saw the Day-Glo reflection of her lava lamp.

Downstairs, the front door slammed. An engine revved and faded. Angel didn't bark. Angel always barked when someone left. Something was seriously messed up.

"Good morning, Alex." The man's voice was deep and booming, like a TV announcer. "Time to get up. My name is Carl Alden. We're going to get you to your program."

"What program?"

"The Birches. The one your parents picked."

"No way. I've seen that rehab stuff on TV." The shows where the family guilt-trips the person into going. At the end, you find out what happened. It almost never worked out.

Alex sat up fast, her stomach roiling, deeply regretting the tuna-sub chaser the three of them devoured in Evan's Corvette, blasting Amphibian. It had been fun, even with bitch Larke squeezing next to Evan, forcing Alex to take the window. She would never sit in the back, no matter how crowded they were.

"The Birches is nothing like that." A female voice floated toward her, and a woman in glasses stepped forward. "I'm Officer Murphy. I'll be in the car with you today." She had a boxy mom haircut and wore all black—not cool black, but black like she didn't give a crap: baggy pants, ski jacket over a turtleneck. *Mock* turtleneck. Alex squinted. Was that a *fanny pack* around her waist?

The woman had the nerve to sit on Alex's bed, motioning to a pile on a storage cube. "Your mom put clothes out. Get up now and get dressed."

Alex's heart began to pound in tandem with her temples. These people were serious. Could they really take her? "Wait a sec. I mean, I have rights, don't I? This is, like, child abuse."

"This is perfectly legal, Alex. I'll leave you with Officer Murphy to get ready," the man said, lifting a camouflage cap to rub his head. "And let's get a move on. No telling how many folks will be headed to New England this weekend."

New England? Alex's palms grew clammy. She'd been crystal clear about her feelings on that subject when her mom dragged her out to the promenade for coffee. *She wouldn't, would she?* Panicked, Alex stared at the man, whose hand rested on her doorknob.

"I'll be just outside the door."

Alex crossed her arms. "I'm going *nowhere.* I already told my mother that. And you guys could be some child molesters, for all I know." She groped around her comforter for a cigarette and lit one. She was forbidden to smoke in the house—to smoke at all, actually—but the heck with that. "Where's my mom? She can't make me do this."

"Actually, she can. You're still a minor." Quicker than Alex, Camo Man neatly deflected the empty Coke can Alex grabbed from beside her bed and leveled at him, dropping it into her wastepaper basket. She didn't even know where her own reflex had come from or when the jackhammers began their assault on her chest. She only knew her heart was beating so hard she was terrified she might pass out.

Camo Man pulled a white handkerchief from a pocket and wiped his hand. "That's not going to help, Alex."

"I don't care. I need to talk to my mom. *Mom,*" she cried. Out of bed now, Alex stumbled over old breakfast dishes and clothes to her door. Camo Man blocked her path and grabbed her wrist—not tight, but still. Mom Haircut was on the other side like a shot.

"Your mom left." His voice was irritatingly calm, like he was talking to a very young child. Or a mental patient. "You can talk to her later. It's time to get dressed and cooperate."

Trapped, she rested her forehead on the door, her stomach in overdrive. *I should puke on their shoes.* "I'll just run away."

"Alex, your mother told me what a smart girl you are," Carl said.

The same bull her mom handed her all the time. "I'm smart enough not to go anywhere with you."

The man's grip loosened. "Look at it this way. At least you don't have to go to school today. Excused absence and everything." Was he busting her behind the aviators? She couldn't tell.

"Right, road trip," Murphy chirped. "We've got movies, snacks—the works."

Bribing her with a load of Disney films. This was turning into a bad comedy routine, a nightmare Dr. Drew. Or maybe it was that other TV doctor, the bald one. She couldn't remember.

They turned her around slowly in a weird three-way dance. "This program will help you figure things out," the man said. "And I can tell you definitively: cooperating is your better option.

> *Let the powers that be warm the path you will tread;*
> *No journey's harder than the one in your head.*

He had to be kidding. The dude was singing the chorus from Amphibian's "Cloud Path." Alex was obsessed with the second track on the Rainmaker album; Cass had covered an entire notebook with the lyrics. Even more surprising, Camo Man could totally sing, nailing the trademark tremor of Amphibian's lead singer, Ace Ackerman.

She glanced at the poster over her bed and bit her lip. No way he was a true Phib; this had to be a head game. She wouldn't give him the satisfaction of even mentioning it.

"I'll leave you now to get dressed." Carl released his grip. Murphy still held her other arm. "And one more thing. Give me that cigarette."

She took a long, defiant drag, staring at the warped version of herself in his stupid sunglasses, weighing her options. Maybe with him in the hall, she could work on the woman. She stabbed her cigarette into a milky cereal bowl on her desk. "Fine."

Nodding to Mom Haircut, Camo Man slipped out of her room. How could her mother do this?! Didn't she realize how super-stressed she was about everything? Alex kicked the clothes off her storage cube. "One thing's for sure. I'm not wearing those. I'll look like a nun."

"Then I'd suggest long pants and a warm top. It's still pretty chilly in New Hampshire."

New Hampshire. That at least narrowed it down a little. Now was her chance. Alex sat on the cube, summoning every fiber of sweetness the early hour would allow. "I think there's been a mistake. I totally planned to go to school today. So if you could just, like, get my mom on the phone, we can figure this out?" Her voice did that question-marky thing at the end that Cass hated. She forced a smile.

"I can't do that, Alex."

Alex's stomach felt like it was jammed on the twisty part of the washing machine. "My dad, then. He'll be cool with me—"

"Get *dressed*, Alex." Mom Haircut's tone was irritatingly final, like her mother's often was.

Alex opened a drawer, deliberately drawing out the process, holding up one bottom after another, settling on leggings. Bending over to pull them on made the walls whirl; she pressed a hand on the floor to steady herself. Why hadn't she stayed home last night, like Shana had?

Behind her, the woman had a chirpy comment about everything. "Lava lamp, huh? I had one when I was your age. Had the incense, beaded curtains, the whole nine yards."

Shut up. Alex dug in her closet for socks. Her mistake had been coming home at all last night; she should have told Evan to keep going.

Evan. He always went to school late. He'd rescue her. One sock on, she lunged for her phone to text him. Mom Haircut beat her to the punch, pocketing the phone and coiling the power cord into a neat bundle.

Alex stomped her bare foot. "You can't do that. If you're gonna drag me all the way to New Hampshire, I at least get to keep my phone."

"These are the rules, Alex." Murphy pocketed the charger, then swept Alex's bag off the floor where she had thrown it last night.

Did this woman think she was airport security? "That's an invasion of privacy. You need, like, a search warrant," Alex protested.

Apparently she didn't. Alex was under eighteen and in her parents' home. And since her lovely parents had given these two permission to ruin her life, Mom Haircut was entirely justified in rummaging through her bag, where a three-pack of condoms rested at the bottom, Alex remembered, squirming. Shana had thrown them in as a joke. Would anything else in the bag incriminate her? She couldn't remember. That was the problem with weed. It was awesome at helping you forget stuff, but sometimes it took away things you wanted to remember. She recalled the humiliation of Evan dropping her off first, before Larke, but beyond that, things were extremely fuzzy.

Mom Haircut handed the bag back without comment. Relieved, Alex found her suede boots under her bed and pulled them on.

"You might want something waterproof."

"These are fine."

When Alex was dressed, the woman opened the door. Alex glanced toward Jack's room. "Can I at least say good-bye to my brother?"

"Jack's not here," the man said. *He knew her brother's name.* Wasn't it like, six in the morning? Where was Jack? Where was everybody?

"We need to go, Alex." The harsh hall light illuminated the woman's gray streaks.

"Wait! I forgot something."

The two exchanged a glance, and with Camo Man blocking the stairs, Alex dashed back and grabbed the purple scarf, looping it around her neck.

Murphy walked downstairs first. Carl motioned for Alex to follow. At the bottom, they each took an arm. *Tell me they're not really going to walk me down the street like I'm a prisoner.*

"You don't have to hold me." She licked sweat forming over her lip.

"We want to keep everyone safe," Carl said.

What was safe about two strangers dragging her off to no-man's land? Her house was eerily quiet. Maybe by some miracle her father was asleep in the basement. "Dad," she yelled.

Camo Man tugged her toward the front door. "He's not here either, Alex."

She cringed as they walked three abreast up her street—her own personal walk of shame. This must be how criminals felt. On the right, the Arnolds' house. She used to babysit their two little girls. Past the Mitchells' and their twin varsity-basketball-player sons. Not that she was big on jocks, but those guys were hot. How mortifying. *Please, please don't be up yet.*

After an eternity, they stopped at a regular black car. Camo Man opened the back door, and the two formed a human wall behind her.

Light-headed, Alex stared into the car's interior. This was not happening. If her mom had staged this crazy show to scare the crap out of her, it was working. She spun and faced them.

"You have to talk to my mom. Tell her I'm trying. I swear." Alex reached into her bag and produced a scrap of notebook paper. "See? Geometry problems. I went for extra help yesterday." She dove in again for *The Giver* and fanned the pages, stopping at a folded-down corner. "And I've been reading. I stopped right here. I even went to a study group to bring my grade up."

"It's too late, Alex."

"It can't be. I get what my mom's doing. I'll do anything she says." She spun, squelching back the tears that threatened. The woman Murphy had to have some sympathy. "Please. Tell her I'll go back to the shrink. To school every day if she wants me to." Alex thought she glimpsed a flicker of emotion behind the glasses. "I'm begging you. Don't make me go."

They pressed closer to her. Without warning, last night roared up into Alex's throat, and she threw up beside the car, vomit splattering the man's boots and the tail of Cass's scarf. Alex hung there, sweating and spitting out the sourness. Mom Haircut shoved a tissue under her face.

"I can't go. I'm too sick."

"You'll be fine, Alex," said Camo Man. "Take some deep breaths."

Were they made of stone?

"Let me grab that scarf, Alex. It's dirty."

Alex swatted away Murphy's hand. "Don't touch it." They wouldn't take that from her, too.

Too queasy to argue, Alex let him shut her in the backseat. He stood guard until Murphy got in the other side, then he slid into the driver's seat. Surely they'd just drive around the block to scare her. "My school's really close. You can drop me there. Watch me. I'll totally go in, I swear. And stay the whole entire day."

Murphy buckled her seat belt, motioning for Alex to do the same.

Camo Man started the car. The GPS glowed into action. "Three hundred and one miles to destination," the computer-generated voice chirped.

Trapped in the backseat, Alex watched the thick blue line creep across the dashboard screen, like the heart line spanning her palm, mapping her destiny. She unclenched a fist, recalling the palm reader pressing her hand open the night of her Sweet Sixteen, tracing the light line from pinky to pointer with a roughened index finger. "Your heart line is quite long, even a little curvy," she had observed.

"Ask her what that means." Cass poked her from behind.

"I *know*." Alex elbowed her back.

"You feel very free to express your emotions and thoughts." The reader glanced up at Alex. "Maybe sometimes too free?"

Cass howled. "Ha. That's so you, Alex."

"Very funny."

One line remained to interpret: Alex's health line, from pinky back up to thumb, stretching like a smile across her palm. "That little square there is a good thing. Protection."

"Protection? Why would I need protection?" Turning to Cass, Alex saw her friend's face had paled. "Let's just go," Cass whispered.

"Why? This is cool. You love this stuff."

"I know, but not this time. She's freaking me out."

"What's to freak out about? She's telling me I'll be safe."

"I don't care, Al. I'm getting weird vibes. Look. I'm all goose-bumpy." She held out her arm, pimply like chicken skin. "Sorry, Al. I know this was my idea. But I'm out of here." Cass jumped to her feet, brushing her head against the tent roof, and melted into the dancing throng, her violet wrap billowing behind her like a sail.

MEG

Pulling the van into the convenience store parking lot, Meg knew she would never forget the pain in Alex's voice as she rushed out of her daughter's room twenty minutes ago.

She checked her watch again. When would Carl contact her? Maybe she should just go back and call the whole thing off.

In front of her, early-morning commuters darted in and out of the market. She wanted their agendas, their petty worries.

Jack stirred in the backseat, Angel curled next to him. The boy had barely protested when she lifted him out of bed a little before six, all warm Spider-Man pajamas, wrapping wiry legs around her waist, so groggy he didn't even question his aunt's presence in the van.

Melissa had been a lifesaver to come early and wait with Jack while Meg led the transporters to Alex's room. Once Meg came out, Melissa headed home. She didn't think she could bear the sight of the transporters escorting her niece out of the house, she said.

Angel leaned his paws on Jack's shoulder and licked him into full alertness. Meg handed him a Styrofoam cup topped with a whirl of whipped cream.

Jack frowned. "You never let me have chocolate in the car. Only Dad does."

"Can't Mommy bend the rules sometimes?" She followed the cup with a handful of napkins.

He sipped, mocha foam rimming his mouth. "Is this a holiday?"

"Nope."

He glanced down at himself. "Pajama day?"

"Nope. Just a regular day." Meg's phone thrummed in the cup holder. *Finally.* She peered at the screen:

```
On our way. Next contact from rest stop.
```

Sighing, Meg dropped her head back against the headrest. Step one accomplished: bedroom door to car door, the most vulnerable time. Wasn't that what Carl had said?

"Mommy, you OK?"

She straightened up and swiped tears from her cheeks. "I'm fine, Jack."

"Was that Daddy?"

"Nope."

"When's he coming home?"

"Not sure, bud."

Jack let Angel lick chocolate from his cup. "Look, Mom. I'm Angel." He made exaggerated lapping sounds while the dog watched, entranced.

"Great. Now I have two doggies to take care of." She reversed the van, ignoring the middle finger of the contractor whose truck she nearly clipped, confident she'd done the right thing.

With Alex safely in Carl Alden's care, the hardest part was behind her.

ALEX

Camo Man glanced at Alex in the rearview mirror. He outlined the day's itinerary like a bus driver on a class trip. Their ETA was around four o'clock, he said; they'd stop for lunch in Massachusetts, halfway to Silver Mountain. "After that, it's pretty much all mountains. There will be some amazing views."

Like I give a crap about the scenery, Alex thought.

They were headed north on Boston Post Road, her high school up ahead on the right. Some ass-kissers streamed in, for extra help or for the prayer group that met every morning at the crack of dawn. Alex slouched down until they were well past the building.

She turned away more tissues from Mom Haircut, who wouldn't let up, sticking a basket in her face. "Something to eat? Might make you feel better."

Sneaking a look, Alex saw chocolate-cherry energy bars, her favorite. Had her mother given them a shopping list, right down to her musical tastes? She felt like Jack, being bribed into good behavior. Sniffling, Alex stared out the window. Murphy leaned between the seats, murmuring something to Carl that Alex couldn't catch. Probably some secret agent language.

They were on Midland Avenue now, passing her store. (*Old* store, she corrected herself.) The surf-shop window was strung with bright bikinis and sundresses, *harbingers* of spring. The SAT prep-class word popped into her head unbidden: *anything foreshadowing a future event; omen.* Alex's immediate future was looking pretty bleak, given this ride to nowhere.

The window display was meant to be all hopeful and optimistic, but right now, it only made her sad. Alex had been stoned that last day when her manager Joanna called her into the stockroom. She hadn't meant to smoke before work. Shana was giving her a ride straight from school. But then that song had come on the radio: Alex and Cass's go-to getting-ready anthem. A block from the store, Alex began sobbing like a crazy person. There was no way she could go to work like that. So she and Shana made a little detour. She'd only been, like, twenty minutes late? But Joanna was pissed.

"I like you, Alex. I know you've had a rough time," Joanna said. "But I need somebody I can count on."

Alex blinked and tried to concentrate. Joanna had really big lips.

"I know. I'm sorry." She genuinely was. The work gave her something to focus on for a few hours. But her boss's patience had run out. Joanna could have the stupid job, Alex had thought, alone in the stockroom. Somebody else could fold their dumb rash guards and hoodies. Her final paycheck was still at the store; she'd been too humiliated to pick it up.

Pressing herself into the corner of the backseat, she tugged at her scarf. Cass's scarf. Camo Man's itinerary didn't include a stop at the cemetery, way on the other side of town. Her mother had no idea she spent so much time there. She would probably think it was unhealthy. Who would take care of Cass while Alex was gone? Shana would never go there without her.

They were at the highway now, merging into I-95, sucked into a nauseating blur of tractor-trailers and buses. The car's overpowering strawberry deodorizer caught in Alex's throat. She covered her mouth, praying her stomach wouldn't revolt again. The Murphy woman watched her, alert as a deer, practically twitching.

With every mile, Alex's life receded into nothingness. They had no right to do this to her. Evan and Shana would be wondering what was up. She had to get her act together and blow off this whole New England adventure her mother had planned for her. *This* was what she meant that day on the promenade, Alex realized, heat flushing her cheeks—the "new start" she had hinted at. No matter what Camo Man said earlier about her "parents'" wishes, this expedition had her mom all over it.

Watch out, Mom. Paybacks are rough.

CARL

Not long after they settled in on I-95, the girl appeared to fall asleep, head rolled back on the seat, open-mouthed and snoring. She'd likely be out for a while. The kids he picked up were usually in pretty bad shape; their parents wouldn't have hired him otherwise.

All in all, the bedroom-to-car segment had gone well, if you didn't count the flying soda can. The verbal abuse came with the territory. These kids were terrified, cornered. Words were their only weapons.

Restraints had not been necessary.

Behind him, Murphy leaned her head back and opened her mouth, imitating the girl. "I hope she doesn't choke on that gum."

Alex gave no sign of having heard her. They took nothing for granted, however. Kids frequently feigned sleep in the car: to avoid conversation, to stew, to plot. Murphy knew never to take her eyes off Alex, no matter how authentic the snoring.

"Jamie still enjoying karate?" Carl asked. Murphy's daughter was ten, a quiet, bookish type. The two lived with Murphy's mother in the mother's Queens apartment.

"Got her yellow belt last week. She was so proud. Her dojo says it's really boosting her self-confidence."

"You've got a good kid there, Murph." Not for the first time, Carl was impressed by the way she juggled single parenting with her full-time job and Begin Again assignments.

They were about a half hour into the drive now. The traffic moved steadily; opposite them, the day's commuters headed into Manhattan from Westchester and beyond. They should have a fairly easy go of it for most of the day, he estimated, with an off chance of catching early weekend traffic around two or three o'clock. He'd built a buffer into his timetable just in case, booking rooms for himself and Murphy tonight near the main highway in New Hampshire. They'd get an early start tomorrow, be back in the city by midafternoon. With any luck, Randall would have his car ready to roll for Sunday's transport.

"Didn't you say the Carmodys were married?" Murphy asked.

"Yes. Why?"

"No reason. Just something Alex said in her room."

Murphy had good intuition. It was one of the reasons Carl had relaxed the rules a bit when he hired her. Murphy more than met most criteria he set for guides: law enforcement training, experience with at-risk youth. Many came from residential-treatment backgrounds, having worked at places like the one they were headed to now and others far more regimented.

But at thirty-seven, Murphy was younger than the usual female guides he hired. Besides their professional qualifications, Carl preferred mothers with teenage children. These women were in the trenches personally; they understood that no matter how developed the client was physically, a sixteen-year-old was still a child. They responded appropriately. As he witnessed almost daily, there was no animal worse than a teenager wronged: all the strength of an adult, minus the maturity.

So Murphy was a little green. Jamie wouldn't show those colors for a few more years—maybe never, if she was lucky.

But Murphy brought other assets to the table. She had proved herself a tech-savvy and skilled investigator during jobs like the one out of Maryland last month, a no-show. The parents were frantic, worried they'd have to abandon their plan. Cool as a cucumber, Murphy flipped open her laptop at the family's home. In a few keystrokes, she had called up the kid's cell phone records, crossmatched some numbers to street addresses and had the transporters knocking on a few doors. By noon, she'd tracked down the boy, who was crashed on a friend's floor. They woke him and ran their drill, transport delayed only a few hours.

Yes, Murphy was a valuable guide. And besides that, there was Jimmy—Jimbo, as he had been known in their platoon. They were tight. Carl had made him a promise.

Movement in the backseat caught his eye, the girl thrashing in her sleep. Murphy clasped her wrist in a light hold. Alex appeared to settle under her touch.

"Bad dream?" Carl raised an eyebrow at her.

"Who knows? I got her." Murphy was facing Alex, primed to react. Carl trained his guides to pick up the slightest nonverbal cue: an eye movement, the way a child sat, a hesitation before answering a question. Each spoke volumes.

Like right now. Even in sleep, the girl's hands were clenched in fists. It didn't take an expert to predict Alex Carmody would wake up in a fighting mood.

MEG

Meg made herself go into Alex's room. She surveyed the mess, inventorying the tornado of dirty dishes, makeup and discarded clothes, including the ones she'd left out for her daughter to wear on the trip north.

On the vanity, the lava lamp was still warm to the touch. Beneath it sat a metallic mountain of discarded gum wrappers creased and folded into *W*s, a curious habit her daughter had adopted. She ignored the temptation to sweep them all into the garbage. Alex would be livid if she knew Meg was in here. She mostly stayed out. *Pick your battles.* Sage advice from the well-thumbed parenting books on her nightstand.

Alex's bifold closet doors were open, shoes and boots blanketing the floor. Through the jumble of leather and suede, she spotted a slice of turquoise. She knelt and grabbed at the fabric, knowing exactly what it was: Alex's Sweet Sixteen dress, the one Meg had stuffed down in the trash at the end of that long night.

Holding the dress, Meg sat back on her heels, recalling her arrival at the accident scene, finding Alex white faced and glassy eyed on the stretcher. Her daughter had been in the backseat, her most serious injury a gash on her cheekbone requiring stitches. Another inch, and it would have been her eye.

A few yards away, another stretcher had borne Cass's still and broken body. Meg had been seized with an irrational desire to pull the sheet back, as though that might alter the outcome. Unsecured, Cass had been thrown from the car by the impact.

Meg fingered the dress's bloodstained neckline. Alex must have pulled it out of the garbage. Why would she want to hang on to such a tragic memento? Meg wondered, tucking the dress back where she'd found it and standing. As she did so, she caught her image in the mirror over Alex's bureau. Curling from the mirror's frame was half a photo strip of Alex and Cass mugging in their Sweet Sixteen finery, a souvenir of the party's photo booth. Across the pictures were scrawled two words: *Happy Corner*. Appropriate words, as the booth had been wildly successful, drawing a long line of kids to that corner of the ballroom.

Meg traced the photos on the strip, wondering about its other half, seized with melancholy at the realization of its likely owner. Backing away from the mirror, she closed Alex's door behind her.

In the upstairs hall, Meg checked her watch again—at least two hours until Carl's next check-in. Meg saw how she would navigate her day. The infusion center's full treatment schedule would be the vehicle carrying her along, Carl's check-ins the mile markers.

Half an hour later, hair damp, she carried her travel mug of coffee out to the van. Their street was quiet. Had any of the neighbors seen Carl and the female guide marching Alex down the street to the car?

Whatever. It was done. Everything would be different, from this day forward.

Her cell phone vibrated on her hip: Jacob touching base. He yelled to make himself heard over the *whrr-whrr-whrranng* of electric saws. "Shouldn't you be at work by now?"

She had planned for this. "Jack's teacher wanted to see me."

"Jack doing all right?"

"Great, actually. She moved him up to accelerated reading." That was the truth; Ms. Traynor *had* e-mailed her about it last week.

"She made you come in to tell you that?"

"Newbie teacher, trying to make nice with the parents."

"Did you see him?"

"See who?"

"Jack, Meg. You know, our son?"

Meg snapped to attention. The last thing she needed was Jacob quizzing Jack on the phone later. "Nope. Kids were in gym. He never saw me."

"OK." He paused. "Alex all right? She get to school today?"

"Out the door bright and early." She bit her lip until it hurt.

"Hah. If she makes it all day, we'll have to give her a gold star."

Meg forced a chuckle. "I hope she makes it the whole day, Jacob. I really do." She heard someone calling him. "I've got to get to work. Call me tonight?"

He cleared his throat. "Actually, you may see me tonight. Ben said we might finish up around two. There's some bad weather heading in."

Panicked, Meg did the calculations. Even if Jacob stuck to that schedule and drove straight through, he wouldn't make it back before seven. Alex should be safely to New Hampshire by then. There'd be nothing he could do.

And after he exploded—which she knew he would—she'd make him see this was the only way to save their daughter.

ALEX

The siren sailing past them splintered Alex's sleep, the midmorning brightness scorching her eyelids. Above her, clouds scuttled past the sunroof at a dizzying speed.

It hadn't been a dream. She *was* trapped in this car. Her neck ached from falling asleep in such an awkward position, and her mouth was dry and sour. And open, she realized with horror, wiping drool from her cheek. The woman tapped her hand, passing a bottle of water.

Probably thrilled to have something to do, Alex thought, guzzling the water. She shielded her eyes. Squinting helped steady the lurching scenery: steepled white churches, clusters of box stores, a lone motorboat pulling out of a marina slip—typical New England stuff she'd passed a hundred times with her family.

When she was younger, they had driven all over, her parents offering up special locations from their combined pasts like jewels in some kind of treasure hunt. And every time, they expected these places to be filled with meaning for Alex and Jack. Didn't they realize their children needed new memories instead of their parents' recycled dreams?

There were road trips almost every weekend, before things got all weird between her parents. Alex's favorite was the visit to a Vermont lodge where her dad vacationed as a kid. The place had been completely redone since his last visit; he was disappointed to find a year-round aquatic center in place of the theater in a barn. According to Grandma Miriam, her father had put on quite a performance there. She insisted Alex inherited her drama gene from him.

Despite the renovation, they'd had an amazing time. Alex loved the lodge and all its hokey details, from the suspenders holding up the waiters' shorts to the delicate white flowers painted on the red bedposts. And it was cool to swim in the middle of winter, then jump onto a sled outside.

There hadn't been a family road trip in a while. She felt cheated. All the kids she knew with divorced parents ended up with two of everything: two houses, two bedrooms decorated exactly the way they wanted, two awesome vacations every year. They spent just enough time with each parent before they got sick of each other. Tons of parental guilt equaled tons of swag, like they were making amends for the divorce or something.

But with Alex's parents, there were no such benefits, only a hypocritical and embarrassing living arrangement that both confused and depressed her. They said it was about the money, but if they could pay for her super-lavish Sweet Sixteen, how bad could things be? And did their staying together in the house mean that they might *stay* together? That they were secretly working on things? The sight of her parents' cars side by side in the driveway at night gave Alex hope. Maybe this would be the night they'd all sit down to dinner again or maybe even orchestrate a jam session in the basement together as though nothing had happened.

But inside it was always still Siberia, the deep freeze. *Upstairs, downstairs.* Her banishment from the basement had been the final insult. And they wondered why Alex was never home.

Even Jack was freaked out by it. If it were possible, her little brother had been more annoying than usual, lurking outside her room at night.

Like the night a couple of weeks ago, when Jack kept knocking over and over while she was going through some private stuff. Alex had caved and let him in. She couldn't help but feel sorry for him.

She closed her eyes again, willing herself anywhere but in this stupid car. Last night at Evan's, she had felt guilty about ignoring her mother's text. But now, knowing what was in store for her, she was freaking glad she had stayed out.

The car changed lanes suddenly; her stomach revolted against the motion. She hadn't sat in the backseat of a car in a very long time. Not since the back of Logan's new car, the night of her party. Since then, Alex had made sure to call shotgun before anyone else. Now she had a hazy flash of Cass planting herself next to her that night and sticking her finger in Alex's face. "Remember, thirty minutes," she'd said, tugging the seat belt across Alex.

Thirty minutes for what? Alex couldn't remember. Whenever she asked Shana, she would only say it was for Slurpees. Shana had a hard time talking about that night.

From up front, the strains of a reggae song filled the car. *Ugh. More lame attempts at Camo Man coolness.* For a moment, the sun went behind a cloud, and she noticed a trinket dangling from the mirror. It was a frog, perched on an unseen rock like a Buddha, its eyes two garnet slits in its golden body. She would have recognized it anywhere.

OMG. Was this another prop in her mother's drama? Had she deliberately positioned this Amphibiana icon to sway Alex into cooperation? *Stop being paranoid, girl.* That would be too much, even for her mom. And Meg wouldn't even know what the frog meant. The only person in her life besides Cass who could appreciate the golden tree frog's significance was her dad, and he would never use their Phibs connection to manipulate her. It was their bond. Although there had been more than one occasion lately when he had gotten all "tough guy" with her and Jack.

Anyway, it didn't matter. An entire rain forest of golden tree frogs couldn't sway her. She wouldn't give anyone connected to this bizarre road trip the satisfaction of acknowledging the trinket swinging next to Camo Man's head. The frog no longer meant anything; that dream would never happen now.

Thankfully, the song ended. But then the silence gave Mom Haircut a chance to ask if Alex had any questions about the school. The way her nostrils quivered when she spoke made the woman look more like a rabbit than a deer, Alex decided.

And no, she didn't have questions. Evan had told her everything she needed to know about places like this. He'd "gone away" the entire summer between freshman and sophomore years. Someplace in Maine near a lake. There was so much forced talking and group sharing that summer, Evan had wanted to jump off a bridge.

"What if you didn't *feel* like talking?" Shana had been sitting with her back pressed against her bedroom door. She was always really paranoid when they smoked.

"They didn't make you," Evan said, "but you got, like, extra points for it. It was like a game. I played along, making up shit, just to get out of there."

Glancing sideways at Mom Haircut, Alex decided to play that game, too.

MEG

Meg flashed her ID badge at the security gate of the Rosswell Infusion Center, a gleaming edifice on the perimeter of Rye Hospital. In the parking lot, she drummed the wheel while a young mother buckled a child into a car seat, collapsed a stroller and slid it into the trunk before relinquishing a space near the entrance. Was it just her, or was the entire world in slow motion today?

"Morning, Meg." Up on her floor, a cheery voice called out to her. Ruthann—absolutely the last person Meg wanted to see today. She'd liked her well enough until the motherly nurse had slipped her the card, *Families Together: Riverport Chapter*.

"Tuesday nights at the Presbyterian Church. Trust me. It helps."

Meg had managed a smile and stuffed it in a pocket. Who was Ruthann to pass judgment? Meg barely knew her; she was a name on a sub sheet, someone to switch shifts with. And although Meg might have complained some about Alex in the lounge, it certainly wasn't enough to warrant Ruthann's interference.

"Morning." Still in her coat, Meg leaned over the desk monitor, typing. The screen flooded with the day's treatment schedule, patients arriving at half-hour intervals. "Are they kidding? Who squeezed in two more day stays last night? Why don't they just invite the whole neighborhood?"

Ruthann pressed a finger to her lips. Meg turned to see a gray-haired man in a cardigan wheel a woman by the intake desk, her lashless eyes disapproving.

"Sorry, Mrs. Rosenthal. Rough morning." In front of Meg, the screen blurred. *I will not cry.* She grabbed a tissue, feeling Ruthann's eyes on her. She would do her best to avoid Ruthann today, Meg decided. Which she did, for the rest of the morning. Unfortunately, the nurse happened to be passing by at the exact moment Meg's third patient of the day yelped, and Ruthann felt compelled to stick her head inside the room. Meg was momentarily frozen, staring at the crimson puddling in the crook of her patient's arm.

"I'm so sorry, Mrs. Ryan." The patient was on the floor for a day stay, her sixth in an eight-week chemotherapy regimen. In Meg's defense, Lara Ryan had been subjected to so many draws by this stage of her treatment that even after making a fist like Meg asked, her over-worked veins refused to respond to Meg's probing.

Ruthann stepped in and pressed Lara's forearm a few times, then carefully reinserted the needle. Meg pinched the line, watching for bub-bles confirming that the Herceptin flowed freely through Lara's veins. Ruthann patted Meg's shoulder and left.

Lara offered Meg a wan smile. Feeling guilty, Meg asked if she'd like to be taken to a group treatment room, for company during the infusion. Lara was alone today; visitors for the day stays tended to drop off after the first few weeks.

"No, thanks, Meg. I've got all the cancer friends I need right now. I brought a book." She tapped a backpack at her feet.

"OK. If you change your mind, let me know. I'll be back in a while to check on you."

Ruthann was waiting for her outside Lara's room. "You OK?"

For the briefest of seconds, Meg considered pulling Ruthann into the staff room and confessing all. Instead, she offered her colleague an exaggerated thumbs-up. Once Ruthann was back at the intake center, Meg ducked into the bathroom, closing herself into a stall and allowing the tears to flow.

ALEX

"How are you doing, Alex?" Camo Man stalked her in the rearview mirror, smiling. Bored, Alex decided to at least pretend to be interested. She stretched. "Where are we?"

"Still in Connecticut," the woman said. "We'll stop in about an hour. You can use the bathroom then."

"Cool." Just the mention of a bathroom made her want to pee. She'd had to go so bad last night when Evan dropped her at home. He must be pissed off by now. It was Friday; people needed supplies for the weekend. Now she had to worry about getting word to him, on top of this magical mystery tour.

Evan was Logan's friend. She'd met him at Shana's, the first time she saw Logan after the funeral. When the two boys showed up, Logan caught her eye, tipping his head at Evan. Alex got it: *Don't talk about it in front of him.* She was glad Evan was there. They needed a neutral party.

"I'm Alex," she'd greeted him as she dropped onto the floor of Shana's room.

"Hey," he returned, taking a seat on Shana's zebra-striped bench. "Is it cool?" he asked Logan. When Logan nodded, Evan dug into his pocket and tossed a joint to his friend. Alex's eyes widened as she watched Logan light it. He inhaled so hard, she was afraid he'd swallow it. Exhaling, he offered it to Alex, who waved it away.

Shana was next. She hesitated, surveying the prescription bottles on her nightstand. "I better not. I'm, like, already buzzed from my pain meds."

Evan took a hit, then held it out to Alex again. The sour-sweet smell tickled her nostrils.

"Come on. It'll mellow you out." Logan, the king of good judgment, sitting back, eyes closed.

Alex wavered. Mellow sounded loads better than she felt right now, her heart hollow, her brain in constant-replay mode. She took the joint, pinching it between thumb and forefinger like Evan had, and inhaled.

"Harder," Evan ordered. "Hold it in as long as you can."

She did as he said, containing the acrid heat in her lungs until she thought they would burst, then exploded in one choking exhale.

"You might not feel anything the first time," Logan volunteered. *What was the point of that?* Alex thought. When it came around again, she took the joint from Evan. Soon, the sharp edges of her anxiety softened, silencing the jackhammers. She floated to a little corner of her brain where there was nothingness. It felt safe.

That was the first night the four of them started hanging. Her mother didn't think their constant togetherness was healthy.

"I'm just suggesting it might be good to hang out with some other kids," she said one Saturday morning.

At the kitchen island, Alex mentally reviewed her "other" options. First, there were the nosy kids, creepers who wanted all the gruesome details: *Was Logan drinking? What was the last thing she said? Did you see her body?*

Alex wished she had the answers; she'd asked Shana a million times what happened that night. When Shana said it was better if she didn't know, Alex tried to fill in the gaps herself, but there were too many blurry bits between Cass's cool touch in the ladies' room and coming to under a fuzzy white blanket covering her like a dusting of snow, straps tight around her waist. A violet silkiness had been tucked under her chin, with no one sure how it ended up there.

Beyond the nosy kids, there were the avoiders, who never spoke to her directly, instead just pointing and staring as though Alex were parading around in prison stripes. The avoiders were right: losing Cass *was* Alex's fault.

Possibly worse than the avoiders were their friends from *before*, all sobby and sad at the funeral, then within a few weeks acting like Cass never even existed, expecting Alex to feel normal, to want to go to the mall on Saturdays like they always had.

Only things weren't like before. Why couldn't her mother see that? Why did she have to act like Alex could just march down to Walgreens and pick out new friends the way she picked out a new lip gloss?

"I worry this Evan boy is a bad influence," Meg had said again that morning.

"You don't know anything about 'this Evan,' Mom. And maybe *I'm* the bad influence."

Her mom scooted around the island to hug her. "Of course you're not." Despite ragging on Alex about her friends, her mother seemed to be trying very hard that morning to avoid a fight. She'd even suggested they do something together. Alex had refused, even though it made her feel bad. Everything made her feel bad.

After releasing her from the hug, Meg grabbed Alex's high school newspaper and flipped it open to a notice about auditions for the spring musical, suggesting she try out.

Alex stared at her mother. How could she not know how ridiculous that idea was, on so many levels? Any play tryouts were dead to Alex now—not just because of Cass's absence, but because her parents had chosen *that* morning, the day the *Annie* cast was due back at school to strike the set, to tell her they were separating.

Their announcement from opposite ends of the living room couch—that the life Alex knew up to that point was over—would forever be intertwined with the dismantling of the show's backdrops, the breakdown of props and costumes, the ceremonial burning of leftover programs.

She would never step onstage again. To this day, Alex couldn't stomach the orphans' lament that taunted her from a constant loop on the school's cable TV channel, the cast singing how throwing in the towel was a lot easier than putting up a fight.

At school that day with the cast, Cass sensed Alex's anguish right away, wrestling the news of her parents' split out of her best friend. By sheer brilliance, Cass gave her hope, by proposing the most incredible idea—a milestone to anticipate and plan and experience together.

Happy Corner.

It became their mantra, whenever things got a little rocky—*Happy Corner, Happy Corner*—bolstering Alex through the initial blow of her parents' separation. Then, in an instant, Cass was no longer around to help decode her mom and dad's confusing behavior. Or to calm Alex's concerns about the future: What if her parents found new boyfriends or girlfriends one day? Would she have to act like she liked their kids? Or, OMG, share a room? There were a bazillion more questions Alex didn't dare ask, terrified of the answers.

So, of course, she found a new crew.

That morning in the kitchen, Alex wrenched the school paper away from her mother. "I'm out of here. My friends know what I need." Shana and Evan could never fill Cass's shoes, but they were all Alex had.

In this evening's performance, understudies Shana and Evan will play the roles of Alex's best friends . . .

Her mother followed her outside to Shana's car, begging her to finish some lame chore first.

"Alex. Alex." A hand was shaking her.

"Leave me alone, Mom. I'll do it later."

"Wake up, Alex. We're here."

Disoriented, she opened her eyes to find Mom Haircut smiling at her. "You slept for quite a while. We're at the rest stop. Time for lunch."

MEG

"So tell me. Is he hot?"

"Is *who* hot?"

"Your new guy." Lara Ryan's blanket had slipped off her shoulders. Meg set down her own lunch tray to rearrange the woman's cover. The treatment rooms' arctic temperatures were designed to ward off the patients' nausea.

"What new guy?" Meg snuck another look at her phone to see if Carl had called from their lunchtime stop.

"You know. The one you were so distracted over earlier?" Lara offered up her bandaged forearm as a reminder.

"Oh, no. You're kidding, right?" Meg pushed some chicken broth toward Lara. "Try to eat some of this. It will settle your stomach." Meg sat down and picked at her own salad. She had chosen her meal carefully from the cafeteria, avoiding any strong odors that might set off sensitive stomachs in the treatment area.

Lara toyed with her soup. "You've been glued to your phone all day like a lovesick teenager. I just thought you might have something . . . you know . . . going on."

Meg laughed. "Like dating? I'm such a hot mess, no one would want me." She fingered the spot where her wedding rings had been until a few months ago, their absence alerting the world to her single status. She still felt their phantom weight sometimes. She shrugged off the twinge of guilt. There'd been nothing wrong with slipping them on yesterday before Carl's visit; she *was* still married.

"I might know somebody," Lara offered.

"So you're a matchmaker now?" Meg teased. "That's sweet. I'll let you know when I'm ready, but don't hold your breath. The truth is, I'm just waiting on news about my daughter. It should be anytime."

"How are you holding up?" Lara asked.

Meg blinked. How could she know about Alex? Then it dawned on her Lara meant the separation, a development her observant patient pulled from her some weeks ago. Things got personal in treatment rooms sometimes. Meg tried hard not to cross the professional line, but you grew attached to some patients. Like Lara Ryan.

"Honestly, I'm still getting used to it," Meg said. "I never thought I'd be one of those women. Anyway, you don't need to hear my problems."

"I don't mind. I've got plenty of time. And it takes my mind off this adventure." She jerked her head at the IV. "So . . . your daughter's giving you a run for your money?"

Meg rolled her eyes. "You know teenagers. It never ends."

Lara leaned forward, and Meg sensed her loneliness. Though Meg had finished her lunch and was scheduled to orient a group of new patients, she inched her chair closer to her patient. "I remember this one time, when Alex was in seventh grade," she began.

Alex's science class had watched a movie about slaughterhouses. Meg described the scene for Lara now: Alex coming home in tears, swearing off eating red meat—and everything else.

"She dragged me through the supermarket, filling the cart with tofu, sprouts, a bunch of very expensive frozen vegan meals."

"Let me guess," Lara said, eyes shining. "She lasted six months."

"Try *one* month. We caught her at Playland devouring a cheesesteak." Meg described Alex's chin, slick with grease. "She said she couldn't help it, that it just *smelled* so good."

"She was back."

"Yes, but that's not the end of the story. I ended up with a freezer full of tofu. *And* a dog." Her fleeting vegan experiment inspired Alex to begin volunteering at the local animal shelter a few weeks after the cheesesteak incident. When Meg picked her up after her first day, Alex wrangled a scruffy Lab mix of indeterminate age on a leash.

"They said we can take her for the night, Mom."

The dog leaped up to lick Meg's arm through the open window. "One night, Alex. That's it. A dog is a big responsibility."

As Meg had known would happen from the moment they drove away from the shelter, Angel's one night turned into forever.

Alex barely volunteered these days. It saddened Meg that since the accident, little inspired her daughter.

"But Alex is good now, right?" Lara asked.

"*Really* good," Meg lied, patting the woman's hand, pleased to have cheered her. Other recollections might not have had the same effect.

Like the day a few months ago when Meg opened the front door to face Alex and a police officer. He had picked her up in the pharmacy downtown, headbands stuffed up her sweatshirt sleeves, he said. The officer knew the Carmodys—Meg monitored his father's prostate cancer treatment—and had convinced the store manager to let Alex off with a warning, a kindness that went unappreciated by her unrepentant daughter, who seemed more upset over being caught. And who couldn't explain to her mother why she would have stolen headbands at all, with bins full of them upstairs in her room.

Finishing her lunch, Meg regretted not holding Alex more accountable for that action.

Or others that followed, usually brought to Meg's attention by an alert from the school's attendance office. The first time, Meg called back in annoyance. "My child is *not* absent today. I dropped her there myself." It had been their usual tense parting at the school curb—Alex's hand on the door while Meg reeled off reminders: after-school dentist appointments, the check for SAT prep class, undone chores. Alex had pulled away from Meg's good-bye kiss and slipped into the school. Hadn't she?

During the frenzied hours that followed, both Meg and Jacob had texted and called Alex, with no response. By late morning, she had been ready to involve the police when Alex texted to say she was back at school and could Meg pick her up after detention.

Detention did not deter Alex. After the next school alert, Meg decided to tail her. After dropping Alex off as usual, she pulled a couple of car lengths ahead and waited. Sure enough, not ten minutes later, Alex emerged from a side door and bounded across the school lawn in the direction of downtown. Following at a discreet distance, she watched Alex slip into Perk Up. Finding her inside alone—who skipped school *alone?*—Meg marched a scarlet Alex back into school herself right as the late bell rang.

Even after that, no amount of detention deterred her daughter's pattern of truancy. Alex seemed to have given up. Meanwhile, the sight of the school ID on her phone could still unnerve Meg, as if she herself had been summoned to the principal's office.

She didn't share any of these memories or thoughts with her patient. "Don't forget to stop by the pharmacy before you leave," she said in parting, tucking Lara's prescription into the woman's purse.

Before her next patient, Meg ducked into the restroom again and called Carl. It rang several times without an answer. *Calm down,* she told the reflection in the mirror over the sink. In the restroom's flat blue light, the folds framing her mouth deepened into crevices. No wonder Jacob wanted a different model.

Meg's phone buzzed in her hand. It was an auto text from Alex's school. Her heart rate skyrocketed briefly before she laughed out loud.

In the morning's excitement, she'd apparently forgotten one key detail: calling school to report her daughter's absence.

ALEX

Outside, the morning's relentlessly bright sky had dialed down to gray. A steady stream of travelers emerged from neat lines of parked cars and tour buses, drawn like lemmings to the faux colonial house that was the Charlton Service Center. The grass border alongside the car was dusted with snow.

"It's chilly. You might want to put this on." Murphy held the lame quilted ski jacket Alex's mother had bought on clearance and left on her bed, another *surprise*. Alex usually tried to suck it up when her mother shopped for her, wearing stuff once or twice to avoid hurting her feelings.

But this was *after*—after her mother made her choose sides in their separation. OK, nobody ever came out and said that, but Alex couldn't help but feel that way. So when she found that coat on her bed, the *bribe*, she brought it down to the kitchen and dangled it in front of her mother, claiming she'd never be caught dead in it, letting it drop to the floor. (Even as she uttered those words, she practically heard Cass tsk-tsking.)

Her mother did her trademark lip-tightening thing. Angel sniffed the coat, then walked away. Alex had waited for that *gotcha!* rush from this moment of rebellion, but she had felt only lingering anger over her mother's belief that a stupid coat would make everything better. And while they were on the subject, why did she feel she could waltz into Alex's room any time she pleased? She had no right to throw away her Sweet Sixteen dress—the first thing Alex looked for when she came home from the hospital. Had she really thought getting rid of the bloodied reminder would make Alex forget? Or that the new coat was a way to kiss and make up?

But it *was* freezing in the rest stop parking lot. And since her mom wasn't there to gloat, Alex took the jacket and put it on. She had bigger things to worry about, like contacting Evan.

Once again, Carl and Murphy reattached themselves like leeches and aimed Alex toward the service center. *If anybody thinks they're my parents, I will literally die.* Inside, a sea of brown and yellow diamond tile led them to a food court, where odors of grease and microwaved pizza assaulted them. There was a McDonald's, where a cheesy fake fireplace burned in a slate wall behind some crayon-colored tables. And something called Fresh City, with wraps and other healthy stuff. Auntie Anne's and Papa Gino's rounded out the remaining food options, unless you counted the vending machine snacks.

Travelers milled around the open space, perusing menus or stopping to play one of the many arcade games.

"Good time for a restroom break," Carl said.

Alex gazed at the McCafe, longing to sit and sip a frappé mocha by herself. "I don't have to go. OK if I walk around?"

"Sorry, Alex. Rules."

Is this woman planning to wipe me, too? Murphy led her toward a chrome "Restroom" sign over by a bank of pay phones. Standing in line with the woman, Alex leaned her head against the tile wall. It felt icy cold, like a brain freeze. Her lungs tightened in that familiar pull, signaling the need for a cigarette. The bathroom smelled like diapers and industrial-cleaning fumes so harsh she could taste them.

No sooner had they gotten in line than a noisy group of teenagers joined them.

"Let's go, girls. We don't have all afternoon." A tall woman in an "I Heart NY" sweatshirt and too-tight powder blue sweatpants caught up to the teens, her laminated ID slapping against her sweatshirt's plastic heart appliqué. *Chaperone from hell.* The girls hung in clumps, giggling and whispering.

Murphy was listing possible lunch choices: burgers, pizza, pretzels. Alex wanted a bagel. And gum. She was almost out of Rainbow Bubble, which was almost as rough as being out of cigarettes. If she couldn't smoke, at least they could replenish her gum. They couldn't expect her to go cold turkey on that, too. It was humiliating, having to ask for every little thing.

"We'll see," Murphy said when Alex asked for it.

Such a mom answer. "Is he, like, your boss or something?"

Murphy smiled. "He pretty much runs the show."

"You guys married?"

This time, Murphy threw her head back and laughed. She had a nice laugh, soft and ending on a high note as though she were surprised, not like her mother's demonic cackle. "No way. We are definitely *not* married. We're just colleagues—you know, people who work together."

"I know what colleagues are," Alex snapped, offended. "I take English honors." *Took,* she silently corrected herself, having been bumped back to regular English for never handing in homework. Now, today's sick conspiracy obliterated any chance of salvaging her junior year.

"I have a daughter," Murphy volunteered. "Younger than you. She's ten. Her name's Jamie." Alex pictured a smaller version of Murphy, a Mini-Me wrapped in her own black trench. She felt sorry for the kid. Murphy dug for her phone and pressed a few buttons. For a second Alex wondered if she'd let her borrow it.

"Here's my girl." She knew what Murphy was doing, like Dr. Fallon *after*. Trying to get all buddy-buddy, *relating*. Alex played along, as she had for a time with the counselor, peering into Mom Haircut's screen. The girl actually was kind of cute, probably took after the dad. Her straight brown hair came to her shoulders, and light pink glasses framed blue eyes. She sat cross-legged on grass, smiling as she tickled the underbelly of a squirming puppy.

"My mother takes care of her when I have to travel for work." Another divorced mom. Wasn't everybody, these days?

"Does she see her dad much?" Probably more than she saw hers, Alex thought.

Murphy cleared her throat. "Jamie's father died. In the line of duty."

"In 9/11?" The question popped out before she could stop it. Her mom had rushed to the city to help that day with a bunch of nurses from the hospital. Alex was six at the time; she didn't remember it very well. They watched the Ground Zero memorial service every year. Their own town lost fourteen people in the attack.

"Oh, my. That was such a tragic day. But no. It was a year later. Jamie's dad was a police officer. In Jersey City."

Alex did the math quickly. "Does Jamie remember him?"

A quick intake of breath. "No, unfortunately. I was pregnant when my husband Jimmy died. Jamie was born a few months later."

Jimmy. Jamie. *Duh.* Named for her father. Like Jack was, for her dad. Except their dad was living and breathing. He might even be in the same state as Alex was right now; she glanced behind her, as though her father might magically stroll out of the men's room.

He didn't. Alex rolled her shoulders, thinking that if he had, he would take her home, no questions asked. At least, Alex *thought* he would. Lately he resisted Alex's charms, always tired and cranky after his tree jobs. Like over that college thing; her entire body stiffened at the memory of that confrontation. It wasn't fair when he changed the rules.

To Murphy, Alex mumbled what hundreds had murmured in her ear as they streamed past her at Cass's service: "Sorry for your loss."

"Thank you. We miss him every day." For the first time, Alex noticed the American flag pin on Murphy's trench.

They were getting along so well, Alex forgot for a second why they were even together. When their turn came, Murphy was all business again, waving her into an empty stall. "Meet me out here by the sinks," she instructed. Alex locked the stall and sat on the toilet. She didn't have to go, just needed a few seconds alone to think. She wished the giggling girls outside the stall would shut up. And she sorely missed her phone. It was like losing an essential organ. She could only imagine the bazillion missed calls from Evan. And Shana must be losing her mind right about now without Alex at the lunch table. Although Alex had skipped so many times, Shana had found other random people to eat with.

Twirling the toilet-paper roll loudly to buy more time in the stall, Alex weighed her options. With Murphy all business again, the moment to ask for her phone had passed.

1. Find a pay phone. The ones right outside the bathroom were too obvious, too out in the open. And if her keepers took her cell, they'd never let her use a pay phone.

2. Make a break for it. She surveyed the stall: Behind her, a sign listed all the gross things you weren't allowed to flush. (*Did* people need a reminder not to dump grease into the toilets, she wondered, reading?) Overhead, the ceiling looked like the ones in all her classrooms: square fluorescent panels set in an aluminum grid with lighting that made everybody look sick. And there were no windows anywhere. In short, the bathroom offered zero possibilities.

3. Push Murphy down and run past Carl through the front door, then hitch a ride or hide on a tour bus. Although she'd gotten good at hitching, the thought of running made her head ache. And Carl was right outside waiting. He'd probably have the place on lockdown in thirty seconds.

Murphy pounded on the metal door. "Alex, almost done?"

OMG. She wasn't a three-year-old. "Be right there." Alex spun the paper roll once more for effect, fuming at the unfairness of being held against her will. She'd read that abducted people sometimes fell in love with their captors. She thought of Camo Man outside the bathroom and almost threw up in her mouth. *As if* she'd get all Stockholm syndrome-y over him.

4. Get a message to somebody. She could slide it across the counter to the coffee guy: *Help! I'm being held against my will!* Then again, Carl and Murphy would probably whip out their badges and shut that one down, fast. Someone would tweet it and she'd end up on the seven o'clock news. Not that her friends ever watched; stuff had to be trending on Twitter or heart-ed by a bazillion followers on Instagram to get on their radar. But their parents watched.

What else? She couldn't think with the girls' stupid laughter echoing in the cavernous bathroom. They must be on a school trip, bored to tears, this rest stop the highlight of the day. Proud owners of Boston whale-key chains.

Alex sat up. It was a long shot, but maybe the message thing *could* work, if one of these idiot girls would help. If the situation were reversed, Alex and her friends wouldn't be able to resist the opportunity, she reasoned. Well, maybe not Cass. She'd be all: *Don't do that. What if you're texting a criminal or something?* As much as Alex loved Cass, she could be a major buzzkill sometimes.

Not Shana. Shana had a pair. Like the week before her Sweet Sixteen, when the three of them tested party makeup in Alex's bedroom, and Shana had pitched her vodka idea again, and for the bazillionth time, Cass shot her down.

"Geeze, Cass, you're such an angel," Shana had teased, turning to Alex. "Come on. It'll be cool, Al. We'll use your prezzies to sneak it in. Gift bags are the perfect size."

"Seriously, Shana," Cass had said. "Why do you always have to create drama?"

There was a glimmer of truth in Cass's words. Shana liked to stir things up a bit—get the party started. But when it came down to it, Shana usually ended up on the sidelines, watching everyone else turn into waste products without partaking much herself.

Yeah, Shana definitely would be game for this, Alex thought in the bathroom stall. So if any of these girls had even an ounce of Shana's guts, this might have a chance of working. Cracking her gum, she pulled her wallet from her purse. Movie stubs, school ID, ATM card, but nothing in the bank account it linked to. She swore she'd had a ten last night, but then remembered she bought cigarettes. There had to be change, though. She shook her bag, rewarded with the clink of coins at the bottom. Peering inside, she separated two wadded-up dollar bills from a mess of gum wrappers and grabbed a couple of quarters. Less than three bucks; she'd have to sweeten the pot a little. There must be something else she could add.

There it was. A smile played at Alex's lips. Evan had given her a little something extra awhile back. Mom Haircut had missed it. Or thought it was a Tic Tac. Yeah, that would definitely seal the deal. It would have been nice to have it for the rest of the ride, but this was more important.

Next, paper and something to write with. More digging: last semester's progress report, a neon blue highlighter. They'd have to do. She put her purse on her lap like a desk, smoothed the paper over it and wrote: *Plze text to 555-897-3320.* Other than her mother's, Evan's was the only number she had memorized. Shana made fun of her for it. She added a brief message for Evan, hoped he'd figure it out. At least he'd know she tried.

She folded the bills, making a little pocket and dropping the coins inside. She added the yellow pill from her purse pocket, wrapped the entire thing inside the note and folded it as small and flat as she could, leaving a little money sticking out. This was for real, not like that trick

Jack liked to play from under the promenade, poking a dollar through the boards to tempt walkers overhead, only to yank it away when they went for it. Every time. Jack would tumble back into the sand cracking up until their mom yelled for him to get out of there.

The last challenge: getting the packet to the girls at the sink without Murphy seeing. Concentrating, she blew a bigger bubble than usual, peeling the residue from her lips and rolling it between her fingers.

OMG. Gum could work. Quickly she wadded her gum and stuck it to the inside of the stall door, then pressed her SOS packet to it. *Voila.* Pleased, she silently unlocked the stall door, opening it just enough to see the line of people waiting. When the next giggling girl stepped up, Alex swung the door open and held it for her.

"About time, Alex." Mom Haircut's arms were crossed; all Alex's sympathy for the woman vanished.

"Sorry. Thought I got my period." Under the woman's watchful eye, she washed her hands and tossed the wet towel in the garbage. "Thanks for waiting." Adjusting the purple scarf around her neck, she gave Murphy her sweetest, most sincere smile. "Let's eat."

CARL

The Charlton rest stop's layout was pretty straightforward: a single set of doors in and out, aside from the emergency exit. From where Carl stood, he had a perfect 360-degree view of the facility. A busload of giggling girls straggled in, a handful breaking off to use the toilets.

He used the wait to check in with the mother, who picked up immediately. "Mrs. Carmody, Carl Alden here. Just wanted to let you know everything is going according to schedule."

Her relieved sigh reminded him how much parents relied on his updates from the road.

"I've been crazy with worry all morning. How did everything go?"

"Like clockwork. We're at a Massachusetts rest stop on I-90, not quite halfway. We're about to have lunch."

The mother haltingly asked for details about the morning pickup: Did Alex yell or scream, fight them in any way?

He measured his words. "There was, shall we say, a certain amount of resistance on her part."

She sniffed. "I bet she had some choice things to say about me after I left."

Again, he edited his response. "She was upset. It's understandable. She wanted to say good-bye to you and her brother."

The mother asked what they'd talked about.

"She's been sleeping, mostly. Maybe we'll chat some at lunch."

Scanning the stream of women exiting the toilet, Carl thought he saw Murphy and the girl coming out. The pair separated, one strolling toward the sunglasses display, the other to the ATM. He'd been mistaken. But he had to remain vigilant. You just never knew. Alex may have been sleeping in the car, or just thinking. He still wasn't sure yet about this one; he had to be prepared for anything.

The mother asked what was happening next.

Carl checked his watch. "After lunch, we'll get back on the road. We're anticipating a little wet weather toward the end of the ride, but nothing that should keep us from the timetable I gave you."

"OK." A few seconds of silence. "Did you give her my letter?"

"Still waiting for the right moment. How are you and your husband holding up?" He knew the day was extremely draining for clients, how much faith it took to place their children in his hands, the stress of waiting for updates.

They needed as much reassurance as the children themselves.

"I'm trying to hold it together and get through work. I feel better, knowing things went OK at the house."

"Glad to hear it. I doubt we'll stop again, so I'll text you once we arrive at The Birches this afternoon. We can talk more tonight, once the school has taken over."

"OK. Please be careful." She sniffed again. "Tell Alex I love her, huh?"

"Of course. Try not to worry, Mrs. Carmody. We're off to a good start."

Ending the call, he flagged the pair, who headed toward him, only Carl reading Murphy's hand on Alex's back as anything more than a guiding touch. He caught the vestige of a smirk on Alex's face before his charge tossed her braid and smiled brightly at him—a little *too* brightly, he thought. Like the mother this morning, leaving her daughter's room.

ALEX

Camo Man set a pill in front of Alex. "Your mother said to take this at lunchtime."

Good old Nurse Meg, Alex thought, rolling it around the fake wood grain of the food-court table. *Aren't you afraid I might sell it, Mom?* Even if Alex had been somewhat creative with the truth lately, her mom had no right to hatch this entire plot based on a teeny-tiny bag of pills.

She could just pretend to take the pill; then again, the meds did mute the jackhammers. She swallowed it with a gulp of soda. "What else did she say?"

"To tell you she loves you." *Way to show your love, Mom. Pay strangers to yank me out of my bed in the middle of the night.*

"Great. Love you, too, Mom," she muttered.

The three now sat at a cramped plastic table with their food. Carl across from her, Murphy to her right, so close their shoulders touched. The woman would probably cut Alex's food if she let her, Alex thought, biting into her bagel. She was starving, jonesing for a cigarette. The whole bathroom scene had primed the jackhammers for a workout.

She forced herself to listen to their chatter. They had checked out Playland and the promenade last night, Carl said.

Alex stopped chewing. "You were around last night? Were you like . . . at my house?"

Camo Man nodded and took another bite of pizza.

So they were stalkers, too. She imagined them in a car outside her school, creeping on her. Everything had happened so fast this morning, she hadn't even thought about where they came from. But now, the sleep and food clearing her head, the logistics of this adventure began to sink in—the scheming her mom must have done to make this come off.

The whole thing made sense now. The bagel turned to cardboard in Alex's mouth.

Peals of laughter made her look up. The giggling bathroom girls passed behind Carl with loaded trays. Did they ever stop laughing? The tallest one stared at Alex for a second, offering an exaggerated thumbs-up before sprinting to catch up to the rest. They sent the message, Alex thought, relieved. But what if they were messing with her? And now they had Evan's number. Strange girls texting him crap would seriously piss him off, killing any chances she had with him. *If* Larke hadn't already moved in on that territory.

The undigested bagel churned in her stomach. Of course, they were messing with her. She'd been a total douche to pull that in the bathroom. Despite the meds, the jackhammers grew louder. She unwrapped her last stick of gum and rolled it into her mouth, staring at the bathroom girls and praying for the power to read lips.

"Why do you do that?" Murphy asked.

"Do what?"

"That thing. With the gum wrappers. I noticed you doing it in the car."

Alex dropped the folded silver *W* onto her tray. "I don't know. Habit, I guess." The action was only a reflex these days. At one time, the silver links were the building blocks of a whole DIY thing she and Cass envisioned—a line of soft-sided metallic phone cases and wallets they would sell on Etsy to subsidize their dream. Alex still had a massive pile of folded wrappers on her vanity, combined fruits of six months of marathon gum chewing. They had planned to get down to business after her party.

The wrappers meant nothing now.

"Nervous habit." Murphy had a blob of creamy salad dressing on her chin, which Alex meanly decided not to mention. She felt sorry for the woman, with her husband gone and all, but she was still the enemy.

"Got any hobbies, Alex?" Carl asked.

Seriously? This guy probably had a whole file on her. Out of nowhere came a stupid urge to impress them. "Yeah. Music."

Why did you just tell him that? He had a way of getting her to talk. She'd have to be more careful.

"You go to concerts?"

She shifted on the hard plastic seat. "Sometimes. I like this band Amphibian." He already knew that; his performance in her room this morning hadn't fooled her. He probably saw her concert poster when he scoped out her room yesterday.

Carl wiped his hands on a napkin. "Ah, Amphibian. Excellent bassist. How about 'Rock of Ages'. . . that ten-minute jam in the middle? I saw it live upstate New York a few years ago."

Alex knew the band's tour history by heart. The guy had his facts straight. "You saw the Grass Is Greener tour?"

He nodded. "Eight thousand people camping for three days. Got nasty the second day, when the skies opened up. Thought for sure they'd shut the whole thing down. But they kept on playing. The crowd went nuts. When the drummer flew out on those wires . . ."

"I know. I watched it online." Alex cocked her head. "Seriously? You were there?" He was certainly old enough—at least her father's age, maybe older. He dressed older.

"What's the matter? Don't I look like a Phib?" Camo Man pulled at his navy shirt. "I know it's not tie-dye."

"It's not that . . ." she started.

"What, then? Everyone's stoned out of their mind the entire time? Can't see me with all those twirlers?"

Her mouth dropped open. She had been captivated by their whirling and wheeling, song after song without a break, powered by some magical fuel. They even had their own section at the shows. She and Cass had tried twirling the length of a single song at home one night, only to flop dizzy and winded onto Alex's bed. Phibs' songs were long.

"Whatever the scene, those guys are superb musicians. Classically trained, actually. I appreciate their performances just fine these days without all the . . ." He paused to clear his throat. "'Enhancements,' shall we say?"

Was her chauffeur admitting he'd put away a few bowls in his day? Maybe Camo Man was human after all. She'd heard the band took care of Phibs who'd had problems with drugs or alcohol, but still wanted to go to their shows. Even held special meetings for them on the road, in tents. Supposedly Adam, the crazy drummer, had had his own issues. He left the band for a while. *Exhaustion,* they said. How cool would it be to peek in that tent, to see Adam up close?

Alex chewed the inside of her mouth. There was no way Camo Man had been coached on her current obsession—he knew way too much. "So, that frog thingy in your car?"

"You mean Rainmaker? That's my traveling buddy. A little memento. You know the place?"

Duh. What self-respecting Phib didn't know the birthplace of *Rainmaker*, the group's first album? Recorded in a college-dorm room, the record catapulted the group to celebrity status in the jam-band realm. Thanks to her dad, Alex could spout Phibs lore like other kids recited nursery rhymes. He even owned a *Rainmaker* original vinyl pressing. She was eight when he showed her the album cover, the tree frog's hypnotic gaze scaring the crap out of her. But then her father picked up his bass and strummed the raw opening chords of the title track, sweeping them both away:

> *We opened our mouths to the manna from above*
> *Sure in our purpose, uncertain in our love*

The double jolt of her father's passion and the music transported Alex, converting her on the spot—the day Alex drank the Kool-Aid, as her mother liked to say. And because they shared everything, it wasn't long before Cass took a sip, too, falling under the band's spell, Amphibian becoming their shared religion. They were practically babies compared to the Phibs' fan demographic, which fit perfectly with Cass's anti-cool take on everything. Who needed one-dimensional boy bands and country singers when there was Amphibian? ("I mean, do those guys *sleep* in those cowboy hats?" Cass used to wonder. She had a teeny snarky streak in her.)

Alex's dad took them to their first Phibs concert after eighth-grade graduation. With his blessing, they wormed their way to the stage, navigating the sea of fans, most old enough to be their grandparents.

Because Amphibian obsessed over its set lists, Alex didn't get to hear *Rainmaker* live until last summer—with Cass, not her father. By that time, he had stopped coming with them. The wait was worth it: the dazzling twenty-three-minute extravaganza of a jam was lush with imagery of desert storms, mushroom clouds (wink, wink), mirages . . .

That was the beauty of the band. Though they'd been around for more than thirty years, if you counted the time they were broken up, they still kept it fresh, every show unfolding like a perfectly choreographed dance. The place had been packed, considering it was Father's Day. Some band members brought their children onstage. The musicians were such gods to Alex it was really funny to think of them as parents, with kids and dogs and houses like normal people.

She felt guilty her father missed that show. It wasn't like she'd completely ignored Father's Day. She left a card—had gotten Jack to sign it, too. Her mother said something about a family barbecue, but Alex just waved her concert tickets on her way out. What were they going to do? Sit at the picnic table and watch her parents stare at each other?

Instead, the friends swayed and sweated in communion with thousands of Phibs at the Long Island amphitheater. Alex was so suffused with bliss she didn't mind that Cass took off without her to celebrate the day with her own dad. Nor did she regret blowing all her cash on a skull-covered cape her mother would freak over.

Nothing mattered because Ace, arms wrapped around his bass like a protective father, sang to her, and only her:

> *Parched and burning, it soothed our souls*
> *Quenched our thirst though it took a toll*

And then, because Amphibian always delivered a big finish, a set of giant sprinklers rose from either side of the stage and sprayed the audience, refreshing and reviving the crowd like a summer rainstorm, a final communal baptism before they all processed to tents and cars in a single undulating, glistening mass.

Rainmaker.

Her dad waited up for her that night, jumping out of the living room shadows, asking how many encores Amphibian played.

"Um, four, I think?"

"That's about right." He pulled a cardboard tube from behind his back and offered it to her. "Open it."

This was *his* day. Why was he giving her a present? Beyond remorseful now, she pried open the tube. Inside was the celebrated Phibs tour poster commemorating *Rainmaker*'s first pressing. She gasped; the posters were like gold—sold out everywhere, even on eBay.

"How did you get this?" she said, breathless.

"I have my connections. Night, Al." He shut the basement door behind him before she could thank him.

She'd stared into the red eyes of the frog on the poster. It was *soooo* frustrating to figure out her dad these days. He was eons away from the guy who had sat between Alex and Cass on the basement couch on the twenty-fifth anniversary of Amphibian's *Rainmaker* recording to watch the live stream of festivities from some far-flung corner of New Hampshire. The three had cheered along with the live crowd as the band unveiled its giant tree frog statue—a twenty-foot version of the amphibian blinking at her from the poster.

So yeah, Camo Man. She *did* know about Rainmaker. She pushed her half-eaten bagel toward him. He could keep his pint-size version of the real thing. *Happy Corner.* Alex would never see it now. That would be the ultimate betrayal. She couldn't hurt Cass again.

Across from her, Carl stood and piled his trash on a tray. "So, my fellow Phib: You know what they say, right? 'One show at a time.'"

Alex didn't like his saying *my* like they were friends. And it was a stupid saying, anyway. Of course you couldn't do more than one show at a time.

He was still talking. "I just follow the green balloons now."

Alex cocked her head. She'd seen bunches of green balloons at shows but wasn't sure what they meant. Maybe they marked a special place for Phibs who'd attended a certain number of shows or were doing something for the environment. Not wanting to act dumb in front of Camo Man, she nodded as if she knew what he meant. Next time they went, she and Shana would get to the bottom of the balloons thing.

In front of her, Camo Man and Murphy did their little shuffle and attached themselves to her again. Making their way out of the food court, they passed the table of bathroom girls. By craning her neck, Alex caught the eye of the tall girl, her heart dropping when the girl stuck out her tongue. Then another girl noticed Alex looking their way and curved her hands into a heart, pressing the shape to her chest, smiling.

Alex smiled back. Maybe the day wouldn't be a complete fail, she thought, letting Camo Man guide her toward the exit.

CARL

What was it about a little rain that turned normal drivers into morons?
Carl wondered as he negotiated I-93 in the light drizzle, staying left
to head toward Concord. All it took was a little common sense. He
tried to pass a tractor-trailer loaded with new cars, including a cherry
Mercedes dangling perilously from the rear. The guy wouldn't cut him
a break, keeping his cab nose to nose with Carl's sedan. Carl stepped on
it, passing him and, for good measure, another charter coach. Headed
to Canada maybe? He didn't know how the driver could see through
the steamed-up windshield.

"That guy would do better with his defrost," he said of the bus,
navigating back to the middle lane. "That's better. Nice open road now.
Just another eighty miles or so."

"Did you feel that? That jiggle?" Murphy asked from the backseat.
"The temperature's dropping a little. Maybe there's black ice."

Carl slowed. "Sorry. This car doesn't handle the same as my
Suburban." As he spoke, the trailer sailed by him again on his left and
slid in front of them. Resigned, he inserted a CD into the player.

"Cool," Alex said at the opening riff. "'Lifeboat.'" Her eyes widened
in the rearview mirror.

"Another *Rainmaker* track. Self-produced in '76. In their college dorm." As long as the girl liked the music, he might as well play it. It would put her in a better frame of mind for her arrival at The Birches, he thought. Behind him, however, the teenager was yawning. "But you know all that, don't you?"

"Kinda. My dad's into them."

Carl flicked at the tree frog, sending it spinning. "He ever been, your father?"

"Nope."

"Been where?" Murphy piped up from the back.

"To Amphibian's *Rainmaker* shrine. Picture a twenty-foot version of this in brass." Carl flicked the frog again.

"Why on earth did they choose a frog?" Murphy asked.

"Their mystical properties. Wanted the album cover to stick in people's minds. They say touching the statue brings you luck, money, fertility. And rain. Lots of rain. Real tree frogs lay eggs close to water. In a foam nest that hardens over time. When it rains really hard, the nests melt, and their eggs drop into the water. That's where the fertility part comes in."

"And where exactly is this monster frog?"

Carl chuckled. "Tucked away in a forgotten little corner of New Hampshire, a place called Happy Corner. About as close to Canada as you can get. The band played a festival there once and loved it. Decided that's where Rainmaker should live. Now it's kind of a pilgrimage for hard-core fans. Something to see." He sought Alex's gaze again. "You know, it's not all that far from your new school."

Alex crossed her arms and stared out her window. Murphy's questioning stare now filled the rearview mirror: *You're not thinking about stopping there, are you?*

He shook his head. Happy Corner was not part of this itinerary. Perhaps once the girl got settled, she'd find a way to visit.

The chorus of "Lifeboat" came around again, and Carl rapped the steering wheel:

> *Horizon before us, nothing but sea*
> *You lookin' all fine sitting right across from me.*
> *The vision changes quickly, from tranquillity to war*
> *Who are these people, the enemy, crashing through the door?*
> *Arrivederci, freedom. Will I feel the pain?*
> *Let me be your lifeboat, so I can see you again.*

The *Rainmaker* album provided the soundtrack for the next hundred miles, Carl dissecting every track. Alex came out of her funk a little, warming to his narration, even contributing a bit of band trivia here and there. His charge had been well schooled; her father, Alex said again, when Carl complimented her encyclopedic knowledge of the band.

The guy sounded cool, Carl thought. Under other circumstances, he might have enjoyed meeting Jacob Carmody, the music providing common ground.

When they got to "Rose Volcano," the second-to-last track, the two clashed. Alex swore it was on the band's set list last year; Carl claimed Amphibian retired the song in Santa Fe in 1978.

"I was there, Alex. They made a big deal about hanging up that song. Even erupted a fake volcano on stage."

"But on YouTube . . ." Alex protested.

"YouTube's not the Bible." He ought to remember; Santa Fe was part of his summer with Diana—the best one of his life, until he blew it.

Silent, Alex spun her braid and stared out her window.

"You really got around in those days, Carl," Murphy commented.

"We had a pretty good gig," he chuckled. Life was simple that summer, Diana's dad loading their van with cases of soda they could sell, stacking the cases so high they could barely see out the back window.

"He probably wanted to make sure his daughter would eat over the next few weeks," Murphy observed.

"You're probably right." They had picked up the tour in Albuquerque, Carl recalled. "Every night, I filled a cooler with soda and ice and rigged it to my skateboard. Just before the encores, Diana and I rolled it out to the exit. People came out so hot and thirsty they'd pay two dollars, three dollars apiece for a drink." He lifted his hat to run a hand over his head. "Profits kept us going the entire tour."

Alex sat up, her eyes admiring. "You're so lucky."

"Only thing was, we never got to hear the encores because we had to run outside to get ready."

"Bummer. Encores are sick," Alex yawned and turned her head again.

"What happened to Diana?" Murphy asked.

Diana, the elegant honor student so far out of his league, the serious sculptress he fell hard and fast for in high school. For her, he'd even cracked the books a little, just to sit beside her and feel the spark when his arm grazed hers. They crisscrossed the country that summer in the borrowed van, chasing music, their eighteen-year-old selves convinced they would spend the rest of their lives together.

Then, the morning Diana found him; the hundreds of miles of a silent ride home once they located their van keys. She told him she never wanted to see him again. By the time he had his act together a few years later and looked her up, it was too late.

"You know. Your old girlfriend?" Murphy prompted.

Carl shrugged. "It was a long time ago. Didn't work out."

In the hour or so since they'd crossed into New Hampshire, the rain had intensified, the traffic a sea of brake lights stretching to the horizon. Carl ejected the CD and searched for a news channel. "Might have a little situation up there." They plugged along at twenty miles an hour for a good fifteen minutes, two lanes of traffic squeezed down to one, a single fluorescent-wrapped emergency worker waving everyone to the shoulder.

Carl spotted the wreck first. "Well, what do you know? Our buddy from before." Up ahead, the trailer that had passed them awhile back lay on its side, splayed across both northbound lanes, its shiny vehicles clinging precariously to the tractor frame. Carl cringed at the damage the cargo had likely suffered. The driver stood in the grassy island, gesturing wildly to a state trooper. Southbound drivers rubbernecked, paralyzing the traffic on that side as well.

"Could have predicted that one. He's lucky he's standing." Carl slowed and rolled down his window.

"Mandatory exit for everyone," the red-faced worker said, rain pouring off his bright orange vest. He pointed to the exit ramp up ahead. "You gotta get off there. Shutting down northbound 93 till we get this cleared." Sirens whined in the distance.

"That could take hours." Carl merged into the stream of cars bumping along the grassy roadside. "We'll need a detour." He tapped furiously into the GPS screen. "Problem is, the exits are further apart up here. There's not another one for twelve miles or so. And we're right up against solid forest here"—he pointed to a thick green mass on the GPS grid—"which pushes us much further east than I'd like." They'd have to go way east, then double back again, he said.

They were off the highway now, in Lincoln, an area thick with shops and hotels and other tourist spots anchoring ski resorts. At the slower speed, the rain plinked off the windshield. He pulled into the next gas station and stopped.

"Probably better to figure this out the old-fashioned way." He pulled a map of Vermont and New Hampshire from the glove compartment and snapped it open, studying it a moment before folding it down and offering it to Murphy. "This right here is 112, the Kancamagus Highway." He traced a route that sliced through the White Mountain Forest. They'd take the Kanc into Conway, then hop onto 302 north up to Silver Mountain. The detour would take them out of their way a little, setting them back maybe half an hour, well within their timetable, he said.

"We could just wait here until they clear the accident and hop back on 93," Murphy suggested.

Not necessary; he'd driven the Kanc many times before. The White Mountains were filled with camps and wilderness programs extremely popular with his clients. Carl knew to avoid the winding highway in winter when the access roads on either side weren't maintained. But it was spring now. Leaving Murphy to hold the map, he smiled at his passengers.

"We'll be fine," he said. "We're just lucky the whole Kanc is open now. A couple weeks ago, and we'd have been in big trouble."

ALEX

Could it hurt to ask? Beneath the mirror, the frog's omnipotent gaze challenged Alex to fire at Camo Man all the burning questions she and Cass had debated endlessly. *Would the Phibs embrace them? Were there sacred dances around the statue?* And most important: *How often did the band visit Happy Corner?*

With the driver's off-the-cuff mention of the place, everything had roared back to the surface: the expectancy humming under Alex's skin, the anticipation and curiosity she'd pushed so far down she'd convinced herself they had disappeared.

But asking would be a betrayal. That pilgrimage to the site of Amphibian's first festival, to Rainmaker's home, was to have been their journey, hers and Cass's—their *raison d'etre*, as Cass described it when she was feeling super-dramatic, which was pretty often. Spellbound by a public radio account of the colony that sprang up from the band's hallowed ground, this was what Cass had proposed the day Alex's parents announced their split: that they visit Happy Corner the summer after high school. Their pact kept Alex going even as her parents' relationship imploded.

Armed with names generated at FindYourInnerHippie.com (Blossom Jade Sweetwater for Cass, Indigo Wren Sterling for Alex), they immersed themselves in Happy Corner lore. Alex fancied herself tending the self-sustaining gardens, collecting fruits and vegetables for locally sourced communal meals, while Cass fantasized about assisting in Happy Corner's school for Phibs offspring, run out of an old barn.

Stoked with excitement, the friends stepped up their gum-chewing, wrapper-folding enterprise, each stick moving them farther along their journey. They worked in Alex's room, with her Rainmaker poster for inspiration.

Anything had been possible with that great golden statue in their future.

In the backseat now, Alex swallowed her questions. She'd sooner die than break the promise she'd made to herself after. And to Cass. Forgetting would be infinitely more challenging now, with Rainmaker so close. Her penance, she decided. Perhaps by virtue of proximity, the statue's energy would radiate to her new prison naturally, which would be perfectly acceptable under the terms of her self-made pact.

Still, she wished Camo Man had never mentioned it.

Alex felt moisture on her face and opened her eyes. Rain sluiced through Camo Man's open window as he plotted their detour on a map. Mom Haircut was all for waiting out the traffic; Camo Man was determined to move forward. Alex smirked. *A little trouble in paradise.*

The driver turned up his coat flaps. "You folks wait here. I want to give the school an update." He disappeared into the little store attached to the gas station, its windows plastered with Mega Ball posters surrounding a blinking "Hot Coffee" sign. A faded plaque outside read "Lynx," a bus bearing the same logo idled in the parking lot while the driver smoked a cigarette outside.

"Why doesn't he call them on his cell?" Alex asked.

"Service is pretty spotty in the mountains."

This was the icing on the cake: her mother sticking her somewhere with no cell service. Alex's phone kept her going, connected—the reassurance somebody was always out there, a lifeline, when her house full of people felt empty.

Beside her, Mom Haircut dug into her fanny pack, extracting an envelope. "Your mother wanted us to give this to you."

Alex grabbed it, recognizing the signature scrawl that greeted her every time she opened her lunch bag. Without Cass at her elbow to chortle over her mom's latest corny sentiment, reading the daily notes was like watching a movie without popcorn, or munching a hundred-calorie snack. Without Cass, something essential was missing. The notes kept coming, though. Alex read them quickly, away from Shana's prying eyes.

Murphy beside her, Alex traced her name on the envelope, pondering its contents. Maybe if she had only texted Evan's address to her mom last night instead of going off the radar, her mom would be saying this stuff in person.

"You don't have to read it now."

Damn straight I won't—not with you sitting there watching me. Alex fake smiled and stuffed the letter into her bag, hoping Mom Haircut wouldn't do something lame like grab her hand, relieved when Camo Man dropped back into the front seat.

"It's starting to sleet." He took off his hat, sending another spray of water Alex's way. "Temperature's dropped a good fifteen degrees since we stopped."

"Maybe we should wait it out," urged Murphy. "It'll only get worse as we go higher up." Worrywart Mom Haircut, scared of a little sleet. Alex was up for anything that delayed the inevitable.

"We'll be fine," Camo Man said, turning to her. "Turnaround's tight tomorrow, remember?"

"You have to think about *her*." Murphy pursed her lips and looked out her window.

Hmm . . . a little like the Meg and Jacob Show, Alex thought. No wonder she had assumed they were married, although Camo Man still sounded obsessed with that Diana chick. If he loved her so much, why hadn't he fought for her, like people in love were supposed to do? *'Til death do us part.* Then maybe he'd have his own kids to worry about today instead of kidnapping other people's for a living.

Peering out her rain-splashed window, she regretted opening up to the driver earlier over the music. Even if he *was* a certifiable Phib, which she was convinced of now, he only used their common passion to manipulate her. The man could turn on her at any moment.

Like her father, who had always been the fun parent, the silly parent, the parent who usually caved when her mom wouldn't. When the tables started to turn, her dad becoming all bad cop, it threw everything off-balance.

Like when he started sleeping in the basement, suddenly all on her case to move her stuff out of there. The basement, where they spent gazillions of hours listening to music, was now off-limits. Her dad, grouchy and moody—when he wasn't away working, he was sleeping down there.

Next, he'd moved on to her makeup. The guy who took her to get her lip pierced suddenly cared about her eyeliner application?

Fast-forward to her Sweet Sixteen: Alex's cheeks flamed just thinking about it. The party was rocking—Shana's toilet activity undetected, thanks to her mother's obsession with getting lame family pictures. Why couldn't they just cram into the photo booth and call it a night, Alex complained. She saw no point in family pictures now.

To her horror, her mother licked a finger right in front of the whole world and went to town on Alex's face. "Hold still, Al. You've got glitter on your cheek."

"Stop, Mom. It's *supposed* to be there." Mortified, she turned to make sure no one had seen. Behind them, the chocolate fountain had begun to give off a burnt smell, the basin lumpy with broken pretzels and strawberry hulls. Her parents posed stiffly on either side of her.

"Smile, Carmodys."

Her mom pulled away suddenly. "Wait. Don't move. We're missing Jack." She dashed off, leaving Alex with her father. He'd looked handsome that night. Alex hadn't been able to remember the last time she'd seen him in a suit. Maybe Grandpa's funeral? He didn't have a suit kind of job. Maybe with the next one, he would.

"I can't believe you're sixteen," he said.

At that moment, Cass had strolled by. "*Soooo* cute. You guys look amazing."

Her dad smiled. "Next thing you know, we'll be taking pictures of you girls at your graduation and sending you away to college."

"That's right. *Away.*" Cass locked eyes with Alex, undulating her hips and waving her hands at her sides, all the while moving away from the pair.

"What the heck is she doing?" her father asked as Cass slipped back into the ballroom.

Alex seized the moment. She was so anxious to know what her parents' crazy arrangement meant for her future. Moistening her lips, she began. "Dad, I found this college . . ." The photographer posed them back-to-back in a cheesy father-daughter shot.

"College, huh? How are those grades doing, by the way?"

"Great. Awesome." She couldn't tell him all the tension at home made it hard for her to concentrate, paragraphs and equations blurring on the page. Alex lifted her chin at the photographer's bidding. "Anyway, this school," she said through a forced grin. "It has exactly the program I want. Marine biology."

Her dad chuckled in sync with the photographer's flash. Later, in the photos, his smile looked totally natural. "You loved scooping stuff out of the bay that summer, remember? So, which college are we talking?"

She'd watched the virtual tour a thousand times, imagined herself strolling to class in the shadow of the Kilauea Volcano, immersed in life below aquamarine waters. That's how you knew it was the right school, wasn't it—when you could see yourself there?

At that exact second, the DJ launched into "Best Night Ever."

"University of Hawaii," she yelled over the music.

"You're kidding, right? We talking college or vacation here?" her dad called over Wale's full-blown rap.

Please be joking, Dad. Alex knew it was far away. But if she didn't get away from the two of them and their mixed-up life, she would suffocate.

"It's great you're thinking ahead, but we're not made of money."

No. No no no no. He couldn't possibly crush her dream on the most important night of her life. She turned toward him, on the brink of tears. "But Dad, there's scholarships. And financial aid. I can work in the summers for airfare and—"

The photographer interrupted. "Miss Carmody, could you turn back to me, please?"

Her father maneuvered her toward the camera. "That's great, honey. But I don't know how we could do that."

"But this party . . ." She waved at the festivities behind her.

"Tonight was a special case," her father said. "I'll explain it sometime."

Alex wasn't able to imagine what those reasons could be, but if she had known her parents couldn't afford a party of this magnitude, she would have scaled it way back. She would have told them to save the money for Hawaii.

Her dad had slung an arm around her for the last photo. "Sorry, Alex. It's just not in the cards right now. Things are pretty tight."

The banquet-hall air felt stale and warm suddenly. Alex longed to yank her father away and make him understand this was the only school she wanted. If they *were* officially poor now, couldn't financial aid fund her dream? But the words wouldn't move past the ginormous lump in her throat.

Her mother had dragged Jack back in time to hear her dad's last comment. Before Alex could plead her case, her parents were off and running:

"Really, Jacob? Is this the time and place for that discussion?" her mom snapped. She tugged at her strapless dress, pressing her lips in an approximation of a smile.

"Alex brought it up. I just want her to know I'm doing everything I can for her and Jack," he said.

"You mean your mother is," her mother whispered, but Alex heard it anyway.

"Meg, please. I'm working on it."

Two cheerleaders stared on their way to the chocolate fountain—seniors Alex hoped to impress. They laughed and touched heads, Alex imagining their snarky observation about her family.

"You don't know anything about what I do," her dad continued. Her parents had stopped posing and now faced each other. "It's all about contacts, word of mouth."

"Fine. Do it your way. Look how well it's working!"

Alex froze. This could *not* be happening. These parents who lived separate existences 24/7 now picked her party to rip into each other? Willing the floor to open up and swallow her, she rolled her eyes at the returning cheerleaders while the bickering continued. Jack wandered over to the chocolate fountain, hands over his ears. Her parents moved apart.

Girl alone, the last shot.

Her father made a show of tapping his watch. Suddenly he had to go; something about Vermont at the crack of dawn.

"You can't leave, Jacob. Alex hasn't cut her cake. Or done the friends ceremony."

Ignoring her mom, he hugged Alex good-bye. "Happy birthday, kiddo. Gotta get some sleep before I go to work." He twirled his keys. "We'll talk more about the college thing. Find a school on this coast, honey. Better yet, county. You can transfer after two years. You get good grades, you go for free."

He slipped through the crowd, tugging at the knot in his tie.

"Mom, please. You have to talk to him."

Her mother didn't hear her. She was already pulling Jack to the bathroom, his chocolate hands raised in surrender. Trembling, Alex peeked into the ballroom. Barely anyone was left on the dance floor. She spotted Cass from the back, the silky violet trailing over her shoulder. *Thank God.* She strode toward her friend, blinking back tears. A few yards from Cass, she stopped short.

Holy crap. Cass was slow dancing with a boy. Cass *never, ever* slow danced. That was, like, rule number one in the Cass playbook. Tucking herself behind a column, Alex watched the pair sway together, her BFF's flushed cheek pressed against his sport-coated shoulder.

Cass looked so blissful, Alex couldn't bear to interrupt. She backed away from the couple, ducking around the other dancers. In the corner, the line for the palm reader spilled out of her tent, the fuchsia decorations they'd carefully chosen now looking gaudy and childish. Alex and Cass had taken their turns before the party started. Not that the woman's prophecies meant a thing anymore.

Thanks for laying out my whole future, Dad.

"Alex, wait," Aunt Melissa called after her. Ignoring her godmother, Alex wiped under her eyes and zigzagged through the crowd, heading straight for the bathroom, hoping Shana had saved some party for the birthday girl.

MEG

Jack was at her elbow, aiming a chicken finger at Carl Alden's picture on Begin Again's home page. "He looks scary, Mom. What's an in-ter-vent . . . ?"

Meg slapped her laptop shut. "Nothing you need to worry about. Finish your plate." *Don't panic.* A dozen different scenarios had raced through her mind when she was unable to reach Carl. She had called The Birches. Like her, they'd heard from Carl at lunchtime and midafternoon and expected him at any moment.

"When's Daddy coming home? He promised he'd hit balls to me after school. Tomorrow's our first practice."

Baseball. Meg had forgotten all about it. She wouldn't win any parenting prizes today. Her son's freckled face crinkled into a frown. "I'm gonna suck."

Meg buried her face in his peanut-buttery neck. "Honey. You will *not* suck. Everybody's rusty at the first practice." She pinched his nose. "Don't worry. Daddy will have a catch with you this weekend, I promise."

"Pinky-swear?"

"Pinky-swear." They entwined little fingers. "How about this: When he gets home tonight, he'll wake you up to figure out your official training schedule."

That solution seemed to satisfy Jack. And bought her more time before she'd have to tell him about Alex, Meg thought. Jacob was always so wired when he got back from these road trips.

Licking his fingers, Jack thought of something else. "Mom, can you come to my first game?"

"Of course. Why wouldn't I?"

"Because you and dad are getting avorced."

"Di-vorced," she corrected. "And why would that stop me?"

Jack shrugged. "'Cause you don't want to hang out with Daddy now."

Meg grabbed his shoulders. "Listen, buddy, when it comes to you and Alex, Daddy and I are a team, you know? Like your baseball team. We'll always be there for you guys."

"I want the whole family to come. Like we did for Alex's games."

"I'd love that, too." Jack couldn't possibly recall those fall afternoons. He must be remembering photos of them lofting him as an infant at Alex's soccer matches, Alex running to the sidelines at every opportunity to kiss her new baby brother.

"How can we? Alex is never here anymore."

"She's getting older, bud. Her interests are changing."

"I know. Kissing *boys*. Smoochy, smoochy, smoochy." Jack zoomed out of the kitchen making kissing sounds.

Alone, Meg fixated once again on Alex. They should almost be at The Birches by now, she thought, grabbing her phone to call Melissa for a sanity check.

Her sister told her in no uncertain terms she was overreacting. "Remember the last time we skied up that way? Our cells never had service." She suggested that Meg try Alex's friends.

Carl had taken Alex's phone this morning, Meg reminded her.

"That must have gone over well."

"I know. She's probably in withdrawal."

Alex and her friends texted each other at all hours of the day and night. Meg always wondered what happened overnight in the teens' social circle that was so monumental it couldn't wait until morning. When Meg lamented her daughter's unhealthy attachment to her phone one day at work, a young nurse diagnosed the condition: FOMO, a crippling "fear of missing out."

"Try that girl Shana," Melissa suggested.

Meg had barely spoken to Shana in months, but she knew how to get in touch with her. Back when their phones were new and the young girls unsuspecting, they'd all given Meg their numbers when she asked. She hung up with Melissa and then called Shana right away, getting voice mail after a curt one-and-a-half rings. *The girl probably hit "Ignore" as soon as she saw the caller ID*, Meg thought. She didn't bother to leave a message—Alex never checked voice mail and Shana probably didn't, either. She sent a carefully worded text instead:

    Hi Shana, it's Alex's mom. Trying to get
    hold of her. Heard anything?

A sudden downpour pounded the canvas awnings outside the kitchen window. She jumped up and closed the ones she'd opened yesterday to let in some spring air. April weather was so fickle. In the dining room, aluminum verticals rattled against glass sliders leading to the deck. Investigating, she found the slider partially open. Odd. She was usually vigilant about locking up when she left, although that morning had been anything but routine.

Give yourself a break, she thought, securing the latch. It felt looser than usual. One more thing for Jacob's growing list. Would he eventually fight her for this house, if they ever got their heads above water financially?

Meg didn't even know if she wanted it. On the one hand, their home overflowed with delicious memories of raising Alex and Jack: loud, messy Saturday breakfasts, Jacob dishing up pancakes bubbling over with blueberries, catching Jack by surprise with the garden hose, planting a summer garden, Alex's squeal at the season's first cherry tomato. For every room, every season, a thousand joyful recollections.

On the other hand, Meg would forever associate this house—the very deck she was staring at, actually—with the defining spring evening last year, a night so warm they decided to barbecue. One minute they were laughing and joking with the kids over a silly YouTube cat video, the next, with Alex and Jack back inside, Meg was slipping through the slider with an armload of dirty plates when Jacob blurted to her back that he no longer wanted to be married.

Somehow, Meg had managed to set the plates on the dining room table before slowly turning back to her husband, praying she had misheard. Jacob's downcast eyes and hollowed cheeks told her she hadn't. He'd been feeling like this for a long time, he said quietly, suddenly absorbed in his nails.

A long time. Three words out of the blue that changed everything. Blindsided, she could only manage one word of her own: *Why?* He still hadn't fully explained, at least not to Meg's satisfaction, other than pointing out all her qualities and quirks that led to his decision. Phrases that always began, "See? This is why . . ." as though needing to justify his decision to himself.

At first, she refused to accept any blame. *She* kept this family humming; *she* picked up the pieces when his business fell apart. In her most self-reflective moments, however, Meg admitted he might be right about some things: She *was* too controlling. She didn't always consult him; her default mode was critical. But those faults and shortcomings shouldn't short-circuit a marriage that had endured as theirs had without some type of intervention, like couples counseling or maybe individual therapy. Jacob refused both.

Meg worried that he wasn't in his right mind. Unemployment could do that to a person. She'd hoped working with Ben would lift his spirits, but if anything, Jacob's moods had grown darker, more mercurial. She heard him sometimes, roaming around the kitchen in the middle of the night, the nocturnal rev of his truck as he drove away. He claimed he had run to the 7-Eleven for coffee when Meg questioned him in the mornings.

There was perfectly good coffee in the house, she countered. Which could only mean something else—or someone else—was percolating.

She'd pleaded with Jacob to reconsider. "How can you not fight for me? For this family?" she asked him that night and many times after.

"Things aren't what they were."

"Of course they're not. We never expected your work to dry up the way it did."

"It's not just that. People change." Jacob more than anyone, she thought, twirling the loose latch. He wasn't the same Jacob she had first met, when the odds had been stacked against them and their unconventional start as a family.

His mind was made up, he said.

Mourning their disintegrating marriage, she nevertheless agreed to present a united front for Alex's and Jack's sakes. Meg was surprised how well Alex had taken the news, running out the door to play practice or whatever the cast did once the show was over. They parceled out their explanation to Jack in small doses.

Meg and Jacob became virtual strangers in their own house. She stopped asking him if there was someone else. *Who else would want the moody bastard?* Meg thought now, jerking the verticals shut against the rain. When the time came, *she* would be the one to start fresh, in a little town house closer to the Sound. She'd get her own promenade bench.

Maybe Shana had called by now. Passing the dining room table on her way to check her phone, she wiped the damaged tea set with the hem of her scrubs. *I'm doing the best I can, Mom.*

Halfway to the kitchen, she stopped. The house had grown uncommonly quiet. Meg went in search of Jack, finding him upstairs in Alex's room, kneeling by his sister's bed.

"Jack, what are you doing?"

"Nothing." His stricken face belied his innocence.

"Doesn't look like nothing. What's up?"

"Alex said I couldn't tell. She'll whip my butt."

"I'll make sure that doesn't happen. Be a good boy and show me what's under there."

"You have to say you made me."

"Deal."

"OK. Sit there." Jack pointed to the floor, and Meg sat as instructed, shoulders tensed. If Alex had put Jack in any danger, she wouldn't be able to bear it.

Jack made a great show of raising his arms and shaking them, like a swimmer warming up on a high dive, before lifting Alex's dust ruffle and slithering under her bed just like Angel would. Reappearing, he pushed a white plastic storage bin toward Meg, then sat back cross-legged, chin propped in his hands, watching her pounce on the box and pop off the cover.

Meg covered her mouth.

"See, Mommy. I knew you'd be surprised."

ALEX

They were back on Route 112 in Lincoln, Camo Man and Mom Haircut still bickering about detours and road conditions. They passed a bunch of restaurants with cutesy names like Mountain Man Inn and Gnarly Gourmet. A movie theater advertised a single film, *A Cabin in the Woods.* Evan, Shana and Alex had seen it stoned months ago. Scary movies were always better that way. As usual, Shana acted paranoid and had to go sit in the car for a while. LOL. Alex had been up for anything that helped her to escape her memories—although her mom seemed to have the opposite intention, dragging her to that horrible therapist.

Her parents should be the ones in therapy, Alex thought now. Maybe if her dad hadn't been such a jerk during the photo session, leaving so abruptly; if her mom had taken a single second to notice that Alex was decimated instead of abandoning her; if her parents could have *for once* treated her like the adult they always insisted she be and tell her the truth about what was happening to their family, she never, *ever* would have made the trail of lousy decisions that eventually trapped her in Logan's backseat. *And* this one. Decisions that cost her *everything.*

Yes, Alex decided. Everything was their fault.

Beyond the Lincoln Theater, large hotels lined the road, advertising indoor pools and game rooms and free breakfasts. Billboards advised passersby to "Take Advantage of Spring Skiing Rates." Within a few minutes, the road went from totally crowded to dead quiet. The highway climbed; they passed a turnoff for Loon Mountain Resort, "Rated Number 3 for Parks and Pipes." *Pipes. Ha.* There were campgrounds carved out of the side of the road, scenic overlooks, a deserted tourist information booth. Alex's ears began to pop from the altitude. Soon there was nothing to look at except trees, trees and more trees, an occasional rain-slicked picnic table on the side of the road.

Bored, Alex shut her eyes. The car wound round a curve. That time, even Alex felt them fishtail. She opened one eye.

Murphy hunched toward the driver's seat. "Carl, I really think you should reconsider. There are loads of places to stay in Lincoln."

OMG. Stay? With these two in a motel room? That was *so* not going to happen.

"We'll be fine. I'm the driver, remember?" Reaching over the seat to pat Murphy's arm, Camo Man sounded half-jokey. At the higher altitude, the rain had become sleet, the slushy mix pinging off the metal roof, glazing the windows like rock candy.

"We can still turn around, Carl. Please stop."

"We're almost there. Relax, will you? I've got this." Camo Man's grin filled the rearview mirror.

Defeated, Murphy sat back and tapped on her window, fake laughing to cover her fear. "Look at that. Pink gas tanks painted like pigs. Who would ever do that?" Alex didn't even bother to look; any acknowledgment might suck her into more unwanted conversation. Carl switched on the news, music appreciation over for now, Alex grateful to Amphibian for making a chunk of the journey bearable.

The satellite signal faded in and out as they climbed, the drone of the newscaster's voice—news and weather, news and weather—lulling Alex back to semisleep. Pig gas tanks, she thought drowsily; Jack would crack up. Guiltily, she remembered her brother's first baseball game. She finally agreed to go just to get him the heck out of her room. Jack would be mad she wouldn't be there tomorrow, but that disappointment she could blame on her mother.

The radio softened to static, white noise against the clink of ice overhead. Then, without warning, Murphy's scream pierced her half dream. "Carl, watch out!" The nightmare replayed in the backseat, the seat belt straining against Alex's chest. Only this time, every one of Alex's senses was sharp, receptive—every nerve on high alert, absorbing and registering every sensation, each jolt.

Her eyes captured each frame, her brain a camera recording high-speed images: first, a dark, impenetrable wall of animal before them, spindly legs supporting barrel body. Next, close-up on its cartoonlike profile. Cut to slo-mo of the steering wheel, the hand-over-hand struggle to maintain control, the car losing traction and spinning crazily.

A single line of dialogue: Carl yelling, "Hang on, everybody!"

Wide shot of the seismic shift of the car, accompanied by the soundtrack of Murphy's and Alex's screams and the crush of metal and glass against unyielding mass. Murphy's side of the car slams into the moose's legs, propelling its half-ton body heavenward, its brief flight shearing off a great chunk of the roof. Cue Alex behind Carl, jack-hammers at full throttle, watching herself at the center of the scene, oblivious to the wind and ice now inside the car, eyes riveted on hooves clinging to the ridge of the gaping roof for interminable seconds before the animal slid off the car in a deadening thunk. Overhead shot of the car ricocheting off the leaden beast like a two-thousand-pound pinball, barreling across the highway into a lush wall of evergreen that mercifully softened its rocky descent.

Spent, finally, in the gulley, the car's crippled right side rested against a cluster of pines. The mournful wail of the car horn, a final, angry spin of wheels. Then crushing silence. *Fade to black.*

MEG

The bin's contents were disorganized, but there, on the floor of Alex's room with Jack, Meg knew exactly what she was looking at: all the notes she'd ever tucked inside her daughter's lunch since seventh grade. Napkins, Post-its, sheets from the bakery block notes they got every Christmas.

There were hundreds. Alex must have saved every single one.

They started when Alex reached puberty. Meg had done everything to prepare her daughter: the talks, the products, an entire shelf in the hall closet stocked with supplies. One day Alex came home from a soccer match paler than usual, a look on her twelve-year-old face Meg couldn't quite read.

"You OK, honey?" She pressed a hand to Alex's forehead.

Her period had arrived during the game, she said.

Meg played it cool. "Everything's on the middle shelf. Let me know if I can help."

Alex walked away from her and into young adulthood, Meg already feeling as though her daughter would need her less.

It was totally ridiculous, and yet it drove her to do something to maintain the connection between them. So each night as she made lunches, she found some scrap of paper to write on and tucked it into Alex's.

She rifled through them now, groaning at the lameness of some. The acrostic of her daughter's name: *A—amazing! L—loving! E—excellent! X—Xtraordinary!* Cheerleading before a test: *Good luck on your geography quiz. Put us on the map!* Every one of them signed *(heart sign) Mom.*

The task grew more painful after the accident; anything Meg wrote seemed trite. She wrote them anyway on the days Alex took lunch. Often it was their only communication of the day.

She had wondered what Alex thought of the notes. In five years, she had never said a word about them. But here they all were, moving Meg to tears. They must have moved Alex as well; if not, why had she kept them?

Meg sat back on her heels, letting the notes fall back into the bin, a paper chain from mother to daughter.

Confronted with Alex's unexpected sentimentality, doubt prickled Meg's arms. Had she made a terrible mistake sending Alex away? For months, she'd tried to crack Alex's shell of grief. She'd given up on talking to Alex about The Birches after only that one heated conversation on the promenade. Should she have tried again? Maybe the Alex who hung on to her mother's lunch notes might have eventually come around to the idea of a fresh start.

Meg snapped the lid on the bin. What had she done?

CARL

Eyelashes brushing cold nylon, Carl awoke to find himself splayed over the air bag. Woozy, he fought toward consciousness, pressing himself upright, registering first a persistent throb over one eye, then needles of sleet spilling through the jagged opening overhead. Beneath him, the air bag had already begun to deflate, its surface powdery under his fingers.

The girl.

"Alex." A maelstrom of wind and sleet swallowed any response. The rearview mirror revealed only darkness. Craning his neck, he swept the backseat behind him as far as he could reach, feeling nothing. Alex had been buckled in; he had a clear memory of verifying the child locks at their last stop. But, of course, the locks would disengage when the air bag deployed.

Wincing, he reached under the air bag and unbuckled his seat belt, and with enormous effort swung his stiff body toward his door to investigate.

Behind him, the back door gaped open. Alex was gone.

The sudden movement dizzied him. He took a moment to catch his breath. *Carolyn.* With difficulty, he turned toward her. The jagged edges of roof overhead made it clear her side had borne the brunt of the impact. "Carolyn," he called. She detested her first name. He never used it when they were on duty; he was unsure why he did so now.

"Carolyn. Can you hear me?" He hit the visor light. Its wan yellow glow illuminated the unnatural angle of Carolyn's head, her eyes closed and her hand resting in a lapful of broken glass.

He swallowed. Carolyn needed help. The girl was alive, out there somewhere. She could send help, if she could make it far enough to do so. But once on her own, would that be her priority? He couldn't be certain.

There were several variables: the length of time he'd been unconscious, the point at which (and in what condition) Alex had exited the car, the options presented to the newly freed teen. He checked his watch through blurred vision: 4:45. He'd been out for about an hour, which gave Alex a decent head start—providing she wasn't injured or in shock. He wasn't a religious man, but he offered an immediate intention for her safety. He would do whatever it took to find her. Straining, he pushed open his own door and stood, taking a few deep breaths before sliding into the backseat next to Carolyn, pressing two fingers into her limp wrist, willing a flutter, a reflex, any sign of life.

Getting no response, he brushed his partner's hair aside to get to her carotid artery, where the body's pulse was strongest. Below trembling fingers, he thought he detected a faint uneven beat.

The next moments would be critical. If there was a pulse, there might still be time. The necessary supplies were in the trunk. He patted her neck and slid away. "Hold on, Carolyn. I'm coming right back." After feeling his way to the trunk, he located a tarp and a flashlight. Beyond the car, the beam illuminated the dense evergreen wall that had slowed the vehicle's trajectory. On Carolyn's side, Carl gaped at the devastation wrought by the animal: the mangled car door, the roof above it ripped from its frame.

Back on the driver's side, he laid the tarp on the ground outside Alex's door, standing the flashlight up like a makeshift candelabra and sliding next to his partner again. From her clammy skin, he couldn't summon the fluttering he felt a few moments ago.

He palpated her neck. "Please, Carolyn. Hold on." In the visor's glow, her flag pin winked at him.

Carl sat back, mulling over the choices. Medics knew never to move accident victims, especially when there was a threat of internal injuries. But he also knew that in the absence of a pulse, he had to attempt CPR, which required laying her flat. He released her shoulder belt; untethered, Carolyn slumped toward him. Supporting her back, he maneuvered her along the backseat and onto the tarp, an effort that drenched him in sweat despite the cold. Beside her, the upturned torch cast ghoulish shadows on the sleet-heavy branches overhead.

Kneeling over her, he removed her glasses and set them on the seat above. Having cleared her mouth and airway, he began the compression sequences he'd done a hundred times, pressing on her chest, shutting off the thought of any internal damage beneath his hands, the pain he might be inflicting. *One, two, three, release. One, two, three, release.*

Carl sat back, imploring her chest to rise. Nothing. He repeated the compressions. *Please, Carolyn. Don't give up.* He lost count of the repetitions, oblivious to the sleet soaking them both and to his raging temple. He had not once regretted this decision to hire her. Until now, when the job had put her life in danger.

He had warned Carolyn about the long, unpredictable days. Across from him in the diner that day, her chin had been resolute. "I know I can do a great job for you. And also I need the money. *We* need the money."

That muddled things; he couldn't leave Jimbo's family in need. He offered financial assistance. When she refused, he let her ride along on a couple of transports, a trial run for both. Carolyn was an astute observer, taking notes, peppering guides with questions after the drop-off. Soon after, they made things official.

One, two, three, release. One, two, three, release. He pictured Jamie's freckled face. He had taken her mother away so often. And he would bring her back this time, as always. After everything the little girl had been through, she needed her mother. *Jamie, I'm trying.*

One, two, three, release. Carl thought of Jimbo, who, after leaving the service, turned down a chance to partner with him in Begin Again. He liked the precinct just fine, he said. Turned out there was a reason for that. He'd met "the one," his burly fingers curled in air quotes: Carolyn Lawler, a twentysomething working the dispatch desk. Carl had been honored to stand up for him at their wedding in 1991.

Eleven years later, he was back at his friend's side in church, a pall-bearer alongside Jimbo's fellow officers. After the funeral, Carl swore to Murphy she could always count on him. *You can count on me now.* He leaned on her chest one more time. He would not leave her to die in this frigid grave. *One, two, three, release.*

It was getting darker. Carl reached over Carolyn and shifted the flashlight closer. Had he imagined it, or had her chest swelled ever so slightly? Encouraged, he resumed compressions. After a few more sets, he was certain Carolyn was responding. He sat back, watching the steady rise and fall of his partner's chest. The dashboard clock measured the passage of five minutes, then ten, of Carolyn breathing on her own. Carl's respiration matching hers. With great care, he lifted Carolyn and laid her on the backseat, wiping her damp face with his handkerchief.

Squatting next to the car, Carl considered the next step. In Carolyn's fragile condition, it would be foolhardy for him to risk transporting her. And he could never manage the steep climb out of the gulley with her. On the other hand, hypothermia would set in quickly in these extreme conditions.

He made a snap decision. Although it pained him to leave her, Carolyn's best chance for survival was to remain here, somewhat sheltered from the elements. He could move faster without her to summon help. From the trunk, he found a stadium blanket and tucked it around her. He then removed his own coat and laid it over the blanket.

As a final gesture, he retrieved the tarp and tossed it over Carolyn's side of the damaged car, securing it along the jagged roof. Leaving the girl's duffel in the trunk, he stuffed Carolyn's purse into his backpack, only to yank it out again and dig for her driver's license. On a gas receipt, he scribbled his name and cell number and wrapped it around her license, tucking both into Carolyn's coat pocket for identification, should help arrive before he returned.

Checking Carolyn one more time, he switched off the visor light and shut the car door gently. Overhead, a sudden gust bent the tree canopy, lashing his face with sleet.

Walking away from the car, Carl took stock of his own injuries for the first time. His lips were salty from his own blood. After touching the bump over his eye, his fingers came away sticky. He couldn't remember the impact, only his futile attempt to right the car after the animal's initial slam, steering into the skid as he'd been trained to do, brakes useless on the skating rink of a road. Perhaps the rest would come to him later. For now, he had to keep moving, focus on seeking help for Carolyn, hopefully finding Alex in the process, as soon as possible.

He could only guess at the direction the girl had gone. The storm had dropped a premature curtain of darkness over the White Mountains. He cast the light in a wide circle over the ground. At first he saw only the car's erratic tracks in the mud, ending in an angry *Z*. Then, dropping to his heels, he caught the faint suggestion of prints in the tracks—following the wobbly trail for a few hundred feet until it slammed him into a steep hillside, where the footsteps disappeared.

Puzzled, Carl cast the flare on the face of the incline, pocked with random indentations and scrapings. Then it dawned on him: She had turned and taken the hill backward. The girl had better instincts than the mother gave her credit for.

Hoisting his backpack, he followed the scrapings, ignoring his head's pounding. Grabbing overhead limbs for support, he made his way up the hill, berating himself for this turn of events. He had known to watch for moose. How many warning signs with the moose silhouette had he passed?

And yet it had happened. Today, trying to make up for lost time, for lost work, had he taken the curve too quickly? The decision could cost him dearly: two lives entrusted to him, the business he had so carefully constructed over twenty years.

At the top of the hill finally, he stepped over the guardrail onto the Kancamagus Highway. The girl's wits had gotten her this far. Here, however, the flash-frozen landscape obscured any further clue. A choice now: Head north or south? To his right, the road climbed higher and deeper into the White Mountain forest. They must have been farther up that hill when they'd left the road, which would explain the wayward car tracks. He remembered the small store they passed only moments before that had caught Carolyn's attention.

Would Alex have remembered? She'd barely grunted when his partner pointed out the pastel gas tanks. But the girl had already proved herself to be resourceful. He hoped she had the sense to seek shelter from the storm. Her light clothing wouldn't protect her for long.

He decided to head downhill toward the store. The adrenaline that fueled him was beginning to fade, replaced by a damp chill that amplified his body's aches. He paused a moment, knowing he needed to remember this spot so he could come back for Carolyn. Sitting on the guardrail, he glanced around for a means of marking the location.

That's when he noticed the slash of violet dangling beneath the guardrail, sodden with sleet.

MEG

Jack was killing her.

Carl hadn't called. Shana hadn't responded. And downstairs, her son now posed in the doorway, strumming his father's prized Fender bass.

"Are you kidding me?" she said. "You know Daddy's rules." It was as though the boy were dreaming up stunts to distract her from her worry. She detached him from the cherished instrument.

"But I want to be in a band like Daddy."

"You can, if you keep practicing your clarinet."

"Clarinet's not cool. Name one band with a clarinet player."

"You know I can't."

Even at seven, Jack's grasp of music eclipsed hers. He danced around now, rocking an imaginary guitar, adding the throbbing bass line himself.

When the time came a few years ago to sign Jack up for music lessons, Jacob had lobbied for guitar or drums. "As I recall, you thought it was pretty hot when I played for you downstairs," he said, sidling up to Meg at the kitchen sink and strumming an imaginary guitar the way

Jack was right now. A witness to the moment, horrified thirteen-year-old Alex made an exaggerated gagging sound and exited.

"It was the hormones," Meg had deadpanned.

Tonight, she called a halt to Jack's air-guitar concert, threatening to withhold his video games if he touched Jacob's instruments again.

"OK. But you better tell Alex, too. She's in Daddy's stuff all the time."

She squatted down to her son's level. "She is?"

"Yup. She has some of his records in her room. She plays the same song every night. Something about rain. It's *really* long." Jack rolled his eyes.

A long song about rain didn't ring a bell, but then again, she was more talk radio than Pandora. "OK. I'll talk to her."

Meg carried the guitar down to the basement and set it back in its stand.

Hormones. She had to smile. Hormones definitely played a part back then, when their entire future was pinned on the secondhand crib and changing table in the freshly painted bedroom upstairs.

Meg's mother had thought she was crazy. And she probably had been, a little, when she placed all her faith in the bassist whose lazy grin she succumbed to that night at the Tiki Bar. She'd been dragged there after work by fellow nurses determined to help her move on once and for all from her ex, a med student who decamped to Australia for his studies. Meg lost track of the number of rounds; drinks were sloshed on the crowded dance floor. As they spun near the band, the bass player's gaze warmed her back. She hung behind to chat while the band packed up. When she went to look for her girlfriends, they had disappeared. She didn't try very hard to find them.

The next morning, Meg clung to her side of the bed, appalled at her own behavior. Type A oncology nurses didn't go around picking up stray musicians. To put the humiliating experience behind her, she threw herself into her work. Which was an excellent coping strategy, until she threw *up* at work.

At first, Meg didn't want Jacob's help with the baby. She wasn't even going to tell him. Melissa said she had to. With her sister waiting in the car, Meg tracked him to a dive bar in Mamaroneck, where Jacob did the most surprising thing: he swore to take care of the three of them. After that, Meg couldn't shake him. He trailed her like a puppy, showing up at the hospital at the end of her shift, at her parents' house, outside her OB-GYN's office.

He even charmed Melissa, no mean feat. To demonstrate his commitment after Alex was born, Jacob dialed down Objects in Mirror to weekend gigs so he could frame houses alongside his father. Walter Carmody kept the contracts coming, and from the father and son's skilled hands emerged beautiful, affordable, working-class homes that dotted this side of Westchester County—including theirs. *The house that Walter and Jacob built,* Meg thought, surveying the finished basement.

Meg and Jacob had built something, too. From that regrettable one-night stand, they cobbled together a life—a life Jacob claimed no longer suited him. It made no sense to her that a man committed to both business and family could allow both to slip through his fingers.

But leaning against Meg at the kitchen sink those few years ago, Jacob had been right about one thing: the musician thing *was* a turn-on. She walked around his old practice area now to make sure Jack hadn't disturbed anything else. There was fresh sheet music on one of the stands. *Was* Jacob playing again?

Maybe that's where all Jacob's insanity was coming from, she mused—midlife regret over abandoning his band before it reached its zenith. Objects in Mirror had never been more than a very popular bar band, but a musician could dream. Anyone could. Maybe once Alex was settled, she would encourage him to have the band practice here again. She'd fire up the slow cooker with pulled pork for them like she used to.

Passing the bar, Meg couldn't help but swat the offending pillow. What if she hadn't stopped down here after the house party? What if Alex had come home that night brimming with remorse instead of attitude? What if her daughter had allowed Meg to pick her up from wherever she had been last night instead of ignoring her?

What if. What if. Over the past few months, her life had become a constant cycle of Monday-morning quarterbacking in which she reexamined her nursing, her partnering, her parenting.

Especially her parenting. If someone had told her the one thing, the secret sauce that would reconnect her with her daughter, she gladly would've done it. Anything to once again have cozy nights on the couch, swirling pretzel rods into Häagen-Dazs. And girl talk at the nail salon, Meg's staid Winkin' Pink and Alex's Black Orchid setting under whirring fans. One day Alex dared Meg to try Phospho-licious, a neon yellow that lit up her fingertips. Meg agreed, thinking her patients would get a kick out of it.

Alex had been particularly chatty that day, confessing to crushing on a boy on the school bus. Like two schoolgirls, they plotted ways Alex could strike up a conversation. Alex's victorious thumbs-up coming off the bus a few days later had elated Meg.

These days, it took more than ice cream or nail polish to woo Alex, especially when fashion dictated that the studiously neglected nail, somber and chipped, was more on-trend.

And yet, there were those notes.

Hand on the basement banister, Meg sighed. Alex had looked her straight in the eye the other night when she denied the pills were hers. And Jacob believed her. Meg herself *had* been very emotional that evening. Once again, she second-guessed herself: Had she jumped the gun with this transport?

If only answers could magically appear, like the fortunes dispensed by the palm reader at Alex's party. For now, Meg would settle for any sign the day had unfolded exactly as Carl had promised.

CARL

Had the marker on the guardrail been any other color, Carl might have mistaken it for something left by a road crew or group of hikers. But its signature shiny purple left no doubt: it was Alex's scarf, the flimsy sash she'd insisted on retrieving before they left the Carmody house this morning.

He stroked the soaked fabric. Whatever her condition following the accident, Alex had the presence of mind—and the compassion—to affix it to the guardrail where they'd veered off the road. *Thank you, Alex.* Carl unwound the scarf and retied it around a tree at eye level so it would be more visible. Its gauzy tails flapped wildly in the wind. For good measure, he snapped off a pair of branches and leaned them against the tree in an *X*, pressing their tips into the ground.

Now he could go for help. As he headed downhill, the open road exposed him to chilling sheets of ice that quickly soaked his woolen shirt. He picked up his pace as much as the slick surface allowed, stepping over more fallen branches, alert for downed lines.

He dreaded the difficult calls ahead of him, conversations with two mothers whose daughters' fates were in his hands. He reached for his cell, but put it back after seeing the no-service indicator in the high-altitude dead zone.

A deafening crack at his left made him jump. Casting his light, Carl saw a thick-waisted oak felled horizontal just beyond the guardrail. A few feet to the right, and it would have crushed him. He sidestepped to the center of the road, waving the light over his head. The fallen tree hadn't taken any wires with it, but the next one might. He followed the road's dashed white lines that gleamed sporadically through the sleet for an hour or more, and was beginning to second-guess whether the store actually existed when a faint glow warmed treetops in the distance. The wind's pitch altered; in the lull between gales, he swore he detected the faint grind of an engine. Heartened, he picked up his pace.

The grind grew louder. Headlights sliced through the soupy mist and a gleaming rig emerged, its overhead light bar pulsing amber. Carl attempted to run toward the emergency vehicle, flailing his arms.

The vehicle slowed alongside him.

"Accident," Carl managed to gasp to the uniformed driver. "My car off the road. There's a woman. Badly injured."

"Headed there now. Someone reported it."

"A teenage girl?"

"No idea, sir. Came in through dispatch." He indicated the door behind him. "Hop in. You can show us where the car went off the road."

Carl hesitated. He wanted nothing more than medical aid for Carolyn, but he also needed to find Alex. "How far ahead is the store?" he asked.

"Quarter mile at most."

"I'm going to head there. I had another passenger. A girl. I need to find her."

The driver eyed Carl's bump. "You sure, sir?"

"I'm sure. Keep your eye out for a purple marker on your right. Maybe a mile down."

At least Carolyn would get the help she needed, Carl thought, watching the vehicle drive away. With any luck, he'd find Alex up ahead at the store. Before long, the airborne glow that had teased him earlier swelled into a full-fledged spotlight shining down on twin gas tanks, their slick fuchsia flanks glistening—the oddity Murphy pointed out a lifetime ago. Beyond the tanks, a neon "Open" sign on a log cabin blinked at Carl. He paused on the cabin porch to catch his breath before pushing the door open, its chimes startling a woman sorting dishes on a table.

"Sorry, sir, we're just about to—" She stopped at the sight of him. "Oh, my goodness. You're bleeding. Are you all right?"

He hadn't given a thought to what he must look like. He felt his head; the bump had swelled to the size of a small egg. Water streamed from his shirt onto the braided rug below.

She called to a man at a far counter. "Cam, come help." She took Carl's elbow and helped him to a bench by the door. "What happened?"

Carl strained to catch his breath. "I hit something. Up the road. Two people hurt."

"Moose, no doubt."

He paused, distracted by the taxidermy dotting the store's walls—white-tailed bucks, deer skulls, the thick-lipped sneer of a moose snout—glass stares accusing. He swallowed. "My partner . . . and there's a girl missing." The man was on his other side with a glass of water.

"Drink some of this, sir. You're looking pretty pale."

"I'm fine." Carl waved him away. The man's iron grip on his forearm was the last thing he remembered before everything gave way to darkness.

MEG

Jack flung open the basement door. "Mom. Phone. Should I answer?"

"Leave it, bud. I'm coming." Even taking the steps two at a time, Meg still missed the call. Relieved to see the New Hampshire area code, she dropped into a kitchen chair to call Carl back.

"Swiftriver Gorge. Iris speaking."

Was the transporter calling from his hotel? Confused, Meg asked for Carl Alden.

"He's right here. Just a moment." The phone changed hands against a jumble of background voices. As the wait dragged on, Meg wondered idly if the driver booked two rooms or one, trying to picture Carl and the mousy woman together. None of her business, she decided. Finally, she heard a man clear his throat.

"Mrs. Carmody." At Carl's defeated tone, Meg's instincts soared to high alert.

"Carl? What's wrong? Where's Alex?"

"I have some bad news." A pause, followed by a ragged breath. "There's been an accident."

Please no. Not again. Not Alex. Meg gripped the back of the chair. "Is Alex hurt?"

"We hit a detour. Some bad weather in the mountains. Something I didn't foresee."

Didn't foresee? In her living room yesterday, he had laid out his meticulous plan. "My daughter, Carl. Tell me what happened to Alex."

His breathing grew more labored. "Alex is missing, Mrs. Carmody. She . . . walked away."

"What do you mean, 'walked away'? As in, 'walked away without a scratch'?" Jumping up from the chair, Meg grabbed a sponge from the sink and swabbed Jack's place at the table. *I will wipe this table exactly the way I do every night, and he will tell me everything is fine. That Alex is fine.*

"Mommy, what happened?" Jack in the doorway.

"Nothing, bud. Go watch TV. Mommy needs some privacy for a bit." Dropping the sponge, Meg shut herself into the powder room and took a deep breath. "Carl, just tell me about Alex."

"She walked away from the accident scene. Which we're taking as a good sign."

"A good sign?" Meg sat on the toilet lid and doubled over, the bathroom floor's black-and-white mosaic blurring as Carl described the impact, the skid, the car careening down the hill, his coming to and realizing Alex was gone. *My baby is missing. I sent my baby off with strangers, and now she's gone.*

Jack banged on the door. "Mommy, you're scaring me. Is Alex OK?" She couldn't hear Carl over Jack's cries.

"Hold on. It's my son." She got up and stuck her head out the door, forcing her mouth into a smile. "Honey, Alex is fine. Mommy just really, *really* needs you to go watch TV. I'll get you in a sec, OK?"

"Why are you yelling? I want Daddy." Jack rubbed his eyes.

"He'll be home soon. Go, Jack." Shutting the door again, she asked Carl what time they crashed.

"Around four."

She checked her phone screen. It was now six twenty. Alex had been wandering alone in the mountains for more than two hours—not in the warm outfit Meg set out for her but in clothes of her own choosing. Shuddering, Meg envisioned her daughter crawling along the icy road in flimsy leggings and a T-shirt, sleet seeping through thin soles.

Fourth grade: Meg racing to pick up Alex after a soccer match, a downpour snarling traffic.

"Why aren't you out looking for her?" she asked Carl.

"I will be as soon as I hang up."

Arriving ten minutes after the bus, Alex waiting for her outside, blue-lipped and soaked, soccer shorts clinging to her legs like a second skin.

"Your partner then? Couldn't she search?"

Carl's voice was hoarse. "Carolyn was in back, next to Alex. Her side took the brunt. She's . . . it's . . . bad."

The powder room felt claustrophobic, the leftover Christmas potpourri cloying as Meg recalled the woman she brushed by in Alex's bedroom this morning.

"I'm . . . I'm so sorry, Carl. I hope she pulls through. But you have to understand. My daughter. You have to find her."

I thought you forgot me, Mommy.

Would Alex's wounded gaze in her bedroom that morning be Meg's final memory of her daughter?

I would never, ever forget you, lovey.

She made herself focus on Carl's words—something about state troopers and a missing persons alert.

"An Amber Alert?" That's what they did when a child went missing.

"Those alerts are for when there is a suspicion of abduction. We don't know that."

"Not *yet*, we don't. Can't they put one of those alerts out, too?"

He promised to ask the troopers, who would set up at Swiftriver Gorge—not a hotel as Meg imagined but a general store Carl had managed to hike to. He had hoped Alex had done the same, but no one had seen her.

Crash. Troopers. Missing person. The straightforward transport he promised her had become a nightmare. "Carl. Tell me the truth. Do you . . . do the troopers think . . . she's alive?"

"She had her wits about her. We know for sure she made it up to the road."

When Carl described the marker Alex tied to the guardrail, Meg lost it. "She never lets that scarf out of her sight. It was her best friend's."

Her heart cracked open. First the lunch notes, now this selfless act by her daughter. It was too much. She had sent Alex straight into this horror.

"We'll find her, Mrs. Carmody. You have my word. I know that doesn't mean much right now . . ." Carl coughed. "If Alex stuck to the highway, someone's bound to see her very soon, whenever this weather breaks."

Meg hugged herself as Carl described the ice storm coating the region. "She . . . she could die out there, Carl. Alex doesn't know what to do on her own." This was a girl who refused to wear a coat to school. Meg bartered with God: *If you bring her back, I'll never nag her about that again.*

"She did take the coat you sent."

The ski coat. The one Alex swore she hated.

Carl's voice was soft. "Alex is tougher than you think."

Numb, she jotted down his location: *Swiftriver Gorge General Store. Kancamagus Highway. Route 112.*

The store would stay open as long as necessary; there was a generator and plenty of wood, in case they lost power, he said. That happened during these ice storms.

"I can't just sit here, Carl. I have to do something. Tell me what to do," she begged.

"Do about what?" Jack asked from outside the door.

"Check with Alex's friends. Facebook, social media. She may have gotten through to somebody by now. It's a long shot, but worth looking into."

Meg thought of her unanswered text to Shana. "Call me the second you hear anything. Anything at all. And Carl . . ."

Jack knocked again. The rain intensified, great gusts of wind scraping branches of an overgrown oak against the powder room window— the same force whipping her daughter along an icy highway hundreds of miles north. "Find her, Carl," Meg choked. "You have to find my little girl."

No longer able to bear the tom-tom of Jack's knocking, she blew her nose with toilet paper and wiped her streaming eyes in the mirror. "I'm coming, bud."

CARL

Handing the phone back to the man, Carl felt drained from the two calls he had just made. Carolyn's mother took the news stoically. He tried not to think about her inevitable conversation with Jamie.

Carl didn't see the girl often. Not long ago, a transport initiated near Carolyn's home, and it made more sense to pick her up there. Jamie half hid behind her grandmother's back when he said hello and blinked back tears as her mother said good-bye. Carolyn had brushed bangs out of her daughter's eyes. "I'll be home Friday to watch TV with you. You help Grandma make the popcorn, OK?" Jamie clutched her grandmother's hand as they'd left.

Then the call to Alex's mother, to say he had quite literally lost her daughter. Her anguished voice stayed with him, beseeching him to find her. He had never in his life felt so powerless.

The woman slid a mug of coffee toward him, her eyes warm with sympathy. "Such terrible news for a parent."

"I'm responsible."

She pushed the sugar bowl forward. "It wasn't your fault."

"I give these families my word when they hire me to transport their children. My guarantee."

"You're not God, you know," she said softly. "Accidents happen." She extended a hand. "By the way, I'm Iris. Iris Bailey. My husband is Cam." Her hand warmed his chilled one.

"Carl. Alden. Thank you for the coffee. For everything. I'm sure you'd much rather close up shop and get home."

"Actually, Swiftriver *is* home." Iris indicated a set of stairs at the back of the store. "We live over this place."

Pulling the borrowed blanket around himself, Carl stood to get a better look around. Could Alex be hiding somewhere? In a basement or storeroom? He strode toward the stairs, and Iris followed. "Mr. Alden, we told you. Cam and I have been here all day. If your young girl came in, we would have seen her."

"It's true," Cam said, descending the stairs with an armload of clothes that he offered to Carl. "You should get out of those wet things. Bathroom's over there. Troopers will probably be here anytime."

Carl took the clothes into the closetlike toilet and dressed quickly. He peered into the garbage and the vanity under the sink; he attempted to raise the window, which refused to budge. Probably painted shut years ago. Nothing in the small bathroom offered any clues about the missing girl. Discouraged, he stared at the bloodshot eyes facing him over the sink. No wonder Iris had been alarmed: dried blood encrusted one cheek, and an angry bump swelled over one eyebrow. He wet a paper towel and wiped the blood off, baring an angry split in his forehead. What injuries had Alex suffered in the backseat? he wondered.

Back outside, he refused more coffee. Skittish as a caged animal, he skimmed a hand over his head. If Alex hadn't come here, she must have headed in the other direction. When the troopers arrived, he'd make sure the search covered the Kancamagus end to end.

"You from New York, too, like the girl?" Iris was at his elbow.

"Yes."

"I love the city," she said, her voice laced with longing. "Which part?"

He had never felt less like engaging in small talk but felt obliged to answer the kind woman.

"Lower Manhattan. Area's changed a lot."

"I'm sure. I've been up here *waaaay* too long." She wiped her hands on a dishcloth. "After I graduated from NYU, I came here, hunting capital of the world." She fingered the hem of a lacy dress hanging rather incongruously from the twelve-point buck above her head. "My little antiques business keeps me sane."

This portion of the store was appropriated for dishes, glassware, other knickknacks. *Cam must be a hunter*, he thought, turning his head to take in the herd of taxidermy. The movement shot needles of pain down the back of his neck.

Iris caught him wincing. "Whiplash, probably. You're going to feel that in a day or two."

He appreciated her concern, but the hot drink and dry clothes had gotten Carl's blood going again, and he could focus only on Alex. What would a sixteen-year-old do? He was about to ask if he could take a look upstairs when a pair of troopers stomped into the store, accompanied by a sleety cold draft, pausing to scrape regulation boots on the bristled rack by the door.

Iris hurried to greet them. "Jordan, is that you?"

"Mrs. Bailey. Good to see you again. Got a report of a missing hiker?"

Already the story was wrong, Carl thought, his forehead throbbing. "There's no hiker. It was a car accident," he said, stepping up to the troopers. "A teenage girl walked away. Two hours ago already."

"I'm aware of the accident, sir. We sent a crew that way. But Mr. Bailey just now told us about the girl. My men are on it." He held out his hand. "Trooper Mendham. And Trooper Lopez." The officer behind him raised a hand in greeting. Neither looked more than twenty-five, Carl thought; Mendham's baby face was ruddy next to the olive uniform. These two were in charge?

"That's a nasty bump you've got there, Mr. Alden. We can get another rig here to take you to have it looked at."

"I'm fine."

"You should never mess around with a head injury."

"I *said*, I'm staying."

The trooper crossed his arms. "So you're refusing medical attention?"

"That's correct."

"Well, then, I'm going to need that in writing." Mendham directed the other trooper to dig out a medical release, then proceeded to make Carl recount the events of the afternoon in agonizing detail. Chafing under the interrogation, Carl stood and buttoned his borrowed wool jacket. "Don't you have enough now? Let's get out there."

The officer raised a hand. "I understand you've had a tough afternoon, sir, but first I need to take you back to the scene. Protocol. Identify the car and all." He gestured to Lopez. "My partner will stay here. He'll monitor the crews for any news about the girl and communicate with us if anything breaks."

The door opened again, and more troopers entered, laden with equipment.

"Hope you don't mind, Mrs. Bailey," Mendham said apologetically. "With Swiftriver smack in the middle of the Kanc, we thought it'd be easier to manage things from here. Roads are pretty slick. Want to keep the crews safe." Carl caught Cam raising his eyebrows before the shopkeeper retreated to the kitchen.

"Of course, Jordan. You can set up over here." Iris cleared a table in her nook for their equipment. Within minutes, they transformed the Swiftriver store into a temporary command post, stringing wires between transmitters to create a portable radio system similar to the one Carl had used in the military. Radios began to chirp updates from emergency crews dispatched along the Kanc.

Mendham asked Carl for a photo of Alex to circulate to search teams and media. Carl detached the girl's photo from the Carmodys' transport form; the trooper photographed it with his phone and sent it to headquarters. "Whenever you're ready, sir. Jeep's outside."

Accepting the parka Iris offered, Carl joined Mendham in the state vehicle. As they pulled out onto the Kanc, a pickup truck pulled in behind them. Two men hopped out—a short driver and a much taller passenger wearing a hunter's cap, its flaps tied up top and under the chin—and shuffled into the store.

"Where did you say the accident call came from?" Carl asked.

"A pay phone in Lincoln. Man wouldn't leave a name."

"And they said nothing about the girl?"

"Not a thing. Described the approximate spot of the crash, then hung up."

Maybe Alex befriended a young man, convincing him to report the accident without giving her away. There were many possible scenarios, but for the moment, he had to focus on Carolyn. In silence, they backtracked several miles to where the violet scarf billowed like a flag. Emergency strobes illuminated this stretch of the Kancamagus; they swirled red and yellow, a surreal light show for the recovery operation. Mendham pulled close, instructing Carl to stay in the Jeep while he conferred with an EMT. Their conversation was brief. Mendham climbed back in the truck, rubbing his hands.

They were getting ready to go down to the wrecked car, Mendham said. "Bit of a challenge to move that equipment down the hill."

"What about the girl? Can't you and I start looking around here?"

"Sorry, sir. I have my orders. Roads are just about impassable. The crews have the girl's description. They're very experienced. A lot of hikers go missing in this forest."

"She wasn't hiking. How many times do I have to tell you?" Carl wiped the fogged-up windshield. He could see nothing from the car. Frustrated, he leaped out of the Jeep, ignoring the sting of sleet on his bruised face, and approached the clutch of emergency vehicles. Beyond, the doors to an ambulance were open, ready to receive Carolyn. He checked his watch; almost ninety minutes had passed since he'd thrown the tarp over the car. *Please, Carolyn, hang in there.*

A rigged torch shone down the hill, where workers maneuvered bulky equipment down the incline, the beams of headlamps ricocheting off the wall of evergreen. Jaws of Life equipment; he'd used it himself in the field. He wanted to yell they wouldn't need its menacing blades to tear at the car; he had already freed Carolyn's body. Carl swallowed at the recollection of Carolyn slumped in the backseat.

The EMTs shouted to each other as they pitched down the hill. Carl longed to leap over the guardrail and guide the extrication himself. The lights of the recovery party dimmed as they moved farther into the wood. Despite Mendham's pleas, Carl refused to return to the Jeep, pacing along the road until, finally, watery lights at the bottom of the ravine signaled the returning rescue procession. The first pair lumbered under the weight of the Jaws of Life. Behind them, two more bore a shrouded form on a canvas stretcher.

Carl held a hand out as if to steady Carolyn's passage over the guardrail and her transfer onto the ambulance's waiting stretcher. An attendant knelt and adjusted the oxygen mask over her pale, drawn face.

"How is she?" Carl asked.

"Very weak. Respiration's shallow. From the state of things down there, we can't rule out internal bleeding. We've got to move fast."

Carl followed the stretcher to the ambulance, where the siren *whoop-whooped* sporadically. Bending over, he fumbled for her hand under the blanket and squeezed it. "Fight, Carolyn," he whispered. "Like Jimbo did. Jamie needs you."

He stepped back to allow the attendants to slide her into the ambulance. The doors clanged shut, and its boxy white shape melted into the night. Behind him, Mendham shouted instructions to the remaining crew. One by one, the remaining vehicles glided out onto the ice-glazed Kanc, lights winking.

Carolyn *had* to make it, he willed, staring after the departing column of cars. Nothing had ever torn at Carl like this. There was no protocol for this scenario, no survival manual to consult. This pain felt achingly personal, knocking down every boundary he'd ever set for himself, sabotaging his excruciatingly precise plan.

He felt unsteady, unmoored, loathing the craving it stirred, the long-suppressed itch needling his skin. He needed to hold himself together to find the girl.

Mendham was waiting for him back at the truck. "Very sorry, sir. I know that was difficult to watch." They'd be getting updates from the hospital, he said. A crew could retrieve the car once the weather cleared.

The car. Maybe he had missed something, a clue that might lead him to Alex. He had been so focused on helping Carolyn that he had paid scant attention to it. "I'll be right back." Before Mendham could object, he grabbed the trooper's flashlight from the front seat and scaled the guardrail, retracing the rescuers' slushy trail to the car. As he slid down the hill, he could hear the trooper yelling right behind him. And rightly so: If anyone had tried a stunt like this back in the day when he was on duty, Carl would have collared the idiot, he thought.

By the time he made it to the car, he was out of breath. Opening the back door, Carl shined the light on Alex's seat, illuminating Carolyn's blood, the shattered glass, the sprinkling of discarded gum wrappers.

Mendham had caught up with him. "I'm going to need you to follow instructions, sir. Otherwise I'll start wondering if that head injury is more than just a bump and find a judge who'll make you go to the hospital." He threw an arm over the driver's door. "This your car then?"

"It is." Carl slid into Alex's spot, trying to imagine the girl's state of mind in those horrifying final seconds: the animal's sickening thump overhead, the ripping open of the roof, the car's descent, the grievously injured Carolyn alongside her.

She would have been terrified—in shock, perhaps. Of course Alex would have run.

Carl sat back, discouraged. It was time to go back and devote full energy to the search. He'd already stretched the limited amount of latitude Mendham had allowed. Leaning his head back, Carl caught sight of the rearview mirror, knocked cockeyed in the crash.

The mirror. Pulling himself up by the headrest, Carl aimed the flashlight at it. His good luck piece that rode along on all his transports, the miniature Rainmaker golden tree frog that captured Alex's interest, was gone.

Carl climbed back into the truck, Mendham's chatter barely registering on the black ride back to Swiftriver. He rolled down his window, scanning the darkness. In the few hours he had spent with Alex, he observed she was sharp and smart—and wily enough to survive this. Perhaps her taking the frog was the misguided girl's final revenge. He turned his face toward the pewter sky. *Alex, where are you?*

A cough of radio static disrupted his musings. Carl yanked his head back inside. "What are they saying?"

"Nothing on the girl, sir, sorry to say. But they have a lead on who called in the accident. Trooper Lopez talking to them now. Back at Swiftriver."

MEG

"Did you pick up the cigarettes?"

"Yeah, but I'll lie if Jacob asks me." Melissa dropped the pack into Meg's lap.

"I don't think that's the lie he'll be worried about. He's going to kill me." Meg stood and wiped the tears from her eyes. "Come with me while I have one."

"What about Jack?"

"I'll leave the slider open so we can hear him." Outside, Meg lit up with shaking hands. "This is a nightmare, Meliss." Meg wrapped her arms around herself, feeling the rain soak her scrubs. "I can't get the image out of my head of Alex walking along some icy highway by herself. What if some creep picks her up and . . ." She couldn't finish the thought.

Melissa hugged her. "Stop. We have to focus on the positive—that she made it out of that car alive."

"I'm trying." Meg wiped her streaming nose on her sleeve. "She's just . . . that woman next to her. How Alex must have felt. Again."

"I know. I thought of that." Melissa dropped into a patio chair, despite the rain that had puddled in the seat. "When did you say Jacob would be home?"

"I don't know. Eight, maybe?" Meg took a hard drag. "How am I going to tell him?" Jacob had called multiple times since Carl relayed his news. She hadn't answered, afraid to talk to him or even listen to his voice-mail message.

"Seriously, Meg, how did you plan to tell him before? You must have thought about that."

"I did. I figured by the time I told him, Alex would be safe and sound."

"You still deceived him."

Meg aimed a stream of smoke into the night. "Could we *not* do this now? You made it pretty clear that night at the diner how you felt."

"OK, fine." Melissa poked her head back into the house to check for Jack. "Anyway, Jacob's first concern will be for Alex. Maybe you should text Shana again. Tell her Alex is M-I-A. Scare the crap out of her."

Obediently, Meg sent another message:

```
Alex is missing. Really need your help.
Please answer me.
```

Jack called from the living room. "Hey, where'd you guys go?"

"Coming, honey." Back inside, Melissa guided Jack upstairs, his head bobbing animatedly in the curve of her arm.

Meg lit another cigarette and moved off the deck, triggering the backyard sensor. For a few seconds, light flooded the area, illuminating the wrought-iron table and chairs like props on a stage before clicking off again. Something was amiss: the table was on an angle, chairs shoved to one side. As though someone wanted to clear a path to the slider.

She'd played with that door latch this morning. Had she bothered to look outside? Meg couldn't remember. Even if she had, she'd have been too distracted to notice the disarray.

Now everything was out of place.

Something had glinted on the ground before the light went out. She moved to reactivate the sensor and knelt. It was a screw, one that could have fallen from the troublesome door latch. Especially if someone had tried to force it. She dropped it into her scrubs pocket, where the screw clinked against her phone. The deck went dark again.

Dizzy from the second cigarette, Meg was stamping it out when two beeps signaled a text—not Shana as she'd hoped, but Jacob, a courtesy heads-up he was half an hour away.

Securing the slider as best she could, she rubbed her neck and headed upstairs. Angel followed her, stationing herself in front of Alex's door.

"Miss your sister? I do, too." Meg rubbed the dog's head. "Now go say good-night to Jack." The dog padded down the hall and nosed open Jack's door.

Meg was washing her face in her bathroom when her phone bleated again:

```
It's Shana. Can I come over? Done work
at 8.
```

```
Of course. Have you heard from Alex?
```

She hit Send with soapy fingers.

```
C u then.
```

Frustrated, Meg hurried to Jack's room and waved the phone at her sister.

"Alex?" Melissa mouthed.

"No. Shana." She leaned down and hugged Jack. He had to be exhausted. "Sleep tight."

"Hey, Mom? Can Aunt Meliss put me to bed every night?"

Meg smiled. "If you can talk her into it."

"If I did that, it wouldn't be special, right, bud?" Melissa slid off the bed and pulled the covers up to Jack's chin, tucking the blankets tightly under the mattress.

"Cool. I like it like this. Like a mummy. Good night, Mummy." Jack giggled at his own joke. "Wait, Mom. Don't forget. Dad has to wake me up. You pinky-sweared."

"I know. Go to sleep now, bud."

In the hall, Melissa immediately cornered Meg. "What did Shana say?"

"She's coming over. She didn't say whether she'd heard from Alex."

Melissa paused by Alex's room and peered in. "Scene of the crime, huh? Doesn't look too bad."

Meg pulled her sister into the bedroom. "Speaking of crimes, look what I found outside." Holding out the screw, she described the broken door. "I'm sure this has something to do with Alex. With those pills. What if somebody came looking for her?"

Melissa dropped onto Alex's bed. "Back up a sec. Why would somebody come looking?"

"When they saw Alex wasn't in school today. Maybe it was a desperate customer. Or her supplier."

Her sister leaned back on her elbows and stared at Meg. "Really? And what supplier would *that* be?"

"That kid Evan, I think. I have a bad feeling about him. She had to get those pills from somebody."

"You aren't making any sense, Meg. It was one bag of pills. It doesn't make her part of some drug cartel. You're not even sure they were hers."

"I know what I saw. Somebody broke into this house." Trembling, Meg dropped onto the bed next to Melissa.

"Why do you even care about this right now?" She sat up to face Meg. "You need to focus on Alex."

"That's what I'm doing. This dealer might know something. Maybe they're working together. I don't even get why Alex needed to get involved with this. She has a job." She slapped her head. "Oh, my God. I'm such an idiot."

"Why?"

"I never thought to call Alex's boss. She might have been scheduled to work today."

Melissa coughed. "I don't think you have to worry about that."

"Of course I do. I wouldn't want Alex leaving on the wrong foot— she'll probably want to work there again when she's back home. I'll call her manager in the morning." Meg got up and toyed with the gum wrappers on the dresser.

"Meg." Melissa stood, catching her sister's eye in the mirror. "You need to know something. Alex hasn't worked in a while."

"Of course she has. She worked this week."

"Maybe she *said* she did."

Meg wheeled around. "Why would she lie about work?"

"Because she was let go."

"Alex was fired? And you knew?"

"She asked me not to tell you. Until she found another job. I gave her my word."

"Seriously? You gave *Alex* your word? What about me? How could you keep this from me, knowing everything that's been going on?"

"I'm sorry. I promised her. She told me when I ambushed her and made her come for coffee a few weeks ago. We got to talking. I thought if I kept her secret for a bit, she might open up to me the way she used to, before the accident. You know, the cool aunt and all."

"Very cool." Meg crossed her arms, jealous, unable to recall the last time she and Alex enjoyed a carefree meal or shopping together. "Why was she fired?" *Please don't let it be for shoplifting.*

"She wouldn't say."

"Hmm. So this *is* her new job. Dealing drugs."

Melissa threw up her hands. "Meg, will you let it go? Can you just for once not jump to some crazy conclusion?"

"Easy for you to say. Your daughter isn't *M-I-A.*"

"No, but my goddaughter is."

"What else haven't you told me?"

"Nothing." Melissa jumped up to leave, pausing in Alex's doorway. "I knew you would react this way. I was trying to help. Sorry. Won't happen again."

Meg pulled at her bangs. How could everyone around her—including a seven-year-old and a stranger who'd only met Alex this morning—know so much more than she did about her daughter? Was she that clueless a mother?

But Melissa was Alex's godmother, after all. And Meg was happy Alex had finally confided in another trusted adult. Maybe she'd do that again today—seek help from the right person. Meg's throat constricted again at the notion of Alex coping on her own, cold and wet, possibly injured.

She jumped up and hurried after her sister. "No, Meliss. *I'm* sorry." Her voice cracked. "I know how much you love her." Meg leaned against the stairwell, panic corkscrewing her gut. "We can't lose her. We can't."

CARL

"I swear. We don't know nothin' about a girl." For the third time, the taller of the two men across from Trooper Lopez maintained their innocence. Carl had had just about enough of the man's arrogance. He lunged toward the pair across the counter, where the trooper had seated them for questioning.

"What about you?" Carl's face was inches from the shorter man, previously identified as the driver of the truck now parked in the Swiftriver parking lot. He'd been silent up to this point. A sour haze of smoke and cheap whiskey hung on the men. "You have anything to say?"

"That's enough, Alden. We'll handle this." Mendham gripped Carl's shoulder and pulled him away. How could the officer remain so calm, with a sixteen-year-old unaccounted for? Even riding back from the accident scene, Carl had to restrain himself from wrenching the wheel from Mendham, the trooper had proceeded so cautiously.

Mendham's subduing of Carl produced a smirk from the taller man. "That's the thanks we get for being good citizens? Maybe we'll think twice next time. Isn't that right, Kyle?"

The man next to him nodded.

The troopers swapped places, Lopez taking his place alongside Carl to observe. The men were the same two who had been heading into the store as Carl and Mendham departed earlier, Lopez explained. When the pair spotted the troopers, the taller man began asking questions—*too many questions*, Lopez thought. He finally got him to admit to calling in the accident. They'd spotted the scarf on the guardrail; when they stopped to investigate, they saw the car tracks. They hadn't wanted to identify themselves because they'd had a few pops along the way, Lopez said, hoisting an imaginary bottle to his mouth.

"You ran a check, I assume?" Carl asked.

"Pure as snow. A couple of potato farmers from Fryeburg, headed to Lincoln for the night. When the storm worsened, they changed their minds and doubled back. Because of the weather, they said."

Or because of something that happened, Carl thought, straining to hear the conversation at the counter. With each second that passed, and each idiotic response from the jester in the orange hat, Carl seethed a little more, the possibility of finding Alex becoming more remote.

The two were creeps, dumb as mud. Anyone could see that. Carl was certain they knew more than they were letting on. Maybe they got their jollies by returning to the scene of the crime, he thought. With the troopers absorbed in the interrogation, Carl slipped out Swiftriver's front entrance, damning the chimes signaling his exit. He ran to the men's truck and yanked open the passenger door, then the smaller one behind it. *Too stupid to lock up. First mistake.*

The cab's interior reeked of smoke, even in the cold. An empty bottle glistened on the front bench. Carl leaned over to read the label: Black Velvet Toasted Caramel. About as cheap a Canadian as you could get. His eyes adjusting to the darkness of the backseat, he made out a coil of rope on the cab floor and a blanket wadded against the far door. He pulled on a glove and yanked the blanket out of the truck, generating a flurry of silver that floated to the ground like confetti. Dropping beside the truck, Carl recognized their distinctive *W* shape immediately:

Rainbow Bubble wrappers, the gum with the cloying fragrance Alex had chewed over almost three hundred miles. He had seen her crease the discarded casings into this signature origami and litter her rest-stop lunch tray and the backseat of his rental with them.

Carl pressed a foil between gloved fingers. *Those men are dead.*

Swiftriver's door chimed again.

"What the hell are you doing, Alden?" Mendham's voice rang out from the porch.

Carl got to his feet. "She was in this truck." He held up the wrapper. "Proof."

The trooper was next to him like a shot. "Put that back. What the hell is wrong with you? You said you're an ex-cop, right?"

"Yeah. So?"

"So you *know* we don't touch anything without a warrant. And so far, we don't have enough to hold these guys."

"We do now." Carl showed him the gum wrapper. "This is Alex's. Her brand. The way the wrappers are folded—it's her thing. I watched her do this all day."

"It's a gum wrapper. Plenty of folks chew gum. We're going to need more than that."

"Then get a search warrant. Get some prints. Do I have to tell you how to do your job? Look inside the cab, for God's sake."

Mendham pushed back his trooper's hat, exasperated. "Remember who's in charge here, Alden. Interfere one more time, and you'll be looking at the inside of a jail." Mendham picked up the blanket with his gloved hand and tossed it back into the cab, shining his flashlight inside for good measure. "I'm sure headquarters will be thrilled to death to cooperate now, given how you've just tampered with all the evidence. Good job. Thought you wanted to find this girl."

"I do. This is a clear-cut case. I can prove those wrappers . . ."

Mendham suddenly leaned forward into the cab. "Well, well," Carl heard him say. "What have we here?"

"What is it?"

"Hold your horses, Alden. You've done enough damage."

Carl paced alongside the truck, kicking slushy gravel.

Finally, Mendham backed out of the cab, holding up his discovery. "Now we're talking."

Carl blinked. Draped over the trooper's pen was a single, long strand of hair. Held high under the glare of Swiftriver's spotlight, the strand caught errant sleet, drooping under the weight, its fuchsia tail glistening.

MEG

Downstairs, Meg sat on the couch and sipped the tea Melissa made her. "Did I tell you what else I found today?" She described the bin of lunch notes.

Melissa squeezed her hand. "See? She doesn't hate you as much as you think." Noticing Meg tear up, she pulled back. "Sorry. Bad joke. It's just . . . she's still there, Meg. When she comes home, we'll find a way to get to her."

"Don't you mean *if*? I'm praying Shana has a clue."

"I wouldn't get your hopes up. Besides, I'm not sure I trust that girl. Ever since Alex's party . . ."

Meg's phone skittered across the coffee table with a text:

I'm outside.

"Well, we'll find out soon enough, won't we?" Meg headed to the door. Didn't these girls know how to use a doorbell? It drove her crazy when they just sailed into her house without knocking. "Alex told me to come in," they'd say, waving their phones and heading upstairs.

At the front door, Shana held her purse over her head against the teeming rain. Once the girl was inside, Meg blinked at her transformation. Gone was Shana's angelic strawberry-blond; in its place a dramatic two-toned style that began with stark brunette on top and finished midshoulder with a thick chunk of orangey-blond.

She looked like a different person.

"What's going on?" Shana asked Meg. "Where's Alex?"

"We don't know exactly. I was hoping you'd heard from her today." Meg led Shana to the kitchen table.

"Not today. Last I heard from her was last night, before I turned off my phone."

Was Shana messing with her? These girls all practically slept with their phones strapped to their chests.

"Then did anyone else hear from her? Like maybe . . . Evan?" Meg strove for nonchalance.

"Why Evan?"

"I don't know. They spend a lot of time together."

"I know, but they're not, like, 'in a relationship' or anything." With artfully chipped nails, Shana placed air quotes around the Facebook stamp of coupledom.

Meg decided to call the girl's bluff. "I found Alex's stash, Shana. The one Evan gave her." She described her discovery the night of the house party.

Shana's heavily lined eyes narrowed. "No way. Alex swore that was over." She clapped a hand over her mouth, as if she hadn't meant to say it.

"What was over?"

"Alex . . . helping him. She stopped, like, eons ago."

Meg chewed the inside of her cheek.

"I'm *serious*." Shana tossed her ombréd hair for emphasis. "Alex hid Evan's stuff here once. *Hid* it. Not sold it. And she never took any, if that's what you're worried about."

Among the many things. "Is it possible Alex continued to help Evan behind your back?"

Shana chewed a chipped nail. "I *guess.* I told her to stop helping him. She said she did." She sat back, folding her arms. "It's not like I'm Cass, though."

There was probably a whole history behind that last comment, but Meg didn't have time to dig. She leaned closer to the teenager.

"Did you know Alex lost her job?"

Hesitating, Shana barely nodded.

"Do you know why?" Meg pressed.

Shana wriggled. "Come on. I feel funny talking about that. Ask Alex."

She would, if she only knew where her daughter was. "OK. That's fair. But tell me. Did Evan hear from Alex today?"

"Yeah. He showed me some crazy texts in study hall, from a weird area code. Maybe Massachusetts?"

Meg stiffened. Massachusetts—where Alden, Alex and Murphy stopped for lunch. "Go on."

"Apparently Alex got somebody to text him about his stuff."

"But you just said she didn't help Evan anymore."

"She doesn't. That's what I'm trying to tell you. Alex didn't have his stuff. Evan just *thought* she did. Until Alex texted today to say she'd dumped everything into Larke's purse last night. When he was driving them both home."

So that's where Alex was last night, she thought. At least her daughter had had a change of heart. "What time was that text today?" Meg asked.

"Study hall's at 1:10, so maybe, right before that?"

Carl's check-in from the rest stop had come in around twelve thirty. Even in his care, Alex had contrived a way to send a message. "Didn't you find it bizarre she texted from a strange phone? From a Massachusetts area code?"

Shana blew out her lips. "Seriously, kids forget their phones *all* the time. I figured she borrowed one."

That was true. And no, Shana didn't know the Massachusetts number. But there was one last thing Shana might be able to clear up for her: if Evan assumed Alex had his drugs, he might have grown frustrated when she wasn't in school this morning and come looking for her—or his property.

"Tell me the truth, Shana. Did Evan break into our house this morning?"

Shana twirled her phone in her lap. "I . . . I don't know."

"Somebody broke my dining room door today. Was it him?"

"I said, I don't *know*. And you still haven't told me what's up with Alex. I swear to God, she never said anything about running away. I would have tried to talk her out of it."

"She didn't run away," Meg said quietly. "She was being taken to a school in New Hampshire." She explained about The Birches, the arranged transport, the accident.

"Oh, my God. She's missing?" Shana pushed back from the table. "Holy . . . why didn't you tell me that first thing?" Her eyes clouded. "And why would you send Alex all the way up there, away from her friends?"

"We both know things haven't been good with Alex for a while. Since the Sweet Sixteen."

"Stop." She scrunched her eyes shut. "I don't want to talk about that."

"I'm sorry, Shana. I miss her, too. Cass was like a daughter to me."

"I know." The girl opened her eyes, her face stony.

"It's just that since Cass died . . ." Meg saw Shana wince at the word, and her heart ached. "We . . . I had to do something to help her."

"But why New Hampshire? Why so far? Isn't there any help around here?"

"I tried. Alex wouldn't talk to anybody."

"She talked to *me*," Shana cried. "We talked to each other. And she talked to Cass."

"To Cass?" Meg imagined ghoulish rituals around a Ouija board.

"At the cemetery. Almost every day."

"How did she manage that?"

"She hitched from downtown."

"When she left school." Meg sat back, comprehending. If she only had waited outside Perk Up a little longer that day, she might have discovered how Alex spent her time away from the classroom.

"Now she can't even do that," Shana raged. "And now you're sending her away and I'm . . . I'm . . ." She twisted a saltshaker on the table. "Totally alone. It's not fair."

Meg stroked Shana's back. "Shana. Honey. You're not alone. You have your family. And us. This is a good thing. Alex is going to get what she needs. A fresh start."

Shana shot the shaker across the table and stood. "How do you even *know* what Alex needs? You have no idea what happened." Shana scooped up her phone and backpack. "I gotta go. My mom needs her car."

"Wait. Don't leave. What do you mean, what happened?" Was she talking about last night? Last year? Meg narrowly beat the girl to the front door. She knew Shana's parents; they'd spent some time together after the accident, trying to figure out what happened that night. "Call your mom. I know she'll understand. I could talk to her."

"I have to go." She attempted to slide around Meg.

"Shana, please." Meg gripped her arm. "We don't know where Alex is. Don't you care about her?"

Shana wrenched her arm away. "Of course I care. Alex is all I have. And now you've ruined that." Breaking Meg's hold on the door, she ran out into the insistent rain.

Meg watched the girl drive away, hating the idea of her behind the wheel in such a state. If Shana's version was to be believed, the good news was that Alex clearly wanted to break ties with this older boy, that her text to Evan meant she was done helping him.

But if Shana was right, and Alex was no longer his mule, then what was the explanation for the pills hidden in her basement pillow?

A tap on her shoulder made her jump.

"You need to see this." Melissa thrust Meg's phone at her. "Jacob's pissed. I think he knows something's up."

CARL

"I'm not saying nothing without my lawyer present." As chatty as Chester had been earlier, he'd clammed up as tight as his buddy when Carl and Mendham came back inside.

Carl itched to throw their discoveries in the suspects' faces. As far as he was concerned, they had them. But before they reentered the store, Mendham had ordered Carl to keep quiet. The trooper was on a mission to proceed delicately, directing his questioning toward the more talkative of the two truckers. More than anything, Carl wanted to know if they had harmed Alex and where she had gone. *At this rate, it would take all night for them to confess*, Carl thought.

Glancing at his watch, he wondered if it was too soon to call the hospital again. Carolyn's state had weakened during the ambulance ride, the EMTs reported. At the hospital in the valley, she was taken directly into surgery; admitting wouldn't know anything for a few hours. Raking a hand over his head, Carl turned his attention back to the interrogation.

"You two sure you want to stick to that story? Finding the scarf and all?" Mendham asked.

"'Course. Why wouldn't we?" Chester said.

So much for saying nothing, Carl thought. *Keep talking, buddy.*

"And you had no right to touch my property," Chester continued. "I know my rights."

"Your property . . . You were the passenger, am I right, Mr. . . . ?" He checked his notes. "Mr. Murray?"

Chester nodded. "That's correct."

"So can I assume the truck in question belongs to your friend Mr. Pressman here?"

Kyle the driver began to rock rhythmically on his stool.

"Correct also," said Chester.

"Thank you. I appreciate your staying with me, Mr. Murray. So it goes without saying, that if there *were* any type of illegal behavior involving that moving vehicle—say, for example, driving with an open container of alcohol, unregistered weapons, illegal goods, maybe—any legal consequences would be suffered by the vehicle owner?"

Chester sniffed. "I guess, if there *was* any illegal behavior. Which there *wasn't.* Was there, Kyle?"

The driver froze in midrock.

Mendham leaned in close to Kyle. "Mr. Pressman, what if I told you we know the girl was in your truck?"

Kyle scraped his face with his hands, then spun to face his friend. "Come on, Chester. Tell him, will ya? We didn't do nothing wrong."

Chester slapped the counter. "Kyle, you stupid—"

"Sorry, man. I don't need any more trouble." He crossed his arms and stared at Mendham. "We gave the girl a ride. Nothing else. I swear."

Chester threw his hands in the air. "We're in the shitter now, Kyle. Nice work."

"You're lying. Both of you." Carl could stay silent no longer. "Where is she? If either of you laid a hand on her, I swear, I'll—"

"Relax, dude." Now that Kyle had started talking, he couldn't restrain himself. "Hell knows where she is. She freaked out. Plain jumped out of the truck while it was moving. A little crazy, that one. Wouldn't you say, Chester?"

"Don't you know when to keep your mouth shut?"

"I'm just tellin' the truth. No law against giving rides, is there?" Downright cocky now, Kyle looked for assurance from the officers.

"Ask them how long she was in the truck," Carl said.

"Easy, Alden." Mendham shot him a warning look, but repeated Carl's question.

"Couldn't have been more than fifteen, twenty minutes total."

Long enough, Carl thought.

"And where'd she jump out?" Mendham asked.

The driver scratched his head. "I dunno. Hard to remember with the storm and all. Somewhere right around this place, I guess." He turned to Chester, now pacing the length of the counter. "Woulda thought she'd come inside here, she was so freaked out, right, Chester?"

Ignoring Kyle, Chester stopped in front of Carl and sneered. "What's it to you, anyway, old man? You her *boyfriend* or something?"

Carl lunged.

"Alden. That's enough." Lopez pinned Carl's arms.

Chester used the opportunity to get right up in Carl's face. "Listen, mister. Up here, if somebody's looking for a ride, we give them a ride. And if for some reason they change their mind, well then, that's fine, too. They can just get out. That's all there is to it." He yanked off the orange hunting cap and tossed it on the counter. "That's it. I'm done talking. For real this time. Until I have a lawyer, which the state of New Hampshire is damn well gonna pay for." He shoved Kyle's shoulder. "You better do the same, if you know what's good for you. These guys are gonna twist everything we say."

Kyle put a foot on the ground to steady his stool. "Guess I'm done talking, too."

Carl could barely contain himself. "Really, Mendham, what more do you need?"

Lopez came up behind Carl and steered him to Iris's antiques nook. "I've got enough to hold you, too, Alden, if you don't back off." He shook a finger in Carl's face. "Stay here and be quiet, or I'll book you on interfering with an investigation."

Steaming, Carl considered going back outside to look for Alex, for any evidence she'd been in the vicinity.

Beside him, the two shopkeepers conferred.

"How long you think this is going to take?" Cam asked his wife.

"I don't know, Cam."

"I feel for him, Iris. I do. For those two families, too. It's just the short season and all. We're the only licensing game in town. Once this ice melts tomorrow, everybody's going to be itching to get out there."

"What's that got to do with anything?"

"What will customers think tomorrow morning, our whole parking lot filled with troopers' cars?"

"You know people around here. They'll want to help. Anyway, they're bound to find the girl soon."

"Have you looked outside? You know how these ice storms go. Roads are getting worse by the minute. This could take all night."

Carl sympathized with the man; he was a businessman himself.

Iris laid a hand on her husband's arm. "And what if it does? What would you do if it were Mia out there? My goodness, this girl Alex is just a bit younger."

"Mia would have better sense than that."

"You'd think so. Sometimes that girl surprises me." Iris turned to her husband. "Speaking of Mia, have you seen her this afternoon?"

Cam shook his head. "She's down in her studio, isn't she?"

"That's what I thought. You would think she'd come up to see what all the fuss was about."

"You know how she is when she gets into her work."

This was the first Carl had heard of another building on the premises. He stepped over to the couple. "I couldn't help but overhear you say something about a studio. Is it nearby?"

"Yes. Behind the store, down the hill a bit. Cam built it for our daughter, Mia."

Carl waved his hat toward the counter. "It seems those men gave Alex a ride earlier. They claim she jumped out somewhere near here. Maybe your daughter knows something."

"I doubt it," Iris said. "She's been working down there all afternoon finishing up some big deadlines for art school." She gestured to a collage of paintings on the nook wall. "Those are all hers."

"Iris, I don't think he cares about Mia's art right now." Cam was giving Carl a look like: *Mothers, you know?*

"Still, I'd like to talk to her," Carl pressed.

"Of course. I'll just buzz her." Iris walked over to a wall phone.

"Installed an intercom when I built the studio," Cam offered. "Can't always rely on cells up here."

The men waited in silence until Iris returned. "Mia didn't answer. Doesn't surprise me, though. Sometimes she's got her music so loud she doesn't hear it."

"Mind if we take a look down there?" Carl said.

Iris's expression changed. "Not sure I'm comfortable with that."

"Please. We know Alex was nearby."

Cam pulled a fleece off a peg on the wall. "I'll take you down there. Anything to move this along," he said to Iris over his shoulder.

Outside, Cam bounced his flashlight down the slick path and off a gleaming wall of glass below them. Up close, Carl saw how Cam had transformed an entire wooden shed: three walls of windows sat on a waist-high brick wall, meeting in a sleek arch overhead. The craftsmanship impressed him.

Cam knocked, then pushed open the studio door. "Mia? I've got someone here who'd like to talk to you."

Following Cam inside, Carl was struck by the earthy tang of marijuana and burnt wood.

An artist's leather portfolio leaned against one brick wall. On the wall opposite, embers glowed in a woodstove. A ceiling fan swirled lazily above their heads; industrial lights glittered on a curved track like a smile, illuminating canvases on a pair of easels below. Overhead, sleet ricocheted off the metal-framed roof.

"Strange," Cam said. "No sign of Mia. I'll check the bathroom." He disappeared through a pocket door, leaving Carl to scan the small kitchen. There were mismatched mugs drying in the dish drainer, granola bar wrappers in the trash that might have been there for days.

"Hey, Alden. Come look at this."

Before Carl could make his way to the bathroom, the entire studio plunged into darkness.

"Give it a second," Cam said. "Generator will kick in."

Sure enough, a generator roared to life almost immediately, flooding the studio with light again.

"This isn't like Mia." In the tiny bathroom, Cam held open the curtain of the small standing shower. On its floor was a heap of wet clothes. Even in the dimly lit bathroom, there was no mistaking the coat topping the pile: Alex's quilted ski jacket, the one her mother had packed for her.

MEG

"I *knew* it." With one look at Meg and Melissa's worried faces, Jacob yanked off his coat, tossing it onto the couch. "When you wouldn't answer, I knew something had happened. It's Alex, isn't it?"

"Yes. But I never wanted—" Meg started.

"She ran away, didn't she? Damn it. I bet it was that Evan guy she's been hanging with. When I get hold of that kid, I'm going to wring his—"

He shoved his hands in his back pockets and paced.

"It wasn't Evan." Meg moistened her lips. "You're not going to like this, Jacob. Alex didn't run away. I . . . I sent her away."

He whirled to face her. "You what?"

"I . . . I sent her to New Hampshire."

"You went behind my back, even after I said I was against that reform school?"

"You barely listened to me that night. You were more interested in the TV than what I had to say. I had to do something. You were ready to let her . . . self-destruct."

"I can't fucking believe this," he said, shaking his head. "But wait . . . if you're both here . . . ." He gestured at the kitchen, where Melissa had retreated when he'd come in.

". . . How did Alex get there?"

Meg took a deep breath. "I hired someone. A transport service."

"You paid a stranger to take our kid? What is she, some kind of package to be shipped off to New England?"

"I had no choice. You said it yourself that night: she'd never go willingly. But Jacob, there's something else." Meg joined him at the fireplace, crossing her arms and shaking off the tears that spilled down her cheeks. "There's been an accident."

"An accident? What the—?" Jacob slammed his fist on the mantel. "How is she?"

"We know Alex got out of the car OK. But she's been missing for a few hours." Skipping over the morning pickup, Meg offered the sparse accident details Carl had provided. "We have to focus on the good news. She walked away from the car. *And* she left Cass's scarf as a marker. That's something."

"Good news, huh?" Jacob rubbed his face. "The only thing I'm hearing is that my little girl is out there alone."

"*Our* little girl." Up close, he looked like hell: bloodshot eyes, fatigue stamped in blue crescent shadows underneath, days' worth of stubble. Guilt rippled through her. "Jacob, I am so, so sorry. I never should have done this. Nothing you can say will make me feel any worse than I already do."

"I've gotta go up there." He started for the hall.

Meg ran after him. "Jacob, you can't. You just drove all that way."

At the powder room, he turned, eyes hard. "Yes, I did. And if you had picked up when I called and told me what was going on, I could have gone right there." He went in the bathroom and closed the door.

His eerie calmness jarred her. "I thought about calling you," Meg lied through the door, "but I didn't want to upset you while you were driving."

Melissa emerged from the kitchen. "Don't make it worse, Meg."

The toilet flushed and Jacob came out. "I'm going. The thought of Alex out there alone . . ."

"Jacob, please stay. You're exhausted," said Melissa.

"This is none of your business," he said to her. "Although I'm sure you were in on it since day one."

Melissa glanced sideways at Meg. "I . . . You have every right to be angry, Jacob. I told Meg to tell you."

Meg's mouth dropped open. "Christ. Throw me under the bus, why don't you?"

"Sorry, Meg, but I told you this was a huge gamble." Her voice softened. "Jacob, at least wait until morning. There's a raging ice storm up there. The last thing Alex needs is for something to happen to you."

"Like that expert driver Meg hired?"

"He came well recommended," Meg said. "Parents wrote testimonials and—"

"You went too far this time."

This was better, Meg thought as his voice rose. She deserved his anger.

"Guys, stop. You'll wake Jack."

Tomorrow. Jack's practice. Meg covered her mouth, recalling her promise to her son.

"Are you serious?" Jacob said after she explained. "I can't chat about baseball right now. *You* explain it to him."

Behind Jacob, Melissa gestured wildly at the steps where Jack was making his way downstairs.

"Explain what?" he asked, rubbing his eyes.

"Nothing, bud. Just mommy and daddy stuff," Meg said. "We have to go pick Alex up."

"Why? Where is she? Daddy just got home. Why does he have to go out again?"

"It's important, honey. We'll see you tomorrow."

"Tomorrow?" Jack dropped onto a stair and began to cry. "Then who's taking me to practice tomorrow? Mom, you promised Dad would. You pinky-sweared."

"I can't tomorrow, bud." Jacob knelt in front of the boy, placing a hand on Jack's knee. "But I will next week. Promise."

"You guys always promise."

"I'll take you, honey," Melissa said. "I was a pretty good slugger in my day." Taking Jack's hand, she helped him to his feet. "So how about we head back to bed, ace?"

Partway up the stairs, Melissa turned and made a shooing gesture. "If you're going, go. I'll take care of Jack. Just let me know what's happening."

Meg waited until Jack was out of earshot to speak.

"Jacob, if you're going, I'm coming with you. You can sleep while I drive." She was slipping into her coat when someone rapped on the storm door. Her mouth fell open in surprise when Shana let herself in.

"I need to talk to you," Shana said.

"Shana, this is a really bad time . . ." Meg began.

"I'm sorry. It's superimportant."

"What's going on, Meg? Is Shana in on this, too?" Jacob twirled his keys at her.

"In on what?" Shana asked, bewildered.

"This scheme involving Alex."

"I told her before. I haven't heard from Alex all day. I just came back because—"

"Give me five minutes, Jacob," Meg said. "*Please.* Trust me."

"Trust you?"

Meg whispered in Jacob's ear. "This must be about Alex. She wouldn't have come back otherwise. Please. Don't leave without me."

Meg led the girl upstairs to Alex's room, Melissa's attempts to soothe Jacob drifting up behind them.

Shana balanced on the edge of Alex's bed. "I . . . I didn't tell you the truth before."

Meg's throat constricted. "You heard something else from Alex?"

"No, no. It's about . . . other stuff."

Meg stood and pressed Shana's knee. "I've got to go, honey. If you want to talk, call me in the car." She lifted the girl's chin. "You're a good friend, you know?"

Shana lips trembled. "No, I'm not. I'm a shitty friend." She grabbed Alex's stuffed unicorn from the unmade bed and clutched it to herself. "It's all my fault."

"How? You told Alex to stop helping Evan. What else could you have done?" Meg stole a glance toward Alex's door.

"Not Evan. *That* night. Her Sweet Sixteen." Shana folded herself over the stuffed animal.

"Meg, let's go!" Jacob called from downstairs.

She couldn't risk Jacob leaving without her. She moved toward the bedroom door. "Shana, please. Whatever it is . . ."

Shana gulped. "It was me. The drinking that night. It was all my idea." Haltingly, she confessed how she smuggled vodka into Alex's party in gift bags, setting up the ladies' room like party central. "Cass tried to talk me out of it. She was so straightedge, pulling Alex around by the nose all the time. I just wanted to Alex to have a little fun, you know, like, YOLO?"

No, Meg didn't know. YOLO sounded like a candy or a boy band. She so didn't have time for this.

"Cass got in my face before the party," Shana continued. "She goes, 'You better pray you only live once, Shana, because I swear to God, I'll make your life miserable.'" Tears streamed down Shana's face. "Cass said she'd friggin' *haunt* me if I did anything."

"I'm sure that was just a figure of speech on Cass's part."

"It wasn't. It feels like she is, every day," Shana sobbed. "Alex had nothing to do with it, I swear. When I offered her the vodka in the bathroom, she took it. It's my fault. I made her."

"Come on, Shana. Nobody *makes* anybody do anything. You've had enough D.A.R.E. assemblies to know that. You were wrong to bring the alcohol that night, but Alex decided to drink on her own."

"But when I saw how mad she was, I pushed her to drink *more*."

Meg frowned. "What was Alex mad about?"

"The fight with her dad. She came into the bathroom crying. Something about a college she liked. He shot her down pretty bad, said the school was too far away or too expensive or something."

Jacob hurled a thirty-second warning up the stairs. Why had he never mentioned this argument to Meg, a discussion that had apparently left their daughter so distraught it triggered the night's events? If Jacob tried to leave for New Hampshire without her, she'd throw herself in front of his car to stop him. "So the fight with her dad made Alex want to drink?" Meg prompted.

"She said you acted psycho, too."

"Me? How so?"

"You fought with him, in front of the photographer and everybody." Shana licked her lips. "Alex lost it. Said she wanted to die. That the party was wrecked. She wished she'd never even had it."

Meg could barely remember sniping with Jacob the way Shana described. Had this forgettable argument cost them their daughter?

Shana twisted the unicorn's horn. "In the parking lot after . . . how could you not know she was drunk?"

Meg *had* thought it strange Alex didn't say good-bye that night. The three friends had emerged from the banquet hall, shoeless, high heels dangling from their wrists like purses. Scary how, even barefoot, they had looked twenty-one, even twenty-three, in sophisticated makeup and fitted dresses, upswept hair. Cass had done most of the talking.

Meg sighed. "You know, Shana, I was exhausted that night. I just wanted to get Jack home. I didn't think a half hour was such a big deal." She'd also been preoccupied, pissed off at Jacob for cutting out early when he should have sucked it up and stayed, for Alex's sake. The girls had been so convincing that Meg relented, allowing them to stay out until eleven o'clock. She had even handed Shana's brother Logan money for Slurpees.

Slurpees. How could she have been so naïve? "I wish I *had* paid more attention, Shana. We all have regrets from that night." She patted the girl's leg again. "Thank you for telling me this. We've all got a lot to think about. Now I really need to go." Meg headed for the door.

"Cass didn't," Shana called.

Meg leaned against the doorframe. "Cass didn't what?"

"She didn't drink that night. She didn't even want to go to that party after."

"What party?"

"A party at Logan's friend's house. Cass only came along to take care of Alex. She thought we *were* going to 7-Eleven for Slurpees. When I told her in the car about the party, she was really pissed off. She started fighting with Logan. She wanted him to take us home."

"But Logan wouldn't?"

Shana shook her head. "They were his friends. He promised. Cass took off her seat belt and threatened to jump out of the car. That's when Logan decided to turn around. He said he didn't want to deal with the drama. But I still wanted to go, so I leaned over and . . ." Shana's words tumbled out in great choking sobs.

Meg pressed a hand on Shana's shoulder. "And what, Shana? Tell me. What did you do?"

CARL

"When did you last see your daughter, ma'am?"

"I . . . I don't know. Around three o'clock, I guess?" Iris dabbed at her eye with a tissue. She had been flabbergasted to learn Mia had disappeared and to hear what Cam and Carl discovered in her daughter's studio. "Mia never leaves without telling us. And she certainly would have told us if some stranger wandered in."

The moment they discovered Mia missing, Cam had slipped out Swiftriver's front door to check the parking lot. Meanwhile, Lopez led Iris to a chair by the makeshift radio center and began questioning her about her daughter's habits and activities. Carl heard nothing that aroused his suspicions about the artist, especially compared to the young people he encountered in his work.

Mia often helped out at Hope Haven, a residential home for teenage girls in Glencliff, about a twenty-minute drive from Swiftriver, Iris explained.

Iris's friend Ellen ran Hope Haven. "It's where I met Mia," Iris said. "And now she's practically a mentor to the girls there." While Iris paused to blow her nose, Cam explained how they had adopted Mia from Hope Haven.

"Has your daughter ever been in trouble before?"

"I don't know what you're implying," Iris flashed. "My daughter is missing, and you're making her out to be some kind of criminal? She's a good girl." She stood up and walked over to study a painting on the wall, as if its subjects, the father and mother walking the young girl up a hill, might offer some answers. She turned to wave an arm at Carl. "I know the kids you work with have issues, Mr. Alden, but Mia's . . . motivated. Head and shoulders above most of the kids around here maturity-wise." She reached to straighten a set of glasses on a shelf.

Lopez swung his notebook open. "So no behavior out of the ordinary lately?"

Hesitating, Iris cradled a crystal decanter. "I don't know if you would call this 'out of the ordinary,' but Mia received an acceptance letter this afternoon from a New York art school."

"What's so unusual about that?"

"I had no idea Mia was applying in the city. We thought she would live with us for a few more years. She loves her studio here and all. But obviously she had other ideas."

"And when she told you?"

"I was a little hurt. We had some words. I may have overreacted just a bit." Iris peered over Lopez's shoulder. "What are you writing, anyway?"

"I'm just trying to understand your daughter's state of mind today, Mrs. Bailey." He flipped to a previous page. "Another thing. Is your daughter in the habit of smoking marijuana?"

Iris flushed. "You'll have to ask her father about that."

Iris looked around for Cam, who was nowhere in sight, then pointed again at Carl. "This is your fault. If you hadn't brought some disturbed girl through here, my daughter would be down in her studio where she belongs instead of—"

"Whoa, Iris." Cam had slipped back inside the store.

"I can't help it. These two are jumping to all kinds of conclusions about Mia."

He put an arm around his wife. "Listen to me. I just went outside to check on our cars. My truck is gone."

Mia had keys to Cam's truck, it turned out. "I always told her my rig handles better in the snow than hers," he said.

Iris glared at Carl. "Your girl stole it, then. Or forced Mia to drive her."

"Alex wouldn't do that."

"You were taking this girl to a reform school, Mr. Alden," Iris said. "How can you be sure?"

Lopez checked his notes. "This Hope Haven facility where Mia volunteers. They might know something."

"I'll call Ellen." Iris used the phone at the cash register. "Ellen, it's Iris. Is Mia there? Good." Iris nodded vehemently to the men. "And the girl with her . . ." Iris frowned. "Really? Are you sure?"

"Tell her to search the house," Carl said.

"I see. That must be difficult. Well, then, let me speak to Mia."

Iris covered the phone while she waited for her daughter. "Mia *did* go there, but Ellen swears she was by herself."

"Not possible," Carl said. "Those were definitely Alex's clothes in the studio."

"I'd have pushed Ellen on it," Iris said, "but they've got their own situation there. An older girl snuck away from a group at the movies. Ellen's beside herself."

Someone came on the line again. "Really? Are you sure?" Iris asked. "But Cam's car is still there? OK. You, too." She replaced the phone. "Ellen can't find Mia. She sent the little ones upstairs to look and everything. She'd just been in the living room two minutes before."

"I'm going over there," Carl said.

"See, I told you. We're innocent," Kyle the driver couldn't resist yelling across the store.

"Shut the eff up," Chester chided.

"Quiet, both of you," Mendham warned. "We still don't know what happened to that young lady when she was in your company."

Carl rubbed his head. "Mind if I borrow that jacket again, Mr. Bailey? Seeing as I don't have a ride, I guess I'll be hiking over to Glencliff."

"That's ridiculous." Cam turned to Lopez. "Can't you get some officers over to Hope Haven to check things out?"

"We will as soon as we can. We're stretched pretty thin tonight, handling other storm-related incidents, too."

"Now that we know where Alex went, you can pull those officers off the road," Carl said.

"Didn't sound to me like anybody over there was too sure about anything, Mr. Alden," Mendham said. "Don't tell me how to run my operation. I'll send somebody as soon as I can."

"I'll take you, Carl." Behind him, Iris had bundled herself into a long, black quilted coat.

"That's crazy," Cam said. "Let the troopers do their job. I'm sure we'll hear from Mia soon."

"I'll be fine," Iris insisted. "You stay here with the store, and we'll take Mia's truck. I need to see for myself what's going on with her." She pushed open the store's door, unleashing another torrent of wind and chimes, and turned to Carl.

"You coming, or not, Mr. Alden?"

MEG

Scraps from Jacob and Melissa's heated exchange drifted upstairs:

"You're always taking her side . . ."

"You can't just get in the car and leave her."

"Watch me."

Meg stroked Shana's hair. "Shana, please. Tell me. After Logan said he'd bring you home, what did you do?"

Shana's face remained planted in Alex's pillow. "I . . . I was pissed off. I really wanted to go to the party. Logan said there'd be all these older guys." Pushing herself up on an elbow, Shana focused on Alex's band poster. "So when Logan said he was turning around, I . . . I grabbed the steering wheel." Fresh tears spilled over her cheeks.

Meg's hand dropped. "You *what?*"

"I just jiggled it a little. I didn't mean for anything to happen. I just wanted to get his attention." Shana wiped her face on the sleeve of her hoodie, leaving a long, black smear. "Next thing I knew, we were on the side of the road. With all those ambulances. And Cass . . ." Shana sat up and hugged her knees. "Cass just wanted to protect Alex. That's the only reason she went that night—to give Alex time to sober up. So you wouldn't find out she was drinking."

Numb, Meg handed Shana a tissue from Alex's night table, rearranging her recollection of that night—a Sweet Sixteen cursed from the start. She covered her mouth. How could she have been so stupid?

"You guys OK?" Melissa stood at Alex's door.

Meg shook her head. "Did Jacob leave? I really need him to wait."

"I'm trying. He's determined."

When Melissa left again, Shana lifted her head. "You must hate me." She pushed herself up against Alex's headboard. "I wouldn't blame you. I hate myself."

Meg measured her next words. There were a million questions she longed to ask. Instead, she grasped the teen's hand. "I don't hate you, Shana. I'm glad you told me."

"Me, too."

"This was an awful lot to keep inside all this time."

"You have no idea."

Things were still silent downstairs. What was Jacob doing? It was a miracle he'd waited this long.

Meg stroked the chipped polish on Shana's thumb, thinking of the hell the teen put herself through over the past few months. "Why didn't Logan say anything?"

"He's my brother."

"But he was the driver. Even knowing he'd be blamed for the accident, he said nothing?"

Shana shook her head vigorously.

"So in effect, Logan covered for you." Whatever Shana lorded over her brother had the potential to be annihilating. "And Alex?"

"Alex was really drunk."

"But is she covering up for you, too?" That kind of stress could explain her daughter's behavior. It could also put a lot of pressure on a friendship.

Shana inched away. "Not exactly."

Meg was confused. It made more sense for the three to stick to the same story—unless one of them didn't *know* the whole story. "Shana, does Alex know what you did?"

Shana's head dropped to her knees. Meg shook her leg. "Look at me. Alex was pretty out of it that night. Does she know what you did? That you grabbed the wheel?"

Downstairs, Jacob had run out of patience, bellowing up the stairs, "I'm going, Meg."

Meg jumped up at the sound of the front door being closed. "I have to go, Shana. Please. What *does* Alex think happened that night?"

Shana drew a shaky breath. "She thinks Cass took off her seat belt. That she fought with Logan about turning around and going home. To protect her. She thinks Cass distracted Logan and caused the accident."

Meg's eyes narrowed. "You let Alex believe that? That Cass died protecting her?"

Shana's eyes overflowed again. "How could I tell her the truth? Alex would hate me."

"So rather than risk losing her friendship, you let her think she was responsible for her best friend's death."

"It sounds horrible when you say it like that."

"But that's how it is, isn't it?" Meg looked around her daughter's room. "So she's been carrying around this guilt since . . ."

In the dim light of Alex's lava lamp, much of the last few months clicked into focus.

"We're all guilty," Shana sniffled. "What if they don't find Alex? I can't lose another friend. I won't be able to live with myself."

You've done a fine job of that so far. Meg bit her lip to keep from saying the words aloud. But Shana was clearly in agony, and no matter how selfish the girl's actions, how pathological her need for acceptance,

Shana was still a child, burdened by devastating secrets. Digging deep, Meg brushed Shana's damp hair from her face.

"They *will* find her, Shana. I have to believe Alex has figured out a way to be safe."

"Me, too."

"And when they do find her, you're going to tell her the truth."

"I will. I promise. I'll tell her everything." Shana hugged her. "I'm sorry. Really sorry."

Meg hugged her back, the embrace feeling like a betrayal of her own daughter.

A horn beeped below Alex's window. Meg ran downstairs, finding Melissa on Meg's phone. "It's him," Melissa said, holding it out. "The man you hired."

While Meg talked, Melissa retrieved Jacob from his truck. Inside, the two crowded Meg while she talked to Carl, shouting questions until she had to walk away, plugging her ear with her finger. Shana came downstairs and trailed Meg into the dining room, toying with the tea set, hovering so near that Meg finally closed herself into a corner to hear.

"They found Alex's coat," she called to her family.

Jacob demanded to talk to Carl. Meg handed the phone over reluctantly. "This is Alex's dad," Jacob barked. "Stop. I don't want any apologies now. Just tell me what's going on." Jacob nodded, his periodic *uh-huh*s torturing Meg as she stood at his elbow.

"I'm coming up there." He glanced at his watch. "By tomorrow morning, early . . . I don't give a shit about the weather. I only care about my daughter. She needs me."

His protective air reminded Meg of the night in the dive bar when she first told him about her pregnancy. Then, as now, his daughter had been his first concern.

Jacob mimed a writing motion, and Melissa retrieved a pen and an envelope from the kitchen. "Log cabin. Pink gas tanks. Got it. And Alden . . ." Jacob's hand shook jotting down the details. "Find her. And have some answers ready for me when I get there." He ended the call.

Meg took back her phone. "That's something, at least. They're on their way to the shelter where she might be. You should wait 'til tomorrow morning to go."

"Don't tell me what to do, Meg. Haven't you done enough already?"

"How many times do I have to say it? I made a mistake. I'm sorry. This is difficult for me, too."

Jacob pushed by her. "I'll be in the car."

"I'm coming, damn it."

"See what she's done?" Jacob said as he passed Melissa.

"I heard that," Meg said, catching up to him. "You left me no choice."

"I was very clear about my feelings that night."

"Clear you wanted to watch the game. Obviously, that took precedence—"

Voices escalating, Meg and Jacob continued the argument, one cutting off the other.

"My children are always my priority."

"Are you sure there isn't another priority out there?"

"Stop! What is *wrong* with you?" The anguished cry came from the living room. Shana stood by the fireplace in front of the family portrait, hands over her ears.

Meg made her way to the girl. "Shana, honey. I know you're upset," she began, stroking the girl's arm.

Shana wrenched away. "Of course I am. How can you guys fight like that? After you just got the best news in the world—that Alex might be safe." She wrapped her arms around herself. "Don't you get how fucked up this is?"

Meg and Jacob looked at each other.

"This is exactly what happened the night of Alex's party. It's literally like déjà vu. This is why Alex is so screwed up." Shana ran past them and up the stairs, slamming Alex's door behind her.

Jacob stared up the stairs after her. "Jesus. What is she, a god-damned teenage shrink?"

Chastened, Meg drew a shaky sigh. Shana was absolutely right. They *were* seriously fucked up.

CARL

As Carl and Iris pulled into Hope Haven's drive, a tall, slim young woman bounded down the steps coatless, her black curls flying behind her.

"I know what you're going to say, Mom," she said, opening Iris's door. "I shouldn't have taken Dad's car. I already told him I'm sorry."

Iris cut off her apology with a fierce hug. "We'll deal with that later. I'm just glad you're safe."

Mia had been in the basement looking around for Alex when Iris called earlier. "It's been nuts here," Mia said. "You remember Reyna, don't you? Anyway, Reyna's gone, and Ellen's frantic."

"We were, too," Iris said.

"Where's Alex?" Carl asked.

"So that's her real name? I was beginning to wonder." Mia looked him over. "You're the guy her parents hired? Dad filled me in when I called the store to say I was OK."

Carl nodded. "We assumed Alex came here with you."

"He knows she was in your studio, honey," Iris added.

"That was my first mistake." Mia turned to Carl. "Alex *was* here. I told her to wait, like, two seconds so I could talk to Ellen. When I came back, she was gone."

Mia led them into Hope Haven's front hall, where a row of coats hung on hooks along one wall. Just then, a young girl of about ten ran out to meet them, stopping short and staring. Behind her glasses, her eyes were red from crying.

"Mia, I gotta ask you something. You know that—"

Carl tapped his watch. "Ms. Bailey, this is very important . . ."

"Of course." Mia knelt and took the little girl's hands. "Reyna's going to be OK, honey. Listen, Ellen needs some help in the kitchen. Go and see her, and I'll catch you later. Promise." The little girl disappeared through a swinging door.

"Let's talk in here." Mia led them into a large sitting room with wood-framed leather couches and flopped cross-legged into a boxy armchair. Carl chose to stand, leaning on the stone hearth, where over the mantel a flat-screen blared the evening news.

"Are you sure Alex isn't here?" he asked.

"I searched this place from top to bottom. I know all the hiding places from having lived here."

"OK, so tell me exactly what happened this afternoon."

"I was in my studio finishing stuff for school when she knocked on my door." Mia hadn't wanted to let her in at first, but she seemed harmless. "And scared to death."

"Makes sense," Carl said, "after all she'd been through."

"Right, except very little of what Alex told *me* matches up with what really happened. Dad told me everything on the phone."

"What did Alex tell you?"

"That she got lost hiking. Separated from her friends. That's when she hitched the ride."

"So she told you about the guys who picked her up?"

"Yes. They sounded sketchy. But she never said a word about the accident."

Carl and Iris exchanged looks. "That makes no sense," Iris said.

"That's what I told Dad." Mia jerked to attention suddenly. "Oh, my God. That's her."

Carl turned to see the photo of Alex he'd given to Mendham filling the television screen, while a somber newscaster detailed the ongoing search. A news ticker crawling underneath spit out an emergency number, urging residents to call or to tweet any information they might have. The teen even had her own hashtag: #FindAlex.

Mia sat back. "This is crazy."

Carl gestured to the TV. "If Alex saw this, it's no wonder she took off. So you believed her hiking story?"

"Of course not. Not the way she was dressed. Although it does happen up here—crazy tourists going into the woods with nothing but a candy bar and a water bottle. They show up at Swiftriver all the time."

"She's right," Iris affirmed.

"I figured Alex was a runaway. That's why my first thought was to come here. I knew Ellen would know what to do."

"Of course," Carl said. "You said Alex talked about the truckers. What exactly did she say?" If they did anything to hurt Alex, Carl couldn't be held accountable for what he might do.

"That they were cool at first. She was psyched. Then things got weird."

"How weird?"

"She didn't say. She just said she freaked and jumped out of the truck not far past Swiftriver," Mia said. "She recognized our distinctive gas pumps, *Mother*."

That much matched up with Kyle's confession, Carl thought. "How the heck did she even find your studio?" he asked. "You're pretty well hidden down there."

"She said she'd been creeping around the back of the store looking for something to eat and found the path."

"Why wouldn't she just come into the store for help?" Iris asked.

Mia had asked Alex the same thing. "I offered to bring her up. Said you guys were chill. But she didn't want to go," Mia said. "She was really anxious to get to the bus depot. It sounded suspicious, but I decided to play along, figuring I'd eventually bring her here."

Mia gave her dry clothes and something to eat. After, the two girls talked a bit.

"And got stoned." Iris's arms were crossed.

Mia's eyes widened. "We did not."

"They searched the studio, honey. Said it reeked of pot."

Mia examined the sleeve of her sweater. "That was mine. I was celebrating earlier. About New York."

"Right."

"I didn't smoke with her, Mom. I swear." There wasn't time for that, Mia said; Alex had another plan. "Some wacko pilgrimage for a band. Rainwater or something?"

"Rainmaker," Carl corrected. *Of course. Their conversations in the car. His missing frog.* Why hadn't he figured it out before?

"Alex is headed to Happy Corner."

"How did you know?" Mia laughed.

"Alex and I talked about the place during the ride up." Carl now keenly regretted ever mentioning the proximity of the Phibs shrine.

"Alex thought she could get there by bus. She knew about the Lincoln bus depot."

The last place they'd stopped before the accident, Carl recalled.

Mia offered to give Alex a ride to the depot. "I had to fake her out. I even gave her bus fare so she'd get in the car with me."

On the way, Mia said she had to make a pit stop and left Alex in the living room while she talked to Ellen. When Mia came back, Alex was gone.

Carl pulled his hood on. "That's it, then. The bus station. Let's go." He thanked Mia for her assistance. "I hope you find your missing friend. Iris, do you mind?"

As her mother got up to leave, Mia pulled on her coat. "Not so fast. I'm coming, too. I have a few questions for my new friend Alex."

MEG

Meg had barely slid into the front seat before Jacob threw the car into gear. They drove twenty miles or so in silence. Finally, Jacob slammed his fist on the steering wheel.

"What the hell *was* that back there with Shana?"

Meg sighed. "I don't know," she lied.

Shana's revelations about the night of Alex's party had brought it all back. She cringed at the memory of their family photo session, the insults hurled at each other over their children's heads. Meg remembered walking away to find Jack, leaving Alex with Jacob. That must have been when they'd fought. And then she'd come back, unknowingly heaping fuel onto the fire.

Beside her, Jacob searched for a radio station.

"I can drive if you need a break," Meg offered.

"I'm fine."

Jacob did in fact seem remarkably alert, given his full day of physical labor and hours of driving. Probably rejuvenated by Carl's encouraging call. "At Alex's birthday party. Do you remember us fighting that night?"

"Fighting?"

"During the family pictures."

"Oh. Yeah. You were giving me shit about my job situation."

Meg squirmed. "When I left to find Jack, did you and Alex get into it?"

"I don't know. Maybe. That guy was posing us . . . Wait a sec. She was talking to me about a college." He shifted in his seat. "Yeah. A school in Hawaii. A pipe dream."

"Is that what you said to her?"

"I don't know, Meg. Probably not those exact words. But seriously, where would she get the idea we could manage that? I mean, the airfare alone. I think I told her to look at schools around here."

"What else did you say?"

He sniffed. "Geeze, Meg. I don't remember."

"I guess it doesn't matter much now."

"Sounds like it mattered to Shana. That was some meltdown. Why was she there tonight, anyway? Was everybody told about Alex's intervention but me?"

"There wasn't an intervention."

"If it wasn't for her, we'd have been on the road twenty minutes ago. What was so damned important upstairs?"

Meg swallowed and looked out her window. "She was . . . upset about Alex. I couldn't just leave her."

"Nice of you to be so considerate."

She put a hand on his knee. "Please. Let's not fight. Not now."

He sighed. "Fine. I just want to get up there, and get Alex."

"Me, too." She took her hand away. "You know, when I was up in Alex's room this morning, I found her dress."

"What dress?"

"Her Sweet Sixteen dress."

"The one she had on in the hospital? I thought you threw it away."

"I did. She must have gone looking for it."

"Oh, my God. That is just so sad." Jacob rubbed his forehead, retreating into his own thoughts.

So much heartbreak surrounded Alex's special night. And Meg was still reeling over the fact that their marital problems, a casual argument they could barely remember, had had fatal consequences. She'd give anything to redo that evening: to avoid the fighting, to convince Jacob to stay until the party finished, to stand her ground about the after-party activities instead of stewing over Jacob's abrupt departure.

And knowing Alex had been oppressed by false beliefs about the accident, Meg now better understood the changes in her—the impenetrable emotional walls, cemetery visits instead of school, her obsessive attachment to Cass's scarf.

And if Meg were brutally honest with herself, she hadn't fully acknowledged the effect of their separation on her children, especially Alex. She naively thought their staying in the same house together would ease the pain of their split—that pulling out all the stops (with Miriam's help) to throw Alex an amazing party would soften the blow.

According to Shana, this was the farthest thing from the truth.

Their family situation had probably been tearing at Alex long before that night, Meg too paralyzed over her disintegrating marriage to see it. Jacob hadn't realized it, either. His shoot-from-the-hip reaction to Alex's college choice that night was thoughtless and ill-timed, but not meanspirited. By steering Alex to a more financially realistic alternative, he'd actually had been trying to be responsible. But Meg could easily see how his behavior must have deeply hurt Alex, who was used to being Daddy's girl.

She glanced sideways at Jacob. His arm was slung over the steering wheel, his cheek pulsing the way it did when he was stressed. He was absolutely entitled to be furious. She never should have sent Alex off without his blessing.

And on the subject of guilt, when the time was right, Meg needed to carefully consider what Shana had confessed about the accident. She wasn't prepared to deal with that right now or the issue of the broken slider door.

All of that would have to wait. First, there was Alex. Meg checked her phone again to make sure she hadn't missed another of Carl's calls. In a pocket of traffic, Jacob shifted into the fast lane, at the same time rummaging in the well between their seats, pulling out one CD after another and straining to read their hand-lettered labels by the light of oncoming traffic before discarding them on the seat beside him. With difficulty, Meg kept her comments about his multitasking to herself.

Eventually, Jacob found the disc he wanted and slipped it into the dashboard player, the car filling with the twangy jam band sound he and Alex loved. Jacob lowered the volume, hoarsely singing along.

> *You called to me, when I was lonely; you sensed my hurt, my*
> *deepest pain.*
> *Your heart is home and gives me shelter, and I will never leave*
> *again.*

Phone curled in her hand, Meg shifted toward her door and tried to doze. When she opened her eyes again, she could swear the same song still played. They were all very long, broken up with lengthy instrumental sections, and mostly sounded alike to her, although Alex and Jacob had gaped at Meg when she said that once.

> *In your safe space, I find my rainbow, my blazing sun, where*
> *troubles cease.*
> *When water's troubled, or storm clouds gather, your joyful*
> *shade can give me peace.*
> *Hap-py Corner, Hap-py Cor-ner, you soothe my soul, you*
> *paint my sky . . .*
> *Hap-py Corner, Happy—*

"Jacob," she interrupted. "What's that you're singing?"

He glanced at her, bleary-eyed. "This song? 'Happy Corner.' By Amphibian."

"I *know* that. But is the song, like, code or something? For getting high, maybe?"

He chortled. "I'd say that's a theme in pretty much every Phibs song."

"But what's it about?"

"Who gives a shit? Why after all these years do you suddenly care about the background of a Phibs song?"

"I just do. What does 'Happy Corner' mean?"

"You've heard Alex and me talk about it. It's a little town in New Hampshire where the Phibs built their *Rainmaker* monument. Satisfied?"

"Yes. Satisfied. Thank you." She sat back. By this point, the number of cars on the road had dwindled. "I only asked because Alex must really like that song."

"She likes all their songs."

"I know, but this one especially."

"Why do you say that?"

"Because she wrote 'Happy Corner' on her Sweet Sixteen pictures. The ones of her and Cass that she hung up in her bedroom. I noticed them this morning."

They sat in silence for a few miles. When Jacob finally spoke, Meg jumped.

"Meg. Get that Alden guy on the phone." His tone was urgent.

She turned to him, startled. "Why? It's not going to do any good to yell at him some more."

"Just get him on the phone. Now." The passing beams of a lone car washed Jacob's face white. "I know where Alex is going."

CARL

Fight, Carolyn.

His partner was out of surgery, Carolyn's mother told Carl when he connected with her on their way to the bus depot. Now all they could do was wait and pray.

Having survived on the hospital's meager updates until this point, he was grateful for the additional details she provided. As Carl had feared, Carolyn suffered massive internal injuries, requiring several units of blood during surgery, leaving her extremely weak and in critical condition. They would know more the following day. His partner's mother and daughter would have arrived at the hospital by then.

"I'm concerned about Jamie," Carolyn's mother said. "I don't know how she'll react, seeing her mom like this."

"I wish I could be there," Carl said, thinking that no child should have to experience that.

"Stay and do what you have to do, Carl. Carolyn would want that."

Feeling helpless, and deeply responsible for the family's anguish, he could only promise to meet them there as soon as Alex was safe. "Let me at least find you a hotel room up here," he offered.

"I can help with that," Iris said from the driver's seat.

Carl relayed Iris's offer.

"That's kind of your friend. Tell her I'm very grateful."

Hanging up, Carl was surprised the call had come through. Cell service fluctuated from limited to none, even at this lower altitude.

Iris placed a hand over Carl's. "I'm sorry, Carl. We're all praying for your partner, if that helps."

"Thanks." Carl turned away. Outside, the sleet had lightened somewhat, but for most of their two-mile journey, they'd plodded along behind a truck that halted sporadically to spit salt onto the road. As they inched along 112, neon logos in taproom windows winked invitingly: "Budweiser," "Sierra Pale Ale," "Dos Equis." Carl swallowed. Beer would be only the beginning for him, a teaser. He imagined lucky patrons warm and dry at the bar, locals during this off-season, cheering the underdog South Florida along the road to the Final Four. What he wouldn't give to be one of them; he bet at least one tourist spot around here hosted karaoke.

There would be no songs for him this evening. Instead, taking advantage of a spurt of four-bar service, he searched online for bus routes available to Alex, so he'd have the information to pass on to the Carmodys when they spoke. He found no direct service to Happy Corner, but a local Lincoln Lines bus hugging the New Hampshire–Vermont border could take her as far as Colebrook, leaving Alex about twenty miles from her destination. One had been scheduled to depart ten minutes ago, Carl realized with dismay. They were now minutes from the bus depot. With any luck, weather conditions had postponed or at least delayed the bus's departure.

At a complete stop now behind the salt truck, Carl was about to jump out and make a run for the depot when his cell lit up with a call from the Carmodys. Stammering with excitement, Alex's father shared his theory about his daughter's intentions, describing how he'd watched Happy Corner's televised unveiling of Rainmaker with Alex and her friend last year, tracked down the rare poster for his daughter.

"The girls were obsessed with it," Jacob finished.

Carl chose not to mention he'd seen the poster in Alex's room yesterday, saying only that the band had provided common ground with the daughter during today's drive and that they had reached the same conclusion about Alex's plans. Listening to Alex's father, he wondered if the two men had attended some of the same concerts, perhaps stood in the same muddy line for a Porta-John. The Phibs world was small.

Carl spoke briefly with Alex's mother, explaining his next steps, raising his voice to hear himself over the fairly heated mother-daughter exchange taking place in the car:

"You could have made some excuse, Mia. Called up on the intercom, at least."

"I just thought Ellen . . ."

"Right. Ellen. I bet *she* knew about New York."

"Mom. Come on. I'm sorry I didn't tell you about New York. But Ellen deals with these girls all the time. It's her job. You've seen her in action. We'd only have ended up at Hope Haven anyway."

"Still, it was irresponsible to drive in that weather."

"It doesn't really matter, does it?" Carl interjected, having ended his call with the Carmodys. "Let's just hope this is where Alex headed."

The salt truck finally turned down a side street and Iris accelerated. "What I don't understand is how Alex could have made it this far alone," she mused. It was too far to walk, and after the girl's experience with those horrid truckers, Iris said she couldn't imagine her hitchhiking again.

Carl harbored the same concerns. There was always the chance they'd completely misjudged Alex's plans.

With relief, he spotted the gas station up ahead. The all-purpose depot looked different at night, the bus company's sprinting stallion logo backlit yellow, as though the mascot might gallop off the wall at any moment. Iris had barely slowed in the parking lot when Carl bounded out of the car and into the store, Mia tailing him. He rushed up to the counter, where a bored clerk was flipping through a girlie magazine.

"The bus to Colebrook? Did it leave yet?" Carl asked.

Sticking a finger in his magazine to hold his place, the clerk twisted to look at the clock. "Ten minutes ago, maybe? It was already gone when I came on." The departure had been late, he added, almost canceled because of the storm. "No more till tomorrow." He opened the magazine again, and Carl slapped his hand on the counter, upsetting a display of cheap neon earphones in the process. "Did a teen girl buy a ticket tonight? Pink braid, lip ring, about this tall?" His hand reached midway up a tower of power drinks on the counter.

"Like I said, I just started my shift." He pointed the magazine toward the rear of the store. "You could ask her, though. She was here when I came on. Maybe she saw something."

Carl and Mia headed toward a back wall lined with glass-fronted refrigerated cases and vending machines. In front of these, a jumble of blue plastic chairs served as the depot's waiting area. All the seats were empty.

Annoyed, Carl strode back to the counter. "Who are you talking about? There's nobody there." The clerk reluctantly put down the magazine and started to come out from behind the counter when Mia called out.

"Mr. Alden. Over here!"

MEG

"Happy Corner." Jacob slapped the steering wheel. "Do I know my girl, or what?"

He dedicated the next forty miles to demystifying the hallowed significance of the Rainmaker shrine for Meg, tying together the words scrawled on the Sweet Sixteen photos to Amphibian's first album, immortalized on their daughter's bedroom poster.

Still, after all Alex had endured today, Meg couldn't buy the idea of her daughter heading to an aging hippie commune to worship a giant frog. "She's been through hell, Jacob. What would she be thinking?"

"She'd be thinking, 'What a great place to escape to.' Same as everybody else who ends up there."

The way Jacob described it, Happy Corner possessed the healing powers of a holy shrine, which sounded ridiculous. Then again, as Jacob pointedly reminded her over the next three exits, Meg wouldn't buy into this logic because she wasn't an Amphibian disciple, a member of the club that counted Jacob and Alex as members—and apparently Carl Alden as well.

Meg couldn't help but acknowledge the poetic justice of it all: this serious, all-business ex-military guy she hired was also a golden tree frog worshiper. The whole thing bordered on cultism, as far as she was concerned. Happy Corner or no Happy Corner, Meg could never put her faith in some toad on a band poster.

Beside her, Jacob hummed something unrecognizable. Meg was unable to relax without another positive update from Carl. Over the next fifty miles, she grabbed her phone once or twice from where it rested on her thigh, certain she'd felt the pulse of a call, only to be mistaken. She would have thought enough time had passed by now to allow Carl to check out the bus depot and get back to her.

Outside her window, the dwindling number of box stores and mega gas stations marked their passage to a less populated north. If Alex *had* taken a bus to a godforsaken corner of New Hampshire, what might she see from the bus window this very moment? Meg leaned her head on the glass, absently reading a bumper sticker for the Vermont Lake Monsters as an SUV whooshed by. *A better name for a band than a baseball team*, Meg thought drowsily.

Baseball. Jack's pinky swear came back to her, along with a surge of guilt at the realization she hadn't left Melissa any instructions. She tapped out a text with the time and location of Jack's practice and a wild guess at where she might find last year's cleats—probably too small, the way the little guy was growing.

Another disappointment for Jack. How many other times in the last year had her second child gotten lost in the shuffle while Alex's drama took center stage? It wasn't fair. Jack deserved as much of them as Alex did. *Things had to change starting now*, she thought, watching the open highway. She'd make it up to Jack once she knew Alex was safe, as soon as they got home. Whether he liked it or not, Jack was about to get a major dose of mother-son bonding. She could pitch to him after school as well as Jacob could.

In fact, there were tons of things the two could do together. She'd make a list and tack it on the fridge when she got home. Meg clicked open Jacob's glove box for something to write with.

"What are you looking for?" Jacob asked.

"Paper and pen." She settled for a stained Dairy Queen napkin and a stubby pencil from minigolf. Smoothing the napkin on a knee, Meg had jotted only a few items when the pencil broke. She dove back into the glove box, rifling through car manuals, maps (who needed those anymore?), the overstuffed pocket of registration and insurance cards, for the pen she swore she placed there back in the day.

"How about putting a note in your phone?" Jacob suggested.

"I'll forget it's there." The pen-shaped object in the back of the glove box turned out to be a Blizzard straw.

"Try your purse."

"I lent my last one to Jack yesterday."

"It's only a friggin' pen, Meg. Do it later."

Ignoring him, Meg yanked the entire glove box contents onto her lap, tossing manuals and maps onto the car floor until only the pocket of auto credentials remained. Abruptly, Jacob reached over, trying to swipe it.

"Is there some woman's picture in there you don't want me to see?" she asked.

"Very funny, Meg. Of course not. It's just that I forgot to pay the insurance on the truck. I didn't want you to see the expired card."

Meg sighed. "I've got bigger things to worry about right now. Just drive, will you?"

Determined now, Meg dumped the pocket's entire contents onto her lap: ID cards, papers, two paper clips, a Band-Aid, an old gas station receipt and a pen embossed with the name of Alex's orthodontist.

"See?" She shook the pen at Jacob, and the gas receipt fluttered to the floor, exposing one last item on her lap. In Meg's second of recognition, a sucker punch; the air drained from the front seat.

"What the *hell*, Jacob?"

CARL

Sprinting past the disinterested clerk, the first thing Carl saw in the back of the bus depot was Mia kneeling beside a large trash can. The second thing he glimpsed was a pair of legs, splayed toward the ATM in the corner.

By now, Iris had come inside. She stopped short at the sight of Mia on the floor. "Oh, my goodness. Is that Alex?"

"No." Mia brushed the hair out of the young woman's face, ashen next to her red ski coat. "It's Reyna." She tapped the girl's cheek gently. "Reyna. It's me, Mia. Wake up."

"Leave me alone." The girl rolled over toward the wall of vending machines, a phone curled in one hand.

"What's wrong with her?" Iris asked.

"Sleeping it off, I think, judging from the fumes." Mia grabbed the girl's jacket and tugged. "Reyna, wake up. I mean it."

The girl blinked, scraping the back of her hand across her mouth. "Hey, Mia." She reached out to touch Mia's cheek, a move the young woman dodged. "Uh-oh. Am I in trouble?"

"You tell me."

The girl struggled to sit up, shrinking at the sight of Carl and Iris crouching in front of her. "No, Iris. Please, please, please don't tell Ellen."

"Reyna, listen to me," Mia said. "Did you see a girl here a little while ago? Waiting for a bus?" Mia began to describe Alex. When she mentioned the lip ring, Reyna's hand fluttered to her own mouth. "Yup. Right there. My friend," she said dreamily. "She bought me this." Reyna looked at her empty hand in confusion. "Wait." On the floor beside her, she spotted a candy wrapper and swatted at it. "I mean that." She waved the wrapper in Mia's face for inspection.

"You talked to her?" Carl asked.

Reyna cupped a hand by her mouth, her head rolling onto one shoulder like a rag doll's. "Who's that?" she asked Mia in an exaggerated whisper, pointing up at Carl.

"My friend. Why did she buy you candy?"

"Cos she wanted to use my phone for a teeny minute." Reyna squinted, pinching her thumb and pointer together and holding them up to Mia.

Mia waved the hand away. "Who did she call?"

"Chill *out*, Mia. You don't have to be mean." Reyna half rolled back to the wall.

"Let me in there." Iris squatted next to the girl. "Reyna, honey, who did Alex call?"

Reyna turned back and smiled. "Iris. Hi. You're so pretty." She pursed her lips. "Who's Alex?"

"The girl with the candy. Who did she call?"

"Her bestest friend in the entire world." Reyna's eyes were dreamy. "To say good-bye." After several tries, she managed to land a wobbly finger on her lips. "Shhh. It's a secret. She said I couldn't tell *anybody*." Her head fell on Iris's shoulder. "I want a best friend."

Reyna's eyes fluttered shut. Carl took advantage of Reyna's state to slip the phone from the girl's hand and flip through it. By some miracle, the device was not password-protected.

Mia tapped Reyna's face again. "Look at me, Reyna. Did Alex get on the bus?"

Reyna swooned. "I *think* so." Her eyes began to close again.

"You're sure?" Iris prompted.

"Ninety-nine point nine nine nine nine nine percent sure. Know how I know? Cos she did this." She held up two fingers in a *V.* "Peace out." She turned her hand to examine the symbol. "And then, poof, she disappeared." Reyna leaned against the trash bin again and closed her eyes.

"Looks like Alex sent a few texts," Carl said. Holding the phone out of sight, he read the first one to Mia:

```
Sorry, I can't help you anymore.
```

"God. So dramatic. What do you think it means?" Mia asked.

"Not sure. Maybe her mother will have an idea. Here's another one, to a different number."

```
Sorry to leave you, Shay-Shay; doing
something I wanted to do for a long time.
```

"Shay-Shay sounds like a nickname. Must be a close friend." Mia commented.

"I'm hoping she was referring to going to Happy Corner. That's still my guess. I'm calling the troopers to stop that bus."

Carl asked Iris if she would mind going to the counter for paper and a pencil so he could note the two phone numbers and messages. In her absence, he continued to scroll the phone's history. "There was also a recent outgoing call to somebody named Lydia," he said.

Mia looked up in surprise. "Lydia is the little girl at Hope Haven. She and Reyna are tight. I'm surprised Reyna had it together to make that call."

As Iris returned with the writing supplies, the store's welcome mat sensor bleated. Mia looked over at the door, then stood up and waved wildly. "Ellen, back here. We've got Reyna."

A tall black woman in a brown velour jogging suit hurried over, her face creased with worry, and knelt beside the sleeping girl.

"How did you know to come here?" Mia asked.

"Strangest thing," she said, rubbing the girl's cheek. "Lydia came to me and said your friend called her."

"My friend?"

"That's what she said."

Ellen said Reyna's name repeatedly, but the only response was a noxious snore. "Well, she's breathing. That's for sure." Sitting back on her heels, Ellen glanced up at Carl. "Who's this?"

Mia introduced him. "It's a long story."

Ellen got to her feet. "Lydia told me it was your friend from the living room. A girl with a pink braid."

Mia turned to Carl. "Lydia must have talked to Alex at Hope Haven. Maybe that's what Lydia was trying to tell me in the hall."

"The two apparently had quite a conversation," Ellen said. "Anyway, she told Lydia that Reyna was in trouble at the bus station and to get help. So here I am."

A snuffle rose from the floor.

"I've got to get her back to the house," Ellen said. With Carl's help, she lifted the girl to her feet, and the two haltingly guided Reyna outside to Ellen's car, with Mia and Iris following. With Reyna buckled into the backseat, Carl handed Ellen the girl's phone.

"I'll definitely be hanging on to that for a while," Ellen said, preparing to drive away.

Mia turned to Carl. "So. What do we do now?"

"We follow the bus to Colebrook." Carl hoped his interpretation of Alex's texts was correct—that she wasn't alluding to anything more dire than a fan's visit to a band's shrine.

ALEX

"Colebrook: 60 miles"

As the road sign whooshed by, Alex perched on the edge of her seat gripping her bag like a grandma, every nerve on high alert, as if she'd chugged three Red Bulls in a row, expecting at any second for the driver to summon her to the front of the bus as if she were a kid acting out on a class trip, demanding a second look at her ticket, booting her off. She had been surprised he'd even let her on at all, considering the soggy mess she was. She supposed he saw all kinds.

Once seated, she waited for a passenger to recognize her—one in particular, a gray-haired lady in thick white socks and Birkenstocks eating a smelly salad two rows up, who gave Alex the stink eye when she passed.

Alex sat frozen like that for miles, twirling her braid. Gradually, as the minutes ticked by and the driver slurped coffee from a giant thermos and riders bent over their lit screens, it dawned on her that no one on the bus gave a crap about her at all.

All anybody cared about was their own journey.

She dropped her braid and settled back into the plush seat, placing her bag beside her. For the first time since this morning, since rolling over to the shock of Camo Man's ugly brown work boots, Alex was free. In control.

Nothing would stop her—not a herd of moose (mooses?—the elusive plural distracted her) charging the highway, not a truckload of creepers, not a two-faced artist, not even that wasted girl in the bus depot. What kind of friends would dump somebody there like that, Alex had wondered. She'd told the store clerk the girl needed help, but the guy had barely looked up from his gross girlie magazine.

Reyna. That had been a bonus, being able to use her phone to contact Shana and Evan.

It had taken Alex awhile to connect the girl to Hope Haven. After all, her number one mission had been to buy a bus ticket, not do the Good Samaritan thing. In fact, had the girl's head not rolled back against the garbage can, Alex might never have noticed her necklace, a scrolly gold version of her name suspended on a chain. Very *Sex and the City*, Alex thought, although those necklaces had been over for, like, centuries in Riverport.

Reyna. Not a common name. Lydia must have said it a bazillion times between sobs, back in Hope Haven's living room, while Alex impatiently channel surfed waiting for Mia. As the little girl stared at Alex (little kids were always mesmerized by her lip ring and colored ponytail), a ginormous image of Alex's own face flashed on the flatscreen behind Lydia—not a Pic Stitched Facebook selfie, but her really, *really* rough high school ID photo, the one with the high pigtails she wore on a dare from Cass, who argued that no one would *ever* see their ID pictures after they graduated, as she collected her own pixie cut into a Pebbles-like arrangement on top of her head.

Sorry, Cass. I love you, but you definitely got that one wrong. As if her hot mess of a picture wasn't embarrassing enough, the television ticker underneath dribbled cryptic details. *(Seriously? Medium weight? How can you tell that from a picture of my head?)* If she had had more time with Reyna's phone, she would have loved to search on the #FindAlex hashtag. Maybe she was trending.

After the shock of seeing the TV coverage, she'd wanted only to get out of Hope Haven *fast* and to find her way to the bus station.

Lydia had followed her to the shelter's back porch, watching as Alex dragged open the shed door, shifting shovels and bags of fertilizer to get at Hope Haven's sad collection of bikes. She chose an ancient model with thick, mushy tires and a rusty basket and wheeled it out.

"You can't ride a bike in the snow," Lydia had said, pushing her glasses up on her nose.

"Watch me. Anyway, it's not snowing, exactly." Dropping her bag into the basket, Alex put up her hood and started down the shelter's sleet-covered driveway, slipping and sliding and leaving a herky-jerky trail in her wake.

She had convinced Lydia to keep her "borrowing" of the bike a secret by promising to look for Reyna in her travels. Later, she'd figure out a way to tell Lydia where she'd left the bicycle: behind the bus depot, wedged between an ice dispenser and a mountain of milk crates. It had done its job, getting her to a gas station, where she asked the guy in the little glass booth for directions to the bus depot. Not that she hadn't been scared shitless sometimes, the road so slick in spots she literally went sideways. Once, on an incline, the brakes failed. *This is it,* she thought, preparing to sail over the handlebars. But she hadn't; something kept her rooted on the bike seat.

Not something. Cass.

Alex had gotten off the bike then and walked with it a bit along the dark road, brittle ice cracking under her thin soles like glass. Sleet had needled her cheeks; the adrenaline began to wear off and a rawboned chill seeped in instead. To take her mind off the panic tickling the back of her neck, she had forced herself to focus on the moonlight filtering through the trees and the lacy patterns it left on the ground—until the designs began to resemble ghoulish claws.

Freaked out, Alex stared straight ahead, periodically touching her neck where Cass's scarf had been. The gas station guy had said the depot was only a little ways up the road, hadn't he? Alex sniffed; what would happen if she missed the bus? She could sleep at the bus depot, but that might be sketchy. She was starting to get hungry, too. There would be abundant food once she arrived at Happy Corner, but what if she had to wait overnight? Her only money was needed for bus fare.

She could remember being this cold and wet just once in her life: the day she waited for her mom after a soccer game. As uncomfortable as that had been, Alex knew that her mother was around the corner and that she wouldn't forget her. What were her parents doing right now? she had wondered. Did they even realize she was gone? Imagining her mother and Jack cozy at their kitchen table, Alex's throat had gone all tight.

Leaning her head on the bus window now, Alex was certain she would have given in to the tears at that moment on the icy mountain road had she not spotted the galloping neon horse on the building up ahead, beaming at her through the sleet.

MEG

In the wan light of Jacob's glove box, the cellophane packet of multicolored pills gleamed like beads from one of Alex's grade school craft kits.

"Pull over." The packet in her palm, Meg's hand shook uncontrollably.

"I can't right now. What if a trooper stops?"

"You should have thought of that before you decided to ride around with this evidence." A salty-sour swirl of wine and chicken fingers coated Meg's throat.

"Evidence? Geeze, Meg. Calm down. I'll get off at the next exit, I promise. You can get a coffee. I'll explain everything."

"How am I supposed to calm down about *this*?" She swung her palm toward him.

"You're making a big deal out of nothing. As usual."

"This is *not* nothing." Meg pressed herself against her door and faced him. "Do *not* turn this one around, Jacob. These are *your* pills. What about the ones in the basement? Are you going to lie to me again?"

Jacob worked his cheek again, the blue-gray vein pulsing. "Just let me get off the highway so we can talk."

Over the next one-point-eight miles, Meg counted the mile markers hurtling by so she wouldn't lose her mind. God help her. The pills were Jacob's, not Alex's. *It doesn't change anything. Alex still did all of those other things.*

But it did change things. This information cast Jacob's reaction in the den last Sunday in an entirely new light. If he'd only been honest and admitted the pills were his, she might have thought things through differently, discussed the situation rationally with Melissa, bookmarked Begin Again's website in her "Alex" folder for a future day.

She would have, wouldn't she?

"How long, Jacob?"

They were off the highway in an unlit weigh station, Meg incapable of waiting until the next official exit. Jacob kept glancing over his shoulder worriedly.

"We'll be in trouble if we're caught here," he said.

"If we're caught, it'll be your fault. I'm asking you. How long have you been using?"

"I'm not *using*. It's a few pills. You make it sound like I have track marks down my arm."

"Answer me."

He laced his fingers behind his neck, staring at the car ceiling. "Not that long. Just since I started with Ben."

That was a good six months, Meg calculated.

The hours and the driving were killing him, he continued. Some guys on Ben's tree crew took stuff to stay awake. "It worked for them, so I figured, what's the harm?" Jacob glanced sideways at her.

"So you were high on the job, using that equipment?" She shuddered, recalling the saw's whine in the background of this morning's conversation.

"It kept me going. You were always up my ass to get more hours."

"Don't do that, Jacob. Don't even *try* to make this my fault." She thought back to the multicolored pharmacy buried in their basement cushion. "What are you taking, exactly?"

Jacob hesitated. "Mostly Provigil."

Meg knew about the medication, having encountered a resident or two over the years dabbling with the drug to make it through grueling twenty-hour shifts. The residents crashed in the lounge after it wore off, sleeping like the dead. Meg always thought it a dangerous game, despite the drug's limited potential for abuse when people took it as directed.

Which Jacob wasn't.

Meg shook the packet at him. "There's more than Provigil here," she said.

Jacob shrugged. "The guys kinda pool their stuff." There might be Ativan (to help him sleep if the Provigil hadn't worn off), Dexadrine (a short-term fix when the Modafinil ran dry), maybe a Xanax or two to chill at home, he guessed.

Speed. Uppers. Xanax, the old faithful. Any one had a deadly potential for abuse, but taking them in tandem, in ragtag dosages, was irresponsible and dangerous. *And* addictive.

He swore there weren't any more drugs in their home; the packet stuffed in the pillow had been it.

"How could you let me think they were Alex's? How could you do that to your daughter?" Meg wanted to scream at the injustice of the deceptions: first Shana, and now Jacob, sacrificing Alex to cover their own asses.

"I didn't *do* this to Alex. I only meant to leave the pills in the basement a day or two. Until I left with Ben."

"A day or two that changed everything. If I had had any idea—"

Meg shifted in her seat to face him. "You could have told me Sunday night in the den. You let me go on and on about Alex—"

"I was planning to get rid of them. To stop taking them altogether."

Wasn't that what every addict said when they were cornered?

"Really. I was," he countered at Meg's raised eyebrow. "I . . . I don't like how they make me feel. I figured blaming it on someone at Alex's house party would be a good enough cover until I could get rid of them. If I created some doubt, you'd let it go. I never imagined you'd send her away over it."

"It wasn't *just* that. But it was the last straw. Don't you see, Jacob? You're the whole reason we're even in this car right now. Why Alex is out there somewhere right now . . ." She wiped her car window and stared out of it.

"That's bullshit, and you know it. Obviously you and Melissa set these wheels in motion a long time ago."

"Melissa didn't . . ." Meg stopped herself, unwilling to involve her sister. "It was me. I did the research. You saw how worried I was that night. And you belittled me, just to cover up your nasty habit."

"A few pills don't make it a habit. I'm not an addict."

"That's good to hear," she sniffed. "Be sure to tell your daughter that when we see her."

"Meg, no. Don't say anything to Alex. I'll take care of this on my own. I promise. Everything will be fine." Jacob's skin gleamed with perspiration.

Meg moved closer to inspect his face. "Are you on something right now?"

"No. I swear. I haven't taken anything since this morning. Go ahead. Check my eyes." He clicked on his visor light and widened his eyes. The car light was too dim for her to get a good fix on his pupils.

She thought back over the past few months: Jacob's nighttime wanderings, his irritability, the uncustomary outbursts with the kids, lack of attention to his appearance. And of course, his surprise announcement on the deck.

She'd chalked everything up to his unemployment. Had it been the drugs all along? Or had his habit propelled his business into a free fall?

Then the fight at Alex's Sweet Sixteen. "Is that why you left early that night, Jacob?"

"Left where?"

"Alex's Sweet Sixteen. Did you leave your daughter's birthday party early to get high?" Meg reached over and yanked the keys from the ignition. "Never mind. Don't even answer that. Get out. I'm driving."

"No, Meg. I'm fine. I swear." Jacob draped an arm over the steering wheel protectively. "Besides, you were drinking wine at the house."

"Half a glass, hours ago. I'm fine. Get out, Jacob." She tossed her phone at him. "You're in charge of that."

CARL

"Colebrook's a straight run north, dude. What else do you want from me?"

With that limited guidance from the disinterested store clerk and a printed bus schedule, the three headed up Route 3, Iris training high beams on the state highway, not much more than a country road at that point and all but deserted. A compact band of sleet built up under the wipers; the weather report indicated they were trailing the storm.

As best Carl could determine from the bus schedule, they were a good half hour behind the coach. Its route rambled up Route 3, with assorted stops at gas stations and even a bike shop.

While Iris drove, Carl and Mia engaged in choppy games of telephone—Carl with Alex's parents, Mia with her dad, relaying updates to and from Swiftriver—sporadically truncated by spotty cell service. Cam said the troopers had shut down operations at the general store, Mia reported. They were shifting manpower to the Colebrook lead, troopers fanning out from Hope Haven and the bus depot, with Mendham, Lopez and several units from the north assigned to track the bus. Attempts to make radio contact with the bus driver were in progress.

On the phone, Alex's mother worried about the officers confronting Alex on the bus. "She'll be terrified. They won't arrest her, will they?"

"Of course not," Carl said. Given her status as a minor and a missing person, the officials could remove her from the bus. But as far as anyone knew at this point, Alex hadn't done anything illegal.

"That drunk girl at the depot—did she actually *see* Alex get on the bus?" Meg asked.

"No," Carl admitted.

"Then did anybody *talk* to the bus driver?"

"We're trying. This storm isn't making things easy."

"So this could still turn out to be a wild goose chase?"

Carl doubted it. "Your daughter was extremely motivated to get to Happy Corner, according to this young woman with me." He shared the two texts Alex sent from Reyna's phone. He was going on the theory that Alex was letting friends know she was headed to Rainmaker, he said.

"What if your theory is wrong?" Meg had asked.

"Then we go back to the drawing board. But we're close, Mrs. Carmody. I feel it." Hanging up, he strained to see through the whorl of sleet for taillights he could tie to either the troopers or the bus. They appeared to be gaining on the storm, if the crescendo of frozen rain pelting the windshield was any indication.

"You know what doesn't make sense?" Mia mused from the backseat. "Why Alex would bend over backwards to help Reyna, but totally skip over the fact she left behind two people trapped in a car at the bottom of a hill."

Carl didn't know how to explain that, either. The omission didn't match up with Alex's actions in the traumatic moments post-crash, when she thought to leave the violet scarf as a marker. The girl he woke from a dead sleep this morning—this morning? Was that possible?— demonstrated remarkable concern for Reyna at the bus station, given her own desperate agenda.

Carl rubbed his head, wincing when he made contact with the bump. There were definitely aspects of this impetuous young teen he hadn't seen during the ride up, a generous and compassionate side. Why she would lie to Mia was perplexing. Then again, Alex was sixteen, her brain years from full development.

Suddenly, the faint whine of a siren interrupted Carl's thoughts.

Iris leaned over the steering wheel. "Folks, am I seeing things?"

ALEX

"Colebrook, coming up in about fifteen miles," the bus driver bellowed.

Inside the overheated bus, condensation clouded Alex's window. She traced a large heart, animating its exterior with lines, like legs on a caterpillar. *Very Keith Haring*, she thought, sitting back to admire her work.

See, Mia? You're not the only artist in the world.

Angered, she wiped out the entire image with her arm. To think she had put her faith in the spoiled painter with the amazing studio, who, judging from the aromatic cloud that engulfed Alex, wasn't above partaking in some serious ganja herself.

The girl's gray eyes had glittered with suspicion (or something else) while she grilled Alex at the door. Once Mia determined she wasn't an ax murderer, she let Alex into the most amazing art studio ever—all glass walls and smooth wood, a sick wood-burning stove, a pair of easels with some seriously good paintings on them, not that Alex really knew anything about art.

Alex wriggled on the bus seat. In hindsight, lying to Mia hadn't been cool. She hated when her friends did that to her. But Mia deserved it for double-crossing her, especially after Alex had sat on the floor in front of that stove and poured her heart out.

Mia had nodded sympathetically the entire time, giving Alex dry clothes and tea and granola—even handing her a folded twenty for bus fare, then offering to drive her to the bus depot.

She should have suspected something when she saw that Mia's friend's house had a name: Hope Haven. Where Alex came from, only rich people out near the country club gave their houses fancy names. There was nothing fancy about Hope Haven. She and Mia had slipped inside without even knocking. ("I spend a lot of time here," Mia had said at Alex's questioning stare.)

The bus's heat was making her sleepy. She curled up on the seat, feeling mostly satisfied with herself and with all of her actions today, and hoping Cass was, too. After all the drama, she was more than ready to be on her own for a while.

Funny, Alex mused, being on her own was kind of what her mother had been suggesting all along.

She must have dozed off, because when she next opened her eyes, the bus had slowed. *Colebrook*, she thought giddily, gathering her bag and preparing to move to the front of the bus so she would be the first to exit. That's when the grumbling of her fellow passengers began to register.

"Sorry, folks," the driver said. "Unscheduled stop. Nothing I can do about it."

Alex rubbed at her fogged window, seeing nothing but darkness. Sleet still drummed the bus roof. Would the weather mess with her plans again? The bus wheezed to a halt, and the driver threw the lever to open the door. Who could possibly be boarding the bus in the middle of nowhere? Alex wondered.

A second later, her question was answered when a uniformed officer stepped aboard, his bulky frame filling the aisle, his park ranger hat grazing the bus ceiling.

"Evening, everyone. Sorry to disturb your journey." The trooper rested his hands on his belt like a cowboy. "Everyone take your seats, please. This won't take long, if everybody cooperates."

MEG

In the passenger seat, Jacob fought sleep, his chin bobbing toward his chest until the last second when he would jerk his head back and shake it. He finally lost the battle as they crossed the border into New Hampshire, his uneven snores now punctuating the silent ride. Meg's phone slipped off his lap onto the seat.

Whatever he'd taken that morning must be wearing off, she thought, sliding her phone closer and wondering what a drug test would turn up in Jacob's system. Would the results match what he'd admitted to?

She wished she had jotted down the texts Carl had relayed to her. One had been to Shana, obviously; the other to Evan, most likely. It saddened Meg but didn't surprise her that Alex reached out to them and not to her parents during her brief window with a phone at the bus depot. Certainly if Alex had reached out to Melissa, Meg would know by now.

When her own phone finally lit up with a text, Meg grabbed it. She rested it on the wheel and attempted to read it, swaying into the empty left lane in the process. The motion roused Jacob.

"Hey, what . . . ?" He grabbed the phone.

"There's a message. Read it to me."

"Hold on. It's from Shana." He read haltingly:

OMG. ALEX TEXTED ME. SO SCARED. DON'T
KNOW WHAT SHE MEANS.

"How could Shana not know about Happy Corner?" Jacob asked once he finished reading. "They were all friends."

"Obviously not as close as we thought. This was clearly Alex and Cass's thing. Tell her she doesn't need to worry."

As Jacob texted a reply to Shana, Meg thought again of her daughter's second text. "Jacob, what was it Alex said to Evan again?"

"Something about not being able to help him anymore."

Meg rubbed her lower lip. "You know, hearing that one again, it sounds kind of final."

"It's not, Meg. It's actually good. She's just trying to shake this guy once and for all."

"I hope so."

Meg shifted into the right lane for the White Mountains turnoff, thinking of her daughter alone on a bus, wishing she could be as certain as Carl Alden and Jacob that Alex was within their reach.

CARL

The siren's wail grew louder. As the gap narrowed between their car and the cluster of taillights up ahead, Carl made out a bus parked on the shoulder, a clutch of SUVs angled beside it. Strategically placed flares framed the coach; its interior glowed softly, silhouetting some standing passengers.

"Do you see Alex?" Iris asked as she pulled over.

"What if she's not on it?" Mia asked.

Carl jumped out and jogged to the coach, its silver exterior slick with sleet. Before he reached the bus, Mia had caught up with him, matching his long strides.

ALEX

At the sight of the trooper, Alex crouched down in front of her seat, pulling her bag with her, jackhammers reactivated and pounding double time. *It's not fair.* They couldn't do this to her now, not after she'd come this far, not when she was so close to Rainmaker she could taste it.

"Just a quick search, folks. Stay right where you are. Appreciate your cooperation."

The trooper's voice was closer now. *Shit.* Squeezed into the small space, Alex wished it were possible to crawl under the seats to the front of the bus, then sneak off. But the footrest dug into her shin in this position, blocking any access. Squatting, she pulled the hood of Mia's sweatshirt over her head to disguise herself and inched closer to the aisle, leaning out just far enough to glimpse the trooper's regulation boots—massive, like monsters' hooves—a few seats away before scooting back again and throwing herself into her seat, curled toward the window and feigning sleep.

Around her, disgruntled passengers continued their complaining.

"How long's this going to take?" a man called out. "We already left Lincoln late."

"Relax, folks. We'll have you on your way in no time."

"They must be looking for that missing girl," a woman said. (The stinky salad one?)

"I heard she just walked away from those poor people," a man answered.

Alex's jaw dropped in indignation. *WTF? I did not*, she mouthed to the bus's steamy window. It took everything she had not to jump up and defend herself to her fellow passengers—to describe the slam of the moose, the sight of the unresponsive driver's head slumped over the pearl moon of air bag, the deadweight of Mom Haircut's arm dropping onto Alex's knee like a zombie's. What would they do if *they* woke up next to a woman with a lap full of glass, sleet pouring in through a jagged, gaping hole in their roof?

She doubted any of them would have had the presence of mind to grab Cass's scarf as she had. Alex was certain Cass was watching over her. It was the only explanation for the car door that miraculously opened in spite of the child locks, and for everything that came after as Alex crawled around the muddy ground behind the car paralyzed with fear, inhaling the faint odor of smoke, practically sobbing when she finally felt the bumpy Braille of tire tracks, following the path on all fours to the bottom of the hill, Cass's scarf trailing on the ground and nearly tripping her in the process.

After a few tries, Alex had given up on scaling the hill. *It would serve her parents right if they discovered her frozen body in the woods*, she thought, slipping to the bottom of the slope. *That* would be cosmic retribution.

So it could only have been Cass who yanked Alex back to her miserable reality, willing her to try again, to inch her butt up the hill, who inspired Alex to loop her scarf around the metal barrier, the shiny wrap a pomegranate kiss against infinite gray.

Had her fellow bus passengers been present in that frosted landscape, they might have understood how it had wounded Alex's soul to part with her best friend's scarf, to leave it billowing in the wind, despite the higher purpose it now served.

They would not have questioned the decision Alex made at that moment—when she glanced back at the violet marker one final time—to fulfill the promise she and Cass had made the day they struck the *Annie* set. Despite her vow after losing Cass, Alex had taken all the events of today as signs Cass wanted her to continue on the journey alone. From that point on, every slippery step along the Kancamagus, every choice made over the course of the day, moved her closer to Happy Corner.

Cass would have been proud, Alex thought, head pressed against the bus window.

The trooper's boots sounded about a seat away now. Alex took another deep breath, wishing she could inhale herself into invisibility, pulling the sweatshirt hood farther over her face.

Up front, the bus door wheezed open again.

The monster feet stopped in their tracks. "Sir, please stay back. No one is authorized to come aboard. Young lady, that means you, too." The boots clomped toward the front of the bus.

Alex strained to listen.

"We have this under control, sir. I need to ask you to wait outside."

Alex thanked the universe for the interference, which gave her time to consider other options. If she could somehow make it outside, she could slip into one of the giant luggage bins below and still get to Colebrook.

Clomp, clomp, clomp. The monster boots marched down the aisle again, now double time as another pair of feet joined the trooper's. In spite of her fear, Alex's curiosity got the better of her. Still curled in a ball, she shifted in her seat, peeking out the tiniest, tiniest bit to see the boots, sounding so close now Alex thought she could reach out and touch them.

That is, if Alex had *wanted* anything to do with the brown work boots she'd spent most of the day trying to escape—boots now so scuffed and filthy they barely resembled the polished pair that showed up unannounced in her Riverport bedroom this morning.

She might have convinced herself they belonged to another disgruntled passenger, were it not for the gratingly familiar voice booming above her head:

"With all due respect, Mendham, Alex Carmody was my responsibility. I'd like to be the one to find her."

REUNION

ALEX

Fists balled, Alex watched the bus to Colebrook ease back onto the highway without her, driving away with her dream. She blew out her lower lip in frustration. Was this her destiny, to be forever in this man's backseat, the ritual click of child locks her soundtrack? There had been a moment when she thought she might finally be free of Camo Man, when the troopers refused to let him take her. But then he started waving that paper he had, and all the adults got on the phone. The next thing Alex knew, she was back in the car with him. Evidently her parents were cool (*cool!*) with Camo Man taking her overnight.

Worse, now that her captor was a passenger, he was free to twist around and interrogate Alex for the entire ride. Right now, she didn't feel like talking to anybody—not to him, to her parents and definitely not to two-faced Mia, her backseat companion for this leg of her joyride. She shifted to face the window.

"I was so worried, Alex," Mia said. "Why did you leave? I wanted to help."

Help me right into a homeless shelter, Alex thought to herself. She didn't answer.

At the next traffic light, they rounded a jug handle and dropped back onto Route 3 South, every mile marker putting more distance between Alex and Happy Corner. She squeezed her eyes tight against the disappointment, wishing she'd just stayed in Camo Man's backseat after the accident and perished from hypothermia.

I'm so sorry, Cass. I tried. I really tried. She'd been *that* close. Mia, the guardian angel Cass placed in her path, turned out to have a set of horns buried in her black curls. To be fair, Cass was fairly new at navigating from beyond; in her place, Alex might also have been fooled. But to have bared her soul to Mia in the studio only to have the girl turn on her? It cut Alex deeply.

"You're fucked up, Mia. You know that?" she said, breaking her silence. "Did you get some sick thrill from tricking me?" Alex fought an urge to lean over and shove Mia.

Mia's eyes rounded. "I wasn't trying to trick you. I just thought Ellen would be a good person to talk to about your plan."

"You sold me out." Alex withdrew to her side of the car. "I told you how badly I needed to go. You're a liar."

"*I'm* a liar? How about you, Miss I Got Lost in the Woods Hiking?" Alex stared out the window.

"How could you not tell me about the accident? About those people trapped in the car?"

Alex twirled her braid double time. "I told the guys in the truck. They called in the accident. They were sending help. I heard them."

"That *is* true, Mia," Camo Man said.

"Why are you defending her? She left you there. That was *so* not cool."

"I don't need anyone to defend me," Alex said. "I know what I did."

"Yeah, and so do a million other people. Pretty much the entire state of New Hampshire was looking for you, and you *forgot* to tell me? No wonder your parents hired him." Mia jerked her thumb toward the front seat.

"That's *so* not fair. My mom has this crazy idea I'm some kind of pillhead, but I'm not." She faced Mia. "And what about you? You're not so innocent. Your precious studio reeked this afternoon. What was it? Sweet Trainwreck? Purple Haze?" Alex reveled in the death look Mia's mother shot her over the seat.

"You know what? I'm sorry I ever let you in." Mia crossed her arms.

"Mia, that's enough. She's just a child," Iris said.

Child? Alex's skin prickled at the word. Would a *child* have made it this far by herself today, in these conditions?

"Well, somebody should tell 'the child' what happened, Mom." Mia pulled herself toward Carl's headrest. "Go ahead, Mr. Alden. Tell her about your partner."

He stared straight ahead. "Now's not the time."

Alex sat up. "The time for what? Tell me."

"That woman in the car with you had to have surgery," Mia said, facing her. "She could have died, Alex. Maybe if you'd done something besides tying a ribbon around a tree like some lame seventies song, she'd be in better shape."

"I *did* do something. I told those guys the second I got in the truck. They swore—"

"It's all right, Alex," Camo Man said. He cleared his throat.

Was he going to *cry*? Of course, he must have had his own horrible moment of seeing his partner injured, just as Alex had. "How is she?"

"She's resting and getting her strength back after the surgery," he continued. "Her mother and little girl will be up tomorrow."

Jamie. Alex's heart tightened at the recollection of the fatherless little girl from Murphy's wallet, with her bright blue glasses, hair falling over the puppy in her lap. What if the absolute worst happened and Mom Haircut *did* die? Jamie was practically a baby, only a little older than Jack. Alex scrunched her eyes against the image of her brother beside an imagined hospital bed, their mom pale and bandaged and wrapped in a tangle of tubes, lines on the monitor beside her going horizontal. Alex would never, *ever* want Jack to go through that.

Was this her fault? Could she have done more? She couldn't bear the weight of another horrendous tragedy. Alex rewound the scene, freeze-framing the moose's drunken lurch, the dead drop of Mom Haircut's arm onto her lap. From nowhere, Alex heard herself sob. "I didn't want to leave them there. You don't know what it was like."

"I'm sure it was terrifying," said Camo Man, reaching over the seat to pat her arm. Alex noticed a nasty, swollen bruise over his eye.

"I thought I was going to die. How could this be happening again?" The images whirled and spun, like she'd applied the dream feature in iMovie. Only now it wasn't Mom Haircut's hand in her lap but Cass's finger in her face, not Camo Man slumped over the wheel but Logan, Shana whimpering beside him. Another sob escaped.

"What does she mean, 'again'?" Mia's voice sounded far away. It was joined by the even more distant sound of a phone ringing. It had to be her parents again. She couldn't talk then. Or now.

"Alex, it's your family."

"I told you. I can't. Tell my mom I'm sorry."

"It's not your mom, Alex." Camo Man held the phone over the seat. "It's your brother. Jack wants to talk to you."

MEG

With the possible exceptions of her children's wondrous births, nothing eclipsed the joy that had filled Meg when Jacob turned to her, eyes brimming, to say Alex was safe. At once, she was whole again. Somehow she'd managed to ease his truck into the shoulder and take her phone from him, its surface slick with his tears, making Carl say the words again.

Given Alex's reticence, it had been a stroke of brilliance on Melissa's part to suggest Jack call his sister, Meg thought now, soaping her face with the doll-size bar of motel soap. The siblings' conversation had been sweet, Melissa told her right after. (Of course, her sister would find a way to listen in.) Alex sounded exhausted but OK, given all she'd been through. She had not asked for her parents.

"Give her time," Melissa advised. "She loves you. You guys will get through this."

Shana had begged to talk to Alex after Jack, Melissa said. Thinking it odd Shana stuck around after confessing and then making such a scene, Meg was grateful her sister hadn't allowed it. In her soul-baring mood, Shana might have unloaded more than Alex could handle right now. There'd be time for confessions later—many sorts of confessions, Meg realized, wiping her face with a threadbare face towel.

They'd checked into the Washington Pines Motel way past midnight, Carl having ceded his reservation to them. The place was less a motel than a cluster of aging log cabins strung around a tiny fenced-in swimming pool. From the configuration of rigs edging the parking lot, Washington Pines seemed to be a favorite of truckers—and transporters, apparently.

She had wrestled with the decision to let Alex stay with Carl overnight. What must Alex have thought of that—their further abandoning her—after all she'd been through? Meg wondered as she headed into the bedroom, where an ancient heater rasped its tepid blend of nicotine and mildew. This would be one more thing to apologize for. They would have reached Alex in another hour or so of driving. But one look at Jacob in the visor light convinced her. She didn't want Alex to see her father like this, with his puffy, reddened eyes and disheveled hair. She had said as much to Jacob, which was what finally wore him down.

Even now, combing his hair in the dresser mirror, Jacob swore he was fine; Meg thought his hands trembled. Maybe she was imagining it. Would it be like this from now on—inspecting his every gesture, parsing every word out of his mouth for slurring? How many times had he walked into their home under the influence without her knowing? At least by stopping here, she could watch him, make sure he sobered up overnight.

Except that now he was threatening to go to Swiftriver tonight without her.

"I want to see her as much as you do," Meg said. "But it's better this way. You promised."

When Carl had called back with Alex safely in the car, Meg had begged to speak to her. Carl had rather awkwardly told her that Alex didn't feel like talking.

Jacob had grabbed Meg's cell. "Please. Tell her we just need to hear her voice."

A moment later, with Jacob holding the phone between them, Meg wept again at the sound of Alex's exhausted voice.

"Daddy? It's me."

"Hello, me." Jacob's signature response to the kids when they called. It usually made them smile, no matter how old they were. Alex didn't sound like she was smiling. "How are you, kiddo?"

"Tired. *Really* tired."

"I bet. Long day."

"Yeah." A long, raggedy sigh. "I just want to sleep."

"Then sleep. We're here. You know we love you, right?"

"Yup." Tangled in her yawn, it came out more like *yawp*.

"Call if you need us, Al. See you tomorrow."

Meeting Jacob's gaze now in the motel mirror, Meg pointed her hairbrush at him. "You promised," she said again.

"I didn't *promise* anything." Jacob plopped onto the twin bed by the window, sending the mattress skidding in a crackle of plastic. "You're just trying to punish me."

"That's ridiculous."

"Is it? Isn't this whole thing, sending Alex away, about sticking it to me? Making me pay for my sins, the separation? You couldn't stand the fact I finally did something for myself after all these years."

"Sorry 'all these years' were such a sacrifice for you. That we were such a burden. All that time, I thought we were building a family."

"We were. We *are*. We'll still be a family."

"You're so full of yourself, Jacob. Today wasn't about you. I wasn't even thinking—"

"Obviously."

"I was taking care of our daughter. But don't worry. Once we get home, you can go back to your trees, and your band, and your . . ."

"My what? I've told you a million times. There's no one else."

"I was going to say 'your pills.'"

Jacob's head dropped. Meg knew it was a vile, vindictive thing to say, but she couldn't help herself. She leaned against the imitation oak dresser. "I told you back in the car. Alex has enough going on without seeing you in this state."

"That's it." Jacob slapped his knees and stood. "Give me the keys, Meg. I'm going."

Meg crossed her arms, keys digging into her armpit. "If you go, I'll tell Alex everything."

"You just said how overloaded she is. I promised I'd tell her when I'm ready."

"Well, you won't have to."

He squinted, gauging her intentions. "How do you think Alex will feel about you wrongly accusing her? That you sent her up here based on a lie?"

"*Your* lie," Meg flashed.

Jacob continued to eye her. Whether it was Meg's threat or his own conscience that swayed him, she sensed him wavering. He sat back down and yanked off a muddy boot, letting it drop to the floor with a thud. "You win. Happy?" Fully dressed, he slid under the covers and turned away from her.

Meg watched him for a while from an Adirondack chair, waiting for the inevitable twitch signaling he was on the verge of sleep. When they were together, she couldn't fall asleep until she felt Jacob's half start beside her. Many times over the last few months Meg had wondered if they would ever sleep in the same room again. In her wildest dreams, she never would have imagined a circa-1970s log cabin with faux fireplace, frayed rugs and wispy-thin towels as the setting for their reunion.

"You don't have to guard me," Jacob called in the dark. "Get some sleep."

She knew she wouldn't sleep, determined as she was to keep an eye on Jacob and consumed with her own guilt. Meg realized she'd given scant thought to how she would justify the transport to Alex, how she would explain that she really *had* believed in The Birches' potential. Instead of the empowering step forward Meg had envisioned, Alex's first exposure to the White Mountains had been nothing short of a nightmare.

Meg had absolutely no idea where they would go from here.

It was chilly in the chair. Still in her scrubs, Meg slipped under the threadbare quilt on her bed. Rolling onto her back, she couldn't banish the nagging worry that, despite Carl's presence, Alex might try to flee again. Or worse. The Alex she'd sent off to New Hampshire this morning wasn't one to follow rules. What Shana told her in Alex's room tonight had helped her to understand why. Meg turned toward the other bed.

"Jacob, what if she *does* try to hurt herself?" she whispered.

"She won't. She was talking about Happy Corner. Let it go."

"I'm trying. It's hard." She couldn't let those messages go, any more than she could erase the events of the past year that had transformed their family or transport them back in time to a happier, safer place. This time last year, she was buying congratulatory bouquets for the *Annie* cast. Six months later, she was choosing a floral arrangement for Cass's service. "Jacob?"

His annoyed sigh rose in the dark. "Yeah?"

"Remember when she was born?"

A beat. "'Course. One of the best days of my life."

"Mine, too."

A crinkle of plastic signaled Jacob's shifting. "For a nurse, you sure gave me a hard time about going to the hospital."

"I just wanted to watch the end of the show."

"You were scared. Admit it."

The night Alex was born, with contractions easily fifteen minutes apart and her hospital bag parked by the front door, Meg sat on the couch, glued to *Jeopardy!*, Jacob beside her holding her hand. "Shouldn't we go now?" he asked.

"I'm good, honey. I know when to go."

When Meg bent over double for the entire commercial leading into Double Jeopardy, he had jumped up. "That's it. Let's go, Mommy." Jacob clicked off the television and pulled her gently to her feet.

Many hours later, still damp from the exertion of the birth and cradling their as-yet-unnamed daughter, Meg giggled suddenly. "I wonder who won."

"Won what?" Jacob was staring at their baby, already in love.

Meg sniffed the baby's head. "You know. Double Jeopardy."

"I think we should focus on naming our child."

"What do you think of Alexandra?" Meg snuggled the swaddled newborn. "We can call her Alex."

"For Alex *Trebek*?" Jacob joked.

"Of course not. Alexandra means 'defender of mankind.'"

"That's a lot to live up to."

"She will," Meg said, handing Alex to her father. "She's ours."

All at once, Meg shivered, despite the motel room heater's valiant cough. How much mankind had Alex defended herself against today, she wondered. "Jacob?"

More plasticky rustling. "What now?" His voice was coarse with fatigue.

"You're right. I *was* scared."

He was silent so long she assumed he had fallen asleep. She might as well try to do the same, she decided, folding the flat pillow in two when he said her name.

"What?" she asked, propping herself on her elbow.

"Remember back in the car, when you found the pills . . . ?"

"Yeah." She sat up, pillow in her lap. "What about it?"

"I lied to you, Meg."

CARL

It was nearly midnight by the time they pulled into Swiftriver, where a rosy halo of ammunition ringed the general store's porch.

"They're Cam's," Iris said. "Got them from a catalog. Lights from authentic fired shells. Go figure."

Inside, Cam had restored order, chaos from the earlier command post all but erased. With Alex steadfastly refusing to see her parents, and everyone too exhausted to argue further, Carl had accepted Iris's offer to spend the night at Swiftriver. It would be a neutral spot for the family's reunion in the morning, she said. Carl fully expected the parents to veto the arrangement, but Meg gave in surprisingly quickly.

Iris said she would make up a couch for Carl; he knew he would spend the night outside Alex's bedroom door.

After Mia led a silent Alex upstairs, Iris swabbed at Swiftriver's already spotless counter with a dish towel. Once he checked on Carolyn's condition, which hadn't changed, and alerted the motel to the reservation change, Carl found himself at loose ends. Business-wise, Begin Again had some transports pending that he should firm up. He started a call, then realized the hour and set the phone down. Anyway, he didn't have it in him at that moment to cheerlead the parents through the exercise.

Once word of this accident got out, he wasn't sure parents would even work with him.

Having checked on Alex upstairs and finding the two young women talking in Mia's room, Carl came back down and rejoined Iris, who was filling stainless-steel coffee urns for the morning. The generator's steady hum was broken by the staccato jangle of silverware poured into plastic bins, the clink of ceramic mugs being stacked three high behind the counter.

Her preparations soothed; Carl was all about rituals and order. The day had shattered him. He was beyond exhausted, on empty, emotionally and physically, numb as the frozen branches scraping the general store's windows.

He allowed himself to be distracted by the mountain landscape on the wall. In the painting, a man and woman clasped a child's hands, leading her up the mountain, its snowcapped summit a pearl smudge in the distance. The woman was unmistakably Iris, in a long skirt and black ankle boots not unlike her outfit now, bracelets stacked up each wrist. Unlike most women he encountered in these parts, Iris wasn't swathed in polar fleece. In fact, the Swiftriver storekeeper looked more like a New Yorker exiting a subway.

Iris caught him looking at the painting. "The view from Swiftriver's porch. As Mia sees it, anyway." She laughed, bangles colliding when she pushed them up her arm. "I don't know what she was thinking. I might be a city girl at heart, but I'd never dress like that for a hike."

She traced the outline of the child in the painting. "When I met her at Hope Haven, I had no idea how much she'd already been through in her young life."

"Is that why Mia ended up there?"

Iris nodded. Eyes misting, she described the night Mia's birth father, in a cocaine-fueled rage, sent her mother hurtling down the basement stairs, where she cracked her head against a cement wall. Crouched in a corner, Mia called 9-1-1, whispering into the phone, terrified he'd come after her.

The paramedics arrived too late to save the woman. The father was arrested and charged; juvenile services placed Mia at Hope Haven, where Iris often volunteered.

No wonder mother and daughter were so invested in the shelter—and why Mia was moved to take Alex there. "Mia's very lucky you were there for her."

Iris smiled and wiped her eyes. The two connected instantly, she said. "It was awful, but when we were waiting to adopt her, I prayed no family would come forward," she confessed.

"What happened to the father?"

"The man had no soul." Iris rubbed her arms, recalling the father in the courtroom in his orange prison jumpsuit, tattooed arms documenting the gruesome tale of his life. The judge put him away for life, she said. "He's never once tried to contact her. I thank God for that, at least." Her eyes went to the wall of pictures. "Painting saved Mia, you know."

"Sounds like *you* saved her."

"You're very kind. But it was actually her court-appointed therapist who suggested art therapy for Mia. To help her work through her trauma. That's when we saw how talented Mia was."

"Mia's certainly gifted," he said. "You gave her a very different life than she might have had."

Iris blushed. "And she us. We feel blessed. And Carl, your work. I imagine you've changed a few lives as well."

"Some definitely changed today." He spun his stool away from her.

"I'm sorry. I didn't mean . . ." She hung the dish towel over the neck of the faucet and came around. "What about you? Anybody special in your life?"

There was once. Iris's question touched a raw place within. When he eventually returned home, his Pearl Street apartment would be empty, as always. He struggled to make his tone neutral. "Never found someone who could put up with my schedule."

Nodding, Iris gathered her hair high over her head. "It's hard to pin your life to somebody else's dream. Look at me. I never pictured myself in a place like this." He glimpsed her slim neck before she released her hair, curls spilling over her shoulders again. She leaned on the spotless counter and sighed. "I'm about done here, Carl. Listen. Cam's been saving some good Scotch upstairs. I'm not much of a drinker, but I could use one tonight. Care to join me?"

There it was: the temptation that had taunted him all day, from his hike along the Kanc to the bar sightings in Lincoln. He licked his lips. At Trinity, singing provided the jolt, and Martin kept the ginger ale flowing, detouring congratulatory drinks sent his way. And he could always find a meeting. They were his backbone. He'd planned to hit the rooms in Woodstock tonight—another anonymous church hall, dinner with Murphy after.

All that had changed. Outside, the world was encased in a steely frost. Carl felt off-kilter. He'd lost control today—of his charge, of his partner, maybe even of his business. From the rear of the general store, the generator surged and moaned, lights flickered, then flared.

Just one. Who would blame him?

Iris disappeared upstairs. He heard heavy footsteps overhead. He made himself a deal: if Cam came back with her, he'd refuse the drink. He rubbed his face, palms cracked and scratchy against his skin. On the counter, water beaded from a pot of defrosting chili into the growing puddle beneath it.

Iris returned alone. She set the bottle in front of Carl and grabbed two crystal tumblers from her nook, peeling off price tags and wiping them on her apron. She filled each halfway and handed him one, clinking her glass against his. "To your health, Carl. And to the girl's."

And to Carolyn, he added silently. The Scotch splashed inside his glass like amber waves. He brought the tumbler to his mouth. The smoky peat mingled with malt under his nose, the tang catching in his throat. He tilted the glass, imagining the liquid spreading over his tongue like honey, the burn in his throat an old friend, the heat in his gut.

Like coming home.

ALEX

Figures Jack's first question would be about the moose, Alex thought, watching Mia make up the trundle bed in her bedroom, where the walls were papered with purple drawings of dragons and butterflies.

"You saw one, Al? Lucky," Jack had breathed when she reluctantly took Carl's phone in the car.

Then someone shushed him—Aunt Melissa?—and he moved to a new topic. Even on a normal day, her brother changed subjects so fast it was like he was flipping channels with an internal remote. "Al, don't be mad. I showed Mom your box."

The notes. Jack *so* couldn't keep a secret. She was actually surprised he'd held out this long. "It's OK, bud."

"*And* I played Dad's guitar. Mom caught me."

Better you than me. "Cool, Jack." She'd faced the car window for a shred of privacy and lowered her voice. "So, what did Mom say?"

"That she'd take my video games if I used it again."

"Not about the guitar. The notes. What did she say?"

"I don't know. Stuff. She cried a bunch. Guess what? Shana's here."

OMG. Why was Shana there?

Jack didn't know. "They talked a bunch upstairs. In your room."

"*Who* talked?"

"Mom and Shana. Now she's sleeping on the couch. I stayed up later than her." Abruptly, he sniffled. "Come home, Al. Everybody's sad. I miss you."

"Miss you, too."

"So now that you're found, you can come tomorrow, right?"

His first baseball game. Obviously, she wouldn't make it. Neither would her parents, leaving Jack with only Melissa in the stands to cheer him, not his whole family as he had asked.

"I'll try, Jack."

"Everybody says that."

"I know. It sucks." She wanted to pump Jack for more details about Shana, but her godmother chose that moment to take the phone from him.

"Here you go, Alex." Mia held out a T-shirt.

"You don't have to lend me any more of your precious stuff."

"Don't worry. It's old."

Alex took it, wadding it under her head like a pillow.

Springs creaked as Mia sat on her bed. "Listen. I've been thinking about before."

Alex stiffened. *Please don't give me any more shit. I've had enough today.*

"In the car . . . I shouldn't have said what I said. I wish you'd told me the whole story, but at least you told *someone.*" Mia crossed her legs and leaned toward Alex. "You must have totally freaked out, with a big moose coming out of nowhere."

"I did. The hole that thing made on top of the car . . ." Touching her cheek, Alex recalled the sleet spraying through the opening.

"It must have been so scary." Mia's eyes softened. "Anyway, sorry I went off on you."

Here it was again: sincerity oozing out of Mia's every pore. Could Alex trust her? She twirled her braid. "I'm sorry, too."

"Get some sleep. I heard your parents are coming at the crack of dawn." She slid under her covers.

"Wait, Mia. Is that girl from Hope Haven OK?"

Ellen was taking care of Reyna, Mia said, reaching up and switched off the light. "I hope that girl figures it out. Reyna thinks running away is the answer, but stuff always comes back ten times worse."

Alex squirmed. She'd heard the gist of what Mia was saying before: from her therapist and from her mom, angry and bleary eyed at the top of the stairs at two in the morning, pulling her fuzzy mom robe around herself. "I know you're hurting about Cass. I can't imagine what that feels like. But you need to face things. Please let us help." Alex had given her mom the finger and slammed her bedroom door. *How about you and Dad help yourself,* she had longed to yell. Didn't they have a clue how much she needed them to be a family right now?

But now, crammed on the trundle bed next to Mia, the artist's words spoke to her heart. ("Truth hurts," Cass used to say to her when they were younger and arguing over stupid stuff.) Maybe Mia was right. In Lydia's tears, in Jack's neediness, even in the serious eyes of Jamie, the girl with the puppy she had never met, Alex began to understand the miserable consequences of a bad decision.

And maybe, just maybe, Alex blaming her despair on her parents was merely an excuse to avoid facing her problems.

Alex rolled onto her back and sighed. Enough reflection for one night. "What's the deal with these pictures, anyway? Were you, like, obsessed with purple?"

Mia chuckled in the dark. "For a while. My art therapist said purple is the color of good judgment. Spiritual fulfillment."

Alex felt the hair rise up on her bare arms. Cass at work again. Was it serendipity or destiny that Cass's parting gift had been purple, too? With a stab of sadness, Alex thought of the lost reminder of happier times.

If only she could conjure a time machine and go way, way back, *before* the vodka-blurred bits, to the start of her Sweet Sixteen, when she and Cass halted at the top of the ballroom steps and shrieked with excitement, drinking it all in: the sea of tables swagged in black and white tulle, the gauzy curtains of the fortune-teller's booth a shot of fuchsia in the corner, the mirrored reflections of the disco ball (retro, but Cass had insisted) dappling floor to ceiling. Cass yanked her down the steps, and the friends circled the room, exclaiming over the photos topping each table that marked a year of Alex's life, Cass essential to many of those moments. They were whooping over year sixteen's— one of Alex, Cass and Shana blowing kisses in Alex's bedroom—when laughter at the ballroom door signaled the arrival of the first guests.

"Oh, my God," Alex squealed. "They're here. Feel my hands."

"Here. Use this." Cass handed Alex a cloth table napkin to dry her palms.

"Thanks." She blinked at her best friend. "Do I look OK?"

"Almost." Cass reached up and righted Alex's tiara. "There. Now you're perfect." She grabbed Alex's hand. "Ready for the most unforgettable night of your life, girlfriend?"

"More than ready."

They stepped onto the dance floor, Alex's crown catching the disco ball's reflection, laying lacy patterns of light on the hardwood.

"Ready for what?" Mia's voice was foggy with sleep.

Alex gasped, horrified she'd spoken aloud. "Sorry. Half-asleep."

Mia groped for the lamp. "Hey, can I ask you something? What did you mean in the car before . . . when you couldn't believe it was happening *again*?"

No. Please don't make me think about that now. "Um, no clue. I was probably, like, in shock or something."

Mia gazed at her a long moment. "OK. 'Night."

In the dark again, Alex suddenly couldn't bear the thought of going on like this for one more second. She desperately needed to talk to somebody right now—the weight of the day and the year was too heavy to bear any longer.

She turned over to face Mia's bed. "Her name was Cass," she whispered.

The lamp back on, Mia rubbed her eyes. "What?"

"Cass." Alex's voice grew stronger. "She was my best friend."

Mia sat up and wrapped herself in a purple afghan.

"I killed her," Alex sobbed. "I killed my best friend."

MEG

How was it possible to live with someone for so long and not notice the signs, the red flags? And she, a nurse. Meg turned on the bedside lamp, a ruby-colored faux hurricane lantern, and sat up to listen while Jacob came clean about his drug use, the origins of which coincided not with his association with Ben but rather with the death of his father, Walter Carmody.

His dad's passing two years ago, when the economy was still firmly entrenched in a recession, sent Jacob into a tailspin, he said. He and his dad were close, and the loss hit him hard.

Meg nodded. It had surprised her at the time that she hadn't seen Jacob shed a tear over the loss. But, then again, everyone grieved in their own way, she had told herself. When she questioned him about it, he had said he needed to be strong for his mother.

"When he died, I not only lost my dad but also my business part-ner," Jacob continued. Having had little exposure to the practical side, which Walter deftly managed until his death, Jacob found himself ill-equipped to estimate costs, manage the books, seek out new projects, especially in a recession. On his own, he vastly underquoted the small jobs he did manage to get, then scrambled to complete them, a vicious cycle that only set him back further.

"Why didn't you ask me for help?" Meg asked.

"I kept thinking things would get better. And you were already stepping up, taking on all those extra shifts," he said. "I needed to do this on my own—to know I could provide for you guys."

"This isn't 1950, Jacob. We're supposed to be a team."

"I didn't feel like a team player. I was depressed. And anxious. So I went to the doctor for something to take the edge off."

"A psychiatrist?"

"No, a regular doctor." Not their family practitioner, but a walk-in clinic, he said. "I didn't need a shrink."

Of course not; admitting that would have placed Jacob squarely on "touchy-feely" turf. But if what Jacob was telling her was true, why hadn't Meg seen any insurance claims?

"I paid for them myself. I didn't want you to worry."

You mean, you didn't want me to know. "I would have understood you were taking care of yourself. There's no shame in taking antidepressants."

He shrugged. The medication costs became more than he could manage. Around the same time the construction work had all but dried up, Ben offered him a place on the tree crew, where drugs were plentiful. From that point on, everything he'd told Meg in the car was true, Jacob said, crossing his arms. "That's the whole story, I swear."

Meg wanted to believe him. He deserved some credit for amending his story. Then again, he'd been living this whole other life, lying to her for over a year, so why should she believe him now?

There was something else, too. The timeline he'd just outlined—the dearth of construction work, Ben taking him on, Jacob's restlessness and irritability—paralleled the disintegration of their marriage. It was a perfect storm of conditions leading to Jacob's pronouncement on the deck that night.

"Is this why you wanted out of our marriage?" Meg asked. "If you were feeling so desperate, why didn't you just tell me?"

"I felt guilty. I messed up so bad, I thought you'd be better off without me."

She sighed. "Damn it, Jacob. You don't get to decide that." She got out of bed, dragging the quilt with her, and walked to the window. Amber streaked the sky over the empty swimming pool. Smoke rose from the trucks' cabs idling in the parking lot. It would be daylight in a few hours. "What are we going to tell her, Jacob?"

When she turned to him for a response, Jacob's lower lip was trembling, just as Alex's did when she was on the verge of tears, their father-daughter resemblance never stronger than at that moment.

"Last Sunday. When you told me about the school. It sounded great. I wanted to help her, Meg. I did." His voice cracked. "I love her so much."

ALEX

"She never would have been in that car if it wasn't for me," Alex finished. "I hate myself."

There. She'd said it out loud. She didn't dare look at Mia, expecting her to totally judge her. When she finally did, the artist's eyes were filled with compassion, not contempt.

"You're making yourself sick over this, Alex. That night was an accident, too. Like today. It was fate."

"Don't even say that." Alex hated that word. The palm reader had spouted a bunch of crap about fate and outside forces and protection.

"If you really feel that guilty, at least channel it by honoring your best friend's memory."

"I am. Look." Alex offered up her forearm to show Mia the tattoo she and Shana had designed: an infinity loop, sprinkled with three stars, one large and two small. "See, Cass's star is the biggest." *It definitely had been worth all the pain and headaches of getting fake IDs and months of hiding the tattoo from her parents,* she thought, running a finger around the loop.

"A tat to memorialize someone is nice, but it's only the start."

Alex yanked her arm away. Mia was right. She'd been taking small steps toward a new life. Maybe it was time for a big one. Was it possible she'd misread Cass's signs? After all, this was a new way of communicating on both sides.

Maybe Mia *was* Alex's guardian angel after all.

Then she remembered Evan. "It's too late. Everything's wrecked already." She told Mia about the older boy, the regretted favors and the message from the rest-stop bathroom—more stupid actions that couldn't be undone.

Mia rolled her eyes. "He's scum, Alex. Tell him to find himself some other mule. And your girl Shana? You might want to start fresh with a new set of friends."

Start fresh. As Mia turned out the lamp again, her advice spun in Alex's head. Somebody else who wasn't high on Shana. Alex sighed and rolled over, and under the watchful gaze of Mia's purple princesses and butterflies she slept, finally, her last waking thought the realization the night had fallen eerily quiet outside Swiftriver.

The storm was over.

She'd barely closed her eyes when someone shook her, calling her name. This could not be starting again—was this *Groundhog Day*, the nightmare edition? *I told you. I'm not going.*

"You have to, Alex."

Alex blinked at the vibrant sunlight pouring through Mia's sheer curtains, illuminating the artist like an angel.

"I've been trying to wake you up for, like, forever. There's troopers downstairs. You have to talk to them."

SATURDAY

MEG

Meg woke to the wheeze of a sixteen-wheeler's hydraulic brakes out-side their curtainless window—and the familiar weight of Jacob's arm draped over her bare stomach. Instinctively, she sucked in her gut.

Neither had intended this to happen. At some point before day-light, Jacob had slipped into her bed, Meg settling against him as if it were the most natural thing in the world, as it *had* been for sixteen-plus years, absorbing his warmth in the drafty motel room, hoping to grab an hour of sleep. Both of them had been fully clothed.

And then they weren't. Their coupling was swift, intense—born of the day's trauma and tragedy, a primal need for release—and nothing more, Meg told herself sternly. Despite their respective resentments, they remembered how to comfort one another, relying on intimate knowl-edge of each other, their shared history. Instinctively, they resumed their natural rhythms, finally dozing off in this habitual position.

What wasn't natural was the waking-up part. Holding her breath, Meg wriggled out from under his arm, so intent on not disturbing him she bumped her head on the headboard in the process. At the noise, Jacob groaned and turned over, blinking at her.

Meg yanked up the sheets to her chin in attempted modesty. "Good morning."

"Morning. Meg, that . . ."

"It's OK, Jacob." She rolled over to grab her scrubs from the floor. "You don't have to say anything."

"I was just going to say, I've missed you. Last night was nice." Yawning, he pushed himself up against the headboard. "Maybe we should just table this discussion until later."

"Of course. Alex." The coffeemaker clock barely registered six. Had it only been twenty-four hours since she sat in the van with Jack and Angel? "Do you think it's too early to go over there?"

"I don't care." Jacob stepped into his pants and boots and hugged himself, bare chested. "What happened to the heat?"

"I don't know." The radiator had given out some time after they'd fallen asleep. When it came to lodging, she and Carl Alden had vastly different standards. While Jacob used the bathroom, Meg checked in with Melissa, surprised to learn Shana had spent the night. She had been a good distraction for Jack, Melissa said.

Outside, Jacob went directly to the passenger side of his truck. Meg gazed at him over her sunglasses. Was he letting her drive to keep the peace? Or had he taken something in the bathroom? His own sunglasses masked his eyes.

When she climbed in next to him, Jacob squeezed her hand. "Let's go get our daughter."

ALEX

The troopers' backs formed a burly, steel olive wall along Swiftriver's counter. Anxious, Alex cleared her throat coming down the stairs, getting their attention.

"Miss Carmody? Sorry to disturb you so early. Just have a few questions for you about yesterday."

Now I'll get what I deserve, Alex thought, heart flip-flopping as she walked over to the counter.

The trooper snapped open a pad. "Let's start with yesterday morning." He grilled Alex on every aspect of the accident, from the hours leading up to the crash to everything after. How long had they driven without a break? Where had they stopped for lunch? Had the adults consumed any alcoholic beverages? Had she seen any weapons in the car? Had she noticed any erratic driving?

Answering, it dawned on Alex it wasn't *her* behavior they were concerned with but Camo Man's.

"Think, Miss Carmody," said the shorter one, fake smiling at her. "Did anything jump out at you?"

Alex folded her hands on her lap, cracking her knuckles. Did they not know what had happened? "Of course. A moose."

The two officers smirked.

"I swear. There *was* a moose. Did he not tell you that part?" She gestured to the bench, where Camo Man nursed a mug of coffee.

"What we meant was, did any circumstances of the accident seem *unusual* to you."

Duh. Jump out at you. Now they pegged her as a wiseass. She could see where this was going: they were trying to nail Camo Man. Alex had walked away from her driver-captor once. Now she had a chance to redeem herself. She sat up straight and flipped her braid over her shoulder.

"He didn't do anything wrong. The road was really slippery. He didn't see the—"

She stopped as the officer scribbled furiously. "Wait. What are you writing? What's going to happen to him?"

"Nothing, unless charges are filed. Let's not get ahead of ourselves." He turned the page of his pad. "OK, let's focus on those men in the truck who picked you up."

Ugh. Alex's skin crawled at the mention of them.

When she'd climbed into the truck, the cab's smoky dry heat had scorched her face like the sauna at Aunt Melissa's gym. Ignoring her parents' warnings about hitchhiking that played like a YouTube video in her brain, she settled on a scratchy blanket in the backseat and told them right away about Camo Man's car in the ravine.

"Don't forget the purple scarf on the guardrail," she'd prompted, as Chester called it in. "You can't miss it." Chester repeated her instructions. The troopers were on it, he promised. Relieved, Alex accepted the cigarette he offered, dragging on its unfiltered tip like it was the last one on earth. Kyle, the driver, was seriously quiet, but Chester made up for his silence with stories about the Kanc and missing hikers and bloody moose impaled on hoods of cars.

That last image freaked Alex out so much she almost accepted Chester's offer of a drink—something potent and caramel-y that she'd never heard of. But she needed a clear head for her journey.

"No worries," Chester said when she turned him down. "Plenty more where this came from, right, Kyle?"

Before long, they stopped for gas, dispensed from the bizarre pink gas tanks Mom Haircut noticed right before the crash. The two got out, talking and pointing to the truck occasionally, Kyle stomping away from Chester at one point.

When they got back in, something felt wrong, like they had unfinished business. Alex brushed off her uneasiness; she needed them. As Kyle pulled out onto the Kanc again, Chester's hand suddenly landed on her knee.

"About time we get to know each other a little better. You got a boyfriend?"

Alex jerked her leg away, her mouth going dry at his touch.

"Aww. You shy all of a sudden? We got a *long* ride ahead of us." He creeped her out the way he lingered on the word *long*.

That's when she knew she had to get out, destiny or no destiny. Gripping her bag, she slid toward the door, wired for the Kanc's next curve. When the truck slowed, she threw open the door and leaped out, landing sideways in icy slush.

The truck lurched to a stop. Chester hung his head out the window. "What's the matter, girl? I scare you? I was just messing with you."

Alex prepared to run, but Kyle gunned the engine and the truck disappeared around the bend. Jackhammers in full throttle, Alex crouched by the side of the Kanc until the only sound was the sleety wind whipping the evergreens—when she felt calm enough to walk back toward the gas station.

That ride had only been a brief detour, she reassured herself; she'd be more selective next time. Even without Cass's scarf, she knew her friend had her back. And besides, she still had one more good luck charm. She pulled Camo Man's plastic figure from her pocket, falling sleet brightening the reptile's scarlet stare, hinting at untold truths. Kissing its bulging cheek, Alex began her skate-walk back to Swiftriver.

"We need to know, Miss Carmody," the trooper pressed. "Did those truckers hurt you?"

Perched on the counter stool, Alex *reached* into her pocket and squeezed Rainmaker for courage. "No. Not at all. It was really stupid to hitch. So I changed my mind and jumped out."

The trooper shut his notebook. "Well, then. That's it. Looks like their story stacks up."

Alex was free to go, they said.

Faint with relief, Alex sat at the counter, picking at pancakes Mia's mother set in front of her. Her entire body felt wrung out; there was an ache in her neck that hadn't been there when she went to sleep.

Reaching for the jug of syrup, she noticed the mud-colored moose lumbering across its label: "Made in New Hampshire." The pancakes turned over in her gut, and she pushed the jug away.

Camo Man's voice came from behind her. "Alex. I almost forgot."

Something tickled her ear. Spinning to face him, she brushed silk. Purple silk.

"My scarf," she cried, grabbing hold of it. "How did you . . . ?"

"I took it last night. Your mother told me it was very special."

Thank you, Mom. "I thought it was lost forever." She pressed the fabric to her cheek, then wrapped it twice around her head. It was never coming off this time.

"Tell your friend it did some good."

If only I could.

Alex slid off the seat and pulled Chester's spare cigarette from her bag. "Just the porch. Promise. It's gonna be a long day."

She sensed Camo Man hovering on the other side of the door as she lit up, just as he had positioned himself outside Mia's room last night.

She'd almost fallen over him on the way to the bathroom. She dragged furiously on the cigarette, hurrying to finish before her parents arrived.

Swiftriver's door opened. Mia slipped out, squinting in the sunlight. She touched the scarf. "Pretty color."

"Thanks. It was Cass's." It felt surprisingly good to say her friend's name out loud. She would do it more often. Turning, Alex aimed her cigarette at the pink gas tanks in the parking lot. "So's that, by the way. *Not.* Who picked that brilliant shade?"

Mia laughed. "My mother." She fake punched Alex's arm. "See? You're not the only one with a lunatic mom. Anyway, the pigs kind of put Swiftriver on the map, you know? You can't miss them."

It was true. The fuchsia tanks with their red tongues and swishy tails had helped Alex find her way back.

Mia leaned against the porch rail. "So, reunion time, huh?"

"Yeah. Any second." Alex ground her cigarette into a sand-filled bucket by the door. "Um, I guess I should thank you."

"It's all good." Mia grinned.

Again, Alex felt the relief of confiding in someone, the dam breaking, the lightening of a burden she'd carried for so long. Her mom had been right, of course: it *did* help to talk about things sometimes, even the saddest things in the world.

"I'll be in New York for school this fall. Maybe we can hang out." Mia lowered her voice. "But don't say anything inside. My mom's not exactly chill with it yet."

"No worries. I've got enough to deal with."

"Like that, maybe?" Shading her eyes, Mia pointed to a vehicle pulling in.

Recognizing her dad's truck, Alex's shoulders slumped. "Yeah. Like that. Think you can stall them a sec?"

Mia crossed her arms. "I *guess.* What for?"

"There's one more thing I have to do."

CARL

Carl was tired of babysitting. His eyes burned from squinting at the two young women through the glass pane bordering Swiftriver's front door.

He needed a meeting. The memory of last night lingered. He was unsure how long he'd gripped the glass Iris handed him, holding it next to his heart while they chatted, anticipating the sip that would numb the ache in his head, the restlessness in his gut. Numb everything.

His hand had tightened around the whiskey, the sleet thrumming steadily on the roof overhead. The storm had heightened everything: sound and light and emotion, changing the rules somehow.

And then Iris asked about Carolyn's family.

Jimmy. All it took was the thought of his friend, the fallen hero. Saying Jimbo's name, the weakness and temptation passed, and Carl's survival instincts kicked in—an unwavering need to feel the loss and guilt and pain of the day's events rather than camouflage those emotions, no matter how wrenching. That was the only way to respect Jimmy's memory, to express his gratitude for having served beside him, for having been invited into his life, however brief it was. The only way to honor the promises he'd made in church and to be there for Carolyn and Jamie in the fullest ways possible.

Carl had sniffed the drink one more time, then set his untouched glass next to Cam's bottle and slid it toward the shopkeeper. "On second thought, Iris, I'll pass."

Skimming his head with his hand, he'd proceeded to tell Iris everything he could remember about the Murphys: their love match at the police station, their abbreviated but joy-filled marriage, the child that remained.

Not too much later, he said good-night, then took his post upstairs, wrapped in an afghan Iris gave him.

And now, in the stark sunlight of the brilliant New Hampshire morning, another family demanded his attention. Leaving Mia to tend to Alex, Carl took a seat at Swiftriver's counter, waiting for the Carmodys to retrieve their daughter.

ALEX

Shana answered on the first ring. "Girl! I thought it might be you! I've been freaking out here." After spending the night at Alex's, she was having breakfast with Jack. Alex didn't mention that her brother had already filled her in.

"Isn't it weird to be there without me?" Murmuring into Mia's phone, Alex moved away from the porch as her parents' voices floated across the parking lot.

"Not really. Jack's so sweet. I might go to his baseball game."

"He'll be glad somebody else is there to watch besides Aunt Melissa."

"Al, you OK? Your mom told me what happened."

"I'm good." She crouched down, watching her parents climb Swiftriver's steps. There wasn't much time. There was something she needed to make sure of before she could face her mother and father.

"Another accident, though. You must have been all, like, déjà vu. Was there tons of blood?"

"It was dark, Shana. It was hard to see. " She couldn't handle going over the gruesome details. "Listen, I've got to go in a sec, but by any chance did you get to the cemetery yesterday?"

"No. I was going to, but then I had this thing, and then it started raining . . ."

You said she was your friend, too. "Listen. I'm pretty sure my parents will put me on lockdown for a while after all this. Could you try to get out there and, like, keep Cass company?"

"Sure, Al. Whenever I can."

"OK, cool." She took a deep breath. "So. What's up with Evan?"

"Nothing. Good move with that text, by the way. He said he's cool with you. You should have seen him yesterday. All over Larke at school, disgusting PDAs in the hall."

"Really." Another person Mia had been right about.

"Listen, Al." Shana's voice dropped to a whisper. "I had the *best* talk with your mom in your room last night. She's so cool—she made me feel really good about everything. Like this gigantic weight lifted off my chest. Did she tell you about our conversation?"

"Nope. Haven't seen her yet." Jealous at the idea of Shana and her mom all cozy in *her* room, Alex remembered her mother's unread letter at the bottom of her bag and felt better. She lowered herself onto a log that edged some shrubbery. "Actually, Shana, how about *you* tell me what you guys talked about?"

MEG

Meg raced into Swiftriver a few steps ahead of Jacob and scanned the store, recognizing the tall man with the white Vandyke striding toward her. "Carl. Where is she?"

"She's here. Don't worry."

Meg's knees weakened, powerless against a fresh wave of panic. The door jangled, and Jacob joined them. Carl spoke before Meg could even introduce the two men.

"Mr. and Mrs. Carmody, let me just say—" he began.

"Save the apologies, Alden," Jacob said, glancing around the store. "Where's my daughter?"

A young woman with a mass of black curls approached them and smiled. "You must be Alex's parents. I'm Mia."

The artist who helped Alex, Meg realized. "Thank you for everything you did for our daughter," she said.

"It was nothing. She's great," Mia said. "She's right outside. I'll go get her."

Carl launched into another apology. "Believe me, if I had a chance to do things differently, to take a different route, I would."

Jacob stepped closer to the transporter. "I had no idea about this scheme of yours, you know that? She set up this whole thing behind my back."

Carl sighed. "That's between you and your wife. I'm just so sorry about what happened."

"I can explain, Carl. I—" Meg went silent as Swiftriver's door swung open again, and the morning sunlight silhouetted her daughter in the doorway.

"Alex," Meg whispered, woozy with relief. She stood still, steeling herself for the inevitable cold shoulder she rightly deserved. *Let her come to you in her own good time.*

She couldn't have been more stunned when Alex bolted across the store and locked her in a hug so constricting it almost knocked the breath from her. Meg sank into the embrace, drinking in Alex's perfume of cigarettes and fresh mountain air, cupping her daughter's head as she had when she was a baby, both of them weeping.

"How are you?" Meg finally murmured into Alex's hair.

"I'm fine now. I'm good." Alex tightened her grip around Meg's waist.

"Alex, I am so, so sorry. I never should have . . ."

"Mom, stop. It's OK."

"It's not, Al. You don't know . . ."

Alex pulled back and gazed at Meg, her bare face glistening. "Yes, I do, Mom. I *know* what I need to know. I'm just so fucking happy to see you." Her hand flew to her mouth. "Sorry."

"It's OK. I'm fucking happy to see you, too." Meg couldn't believe she was laughing. *And* crying. *And* that her daughter was hugging her. *Hugging* her. She pressed Alex away to drink in the sight of her. Even with the sterling lip ring, Alex looked years younger than the snarling teen she'd woken yesterday, her face scrubbed of makeup, Cass's silky purple scarf having somehow resurfaced and now wound around her daughter's head, giving Alex the colorful air of a gypsy.

"What about me?" Jacob had been standing to the side, watching them.

"Daddy." Alex flung herself onto him, then pulled her face away, touching her cheek. "You're all bristly. What's up with that?"

"Sorry. I've been in the car forever." Jacob rubbed his salt-and-pepper stubble. "You scared the crap out of us, you know?" he asked, his voice cracking.

"I'm sorry. I can't believe you both came up here. Together." Her eyes were questioning.

"We love you, Al. We had to make sure you were all right."

Meg relaxed, grateful Jacob was attempting a united front for Alex's benefit.

"I'm good." Alex pressed her face into Jacob's shoulder. "Daddy, I was so scared. I just had to get away from that car . . . I couldn't deal with it again if someone . . ."

She went quiet. Turning from him, she reached out to a table of knickknacks, picking up a silver sugar bowl and twirling it in her hands.

"What was that girl thinking, taking you out in that storm?" Jacob asked.

"Mia tried to help me, Dad. She took me someplace safe."

"A homeless shelter, I heard. Probably full of drug addicts."

Meg stared. Had Jacob actually said *drug addict*?

"Oh, my God, Dad. Forget it. You don't even know what you're talking about. Anyway, *I* was the one who left Hope Haven."

Jacob took a step toward Alex. "You're right. I'm sorry. Al, I remember you, Cass and me watching that Phibs' unveiling on TV and all. But what were you planning to do in Happy Corner once you got there?"

Alex took the tissue Meg offered and blew her nose. "It doesn't matter now."

"I guess not," he said, studying Alex's face a moment. "What matters is you're safe. Now let's get you home." He looked around. "You have a suitcase or anything?"

Carl stepped up and handed Jacob the duffel Meg had packed for Alex barely two nights ago. "The tow truck operator dropped it off this morning," he said.

Alex intercepted her bag. "Hold on. I need to tell you guys something." She paused. "I've made a decision. An adult decision that I need to share with you. Both of you." Alex glanced over her shoulder at Meg. "Don't freak out, Mom. It's all good."

Warily, Meg moved closer to her daughter.

"I've decided to stay," Alex said, her eyes shining.

"Stay here?" Jacob said. "What the . . ." He wheeled and jabbed a finger toward Mia, who had been listening quietly next to Carl. "Did *you* talk her into this?"

Mia recoiled. "Me? I have no idea what she's talking about."

"Dad, chill out. I'm not staying with Mia. I want to go to The Birches." Silence filled the room.

"Oh, Alex." Meg covered her mouth.

"That's ridiculous," Jacob said. "After everything you've been through, you just need some family time. We'll go home, grab some sleep, head out to Playland. Beat the lines for the Dragon Coaster."

"It's not even open yet. Anyway, I can't, Dad."

Jacob massaged his jaw. "OK, then. We'll go bowling. I took Jack not too long ago. Disco ball, retro music. When you bowl, the ball goes right under the stage." He reached for a handle of her bag.

"Sounds cool. But no." Alex widened her stance. "No Dragon Coaster. No bowling. Believe me, I'd love to just go home and forget everything that's happened. But if I do that, nothing will change. And I *want* things to change." She sniffed. "I know I . . . seriously messed up." She turned to Meg. "I totally hated you and Dad yesterday morning, but I kinda get why you did it."

"Alex, I didn't—" Jacob started.

"Jacob, please. Let her talk." Meg preferred to confess her role to Alex during a less confrontational moment.

"So I made up my mind. I'm doing this. I'm staying." She tugged lightly on the duffel. "Let go of my bag, Dad."

Jacob made no move to loosen his grip.

"Mom, please," Alex pleaded over her shoulder. "Tell him. You know." Leaving one hand on the duffel, she reached into her satchel with the other, retrieving a piece of paper and waving it at Meg. "I *know* you do."

Meg started at the sight of her letter, the message she never expected Alex to read.

"What's that?" Jacob's face was white with fatigue. Despite his transgressions, Meg truly regretted all she'd put him through: the deception, the stressful waits for information, the tension and anger building up mile by mile on the ride up. And now a letter he knew nothing about.

Of course, Jacob wanted to take his little girl home. It was only natural. But he had to understand there were no winners here—only a child who sorely needed their support.

"Tell him, Mom. Tell him what you wrote."

Meg took the letter from Alex. "I . . . I just told her how much we both loved her."

"Read it, Mom." Alex's voice was near breaking.

"OK, honey. If you really want me to." Head down, Meg cleared her throat a couple of times before she began reading, at a level meant only for Alex and Jacob.

> *"Dear Alex,*
> *I love you. If you remember nothing else from this letter,*
> *please know that.*
> *You probably hate me right now. I can just hear you:*
> *'Mom, you're psycho.'*

Jacob's chortle momentarily rattled Meg, but she forced herself to continue.

> *Maybe I am. But if that's what it takes to protect you, to help you, I'll fly my psycho flag proudly.*
> *I know the last year has been horrible on many levels. We have all made mistakes.*

The words blurred as Meg's eyes filled with tears.

> *We are human; we fuck up sometimes. (Yes, that's your mother dropping an F-bomb.) Know that no matter what happens with Dad and me, we'll always be here for you.*

Meg paused, acknowledging how much more loaded that statement had become since she had scrawled it two nights before.

> *I'm praying you make the most of the next few months. (Don't freak out! They will go fast, I promise.)*

She looked up and smiled at Alex.

> *The choice is yours to accept this help. Not for anybody else, but for you.*
> *For now, please take care. Because you truly are my precious cargo.*
> *Love, Mom xo"*

Allowing the letter to fall to her side, Meg clasped Alex's hand. "Listen to her, Jacob. This is excruciating for me, too. But please hear what she's saying."

Alex stared at their intertwined fingers, then laid her head on Meg's shoulder, triggering more tears on Meg's part. "Please, Daddy."

"Really, Meg? After yesterday, not knowing if we'd see her again, you're on board with this?" He crossed his arms, frowning. "Well, of course, you *would* be, since it's what you wanted from the beginning."

"You're right. I did, until yesterday. But I came here today ready to bring Alex home. Truly," Meg said.

Jacob cocked his head. "Alex, do you know what you're in for? You won't see your friends. You'll hardly see us."

"The Birches really isn't that regimented," Meg began.

Alex raised their clasped hands. "God, Dad, it's not like we do the family-bonding thing that much anyway. Mom and I fight all the time. Maybe the distance will be good for *all* of us."

"There's been too much distance already, Alex. I want to fix that."

"Dad, do you hear yourself? I'm asking for help, and you're trying to talk me out of it. Isn't that, like, messed-up parenting?"

"It's just . . . your mother sprung this whole thing on me," Jacob said. "I'm still trying to get my head around it."

"Tell me about it." A smile played at Alex's lips. Meg realized Alex suspected her all along. "I'm the one he kidnapped." She angled her head toward Carl, who, along with the shopkeepers, watched their family from a discreet distance.

Finally, Jacob let go of the duffel in surrender, the bag landing with a soft thud at Alex's feet. "If that's what you really want, Al . . ."

"It is. I swear. Will you guys take me?"

"Of course," Meg said. Wasn't that the ideal scenario Carl described the day he toured Alex's room?

Releasing Meg's hand, Alex made her way to the transporter. On the way, Mia fist-bumped her.

Observing the interaction, Meg wondered if the two girls would stay in touch or if the past twelve hours would remain some bizarre footnote in both their lives.

"Sorry I was so much trouble," Alex mumbled, standing in front of Carl.

"I'm sorry, too, Alex," Carl said. "If I could take it all back, I'd—"

"It wasn't your fault. It was an accident. You heard me say that to the troopers this morning. I'll tell them, too, in case they're mad at you." She jerked her thumb at Meg and Jacob.

"Your parents have every right to be upset."

"Not about that. Anyway, I'm gonna go to that place you were taking me to." She looked back at her parents. "Even though I'll probably hate every second. And if they tell me I can't smoke or wear my lip ring, I'll have to go on a hunger strike or something."

Meg hid a smile. *The Alex I know and love.*

"I hope it doesn't come to that," Carl said.

"And I almost forgot. I have something for you." Alex opened her palm, revealing a small plastic frog on a string.

"Rainmaker," Jacob murmured.

"You said it brought you luck, so I thought . . . Anyway, I'm sorry," Alex said. "I shouldn't have taken it."

"It's OK. You can keep it. It's done its job. You can pass it along one day."

"Cool. Like karma." The frog went into Alex's pocket. "I hope Mom Hair . . . I mean Officer Murphy . . . gets better soon."

"Me, too." Carl held out his hand. "I wish you luck, Alex Carmody. And I hope you get to Happy Corner one day. Just remember what I said yesterday."

She frowned. "Which part? You said a bunch of stuff."

Carl chuckled. "I did, didn't I? At lunch. The concerts? The Phibs' mantra?"

It took a few seconds before Alex's face flooded with understanding. "*Riiiight*. The whole 'One show at a time' thing."

One show at a time. Not a bad motto for life, Meg thought, observing her daughter's solemn nod. Meg had never embraced energies or chakras or other New Age-isms, but perhaps there had been some cosmic reason Meg had stumbled upon Begin Again's services. She never should have arranged the transport behind Alex's and Jacob's backs, but watching their exchange now, she understood that for all those hours Alex spent in the backseat of Carl Alden's car, and even for all the hours she had been missing, her daughter had been in very capable and very wise hands.

Of course, Meg didn't dare say that to Jacob. Instead, she leaned over to him now and whispered. "Figures. Phibs fan."

"I know. They're all crazy."

Alex laughed at something Carl said. "Maybe I'll see you at a show sometime."

"You never know. Look for the green balloons."

"What's he talking about?" Meg whispered.

"It's the spot where recovering addicts meet up."

Before Meg could absorb Carl's matter-of-fact admission, Jacob stepped up to the transporter.

"Hey, Alden," he started.

Meg squeezed his arm. "Not now, Jacob. We really need to go."

"I *know*, Meg." He put out his hand to the transporter. "Just . . . thanks. Thank you for bringing her back to us." The two men shook hands, then the couple moved along to the Baileys.

"We're so sorry to have disrupted your business," Meg said to Iris.

"It's nothing. Our kids are everything, aren't they?" Iris looked over at Mia, who was hugging Alex good-bye. "We're close by, if Alex needs anything."

"I appreciate that." Meg swallowed the lump in her throat.

Behind her, Jacob now had an arm around Alex, her duffel slung over his shoulder, as he herded them both toward Swiftriver's door.

Alex turned. "Mom, you coming?"

"One sec, honey." Meg waited until the two were outside. "Carl, I owe you an explanation. And an apology."

"Not necessary. Save it for your family."

"I'll take care of that, I promise. But there's one other thing."

"If it's about the money, you'll get my entire fee back."

"We can talk about that later," Meg said. She pulled out her phone. "I have another question for you."

ALEX

It's done, Alex thought, closing her eyes in the backseat. The cloud of confidence buoying her back at Swiftriver was melting into a puddle of panic. She wondered if her mother had brought more medication; she might need it at her new school. Or sooner. Evan bragged he'd gotten good and shit-faced the night before his parents dragged him off to Maine that summer. He was actually proud of the fact he couldn't remember a single detail.

This voyage, however, would be burned in her brain, Alex decided.

She glanced out the window. Maybe it wasn't too late. They could still go home. It didn't help matters that they'd soon pass the spot where Camo Man's car had skidded off the road. She looked away.

Stop. You're doing the right thing. She'd all but made up her mind last night after talking to Mia; Shana's spilling her guts had only sealed the deal. What if she hadn't called Shana today, Alex wondered angrily, nibbling a cuticle. How long would her so-called friend have kept her in the dark? It *was* time for Alex to move on—to clear out everything that didn't serve her, as Aunt Melissa liked to say. While Shana's confession certainly didn't erase all of Alex's guilt, it at least lightened the sadness on her heart to learn that she wasn't directly responsible for the accident.

Because Shana was.

Shana, who by avoiding Alex's questions and glossing over the night's details for the past nine months, had inflicted deep, unrelenting pain. And had made their friendship a total sham.

All of Shana's behaviors made sense now: the overnight Amphibian passion, the willingness to drive Alex anywhere, anytime; her oversolicitous texts. All along, Alex had the uneasy feeling Shana was trying to make up for something. Now she knew what it was.

The depth of her friend's deception had been too massive to process; Alex couldn't even recall ending their conversation outside Swiftriver. She'd stared at Mia's phone a few seconds, then remembered her mom's letter, balancing on the log to read it. By the time she got to "the choice is yours" part, she was certain what she had to do.

Rereading the letter now in the car, Alex twirled her braid. *Precious cargo*—a phrase her mother used practically since birth: clicking Alex into her car seat, reminding her from the front seat to buckle up, yelling it from the front door whenever she got in a friend's car. *So* embarrassing.

Mom Haircut had been precious cargo. So had Cass. Both had sat beside her on the days of the accidents for the same reason: to protect her.

She'd had no control over what happened to Officer Murphy, or even to Cass. Today, she could begin to hate herself less for losing the most precious cargo of all, her best friend—even without the healing hands of Happy Corner.

"Sorry, Cass," Alex whispered, shoving the letter back in her bag, alongside the crumpled Swiftriver food check with Mia's scrawled cell phone number—a lifeline to get her through the next few months. Suddenly she remembered her own cell, stuffed in Mom Haircut's pocketbook. It might take some time to reunite with it. Then again, maybe it wouldn't be the worst thing in the world to be off the grid for a little while. She'd managed OK for the last twenty-four hours, hadn't she?

"What sounds good, Al?" Her mom beamed her Nurse Meg face at Alex in the rearview mirror. She was driving to give her dad a break, she had said when she hopped in the driver's seat back at Swiftriver. Right now her mother oozed with goodwill, scanning radio stations and stopping at each for Alex's opinion.

"I don't care. You pick." Alex was perfectly content to chill.

"Interstate's coming up, Meg," her dad said, straightening up. "If you don't get over now, you won't make the exit."

Her mother made no move to change lanes. "We're already a day late. The school can wait a few more hours. Right, Alex?" Her mother beamed again in the mirror, sailing right by the exit.

"What?" Alex sat up and stared out the window as the exit receded. She didn't know where the school was, but now that she'd made her mind up to go, she'd just as soon get there. She mimed a smile; maybe there was another nearby spot from her childhood her mother wanted to show her.

"If you're thinking about stopping for food, Iris gave us enough to feed an army." Her father held up the care package Mia's mom pressed upon them when they left Swiftriver.

"I was thinking more like, food for the *soul.*"

"If this is another crazy scheme," her dad began.

"Trust me. It's not crazy."

"Just tell us, Meg," her dad said. "I'm kind of over surprises at this point."

"Stop *raining* on my parade. I promise. It'll be worth the wait."

ALEX

Happy Corner, New Hampshire

Staring up at Rainmaker's magnificence, Alex had no words. Nothing—not Camo Man's souvenir tree frog, not her bedroom poster, not even the videos playing on the Phibs' giant concert screen—had done it justice. Camo Man was right: You had to see Rainmaker in person. It was the only way to truly appreciate the immense brass frog with glittering garnet eyes the size of bowling balls bulging over rounded cheeks, its webbed feet clinging to a cement base the size of a small car.

The statue was so massive, its brassiness so blinding, that its disciples had to circle it a few times in order to absorb the monument's full impact and receive the supersize amphibian's rumored luck and blessings.

Even after she and her dad completed their circuit, Alex struggled to speak. "I . . . I can't believe we're here."

"Me, neither. I'm so happy to be here with you. We can thank your mother for that." Behind them, her mom hadn't stopped smiling since she ended the guessing game, waving her phone with the directions she'd gotten from Carl.

Her mom stepped up to the statue now and rubbed Rainmaker's flank. "So this is what I've been missing all these years." Around them, other Phibs disciples hovered, drinking in the powers associated with the golden tree frog: fertility, wealth and most of all, tons of rain—the part Camo Man had droned on about at lunch. But today, without Cass beside her, there was only one Rainmaker blessing that mattered to Alex: the idol's promise of a happy afterlife, an ancient belief about golden tree frogs held by some Indian tribe. Cass had shared it with her.

That was Alex's prayer today for her friend—peace and contentment for infinity. Gazing past Rainmaker's golden reflection at the blue expanse beyond, Alex felt in her bones that her intention had been heard. "We made it, Cass," she mouthed.

She was ready to move forward.

Feeling happier than she had in months, Alex called to her parents, eager to explore the rest of Happy Corner in the hour limit they'd set for the visit. The three strode across the square to the edge of a massive field that stretched out as far as she could see. Squinting, Alex made out dozens of white tents pitched around a red barn—the barn that housed the school, she realized giddily, recalling pictures Cass had unearthed. From this angle, set against the cloudless sky, Happy Corner resembled a magical kingdom.

"Faster, guys," she urged.

"Relax, Al. This place isn't going anywhere," her mom said.

But I am. She skipped ahead, pausing at the first row of tents, where all the flaps were closed. Alex hesitated, unsure how to summon the Happy Corner residents. Should she knock, yell, ring a bell, maybe? Up close, the tents were stained and dirty; the one in front of her had holes in it the size of her fist. She stuck a hand through one. The flap lifted suddenly and a little boy sprinted by her, wearing nothing but a diaper.

"Sage, get back in here," a female voice called from within. "Sahara, go get your brother, will you?" A girl about twelve, also barefoot, long hair flying, dashed after the toddler, tackling the boy and bringing him back, both of them slipping into the tent. Inside, Alex heard the mother berate her son.

A second later, the flap lifted again and a woman stepped out. "Can I help you?"

Alex stepped back at her unfriendly tone. Her hair was long like her daughter's, but greasy and streaked with gray. Grass stains smudged her long, shapeless dress; the toes peeking out beneath it were caked with mud.

"We're just visiting," Alex said. "I've always wanted to come here. It's, like, a legend." By now, her parents had caught up.

"Legend, huh? They with you?"

When Alex nodded, the woman grudgingly said they could have a look around, as long as they didn't touch anything. "You wouldn't believe what those groupies think they're entitled to," she said.

Alex glanced back at Rainmaker. The tree frog looked much smaller from this perspective. "What time are you guys going to dance?"

The woman frowned. "Dance?"

"You know. The ceremonial dances around Rainmaker?"

She laughed. "We haven't done that in years. You're welcome to dance yourself, if you want. There's always some tourists who do."

"That's OK. I'll pass. Would it be cool if we peeked at the school?"

"Go ahead, but there's not much happening on a Saturday. Most of the bigger kids take a bus to the town school now anyway."

"But what about the homeschooling? The one-room schoolhouse where everyone learns together?" Alex asked.

"State shut us down. The kids weren't doing too well on the standardized tests."

Behind Alex, her mom cleared her throat. "What *is* open, then? We came all this way."

"What about the gardens? Or the fields? Could we sample some of Happy Corner's homemade products?" Alex asked.

"Outsourced. Too much feuding over profits. Anyway, there wasn't much to sell this year. Our crops caught some kind of bug last season. We're giving the fields a rest."

Alex twirled her braid. "So if there's no dancing and no school and no garden," she said slowly, "then what exactly do people do at Happy Corner?"

The woman scratched her head. "Frankly, honey, I wait for the mail, and my check—try to figure out a way to get by with my kids."

Alex felt her dad's hand on her shoulder. She gazed down the row of tents. "What about all the others?" she asked.

"Empty. Summer people, mostly. We rent them out. College kids, city hipsters coming up to camp. It's cheaper than a hotel," she said with a shrug. "We added Wi-Fi in the barn. They wouldn't come otherwise."

"But the concerts. They must come for the music."

Again, the woman's face went blank as stone.

"The band. Amphibian," Alex prompted. "I saw them playing here in a video."

"They played once, back in the day." She crossed her arms and stared out into the field. "They always say they'll come back, but the town wasn't too happy the last time. Said they ruined the roads and the septic." The little boy came out again, wrapping himself around his mother's leg. "Anyway, the band doesn't bother with this little place. They like the bigger venues now. Big festivals. Stagecoach or something?"

"Coachella," Alex corrected.

"Whatever. Although they let us sell CDs. I've got some inside. You want to see?" She held open the tent flap, and Alex peered inside. Sleeping bags were spread on bare ground; the young girl lay on one of them. Seeing Alex, she sat up and hugged her knees. Alex stepped back outside, feeling like an intruder.

"You know, I'm good—iTunes, you know?"

"Fine." The tent flap dropped as quickly as it had opened, leaving Alex and her parents alone in the field.

Alex's mom squeezed her shoulder.

"I think we can go now," Alex whispered.

She was silent on the walk back, kicking a stone across the field. Happy Corner was nothing like they had envisioned. In fact, if you didn't count Rainmaker, Happy Corner was downright miserable. How could she and Cass ever have imagined a life here?

Her dad caught up to her. "This place must have really been something in its day."

"It's not fair, Dad. I was so sure I'd fit right in. That it would be perfect."

Her mother turned to look back at the tent colony. "Is anything ever really perfect, Al? Anyway, Sahara? Sage? If you wanted to stay here, you'd have to do something about your name."

Alex twirled her braid again. "I did kind of pick one out."

She had to give her parents props. Neither cracked a smile when she told them.

They were almost back to the statue. It was time to say good-bye to Rainmaker. Alex reached up and slowly unwound Cass's scarf, grateful once again it had found its way back to her after the storm. She felt as though the sleet and ice of that journey washed away all its bad karma, just as the rain melted the hardened nests of golden tree frogs.

See, Camo Man. I was listening.

Walking around to the bronze plaque under Rainmaker's four-toed feet, Alex dropped Cass's scarf onto the communal pile of flowers, candles and other offerings. "Be happy, my friend," she whispered.

Placing her hand on the statue, Alex willed its warmth and energy to soak through her skin so she could begin to embrace the universe's faith in her own potential.

Cass would want that.

"Hey, Indigo Wren, how about a picture?" her mom called from the other side of Rainmaker.

"Let's get someone to take the three of us," said her dad.

"It's called a selfie, Jacob." Her mom maneuvered her phone to position them both in the picture. "OK, got it. Come here, Alex. There's room for you now."

She watched her parents touch heads and smile, so unlike their last family photo. She wanted to remember them just the way they were at that moment.

"You guys go ahead," she called. "I'm good."

She really *was* good, she realized, better than she'd been in ages. Her fingers curled around Camo Man's frog—all the Rainmaker she would need from this point forward.

SEPTEMBER 2012

CARL

Carl reviewed the provisions in his trunk, which now included an over-size spotlight and a portable defibrillator. He was debating whether he had time to catch a meeting at the Seaport before getting on the road when a trill of feminine laughter wafted down his block.

"Don't treat me like some sort of bumpkin, honey. I lived here, remember?"

"I *know*, Mom. You keep reminding me."

He knew their voices instantly: Iris and Mia, strolling arm in arm down Pearl Street toward him.

"Carl Alden. My goodness. What are the chances?" Iris raised her sunglasses.

"Small world, I guess."

"Mia's in school here now," Iris said. "I had to come down and check on her."

Mia surprised him by stepping up and hugging him. "It's good to see you, Mr. Alden."

"You, too, Mia. How's the painting going?"

"Not bad."

"My daughter's being very modest," Iris said. "From the work she showed me this weekend, New York is clearly her new muse."

"Mom. Please stop." Mia squirmed at her mother's praise.

Of course New York would inspire the girl—*especially this time of year,* Carl thought. Manhattan trees toasted cinnamon and amber against cerulean skies; glass towers glittering like diamonds, mirroring it all; secret green pockets softening steel and concrete.

It was a magical place to find oneself—or lose oneself, if life required that.

Out of politeness, he invited them inside for a cold drink, which they refused.

"We have a brunch reservation," Mia said quickly.

Iris gestured to the packed car. "Looks like you're headed out as well. Where to this time?" She smiled, her eyes warm with interest.

"Pickup in Connecticut, outside Hartford." This transport was a seventeen-year-old male, heroin addict. In recent weeks, Carl had broken in a new partner—Josh, a twenty-eight-year-old probation officer. The single ex-football player was physically strong and emotionally nimble, with no ties. He bonded well with the boys; Carl was accepting only male transports for the moment.

Carolyn was making great strides, he said when Iris asked after her. His partner insisted she'd be back to work within the month, although Carl knew her mother and daughter took issue with that.

"How's her little girl? Jamie, wasn't it?" Mia asked. Since her mother's injury, Carl had begun to visit Jamie regularly, he said, taking her to minigolf, Coney Island. Kid stuff, keeping it light. Jamie had even invited him to her karate competition, and he rearranged his schedule to be there.

And though he didn't share this with the women, when the time was right, he planned to tell Carolyn about the account he'd set up for her daughter, in Jimbo's memory. Perhaps even broach the idea of the art therapy that had been such a tonic for the young Mia.

Iris raised a hand to shield the sun, her bangles lining up neatly at her elbow. "I see your forehead healed nicely."

"Not even a scar."

Mia checked her phone. "Sorry, Mom, but I don't know how long they'll hold our table on a Sunday."

"Go ahead and let them know we're here." Iris gave Mia a gentle push. "I'm right behind you. Promise."

"Nice seeing you, Mr. Alden." Wiggling her fingers at him, Mia turned and bolted across the street as the light changed.

"She looks wonderful." Carl leaned against the trunk, genuinely pleased at seeing the shopkeeper again.

"She's a little annoyed with me," Iris said. "I told her I'm closing my nook—you know, those trinkets I sell at Swiftriver? Her dad and I have been talking about some changes." Iris looked down at the sidewalk.

"Anyway, Mia said it would be like Washington Square Park without the arch, or some such thing." Iris threw back her head and chuckled. "So theatrical. Can you imagine?"

"I'm sure the store holds fond memories for her."

"We're talking about some old junk in a general store, not a national monument." Iris adjusted her sunglasses. "I told her to focus on school, and her dad and I would figure out the rest."

"She'll adjust. Just as you've adjusted to her being in New York."

"I'm still working on that. I couldn't bear to watch Cam pack up her studio. But now that she's here, and I'm here . . ." Iris sniffed the air appreciatively. "I've just missed New York so much—especially the fall. Something about the light, you know?" Her face grew serious again. "Anyway, I sent Mia ahead so I could ask how you're doing." She pointed to the loaded car. "I guess everything worked out with the business?"

"More or less." He had taken some time off after New Hampshire to regroup, he said. The publicity from the accident had been minimal.

If anything, calls to Begin Again had increased. From the easing recession was emerging a whole population of parents needing his help, apparently.

Iris hesitated. "About New Hampshire. I don't know if you're in touch at all, but Alex is doing well. She's still at The Birches."

"I'm glad to hear that. I wish her the best."

Alex's decision to go on to The Birches had surprised and cheered him. He knew the bright girl would succeed there. Her parents had settled amicably with him in the end. There'd been one angry, incoherent call from Jacob Carmody late one night after Carl returned their money. Carl had been certain he was under the influence.

At any rate, the book on the Carmody transport was closed, all parties (including the New Hampshire authorities) accepting the events that transpired on the Kancamagus that afternoon as a tragic accident, an uncontrollable combination of elements and circumstance.

It was what Iris had tried to convince him of that night at Swiftriver, what his sponsor kept telling him. Carl was working to make peace with it himself, a day at a time. Some days, it was an hour at a time.

Getting back to Trinity had helped. Accustomed to his comings and goings, Martin didn't even ask Carl where he'd been for the last few months—just dropped a stirrer in an extra-tall ginger ale and set it in front of him at Trinity's bar. On his first few visits back, Carl shrugged off DJ Ken when he motioned him to the stage. He wasn't ready yet; things were still too raw. But in recent weeks, Carl had been polishing a new number, a slower, more reflective song with a refrain that haunted him during the long, solitary ride home from New Hampshire, after visiting Carolyn.

He remounted Trinity's stage one Thursday in August. DJ Ken released the first strains, obligingly slowing it down a little for Carl. The customers leaned back on barstools as he began to sing:

Fork ahead, that's my daily bread, ride the shoulder if you dare;
Some folks fear the detours but my ride's no worse for wear.
Four walls is nice, count my blessings twice, but what's the
point if I'm alone.
We never know where roads may lead; what heart will call
you home.
Happy Corner, Happy Corner. You soothe my soul, you paint
my sky . . .
Happy Corner, Happy Corner . . .

Looking out into the half-filled bar, Carl had felt the pull of the many roads ahead of him.

Like the Connecticut itinerary beckoning today. A passing taxi horn blared. Distracted, Carl and Iris both spoke at once.

"I really have to get on the road."

"I should meet Mia."

They laughed. Carl lifted his hat and rubbed his head. He was overdue for a haircut; the smooth hair felt foreign under his hand. "If you're in the city again, I'd love to buy you both dinner. For all your help last spring." He drew a business card from his wallet and handed it to Iris.

"I'll be back. That's for certain." She examined Carl's card. "Funny. All those hours we spent together, and I never did ask the name of your business. Begin Again. How appropriate." She slid the card into a pocket. "Be well, Carl Alden. I wish you safe travels."

With a quick clasp of hands, Iris was gone.

Inexplicably, her departure pained him. Leaning against his car, Carl watched Iris walk down the block, *his* block—past the bodega, the new nail salon, Trinity. Slamming the trunk shut, he felt again the longing to share his neighborhood, his life, with someone.

In his pocket, Carl's BlackBerry buzzed. He ignored it, letting it go to voice mail, and watched Iris Bailey disappear into the shimmering city afternoon.

OCTOBER 2012

MEG

Sitting beside Alex on her twin cot in The Birches dorm room, Meg stroked her daughter's braid, now an electric blue. They had just come from watching the regular Saturday night movie in the school's community room.

Alex grinned. "Relax, Mom. It's not permanent."

"Of course not. Not like a *tattoo* or anything."

"It's pretty, isn't it?" Alex offered her forearm. "Come on, Mom," she said when Meg didn't answer. "We could have gone *way* bigger."

"That's true." Meg scooted closer to examine the design.

"You see this spiral? It's infinity. It means Cass and me go on forever. For eternity."

Meg swallowed. Eternity was a very long time. Apparently Shana had ink to match. She didn't even *want* to know how two underage girls had managed to get themselves tattooed. "It's beautiful, Alex."

"Don't worry. It's all good karma." Alex's eyes were clear and honest. "It makes me feel like Cass is always with me."

Strangely, that same sensation had washed over Meg on her last cemetery visit. She faithfully visited Cass's grave each week, something

Alex had asked of her when they dropped her at The Birches. "I can't count on Shana to go, Mom. You have to do this for me."

That good-bye at Alex's initial drop-off had been too emotional for Meg to compound it by sharing Shana's confession with her daughter. But over the weeks at The Birches, Alex had let her know, in bits and pieces, that Shana had told her everything.

These days, Alex barely mentioned Shana. She was slowly making new friends at the school and was even thinking about joining an improv group, she told Meg on her last visit. There was a newfound buoyancy in her daughter's demeanor, a light in her eyes and in her laugh. The Birches was working its magic, just as Meg had hoped it would. Time could heal.

Meg hadn't done anything with Shana's confession. Perhaps there was a legal or moral duty there somewhere, but right or wrong, Meg's focus was her family.

She was doing her best to focus on things in life that she *could* control, a strategy she picked up from her Family Together meetings. After a few weeks back home with Jacob, she resurrected Ruthann's card and located a meeting a few towns away, having zero desire to bump into her coworker at the Riverport Presbyterian chapter. Meg did nothing but listen the first night—and the second and the third. Two messages came through loud and clear. One: despite myriad factors driving a loved one's substance abuse, the fallout rarely varied—ravaged families, blame and self-doubt, a vast, deep well of despair. And two: since there was precious little a person could do about someone else's choices, the shortest route to sanity was simply taking care of oneself.

It was that basic—and that daunting. Meg drew a bizarre comfort from the group members' common terrain. They were in the trenches together. Maybe one night she'd find the courage to speak.

Things on the home front were complicated. Meg and Jacob resumed their separate living arrangements, without a word about what happened between them that night at the Washington Pines motel.

There were superficial bright spots: Jacob occasionally reprising his culinary adventures with Jack, putting out more feelers for construction work, getting a haircut.

On the other hand, Jacob had not yet come clean with Alex about the pills as he had promised, always pushing off his confession until his next visit. Meg could imagine how hard that admission would be for him, but his procrastination fueled her suspicions he was still using.

Her accusations put him on the defensive. He was handling it his own way, was all he'd say. Meg only knew that if Jacob *was* using, he could no longer remain in the house. Melissa had offered to put up Jack and Meg so they could rent out their house, if it came to that. Meg hoped it wouldn't.

In any case, she would make no moves without telling Jacob first. That much she had learned.

All of a sudden, Alex jumped off the bed. "Mom. Wait till you see what Dad sent me." She thrust a brochure in Meg's face. "It's from the University of Miami. It's a state school, so it's way cheaper. Dad said they have a junior year exchange with *Hawaii*." Alex's voice leaped up at the end, her hips rotating in an approximation of a hula.

Meg grinned and said nothing. There was time enough to figure out the college thing, and it was just so delightful to see her daughter smile. Alex had been doing that a lot lately, appearing more relaxed and happy than she'd been in ages. You couldn't ask for a more supportive environment. Most of The Birches faculty lived right on the grounds. After a late-night raid on the dorm's vending machines, Meg returned to the motel recommended by The Birches. (Washington Pines did not appear on the school's list, she had noted.)

The next day, she was back at The Birches in time for brunch. After, the two strolled the lush grounds, needing only sweaters, even on this Columbus Day weekend, stopping to sip bottled water in a gazebo near the administration building. Overhead, Meg noticed a bird's nest tucked in its rafters. She couldn't imagine how it hadn't tumbled off the narrow beams by now. *Mother Nature was nothing if not determined,* she thought. She slapped Alex's knee playfully. "So . . . what do you want to do this afternoon?"

With permission to take Alex off the grounds for a few hours, Meg hoped she would suggest shopping or a movie, but all Alex wanted to do was go back to Swiftriver.

"Mia's home on fall break. She said to come by."

Meg toyed with her bangs. The young woman had been immensely helpful, but she wasn't sure she wanted to encourage the friendship.

But Alex insisted they go. Resigned, Meg signed Alex out. They drove out of the school gates, radio blasting hip-hop, Alex's new obsession, her daughter's Teva-clad feet scraping the dashboard. Meg resisted the urge to correct her. *Talk to them like they're someone else's kid,* the school counselors suggested in a parents-only workshop. Even though Meg was reasonably certain she would tell somebody else's kid to put their feet down, she kept quiet.

Driving along the Kanc, Meg didn't ask if they passed the scene of the accident.

After a bit, Alex shouted excitedly. "There they are. The pig tanks." She directed Meg into Swiftriver's parking lot, past a pair of stomach-churning pink gas pumps, leaving Meg to wonder how she could have missed the whimsical landmarks last spring.

Inside, Iris smiled in welcome, throwing her arm around Alex. Apparently the shopkeeper made a point of visiting her daughter some weekends. "Mia's down in the studio with her dad, Al. You know the way."

Alex flew out the back door, Swiftriver's screen door flapping behind her.

Alone with Iris, Meg felt uncomfortable. The two had barely been introduced in April. To cover her awkwardness, she moved toward an antiques-covered table. "You have some beautiful things here," she said, stroking the teapot of a silver tea set.

"I'll give you a good price. I'm cleaning things out."

Meg smiled. "Thanks. I'll think about it."

They sat at the store counter, sipping seltzer Iris offered. Meg was hearing all about Mia's move to Manhattan when the two girls returned to the store, Mia bubbling over with stories about her new life in the city.

"Can you tell how much she misses us?" Iris deadpanned.

"Stop, Mom. We have a plan, remember?" Mia ticked off the itinerary for Iris's December visit: a stroll on the High Line, Chelsea Market, a new modern hotel nearby with an ice-skating rink outside. "Oh, Mom, did you tell Alex's mom who we—"

"Nope. No need." Iris refilled Meg's glass. "Two months in New York and she's the guide now. Mia, what was that new Asian fusion place you liked?"

Listening to the easy banter flowing between mother and daughter, Meg couldn't help but feel a little jealous. Would she and Alex ever get to that place? To her daughter's credit, Alex's time in New Hampshire was such a leap—progress she might not have made without Mia's help. Meg turned to the young woman. "You know, we're not far from Manhattan," Meg heard herself saying. "If you ever need a home-cooked meal while you're at school, I can come get you, or you could take the train and . . ."

"Home-cooked meal? You, Mom?" Alex teased.

"You know what I mean. A break from the city."

Mia smiled. "I'd love that, Mrs. Carmody."

"Please. Call me Meg."

"Watch out. Jack will drive you crazy," Alex warned.

"I spent an entire day with *you*, remember? Jack should be a piece of cake."

At the mention of her son, Meg stood and checked her watch. "I've got to get you back, honey. I promised your brother I'd be home before he goes to bed."

It would be a beat-the-clock ride back to Riverport, but Meg was trying to keep her promises to Jack these days.

There were more thanks and hugs all around. Meg and Alex were almost to the car when Alex stopped. "One sec, Mom. BRB." She ran back inside, returning with a crumpled paper bag.

"What's that?" Meg leaned over, sniffing unobtrusively.

"Crack, Mom."

"Ohhhh." Meg struggled for nonchalance. "Enough for the whole dorm?"

"Chill, Mom, it's nothing. Just snacks." Alex shoved the bag down by her door.

Meg's stomach lurched. Was Alex's joke a screen to cover Mia giving her something to take back to school? Using at The Birches would get Alex kicked out. Her daughter seemed too happy there to risk that. Then again, she was barely seventeen. Meg snuck a sideways glance. The bag was too bulky for pills; it must be wine, then. Or hard alcohol. Meg's mind raced with the possibilities.

Beside her, Alex chattered about meeting Mia in New York one day. "She said I could stay in the dorm with her, Mom. That would be sick."

Sick, all right: fake IDs, staying out 'til all hours, Alex locked in a cell with common street criminals and drug dealers in a filthy city police precinct.

Stop, stop, STOP. Meg slammed the brakes on her runaway thoughts. She had to leave things up to Alex now. *And* to Jacob. Allow them to experience the natural consequences of their actions. There was little point in worrying about things that might never happen. She and Alex had just had a lovely day together, and Meg was determined to enjoy its remaining moments. The thought of saying good-bye summoned a lump to Meg's throat.

At her dorm entrance, Alex thrust the bag at Meg. "This is for you."

"Snacks? For me?"

"They're not snacks, Mom. Open it."

Meg unrolled the bag; inside was a silver sugar bowl, part of the set she admired back at Swiftriver. "Honey, that's so sweet." She held Iris's bowl up in the fading afternoon sun filtering through the overhead pines.

Alex beamed. "Do you like it? I saw it the day you picked me up. I bought it out of my school allowance. Which kinda means, *you* bought it? Anyway, Iris is putting the other pieces aside for me."

"It's lovely." Meg tilted her head. "But why . . . ?"

"I know you have Grandma's tea set. But after the house party . . . well, I know it got messed up. I thought maybe this could be the start of our special set." Her eyes glowing against golden skin, a testament to The Birches' healthy living, Alex permitted Meg to hug her.

"I love it, honey. I really do." Meg sniffed. "And now I have to go."

"Please, Mom. Don't cry." Alex rubbed her mother's arm. "I'll get you the rest. I promise."

"You know what, Al? I believe you will." Meg tugged Alex's cobalt braid. "I love you."

"Love you, too."

It was a phrase Alex and her friends exchanged carelessly, a stock sign-off, yet hearing it again from her daughter made Meg's tears flow, despite Alex's objections.

"And make sure Dad comes next time."

"I'll do my very best, honey."

As she navigated the school's rocky winding drive, Alex's wave receding in the rearview mirror, Meg acknowledged that her best was all she *could* do—and all anybody should expect.

Turning onto the Kancamagus, Meg readjusted the mirror and focused on the winding road ahead. There was no longer a need for the GPS. She knew her way home by heart.

ACKNOWLEDGMENTS

I am indebted to the following individuals for their contributions during the writing of this story:

My instructors and fellow fiction writers at Gotham Writers Workshop in New York for kick-starting this journey;

The Book Doctors, Arielle Eckstut and David Henry Sterry, whose Pitchapalooza award propelled me to write this story;

My beloved book club, for coming out of retirement expressly to read my novel: Angela Flarity, Susan Kuper, Lisa Muir, Patty Nolan, Ginny Stewart and Nancy Swanson. Your heartfelt support around my dining room table reminded me our book club always was as much about friendship as it was about literature;

My cadre of early readers, whose thoughtful feedback added dimension to these characters, including: Deborah Albury, Karen Cassano, Mita Chatterjee, Jennifer Clark, Teresa Cooper-Kislik, Maurice Donovan, Molly Donovan, Ellen Easton, Judi Feldman, Denise Harkness, Lori Hartman, Barbara Lyons, Mary McNeill, Deirdre McGuinness, Cheryl Miller, Jenifer Morack, Austin O'Malley and Lisa Vlkovic;

Sherry Anderson of USA Guides for insight into the transporter experience;

My agent, Elisabeth Weed of The Book Group, for nurturing this manuscript and finding the ultimate home for *Deliver Her*;

My editors: Susan Breen for her astute early evaluation, and Marianna Baer for her keen-eyed final review and judicious suggestions. Both made this book better;

Danielle Marshall, Gabriella Dumpit and the entire Lake Union Publishing team for making my first publishing experience so seamless and enjoyable;

My parents, who had faith I'd eventually get around to doing this, and my extended Irish family for their encouragement and support;

My daughters, Molly and Nora, whose souls and individuality inspire me every day;

And finally, to Maurice, whose bottomless love and encouragement empower me to indulge my passion and navigate all of life's journeys. This *word picture* is for you.

ABOUT THE AUTHOR

Photo © 2015 Benjamin Russell

Patricia Perry Donovan is a journalist who writes about health care. Her fiction has appeared in *Gravel Literary, Flash Fiction Magazine, Bethlehem Writers Roundtable* and other literary journals. The mother of two grown daughters, she lives on the Jersey shore with her husband.

Learn more at patriciaperrydonovan.com.